Tales and Stories by Hans Christian Andersen

Tales and Stories by
Hans Christian Andersen

Translated, with an Introduction, by
Patricia L. Conroy and Sven H. Rossel

University of Washington Press
Seattle and London

Text illustrations are by Vilhelm Pedersen and Lorenz Frølich (see p. xii). Illustration facing Introduction is from the title page of *Historier af H. C. Andersen,* with illustrations by Vilhelm Pedersen (Copenhagen, 1854).

Library of Congress Cataloging in Publication Data
Andersen, Hans Christian, 1805–1875.
    Tales and stories.

    Bibliography: p.
    I. Conroy, Patricia.   II. Rossel, Sven Hakon.
PZ3.A544Tal   1980   [PT8116.E5]   839.8'136
ISBN 0–295–95936–3   80-50867

To Elias Bredsdorff and Erik Dal

Contents

Translators' Preface

In recent decades the tales and stories of Hans Christian Andersen have attracted a growing audience of adults. The present collection has been selected and translated with the needs of such readers in mind. Although Andersen himself wrote for an audience which he envisioned as containing both adults and children—indeed, one of the chief fascinations of his style is his success in addressing both groups at once—most of the previous translations have been intended exclusively for children. A main goal in the present translation has been to preserve for the English-speaking audience the engaging duplicity of Andersen's style, the tension of play between his sympathetic conversational tone and his use of the studied effect.

Especially in his early tales, Andersen's style may be characterized as simple and direct, verging on the informal, full of explanations and exclamations. Many passages can be translated successfully with a rather familiar, almost intimate, English: "Still, it was quite spunky of him to dare to say to the emperor's daughter, 'Will you have me?' But he dared all right because his name was famous far and wide, and there were a hundred princesses who would have been glad to have him. But do you think she was?" ("The Swineherd").

It is when Andersen's familiarity verges on the colloquial and his lightly amused tone comes to depend on satirical allusion that problems for the translator arise. For example, in his sentimental moralizing tale " 'She Was No Good,' " Andersen uses the phrase "i Tugt og Ære," which translates readily enough as "chastely and honorably"—but there is no way to indicate that this phrase comes from Danish ballad tradition and that Danish readers would hear not only the words but the echoes of conventional ballad stereotyping. With the phrase "i Aand og Sandhed" from the same story, the translator's success depends somewhat on the reader. Danes would be familiar with the phrase from the Lutheran catechism, as well as from the Bible, but English speakers would only know it from John 4:23–24, the story of the woman at the well. The translation "in spirit and in truth" is itself a quotation from the King James version. Sometimes more is lost in translation than just the allusion. In "The Snow Queen" Andersen plays with the words of a proverb well known in Denmark: "Morgenstund har guld i mund" ("The morning hour has gold on its lips"); of a child's kiss he writes that in it was "gold from the heart . . . gold in the earth, gold in the morning hour." Since the proverb is unknown in English, the allusion to it is meaningless, but vanished also in English is Andersen's elaboration of the proverb's rhyme: "Guld paa Munden, Guld i Grunden, Guld deroppe i Morgenstunden."

Indeed, Andersen's frequent use of rhyme and alliteration has posed problems. Some translations have been successful: "Luk dine Blomster og bøi dine Blade" comes across nicely as "Close your blossoms and bow your blades" ("The Buckwheat"); but there is no way to capture the chiastic alliteration of "Stakkel, hvor Du slider og slæber og staaer i det kolde Vand!" in English: "Poor thing, how you moil and toil in the cold water!" (" 'She Was No Good' ").

Nor has it always been possible to reproduce Andersen's puns and joking use of near homonyms. For example, he is fond of making puns out of bird calls. In "The Ugly Duckling" his pun on the cry of a duck (*rap* in Danish) and the verb "to hurry" (*rappe sig*) in " 'Rap! rap!' sagde hun, og saa rappede de sig" (" 'Quack! Quack!' [Hurry! Hurry!] she said, and they hurried") proved impossible to convey. Perhaps more successful is the translation of the crows' cries in "The Gardener and the Lord and Lady." "Caw" is *kra* in Danish; Andersen has the rooks and crows screech a variation—"Rak! Rak!"—down at the hunters, or "Rabble! Rabble!" in Danish. The translation reads, "Riff! Raff! Raff!"

In his use of informal language, Andersen habitually piled on intensifiers—very, quite, just, extremely, terribly, awfully, entirely, much—which are more obtrusive in English than in Danish, and sometimes it seemed better not to render them. For example, ". . . they must also die, and their lifetime is even much shorter than ours," which is awkward in English, has been translated simply as "even shorter," which sacrifices a certain childlike quality in Andersen's Danish ("The Little Mermaid").

Another set of translating problems is caused not by the words but by the fact that readers may not know Danish history or culture. Annotation may solve some problems: in "The Tinderbox" the dog sitting on the chest of gold coins has eyes as big as the Round Tower, and a note can explain that this is an astronomical observatory which dominated the skyline of nineteenth-century Copenhagen. But where Andersen playfully draws out satirical metaphors involving Danish customs, sometimes there is no satisfactory way of dealing with the passage. In "What People Do Think Up," a tale about a young man who wants to become a poet by Easter, the old woman says that even if he can never become a poet, he can still earn his living from poetry, not just by Easter, but by Lent—by beating poets from the barrel" (a Lenten children's game is called "Beating Cats from the Barrel")—and that his reward will be many *boller* (something like hot cross buns). Here it is impossible to render the Easter imagery, and translators are forced to interpret the metaphor itself and speak directly about the young man's becoming a critic.

Since the impact of the tales on children has not been a concern in this collection, the translators have not sought to censor or otherwise interpret any of Andersen's expressions of his attitudes about sex, race, and class. Indeed, one function of the present collection may be to draw attention to the opinions among which middle-class Danish children of the mid-nineteenth century did their growing up.

The present volume includes tales that reflect as many facets of Andersen's authorship as possible, from parable to science fiction. Because the general reader as well as the student may be interested in seeing Andersen's development as one of the main exponents of the literary tale, this collection has been presented in chronological order. Each tale is provided with an endnote containing publication data and, whenever possible, information about the genesis of the tale and comments that Andersen, and sometimes others, made about it. Also provided is a bibliographical guide to Andersen scholarship, to English translations of other works by Andersen—including letters and autobiographical writings—and to the biographical and critical literature in English.

The graphics in this volume reproduce the original illustrations by Vilhelm Pedersen (1820–59) and Lorenz Frølich (1820–1908) for collected editions of Andersen's tales published in 1848 and after. When selecting an illustrator for the first collected edition, Andersen and his publisher considered a number of artists, among them Frølich, whose youthful attempts at illustrating scenes from "The Little Mermaid" were already known to the author. Frølich was currently living in Rome, however, so the choice fell upon Vilhelm Pedersen, a young naval officer whose informal, familiar style appealed to Andersen. After Pedersen's death in 1859, Frølich was chosen as his successor, despite the fact that he still resided abroad. (In this volume Frølich's illustrations are to be found in "The Old Oak Tree's Last Dream" and all succeeding tales.) Although Frølich is considered by many to have been the more imaginative of the two artists, Vilhelm Pedersen is the more famous because it was he who illustrated the most popular of Andersen's tales, stemming from his early career.

In preparing this volume the translators have worked with the five available volumes of Erik Dal's and Erling Nielsen's projected seven-volume critical edition of Andersen's tales and stories: *H. C. Andersens Eventyr* (Copenhagen, 1963–). Also of use were the two collected editions, containing comments by the author: *Eventyr og Historier,* 2 vols. (Copenhagen, 1862–63), and *Nye Eventyr og Historier,* 3 vols. (Copenhagen, 1870–74).

The translators would like to express their thanks to T. C. S.

Langen for her able assistance, to Robert Monroe and Dennis Andersen of Special Collections in Suzzallo Library, and to the editors and readers of the University of Washington Press for their assistance in preparing this volume for publication.

Patricia L. Conroy
Sven H. Rossel
Seattle, April 1980

Introduction

Hans Christian Andersen's
Life and Authorship

SVEN H. ROSSEL

When, at the age of fourteen, Hans Christian Andersen left home to seek his fortune in the big city, his worried mother exclaimed, "Whatever will become of you?" He confidently replied, "I shall become famous." Years later, in his autobiography, *The Fairy Tale of My Life* (1855), experience led him to say it this way: "First you go through an awful lot, and then you become famous." Single-minded in pursuit of art and recognition, Andersen as a child of the working class, with only a rudimentary education and no social connections, had even more to go through than most struggling young artists. His conviction that he had been gifted at birth with extraordinary talent, however, saw him through much. As he says in "The Ugly Duckling": "It doesn't matter if one is born in a duck yard, when one has lain in a swan's egg!"

Andersen was the first prominent Danish writer of proletarian origin. Although he moved in bourgeois and aristocratic circles—in his day this was the only way for a writer to gain recognition and support—he never disguised his background but always considered himself an outsider and kept a sharp eye for the shortcomings of the bourgeoisie and aristocracy. In tales such as "The Nightingale" and "The Gardener and the Lord and Lady" Andersen's biting satire is aimed at the arrogance and selfishness of the aristocracy and court circles. Royalty itself, however, he places above criticism: when the nightingale says of the emperor of China, "I love your heart better than your crown," it continues, "and yet your crown has a scent of sanctity about it." Thus, Andersen did not become a great social writer like Charles Dickens, whose background was similar to that of his

Danish friend and contemporary. Andersen does not express any opinion on current political issues, even though a number of important events took place in his lifetime.

In 1801 a naval battle against the English fleet off Copenhagen ended with a decisive victory for the Danes. The wave of national self-confidence, however, was soon shattered by subsequent defeats that forced Denmark into an ill-starred alliance with Napoleon. The Napoleonic Wars exhausted the country to such an extent that national bankruptcy was declared, and with the French collapse in 1814 Denmark was forced to cede Norway to Sweden. Despite the difficult political and economic situation of the following years, Denmark experienced a cultural "golden age" with its center in Copenhagen, a city of 100,000 inhabitants. In the 1830s, however, the idyllic atmosphere was destroyed by the growth of political pressure for a liberal constitution that would limit the power of the monarchy. King Frederik VII yielded to these demands, and in 1849 the first democratic constitution with wide suffrage was introduced, and other reforms followed. Another cause of political unrest in these years was the Schleswig-Holstein question: the two duchies were supported by Prussia in their revolt against four centuries of Danish rule. Despite Danish victories in 1848–50, years of chronic government crises followed, and Denmark finally lost the duchies to a superior invading force of Prussians and Austrians in 1864. Only very slowly did the country recover from this setback.

None of these events are reflected in Andersen's tales, yet international politics had cast its shadow even over his immediate family. His father's hero was Napoleon. Striving for social advancement, the Danish shoemaker joined the war in 1812 as a volunteer, only to have his dreams of glory smothered by the peace two years later.

Hans Christian Andersen was born on 2 April 1805, in Odense, a town of 5,000 inhabitants on the island of Fyn. His father had acquired an elementary education in spite of the limited opportunities available to working people in those days. He was well read but a dreamer, embittered by frustrated hopes of social advancement. Openly skeptical in religious matters, he was also vaguely radical in politics. In the evenings he would read to his son from his favorite books, the *Arabian Nights,* the *Fables* of La Fontaine, and the comedies of the eighteenth-century Danish playwright, Ludvig Holberg. He also made various toys, paper cutouts, and a puppet theater. Andersen's mother was very different from her husband. She was a strong but naïve and superstitious woman who could not write at all and could scarcely read. But she was an affectionate mother and a good housewife and managed to hold her home together despite economic hardship. In his autobiography Andersen gives this description of his parents: "In a poor little room in Odense in 1805 lived a newly married couple who were extremely fond of each other, a young shoemaker and his wife: he barely twenty-two, a richly gifted man, a truly poetic character; she, a few years older, ignorant of life and of the world, but warm at heart."

Yet we know that six years before her marriage Andersen's mother had had a daughter by a married pottery worker who deserted her. The baby had been put out to nurse. Andersen never mentions his half sister in any of his writing. He feared that she had become a criminal or a prostitute in Copenhagen and would suddenly show up and compromise him—a thought that haunted him for many years. In fact, she maintained herself as a washerwoman and did not enter his life until 1842, four years before her death, when she asked him for and received financial support.*

After her husband's death, Andersen's mother began working as a washerwoman, and Hans Christian was sent to the city school for poor children. In 1818 she married another shoemaker, who died a few years later, leaving her in even greater poverty. She spent her last years as an alcoholic in the Odense workhouse, where she died in 1833. The story " 'She Was No Good' " is Andersen's stirring tribute to her. He visited her

*See H. G. Olrik, *Hans Christian Andersen: Undersøgelser og Kroniker 1925–1944* (Copenhagen: H. Hagerup, 1945, pp. 66–75.

three times in Odense, in the summers of 1829, 1830, and finally 1832. How regularly Andersen corresponded with his mother is not known; however, the letters from her (as she was illiterate, these were written for her by someone else) that have been preserved show that Andersen gave his mother extensive financial support.

As a boy, Andersen spent most of his time dreaming and reading. He could not spell or write a clear sentence, but he devoured any book he could get hold of and learned entire passages and scenes of plays by heart. He made friends with a distributor of theater bills at the Odense Theater; the boy would hand out bills and in return be allowed to keep copies for himself. With these as models, he began to make up little plays for his puppet stage, even going so far as to write an entire tragedy. When the Royal Theater visited Odense in 1818, Andersen was given a walk-on part and a couple of lines to speak. He was now firmly convinced that his future lay on the stage, and he decided to go to Copenhagen to make his fortune. His mother wanted him to be apprenticed to a tailor, but he would have none of it. In the end she gave in, but only after she had consulted a fortuneteller, who predicted that her son would become a great man and that Odense one day would be illuminated in his honor. Shortly after his confirmation, Andersen left Odense.

On 6 September 1819, the fourteen-year-old boy arrived in Copenhagen. He did not know anybody there, and a letter of introduction to the Royal Theater's leading ballerina, Anna Margrethe Schall, was of no use; after watching extemporaneous demonstrations of his skills as an actor, dancer, and singer, she took him for mad and threw him out. Even more disappointing was an interview with the theater's manager, who stressed that he could only employ people with an education. The situation seemed hopeless, and as a last resort Andersen sought out the director of the theater's singing school, the Italian Giuseppe Siboni, whose name he had heard in Odense. The young man's enthusiasm appealed to Siboni, who promised to train his voice, and on the initiative of the composer C. E. F. Weyse, a collection was taken up to support him. After six months, however,

Andersen's voice broke, and Siboni lost interest in him. Another benefactor, the poet Frederik Høegh-Guldberg, appealed successfully to various persons to contribute to a fund to support Andersen, and he was sent to the theater's dancing school. In 1821 he entered the singing school and managed to get various walk-on parts. Finally, however, in 1822, Andersen was dismissed from the Royal Theater altogether.

His faith in his own destiny now led Andersen to decide to conquer the theater as a dramatic writer. He had already submitted a play in 1821, *The Robbers of Vissenbjerg,* based on a Danish legend, which had been rejected with the comment that the management "desired to receive no more pieces which, like this one, betrayed such a lack of elementary education." In 1822 one of the actors at the Royal Theater introduced Andersen to a compositor in a Copenhagen printing company. This company agreed to print his next play, the tragedy *Alfsol,* together with a short story, "The Ghost at Palnatoke's Grave," in a volume entitled *Youthful Attempts* (1822). The pseudonym Andersen used, William Christian Walter, was his own middle name coupled with the first names of two of his literary heroes, William Shakespeare and Walter Scott. Hardly any copies of the book seem to have been sold, and eventually all the printed sheets were used as wrapping paper.

Although *Alfsol* also failed to gain acceptance at the Royal Theater, this time the rejected manuscript was accompanied by an encouraging comment that the author might one day be able to produce something of value, if only he could be given an education. The first step to that end was taken in 1822 by a member of the theater's board, Jonas Collin, a senior government official, who secured a royal grant for Andersen. Collin chose to send him to a grammar school at Slagelse, a small town ninety kilometers southwest of Copenhagen. At the age of seventeen, Andersen, who had no basic education, had to begin in the second grade, and the next five years were probably the unhappiest of his life. The headmaster, Simon Meisling, was a well-known classical scholar and translator, but he completely failed to understand Andersen's hypersensitive and highly strung nature and bullied him constantly, even though he worked very hard. Andersen's letters to Jonas Collin demonstrate that he was eager to achieve the best results possible, and in certain subjects he made good progress; but in the Greek and Latin taught by Meisling, Andersen showed no aptitude at all.

When Meisling was transferred in 1826 to Elsinore, Andersen went with him, and here things went wrong indeed: "Every day he told me that nothing would ever become of me, that I was stupid, that I would get nowhere," Andersen writes. The following year Collin took him out of the school and sent him for private tutoring in Copenhagen, where, in October 1828, he passed his university entrance examination. But all attempts to make Andersen continue his studies failed.

Andersen's heart was set upon a literary career. In 1827, while he was still at school, a Copenhagen newspaper published anonymously one of his poems, "The Dying Child," which has gained an extraordinary and lasting popularity. The most important of Andersen's early works, however, is a collection of sketches in the capricious manner of the German Romantic, E. T. A. Hoffmann, entitled *A Walking Tour from Holmen's Canal to the Western Point of Amager* (1829)—a loosely structured and witty account of the daily walk Andersen made across Copenhagen to his tutor. In the same year he made his debut as a playwright at the Royal Theater with a vaudeville play, *Love in Saint Nicholas Church Tower* (1829), parodying the heroic Schilleresque tragedy. In 1830 Andersen published a volume entitled *Poems,* which concluded with his first tale, "The Dead Man," based on a Danish folktale which he later rewrote as "The Traveling Companion."

Andersen had now gained some reputation as a promising writer but was soon attacked by the critics for his lack of artistic discipline. Extremely sensitive to criticism all his life, Andersen was upset and bitter about these attacks. His friend Collin advised him to go abroad and recover his spirits, and on this trip, the first of twenty-nine foreign journeys in all, Andersen spent five weeks in Germany. In Dresden he met the poet Ludwig Tieck, and in Berlin, Adelbert von Chamisso, who was to be

Andersen's first German translator, and whose own tale *Peter Schlemihl* (1814) would later suggest the theme of Andersen's "The Shadow." After he returned to Denmark Andersen wrote the first of his travel books, *Shadow Pictures from a Journey to the Harz Mountains and Saxony* (1831), a collection of sketches, in prose and poetry, in which he shows himself strongly influenced by the German Romantic Heinrich Heine. In December 1831 a new volume of poetry was published, containing a number of melancholy poems to Riborg Voigt, whom he had met and fallen in love with while visiting her brother, a fellow student. His financial needs forced Andersen to devote most of his time to translating and to writing libretti for operas, until once again Collin came to his assistance with a royal grant. In April 1833, Andersen set out on another journey, which proved to be the turning point of his career.

To Andersen the powerful Jonas Collin had taken the place of a solicitous father; the Collin house was open to him at all times, and he was treated almost as one of the family, even though the Collins never fully appreciated his artistic genius. Andersen on his part objected to their inclination to "educate" him. Especially conflict-ridden was his relationship with the second son, Edvard, who was his opposite in every respect. Unemotional, cool, and reserved, he rejected Andersen's fervent wish for a more personal friendship. Nevertheless, Edvard became Andersen's invaluable business adviser, arranging his financial affairs, helping him negotiate contracts with publishers, and correcting his manuscripts, which were laden with spelling errors. On New Year's Day 1833, Andersen's feelings of rejection were heightened when, having fallen in love with eighteen-year-old Louise Collin, he heard the announcement of her engagement to someone else. Both the rebuffed Andersen and the Collins must have felt relief when the author left Denmark in 1833.

Andersen spent the following two years in France, Switzerland, Italy, and Austria. While in Switzerland he completed a romantic play, *Agnete and the Merman* (1834), which dramatized his infatuation with Louise Collin. It proved to be a complete failure, and it was not until Andersen reached Italy that he began to produce his best work. Inspired by the countryside and the picturesque folk life, he completed the novel *The Improvisatore* (1835), his first international success. It is his own story as it had been and would turn out to be—its hero is a poor boy who, after many adversities, becomes a famous artist.

When *The Improvisatore* was in the hands of the publishers, Andersen turned to other ideas. In a letter to a friend in February 1835, he said: "I have started some 'tales told for children' and seem to be making good progress with them. I have done a couple of the stories I remember having liked when little, and which I think are not generally known. I have written them exactly as I would tell them to a child."

The small volume, published in May 1835, contained "The Tinderbox," "Little Claus and Big Claus," "The Princess on the Pea," and "Little Ida's Flowers." In the opinion of the critics these tales were completely unsuitable for children because they were immoral and without any pedagogical value. In addition, the style was condemned as being too colloquial. However, a friend of Andersen's, the scientist Hans Christian Ørsted, declared that if *The Improvisatore* made Andersen famous, the tales would make him immortal. Andersen did not at first agree with this prophetic judgment and continued to write in other literary genres while also publishing small volumes of tales and stories. During this period he wrote two novels, *O.T.* (1836) and *Only a Fiddler* (1837), both, like *The Improvisatore,* renderings of his own life, but this time set in Denmark. In *Only a Fiddler* the hero fails in his quest for fame and dies an impoverished village fiddler. One of the harshest critics of the sentimentality and self-pity of the book was the philosopher Søren Kierkegaard, who reproached Andersen for not having a consistent philosophy of life. Twenty years later this criticism still rankled. *To Be or Not To Be* (1857), a novel attacking the emergent materialism of the 1850s and sketching a young man's philosophic progress from atheism to a nondogmatic Christianity, constituted Andersen's reply to Kierkegaard.

After *Only a Fiddler,* Andersen again returned to his first love, the theater, and in 1840 *The Mulatto*, his first major stage play, was produced. The hero of this romantic melodrama, a social and racial outcast, was still another self-projection. The play was a great success, and Andersen followed it shortly with a second melodrama, *The Moorish Maid* (1840), which to his disappointment ran only three nights. In spite of much negative criticism Andersen would never admit his failure as a playwright and continued to turn out new plays for many years. His last novel, *Lucky Peer* (1870), is mainly based on his early struggles to be admitted to the theater and tells the story of a singer and composer who dies at the very moment of his greatest success.

From the late 1830s Andersen's literary career flowered. As early as 1835 *The Improvisatore* appeared in Germany; in 1845 it was published in England and the United States, and by 1847 his collected works began to appear in Germany, though not in Denmark until seven years later. Andersen had now become a frequent guest at manor houses throughout Denmark, where a large number of his tales were created. In 1848 he published *The Two Baronesses,* his best novel after *The Improvisatore.* The royal family invited him to stay with them, and on his many travels abroad he met with Europe's leading artistic personalities—the writers Heine, the Grimm brothers, Victor Hugo, Alexandre Dumas, and the composers Schumann, Mendelssohn, and Liszt. In 1840–41 Andersen made his most ambitious journey, to Italy, Greece, and Turkey. Even though in daily life he was extremely timid and suffered from all kinds of phobias, he was willing to face the greatest difficulties on his travels. The result of this extensive journey was *A Poet's Bazaar* (1842), the best of Andersen's lively travel books. It is witty and poetic, sharp and precise in its descriptions of scenery and atmosphere. In 1843 Andersen went to Paris and in 1844 made a triumphant visit to Germany. The following year in southern France he met the Norwegian violinist Ole Bull, who had come from the United States and could tell of Andersen's fame in the New World. In 1847 he went to Holland, England, and Scotland. In England he met the contemporary English author he most admired, Charles Dickens; and Andersen's second visit to England, in 1857, was the result of an invitation to stay with the Dickens family. After a trip to Sweden Andersen published another excellent travel book, *In Sweden* (1851), and other travel descriptions would follow: *In Spain* (1863) and *A Visit to Portugal* (1868). Andersen was to remain an untiring tourist almost to the end of his life. He traveled by every available means, by steamship and stage coach, on horseback; and later, always an admirer of modern technology, he was an enthusiastic traveler by train.

In his private life Andersen encountered a new defeat. In 1840 he had met the young Swedish soprano Jenny Lind, known worldwide as the Swedish Nightingale. Three years later he proposed to her, but she refused. They continued to be friends, and she exerted a tremendous influence on him. Andersen felt they had a spiritual kinship and saw Jenny Lind as a kind of musical parallel to himself, another born artist.

The climax of Andersen's increasingly successful career came in 1867, when he was made honorary citizen of Odense, and the town was illuminated in his honor, just as the fortuneteller had predicted. In 1861 Jonas Collin had died, and though Andersen continued his contact with the family—with Evard in particular—the closeness was no longer there. In these later years he also built up a circle of new friends, mainly rich business families who only knew him as the celebrated writer. Among these admirers Andersen spent his last summer in a country house near Copenhagen, where, after a prolonged period of failing health, he died on 4 August 1875.

As a child Andersen had heard retellings of old stories and tales; his father had read the *Arabian Nights* to him, and later he had become acquainted not only with the German Romantic literary tale as written by Ludwig Tieck, E. T. A. Hoffmann, and Adelbert von Chamisso, but also with the folktales collected by the Grimm brothers and with Mathias Winther's *Danish Folktales* (1823). All these sources are reflected in the first collection of tales in 1835, of which the first three are retold folktales.

The fourth and weakest tale, "Little Ida's Flowers," is Andersen's own invention, but still dependent on a tale by Hoffmann, *Nutcracker and Mouseking* (1819). The discovery of the folktale became the chief element in Andersen's search for artistic independence. Here he found what he had previously lacked, the short form and firm structure. Here he found the technique of retelling the same episode three times—often with increasing effect—as in "The Tinderbox" (1835), "The Traveling Companion" (1835), and "Clod-Hans" (1855). As in the folktale, so in Andersen's tales there is usually only one main character, and all antagonists of this hero or heroine play subordinate roles. The main character suffers hardship, but usually Andersen's tales, especially those based directly on folktales, have a happy ending.

The first six collections of tales were subtitled "Told for Children." Andersen's statement that he had written them exactly as he had heard them as a child reveals his ingenious discovery that the tales and stories have to be *told*. Andersen's tales seem so simple, but the manuscripts tell of all his patient labor to find the exact expression that would fit his intention. He read recently finished tales and stories to friends to find out if the words would fall as they should and to register the reactions of his listeners. By 1844 Andersen had dropped the subtitle. He began to write tales of greater length, and the three collections of 1852–55 bear the title "Stories." They contained such different texts as the science fiction fantasy "In a Thousand Years' Time" (1853) and the social commentary "'She Was No Good'" (1855). But Andersen did not give up the tale, and the last eleven volumes—from 1858 on—bear the title "Tales and Stories."

Andersen's early tales vary greatly in quality. In fact, only a third of the 156 tales and stories represent him at his best, and most of these date from the 1840s. "The Nightingale," "The Sweethearts," and "The Ugly Duckling" appeared in 1844; three of the finest tales, "The Snow Queen," "The Fir Tree," and "The Bell" in 1845; "The Little Match Girl" in 1846; "The Shadow," "The Drop of Water," and "The Story of a Mother" in 1847. As a whole, the production after 1850 does not reach the quality of the masterpieces from the preceding decade. However, we still find some excellent though less known texts, such as "In a Thousand Years' Time" (1852), "'She Was No Good'" (1853), "The Old Oak Tree's Last Dream" (1858), "The Butterfly" (1861), "The Snail and the Rosebush" (1862), "What People Do Think Up" (1869), "The Gardener and the Lord and Lady," "The Cripple," and "Auntie Toothache" (1872).

In his fragmentary but valuable comments on the tales printed in the collected editions of 1862–63 and 1870–74, Andersen continually emphasizes the reality behind his imaginative treatment. He once stated: "Most of what I have written is a reflection of myself. Every character is taken from life. I know and have known them all." In "The Ugly Duckling" we find the glorification of the author's own genius, whereas "The Fir Tree" is a rather harsh judgment of himself as the ambitious, always discontented artist afraid of having passed his prime. Idealized reminiscences of Andersen's childhood can be found in the opening of "The Snow Queen." We see self-portraits in the fortune-hunting soldier of "The Tinderbox" and the hypersensitive title character of "The Princess on the Pea." Andersen's affairs of the heart can be followed in several tales: "The Sweethearts" describes a meeting with Riborg Voigt thirteen years after his unsuccessful courtship; Louise Collin is probably the model for the proud princess in "The Swineherd," in which the swineherd, who turns out to be a prince, is Andersen himself; "The Nightingale" in its contrasting of the real and the artificial is a tribute to Jenny Lind; finally, he deals with his resignation to lonely bachelorhood in the witty parable "The Butterfly." Portraits of friends and acquaintances can also be found. It has been suggested that the prince in "The Bell" is Hans Christian Ørsted, the loyal friend who praised Andersen's first tales and who was also the discoverer of electromagnetism: in "The Bell" the prince represents the scientific mode of approaching the Divine, while the poor boy, another self-portrait of Andersen, represents the poetic mode. It has also been posited that the poet in "The Shadow" represents Andersen, and the title character has the features of Edvard Collin, just as in "The Ugly Duckling" the cat, the hen, and the old woman portray the Collin family. Andersen also carried on literary combat in his tales. It has been suggested that "The Snail and the Rosebush" is another reply to Kierkegaard's harsh criticism of *Only a Fiddler* (the snail, of course, is the philosopher, while the blooming rosebush is the poet himself), and "The Gardener and the Lord and Lady" is regarded as Andersen's final and wittiest settlement with his Danish critics.

But the tales are more than disguised autobiographies and more than simple entertainment. "I seize an idea for older people—and then tell it to the young ones, while remembering that father and mother are listening and must have something to think about," Andersen says. "I write about what is true and good and beautiful," says the learned man in "The Shadow," stating Andersen's own ideal of art, which reflects the Romantic philosophy of his time. But the bitter irony of "The Shadow" is that everyone disregards the learned man and his values, choosing to follow the title figure, undoubtedly the most demonic character in Andersen's writings. By the end of the story there is nothing left of the Romantic belief that the goodhearted person, such as John in "The Traveling Companion" or Gerda in "The Snow Queen," has nothing to fear from evil: all human efforts are absurd. This is also the main theme of the tale "The Story of a Mother," a tribute to maternal love but also a demonstration of the mercilessness of life. Here we are far from the light gaiety of "The Tinderbox" or the optimism of "The Ugly Duckling."

It is characteristic of Andersen's tales and stories that one idea evokes its counterpart, and this duality in his mental and spiritual make-up is recognizable in all his works. The tales deal with optimism *and* pessimism. In opposition to those which posit a belief in good fortune ("The Tinderbox," "The Traveling Companion," "The Flax," "Clod-Hans"), in the power of goodness of heart over cold reason ("The Snow Queen"), and in the possibility of human experience of the Divine ("The Bell"), we can cite many tales that are hopeless in their pessimism: "The Fir Tree," "The Shadow," "The Little Match Girl," "The Story of a Mother," and "Auntie Toothache." Thus Andersen's intense love of life alternates with a preoccupation with death: unable to accept the course of nature, he continually emphasizes immortality and fights death, as the mother does in "The Story of a Mother" and art does in "The Nightingale." The complete absorption in life as represented by the tiny mayfly in "The Old Oak Tree's Last Dream" remained Andersen's ideal.

But when Andersen aimed his satire at various inequalities in society, he never vacillated. Thus "The Nightingale" and "The Swineherd" should not only be interpreted as allegories, setting true poetry against rigid academic convention, but also as highly ironic depictions of human behavior, a critical tendency which is carried further in the social accusations in "The Drop of Water" and "'She Was No Good.'"

Andersen was no romantic dreamer with contempt for his own times. On the contrary, he welcomed many new events in art and science. He fantasizes about aircraft in "In a Thousand Years' Time" and about a magnifying glass in "The Drop of Water." What he welcomed was the victory of spirit over matter, and he was interested in every new discovery that seemed to represent that victory. His own contribution along these lines was the renewing of the genre of the literary tale: "The tale is the most extensive realm of poetry, ranging from the blood-drenched graves of the past to the pious legends of a child's picture book, absorbing folk literature and art literature; to me it is the representation of all poetry, and the one who masters it must be able to put into it the tragic, the comic, the naïve, irony and humor, having here the lyrical note as well as the childish narrative and the language of describing nature at his service" (*To Be or Not To Be,* part 2, chapter 6).

If Andersen himself was able to fulfill these, his own, demands, it was primarily because he, in contrast to the German Romanticists, was able to preserve that primitive immediacy that establishes direct contact with the world around him. His myth-creating imagination, which broke with all literary conventions, knew how to animate the inanimate. His acute power of observation and strong sense of reality endowed the most fantastic beings with realistic traits, forcing the reader to believe in them. Andersen's point of departure is local, Danish—yet his tales and stories live on, even though their creator has long since died.

"Will all beauty in the world die when you die?" the little fly asks the tree. "It will last longer, infinitely longer, than I can imagine!" says the great oak tree.

The Art of Hans Christian Andersen's Tales and Stories

PATRICIA L. CONROY

Hans Christian Andersen was not the first modern European author to happen upon the idea of retelling folktales and nursery stories or of composing his own original ones for a reading audience. As early as 1676, Mme de Sévigné had commented on the popularity of fairy tales at the French court, and by the end of the century there was a notable group of fairy-tale writers working in France. Foremost among them was Charles Perrault, whose *Histoires ou contes du temps passé avec des moralités* (Amsterdam and Paris, 1697) contained such stories as "Cinderella" and "Little Red Riding Hood." Indeed, later in his career, Andersen was to find himself advised by his detractors to take a close look at the French school if he wished to improve his tales. His practice of not pointing a moral at the end of each tale as Perrault had done, but allowing the allegorical and ironic levels of his narratives to speak for themselves, was to become another favorite theme of his detractors, who seem to have been looking for another La Fontaine. Instead, Andersen's own admiration centered more strongly on the writers of the German Romantic school—men like Ludwig Tieck, E. T. A. Hoffmann, and

Adelbert von Chamisso—and on his compatriots, Adam Oeh-lenschläger and B. S. Ingemann. These writers drew inspiration not from the nursery story but from the folktale, and were interested in developing the psychological, symbolical, and even satiric aspects of a literary genre of "folktale." *

Apart from one youthful imitative endeavor, "The Dead Man" (1830), Andersen showed himself even in his earliest work to be an innovator within the tradition of the literary tale. A great deal of what is sensed to be fresh and new in Andersen's tales stems from the fact that he strove to compose them as though he were telling them to children rather than writing them for adults. And a master teller he is! Compare the scene portraying the death of young John's father in "The Dead Man," in which Andersen imitated earlier writers of the literary tale, with the same scene from his later, and for him more characteristic, rewritten version entitled "The Traveling Companion (1835):

["The Dead Man"] It was already completely dark in the cloister, but from the little cottage in whose garden the hawthornes were planted, there still flamed the light of a lamp through the small windowpanes. Inside the bare clay walls lay an old farmer on his deathbed; his son John sat at the side of the bed by him and pressed hard the dying man's cold, clammy hand to his lips. The lamb bleated so porten-

*Interested readers may wish to consult the following translations of some of Andersen's precursors: Charles Perrault, *The Fairy Tales of Charles Perrault,* trans. Angela Carter (New York: Avon, 1979), and *Perrault's Popular Tales,* ed. and trans. Andrew Lang (Oxford: Clarendon Press, 1888), which contains an interesting introduction and notes on sources; Johann Wolfgang von Goethe, *The Parable,* trans. Alice Raphael (New York: Harcourt Brace, 1963), and Adelbert von Chamisso, *Peter Schlemihl,* trans. John Bowring (Philadelphia: David McKay, 1929), which both make use of the same motif employed by Andersen in "The Shadow"; Friedrich Heinrich Karl de la Motte-Fouqué, *Undine,* trans. Paul Turner (London: John Calder, 1960); E. T. A. Hoffmann, *Three Märchen of E. T. A. Hoffmann,* trans. Charles E. Passage (Columbia: University of South Carolina Press, 1971); *German Romance,* ed. and trans. Thomas Carlyle, 2 vols. (London, 1827), a collection often reprinted, both in England and America, containing tales by Musäus, Tieck, Hoffmann, and Richter, as well as introductions dealing with each author.

tously in the corner, the lamp was almost burned out. The old man looked yet again with a great, stiff gaze at his son, squeezed his hand as if in a cramp, and passed away to the Lord.

["The Traveling Companion"] Poor John was so sad, for his father was very sick and could not live. There was no one at all except the two of them in the little room. The lamp on the table was about to burn out, and it was very late in the evening.

"You have been a good son, John!" said the sick father. "Our Lord will surely help you on in the world!" And he looked at him with grave and gentle eyes, drew a very deep breath, and died. It was just as if he slept.

In "The Dead Man" Andersen opens his tale much in accord with the conventions of his day. There is an extended description of the district in which John and his father live—the remarkable, ancient hawthorne tree, the darkly medieval cloisters nearby, and the marsh alive with spirits and supernatural beings. When he focuses on the death scene, the point of view is still exterior to the characters, and the language is stiff and mannered. In "The Traveling Companion," however, he begins the tale directly with the death of the father. He has dispensed with the scene-setting—the creation of an unusual, often eerie atmosphere—so dear to other writers of the literary tale. The pathetic description of the lamb is gone, too: the pathos springs from the interaction of the two characters themselves. The language is simple, reflecting the thoughts of the child John.

In the following passages from "The Dead Man" and "The Traveling Companion," it is easy to see how Andersen tried to adapt the latter to the experiential world of the child:

["The Dead Man"] John spoke, but he did not know himself what he said, for the princess smiled so delightfully at him and stretched out her white hand to him for a kiss. His lips burned, he felt his whole inner self electrified; he could enjoy none of the refreshments that the page bore before him. . . .

["The Traveling Companion"] . . . so they went over to her and said, "How do you do." She looked so pretty, shook hands with

John, and he loved her even more than before. She certainly couldn't be the bad, wicked witch everyone said she was. They went up into the hall, and the little pages offered them jam and gingersnaps, but the old king was so sad that he couldn't eat anything at all, and the gingersnaps were too hard for him anyway.

In the earlier version Andersen describes John's passionate emotional response to the beauty of the princess in a way that is reminiscent of an adult's romantic attraction. In the reworked version he depicts John much as if he were a little boy who naïvely assumes that beauty cannot go hand in hand with evil. Andersen then rounds off the scene with gentle humor and irony by contrasting John's youth and optimism with the king's infirmity and despair. He also simplifies his vocabulary, changing abstract expressions like "refreshments" to more concrete ones like "jam and gingersnaps." In his use of vocabulary and syntax he reflects the usage, rhythms, and spontaneous wit of the spoken language.

The springboard of Andersen's success as an author of literary tales was his retelling of traditional folktales, such as we find in "The Traveling Companion," "The Tinderbox," and "The Princess on the Pea," and of *fabliaux,* or jocular tales, such as "What Father Does Is Always Right." However, a brief survey of his tales and stories reveals that he experimented in most of the shorter genres. He wrote realistic short stories, such as " 'She Was No Good' " and "The Gardener and the Lord and Lady." In "The Buckwheat" he tried his hand at composing a Christian parable about the foremost of the seven deadly sins. He was clearly inspired by fable literature in his use of animal and inanimate protagonists in short, concise narratives that convey a lesson, and his "The Snail and the Rosebush" and "The Butterfly" are fables as good as any of Aesop's, although somewhat longer. He was particularly given to the lyrical sketch, a number of which originally appeared separately or in his travel books, later to be included in his collected tales—for example, he wrote "A Rose from Homer's Grave" for *A Poet's Bazaar*

(1842) and introduced it into an edition of his collected tales in 1862–63. He delighted in recasting myths: in "The Garden of Paradise" he retold the Christian story of the ejection of Adam and Eve from the Garden of Eden, and in "The Story of a Mother" he composed a very free and Christianized retelling of the classical myth about the journey of Orpheus to the region of the dead. Among Andersen's collected tales are also to be found a few works of science fiction. "The Drop of Water" is the satirical tale of an imaginary voyage—the "traveler" observes by means of a magnifying glass the vicious behavior of the microorganisms in a drop of ditch water and mistakenly concludes that it must be Copenhagen. In the tale "In a Thousand Years' Time" Andersen anticipates Jules Verne in his vision of how people will one day be able to travel by air around the world in no time at all.

As we have said, Andersen distinguished himself from other writers of the literary tale in part by a new use of setting. As opposed to Tieck, whose settings give ominous hints about the future, or to E. T. A. Hoffmann, into whose realistic settings the supernatural suddenly intrudes, Andersen did not employ such Gothic motifs, possibly because his concern was to involve the reader principally by means of allegory and humorous irony rather than sensationalism and suspense. He constructed his most characteristic settings out of homey, everyday details that evoke in the reader a sense of intimacy, which is maintained throughout the tale.

Even in Andersen's first collections of tales this fondness for reassuring, familiar detail is evident. In his early rewritings of folktales he describes the never-never land in such a way as to bring it very close to everyday experience. In "The Princess on the Pea" it is the queen who, just like any good housewife, makes the bed for the bedraggled visitor. In "The Traveling Companion" the king himself answers the knocking on his castle door in his bedroom slippers. In the somewhat later tale "The Swineherd," the king in his castle has become even more domesticated. He, too, answers the door and wears slippers around the castle, but here he practices common household economies and wears his slippers until they are run down in back.

In most of his tales Andersen focuses on that part of the world that everyone, especially the child, knows best—the home and its immediate environs. He often places his characters in the kitchen, the playroom, or the drawing room; in the garden or poultry yard right outside; or on the street or road just beyond. This is especially true in the more allegorical tales in which animals, insects, and plants are the main characters. Andersen delights in translating a particular human type into an appropriate and familiar, often wittily chosen nonhuman surrogate, and then describing the world from that point of view. In this way the everyday world we find in many of Andersen's tales never seems stale or tiresome—it is always presented from a new and unusual point of view. In "The Fir Tree" we see the celebration of Christmas Eve through the eyes of the Christmas tree, and in "The Ugly Duckling" we discover what the poultry yard is like if one is a duck. Andersen is especially witty when he describes the setting for an unlucky love affair in "The Sweethearts": the top and the ball first meet in a drawer in the playroom and then many years later happen upon each other again in a trash bin.

Even in some tales set in faraway lands Andersen may draw his imagery from the everyday world of his audience, using it for humorous, ironic, or allegorical effect. For example, "The Nightingale" is set in far-off China, but a China that is a tongue-in-cheek extrapolation of the Chinese porcelain and prints found in bourgeois drawing rooms in nineteenth-century Europe. In "The Snow Queen" Gerda journeys to a Lapland and Finland that are humorous and fanciful combinations of popular notions of these places. In "The Story of a Mother" a mother in search of her dead child travels all the way to the realm of the dead, which is described as a greenhouse, a familiar sight in the gardens of the Danish upper middle class.

But in a number of tales that take place in settings far removed from the everyday world of his audience, Andersen has been deliberately vague in his depiction of a foreign or alien locale. These tales tend to be abstract in their statements about humankind and its spiritual condition, and the nonspecific foreign setting enhances the everyman and everywhere flavor of his ideas. "The Shadow," a tale about the struggle between the altruistic artist and his self-seeking shadow, is set in unspecified "hot countries" and unnamed "spas." The description is vague but realistic: we know these are real places, but what places they are we do not know. We are led to speculate on the meaning of the setting as well as its locale. In "The Bell" the difficult journey of the two young seekers through a forest that grows more and more alien is an allegory of the travail of the soul in its search for the Divine.

The theme of the quest is a frequent one in Andersen; and among the many types of characters in his tales, the searcher recurs again and again. He may appear as a young adventurer out to find himself fame and fortune and a wife—such as the soldier in "The Tinderbox" and John in "The Traveling Companion." The figure of Clod-Hans in the tale by that name is a burlesque of the same prototype. In "The Swineherd" and "The Butterfly" the young adventurer's failure in his quest becomes a vehicle for satire. In "The Swineherd" Andersen pokes fun at the aesthetic tastes of the well to do. The princess refuses the honest prince and his beautiful gifts, whereupon the prince gets his revenge by undertaking to reveal how crass the princess really is. In "The Butterfly" Andersen satirizes the "young adventurer" who cannot make up his mind about a wife.

Sometimes the young adventurer's quest is a more philosophical one—a search for God. In "The Bell" the two young searchers are both called by the ringing of a great, unknown bell and the promise of divine revelation that its tones contain. In "The Snow Queen" there are two young adventurers, each on a different quest. Little Kay mistakenly searches after eternity through cold reason and rationality and is in danger of suffering the death of his soul. His loving playmate, Gerda, tries to save him from his fate and is able to overcome all obstacles because of her innocence and goodness of heart. It is in the description of Gerda that we find Andersen's clearest formulation of the qualities of the ideal young adventurer: someone who succeeds in the face of adversity because of goodness and simple faith.

As interesting to Andersen as the young adventurer was the figure of the artist. The nature of the creative personality was a question which concerned him greatly and which he discussed in several allegorical tales. In "The Nightingale" the true artist, in the form of a real nightingale from the emperor of China's own woodland, is compared with the false—the gem-studded mechanical songbird sent from Japan. In "The Snail and the Rosebush" the artistic spirit of the unselfconscious and joyously creative rosebush is contrasted with the critical and analytic intelligence of the snail, who refuses to produce anything himself because he despises the world. In "The Gardener and the Lord and Lady" it is the humble gardener as artist who is able to see beauty in the world and understands how to "cultivate" it. Although many recognize his genius, he is never appreciated by the lord and lady, who have no aesthetic sense and are prejudiced against him because of his low station. In other stories Andersen describes the defeat of the artist by both internal and external foes. In "Auntie Toothache" an imaginative student, not unlike Andersen in his youth, is frustrated in his ambition to become a poet by his own weakness and hypersensitivity.

It is precisely because of Andersen's ability to translate his ideas and personal experiences, as in "Auntie Toothache," into allegorical tales about life's most important problems that he continues to be read. The tension between the suggestiveness of the allegory and the simplicity of the presentation has fascinated readers throughout the world.

Tales and Stories by Hans Christian Andersen

The Tinderbox

A soldier came marching down the road—hup, two! hup, two! He had his rucksack on his back and a sword at his side, for he had been to war and was now on his way home. Then he met an old witch on the road. She was so hideous her lower lip hung all the way down to her chest. "Good evening, soldier!" she said. "What a fine sword you have, and what a big rucksack! You're a real soldier! Now you are going to have all the money you want!"

"Thank you, you old witch!" said the soldier.

"Do you see that big tree?" said the witch, and she pointed to a tree that stood beside them. "It's all hollow inside! You must climb to the top. There you'll see a hole you can slide through and get down deep into the tree. I'll tie a rope around your waist so I can pull you up again when you call me."

"What'll I do down in the tree?" asked the soldier.

"Fetch money!" said the witch. "Now listen! When you get to the bottom of the tree, you'll be in a large hallway; it's well lighted, for more than a hundred lamps are burning there. Then you will see three doors. You can open them—the keys are in the locks. If you go into the first chamber, you'll see a big chest in the middle of the floor. On top of it sits a dog, and he has a pair of eyes as big as teacups. But don't let them bother you! I'll give you my blue-checked apron. You must spread it out on the floor, then go over quickly, take the dog, and put him on my apron. Open the chest and take as many pennies as you like. They're all of copper. But if you'd rather have silver, you must go into the next room. There sits a dog with a pair of eyes as big as mill wheels. But don't let that bother you! Put him on my apron and take what you want of the money! If you want gold, on the other hand, you can have that too—as much as you can carry—when you go into the third chamber. But the dog that sits on the money chest there has two eyes that are each as big as the Round Tower! That's a real dog, let me tell you! But don't let that bother you! Just put him on my apron, and he won't hurt you. Then take as much gold out of the chest as you like!"

"That's not so bad!" said the soldier. "But what do you want from me, you old witch? You expect something out of this, I'm sure!"

"No," said the witch, "I don't want a single cent. Just bring to me an old tinderbox that my grandmother forgot the last time she was down there."

"Well, then, let me have the rope around my waist!" said the soldier.

"Here it is!" said the witch. "And here's my blue-checked apron."

The soldier then climbed up the tree and let himself drop down through the hole, and there he stood, as the witch had said, in the great hallway where many hundreds of lamps were burning.

Now he opened the first door. Ugh! There sat the dog with eyes as big as teacups, glaring at him.

"You're a fine fellow!" said the soldier as he put him on the witch's apron and took as many copper pennies as his pockets would hold. He closed the chest, put the dog on it again, and went into the second room. Eek! There sat the dog with eyes as big as mill wheels.

"You shouldn't look at me so hard!" said the soldier. "You might strain your eyes!" Then he put the dog on the witch's apron. But when he saw all the silver coins in the chest, he threw away the copper money and filled his pockets and rucksack with silver. Then he went into the third chamber. Oh, it was hideous! The dog there really did have two eyes as big as the Round Tower, and they spun around in his head like wheels.

"Good evening!" said the soldier and touched his cap, for he had never seen a dog like that before. But when he looked at him more closely, he thought, "Now, that's enough!" So he lifted the dog down to the floor and opened the chest. Oh! Good heavens! What a lot of gold there was! With it he could buy all of Copenhagen and the cake woman's candy pigs and all the tin soldiers, whips, and rocking horses in the whole world. Yes, that was really a lot of money! Now the soldier threw away all the silver coins he had filled his pockets and rucksack with, and took gold instead. Indeed, his pockets, rucksack, cap, and boots were so full he could hardly walk. Now he had money! He put the dog on the chest, closed the door, and called up through the tree.

"Now pull me up, you old witch!"

"Have you got the tinderbox with you?" asked the witch.

"Right!" said the soldier. "I completely forgot." And he went back and got it. The witch pulled him up, and he stood back on the road with pockets, boots, rucksack, and cap full of money.

"What do you want with the tinderbox?" asked the soldier.

"That's none of your business!" said the witch. "You have your money now—just give me the tinderbox."

"Rubbish!" said the soldier. "Tell me right now what you want it for or I'll draw my sword and cut your head off."

"No!" said the witch.

So the soldier cut off her head. There she lay! But he just tied up all his money in her apron, slung it on his back like a sack, put the tinderbox in his pocket, and walked straight to the town.

It was a splendid town, and he put up at the finest inn and ordered the very best rooms and his favorite food, for he was wealthy now that he had so much money.

The servant who had to clean his boots thought, to be sure, that they were queer old boots for such a rich gentleman, for he hadn't bought new ones yet. The next day he got boots that were good for walking in and nice clothes. Thus the soldier had become a fine gentleman, and everyone told him about all the fine things in their town, about their king, and about what a lovely princess his daughter was.

"Where can one go to see her?" asked the soldier.

"She is not to be seen at all!" everyone said. "She lives in a big copper castle with many walls and towers around it. No one but the king may go in and out, for it has been prophesied that she will marry a common soldier, and the king doesn't like that one bit!"

"I'd really like to see her!" thought the soldier, but this was, of course, out of the question!

Now he lived a merry life, went to the theater, drove in the king's park, and gave a lot of money to the poor; and that was very good of him! He remembered all too well from the old days how hard it was to be penniless! Now he was rich and had fine clothes and many friends who all said he was a fine fellow and a real gentleman, and the soldier certainly liked to hear that! But since he spent money every day and didn't get any back, he had at last only two pennies left and had to move out of the fine rooms where he had lived to a tiny, little garret way up under the roof. He had to brush his own boots and mend them with a darning needle, and none of his friends came to see him, for there were so many stairs to climb.

It was a very dark evening, and he couldn't even buy himself a candle. Then he remembered that there was a little stub in the tinderbox he had taken out of the hollow tree that the witch had helped him down into. He got out the tinderbox and the candle stub, but the instant he struck a light and the sparks flew from the flint, the door burst open, and the dog with eyes as big as teacups that he had seen down under the tree stood before him and said, "What does my master command!"

"What's this!" said the soldier. "It's certainly a funny tinder-box if I can get everything I want with it! Bring me some money," he said to the dog. And whoosh! The dog was gone! Whoosh! It was back again, holding a big sack of pennies in its mouth.

Now the soldier realized what a marvelous tinderbox it was! If he struck it once, the dog that sat on the chest full of copper coins would come; if he struck twice, the one that had silver came; and if he struck three times, then came the one that had gold. Now the soldier moved back down into the fine rooms and dressed in good clothes, and all his friends recognized him right away, and thought so very much of him.

Then one day he thought, "It's really very strange that one cannot get to see that princess! Everyone says she is supposed to be beautiful! But what good is that if she always has to sit inside that big copper castle with all the towers! Can't I get to see her at all? Where is my tinderbox!" And then he struck a light, and whoosh! There appeared the dog with eyes as big as tea-cups.

"I know it's the middle of the night," said the soldier, "but I'd so much like to see the princess for just a single moment!"

The dog was out of the door in a flash and, before the soldier could think twice, he was back with the princess. She sat on the dog's back and slept, and she was so beautiful that anyone could see she was a real princess. The soldier just couldn't resist kissing her, for he was a real soldier.

Then the dog ran back with the princess. But when morning came, and the king and queen were drinking their tea, the princess said that she had had such a strange dream during the night about a dog and a soldier. She had ridden on the dog, and the soldier had kissed her.

"That's a pretty story!" said the queen.

The next night one of the old ladies in waiting had to keep watch by the princess's bed to see if this was really a dream, or what it could be.

The soldier longed so terribly to see the beautiful princess again, so the dog came during the night, took her away, and ran as fast as he could. But the old lady in waiting put on rubber boots and ran just as fast after him. When she saw them enter a big house, she thought, "Now I know where it is!" and with a piece of chalk drew a large cross on the door. Then she went home and went to bed, and the dog came back with the princess. But when he saw a cross on the door where the soldier lived, he likewise took a piece of chalk and put a cross on all the doors in the whole town. That was a smart thing to do, for now the lady in waiting couldn't find the right door, because there were crosses on all of them.

Early in the morning the king and queen, the old lady in waiting, and all the officers went to see where it was the princess had been.

"Here it is!" said the king, when he saw the first door with a cross on it.

"No, it is over there, my dear husband!" said the queen, who saw a second door with a cross on it.

"But there's one, and there's one!" they all said, for wherever they looked there were crosses on the doors. Then they all realized there was no point in searching anymore.

But the queen was a very smart lady, who could do more than just ride in a coach. She took her big gold scissors, cut a large piece of silk into pieces, and sewed a lovely little bag. She filled it with fine buckwheat grains, tied it on the back of the princess, and when that was done, she cut a little hole in the bag so the grains could dribble out all along the way wherever the princess went.

In the night the dog came again, took the princess on his back, and ran with her to the soldier, who was so fond of her and would gladly have been a prince so that he could marry her.

The dog did not notice how the grain had dribbled out all the way from the castle to the soldier's window, and he ran up the wall with the princess. In the morning the king and queen saw clearly where their daughter had been, so they arrested the soldier and put him in jail.

There he sat. Oh, how dark and dreary it was there! And they said to him, "Tomorrow you are to be hanged." That wasn't nice to hear, and he had left his tinderbox at the inn! In the morning, looking out between the iron bars of the little window, he could see people hurrying out of town to see him hanged. He heard the drums and saw the soldiers marching. Everybody rushed off, among them a shoemaker's apprentice wearing his leather apron and slippers. He went so fast that one of his slippers flew off right at the wall where the soldier sat peering through the iron bars.

"Hey you, shoemaker's apprentice!" the soldier called to him. "You don't have to rush like that, nothing will happen before I arrive! But if you'll run to the place where I used to live and bring me my tinderbox, you'll get four pennies! But then you'll really have to shake a leg!" The shoemaker's apprentice wanted those four pennies a lot, so he darted off after the tinderbox, brought it to the soldier, and—well, now we'll really hear something!

Outside the town a great gallows had been built, and around it stood the soldiers and many hundreds of thousands of people. The king and queen sat on a splendid throne opposite the judge and the entire council.

The soldier was already on the ladder, but as they were about to put the rope around his neck, he said that the custom was to grant a sinner an innocent wish before he suffered his punishment. He wanted very much to smoke a pipe of tobacco. After all, it would be the last pipe he would smoke in this world.

Now, the king didn't want to say no to that, so the soldier took his tinderbox and struck a light. One—two—three! And there stood all the dogs—the one with eyes as big as teacups, the one with eyes like mill wheels, and the one whose eyes were as big as the Round Tower!

"Now help me, so I won't be hanged!" said the soldier, and the dogs flew at the judges and the entire council, seized one by the legs and another by the nose, and tossed them many feet into the air, so they fell down and were broken all to pieces.

"I will not!" said the king, but the biggest dog took both

him and the queen and tossed them after the others. Then the soldiers were frightened and all the people shouted, "Little soldier, you shall be our king, and marry the beautiful princess!"

They put the soldier into the king's coach, and all three dogs danced in front shouting, "Hurrah!" The boys whistled through their fingers, and the soldiers presented arms. The princess came out of the copper castle and became queen, and she liked that very much! The wedding lasted a week, and the three dogs sat at the table and made eyes at everybody.

The Princess on the Pea

There was once a prince. He wanted to find himself a princess, but it had to be a real princess. He traveled all around the world to find one, but everywhere there was something wrong. There were plenty of princesses, but whether they were real princesses he couldn't quite find out. There was always something that wasn't quite right. So he came home again and was very sad, for he wanted a true princess so much.

One evening there was a terrible storm. There was lightning and thunder, and the rain poured down. It was just awful! Then there was a knock at the city gate, and the old king went over to open it.

A princess was standing outside. But Lord, how she looked because of the rain and bad weather! Water poured from her hair and clothes and ran in at the toe of her shoe and out at the heel, and then she said she was a true princess!

"Well, we'll soon find out about that!" thought the old queen, but she didn't say anything. She went into the bedroom, took off all the bedclothes, and put a pea on the bottom of the bed. Then she took twenty mattresses, laid them on top of the pea, and put twenty eiderdown quilts on top of the mattresses. That's where the princess was to sleep that night.

In the morning they asked her how she had slept.

"Oh, just dreadfully!" said the princess. "I hardly closed my eyes all night! Lord knows what was in that bed! I've been lying on something hard so that my body is black and blue all over! It's simply dreadful!"

Then they could see that she was a real princess, since she had felt the pea through the twenty mattresses and the twenty eiderdown quilts. Nobody could have such delicate skin except a true princess.

So the prince took her to be his wife, for now he knew that he had a real princess. And the pea was placed in the museum, where it can still be seen, if no one has taken it.

See, that was a real story!

The Traveling Companion

Poor John was so sad, for his father was very sick and could not live. There was no one at all except the two of them in the little room. The lamp on the table was about to burn out, and it was very late in the evening.

"You have been a good son, John!" said the sick father. "Our Lord will surely help you on in the world!" And he looked at him with grave and gentle eyes, drew a very deep breath, and died. It was just as if he slept. But John wept, for now he had no one in the whole world, neither father nor mother, sister nor brother. Poor John! He knelt down beside the bed and kissed his dead father's hand, weeping many bitter tears. But at last his eyes closed, and he fell asleep with his head against the hard bedpost.

Then he dreamed a strange dream. He saw how the sun and moon bowed before him, and he saw his father strong and well again and heard him laugh as he always laughed when he was really pleased. A lovely girl with a golden crown on her long, beautiful hair held out her hand to John, and his father said, "See what a bride you have won! She is the loveliest in the whole world." Then John woke up. All the beauty was gone.

His father lay dead and cold on the bed, and there was no one at all with them. Poor John!

The following week the dead man was buried. John walked close behind the coffin and could no longer see his good father, who had loved him so much. He heard them casting earth on the coffin, and glimpsed only the last corner of it before the next shovelful of dirt was thrown down and covered it completely. Then John felt as if his heart would burst with sorrow. A hymn was being sung; it sounded so beautiful that tears filled John's eyes. He wept, and his tears eased his sorrow. The sun shone brightly on the green trees as if to say: "You shouldn't be so sad, John! Can you see how beautifully blue the sky is. Your father is up there, praying to the dear Lord that all may go well with you forever!"

"I will always be good," said John. "For then I shall go to heaven to my father, and what joy it will be to see each other again! How much I shall have to tell him, and he will show me so many things, and teach me so much about all the lovely things in heaven, just as he used to teach me here on earth. Oh, what joy it will be!"

John saw it all so clearly in his thoughts that he smiled while the tears were still running down his cheeks. The little birds sat in the chestnut trees and twittered, "tweet-tweet, tweet-tweet." They were so cheerful, even though they were at a funeral. But they surely knew that the dead man was now up in heaven, that he had wings far larger and more beautiful than their own, and that he was happy because he had been good while here on earth. That is what they were pleased about. John saw how they flew from the green trees far out into the world, and he felt such a longing to fly away with them. But first he made a large wooden cross to put on his father's grave; and when he brought it there in the evening, he found the grave had been decorated with sand and flowers. This had been done by other people, for they had all been very fond of the dear father who now was dead.

Early the following morning John packed his little bundle and put under his belt his whole inheritance, consisting of fifty dollars and a few silver coins, and with these few things he was about to set out into the world. But first he went to the churchyard to his father's grave, and there he recited the Lord's Prayer, and said, "Goodbye, dear father! I will always be a good person and then you can safely pray to the good Lord that all may go well for me!"

Out in the field where John walked the flowers bloomed so fresh and beautiful in the warm sunshine. They nodded in the wind, as if to say, "Welcome to nature! Isn't it lovely here?" But John turned round once more to look at the old church where he as a little child had been baptized and where he had gone every Sunday with his old father and had sung his hymns. Then, looking far up in one of the holes in the tower, he saw the church elf standing, with his little red pointed cap, shading his face with his bent arm because otherwise the sun would shine in his eyes. John nodded goodbye to him, and the little elf swung his red cap, laid his hand on his heart, and kissed his fingers many times to show that he wished him well and hoped that he might have a pleasant journey.

John thought of the many beautiful things he would see in the great splendid world, and walked on and on, farther than he had ever been before. He didn't know the towns he passed through or the people he met. He was now far away among strangers.

The first night he had to go to sleep in a haystack in a field, for he had no other bed. But it was really lovely, he thought; a king couldn't have a nicer bed. The whole field by the river, the haystack, and then the blue sky above made a beautiful bedroom. The green grass with tiny red and white flowers was the carpet, the elders and the wild-rose hedges were bouquets of flowers, and he had the whole river as a washbasin with its clear fresh water, where the reeds bowed, saying both good evening and good morning. The moon was a big night lamp high up under a blue ceiling, and it wouldn't set fire to the curtains! John could sleep quite peacefully, and so he did. He did not awaken until the sun rose and all the little birds around him sang, "Good morning! Good morning! Aren't you up yet?"

The bells rang for church. It was Sunday and people were on their way to hear the minister, and John went with them. He sang a hymn and listened to the word of God, and he felt as if he were in his own church, where he had been baptized and had sung hymns with his father.

In the churchyard outside there were so many graves, and some of them were overgrown with high grass. John thought of his father's grave, which might get to look like these now that he was not there to weed it and put flowers on it. So he sat down and pulled up the grass, raised the wooden crosses that had fallen over, and laid the wreaths, which the wind had blown away from the graves, back in place, thinking that perhaps someone would do the same for his father's grave now that he couldn't.

Outside the gate of the churchyard stood an old beggar, leaning on his crutch. John gave him the few silver coins he had, and then went happily and cheerfully on into the wide world.

Toward evening a bad storm came up, and John hurried to find shelter, but it soon grew dark. Then at last he reached a little church standing all alone at the top of a hill. Luckily the door was ajar, and he slipped inside. Here he would stay till the storm was over.

"I'll sit here in a corner." he said. "I'm very tired and need a little rest." So he sat down, folded his hands, and recited his evening prayer, and before he knew it he was asleep and dreaming, while it thundered and lightninged outside.

When he awoke again it was the middle of the night, but the storm had passed and the moon was shining in upon him through the windows. In the middle of the floor stood an open coffin with a dead man in it who had not yet been buried. John was not afraid at all, for he had a good conscience and knew that the dead harm no one; it is the living, evil people who do harm. Two such wicked living persons were standing close beside the dead man, who had been placed in the church before burial. They wanted to do him harm; they wouldn't let him rest in his coffin but meant to throw him outside the church door. The poor dead man!

"Why do you want to do that?" asked John. "It is evil and wicked. Let him rest in peace in the name of Jesus!"

"Oh, fiddle-faddle!" said the two nasty men. "He has cheated us! He owes us money, which he couldn't pay back, and now he's dead on top of that, so we'll never get a cent. That's why we want revenge! He'll lie like a dog outside the church door!"

"I have only fifty dollars," said John. "That is my whole inheritance, but I will gladly give it to you, if you will honestly promise me to leave the poor dead man in peace. I can get along all right without the money. I am strong and healthy, and the Lord will always help me."

"Very well," said the villainous men, "if you will pay his debts, we certainly won't do him any harm, you can be sure of that!" Then they took the money that John gave them, laughing loudly at his goodness, and went their way. But John laid the body straight again in the coffin, folded its hands, said goodbye, and went on through the forest, quite content.

On all sides, wherever the moon could shine through the trees, he saw the pretty little fairies playing merrily. They were not disturbed by John, for they knew very well that he was a good, innocent person; and it is only evil people who are never allowed to see the fairies. Some of them were no bigger than a finger, and they had long blond hair fastened with golden combs. Two by two they rocked on the great dewdrops that lay on the leaves and tall grass. Sometimes the drop rolled away and the fairies fell down between the long blades of grass, and then there was much laughter and uproar among the other little folk. It was great fun! They sang, and John clearly recognized all the pretty songs he had learned as a little boy. Great dappled spiders with silver crowns on their heads spun long suspension bridges from hedge to hedge, and made palaces which, when the fine dew fell on them, looked like shining glass in the bright moonlight. Thus the time passed until the sun rose. Then the little fairies crept into the flower buds and the wind caught their bridges and palaces, which floated away into the air like great cobwebs.

John had just come out of the forest when a strong male voice called behind him, "Hello there, comrade! Where are you go-ing?"

"Out into the wide world," said John. "I have neither father nor mother. I am a poor boy, but the Lord will surely help me!"

"I'm going out into the wide world, too," said the stranger. "Shall we keep each other company?"

"All right!" said John, and so they walked on together. They soon grew to like each other very much, for they were both good persons. But John soon saw that the stranger was much wiser than he: he had traveled almost all around the world and was able to talk about every conceivable thing there is.

The sun was already high when they sat down under a large tree to eat their lunch. Just then an old woman came by. She was very old and bent and leaned on a crutch. On her back she carried a load of kindling that she had gathered in the forest. Her apron was fastened up, and John could see the ends of three large bundles of fern and willow switches sticking out from it. When she was close to John and his companion, her foot slipped, and she fell down with a loud shriek; she had broken her leg, the poor old woman.

John wanted to carry her to her home at once, but the stranger opened his knapsack, took out a jar, and said that here he had an ointment that would make her leg well and strong immediately, and she would be able to walk home by herself as well as if she had never broken her leg. But in return he wanted her to give him the three bundles she had in her apron.

"That's a very high price!" said the old woman, nodding her head in a rather strange way. She did not like to part with her bundles, but neither was it so nice to lie there with a broken leg. So she gave him the bundles, and as soon as he had rubbed the ointment on the leg, the old lady got up and walked much better than before. That's what that ointment could do! But it wasn't to be had at any pharmacy.

"What do you want those bundles for?" John asked his trav-eling companion.

"They will make three fine brooms," he said, "and I am particularly fond of brooms, for I am a strange kind of fellow."

Then they walked on for a good bit.

"Just look at the storm coming up!" said John, pointing straight ahead. "Those are terribly heavy clouds!"

"No," said the traveling companion, "those aren't clouds. They're mountains, the great beautiful mountains, where you can climb high up above the clouds into the fresh air! Believe me, it's beautiful to be up there! By tomorrow we shall have gone that far out into the world!"

But they were not so close to them as it seemed; it took a whole day before they reached the mountains, where the dark forests grew right up to the sky and where there were boulders as big as an entire town. It was certainly going to be a tough job to reach the other side, so John and his traveling companion went into an inn to rest and strengthen themselves for the next day's journey.

Many people were gathered in the large taproom at the inn, for there was a man with a puppet show. He had just set up his little theater, and people were sitting all around waiting to see the play. Right up in front, in the best seat, sat a fat old butcher. His great bulldog—ugh! how ferocious that dog looked—sat by his side. It was all eyes, just like all the others.

Now the play began, and it was a nice play, with a king and a queen in it who were sitting on the most lovely throne and wearing golden crowns on their heads and long trains on their robes—for they could well afford it! The prettiest wooden dolls, with glass eyes and big mustaches, stood at all the doors, opening and closing them to let fresh air into the room! It was really a lovely play, and not at all sad, but just as the queen got up and walked across the floor, then—heaven knows what the great bulldog thought, but since the fat butcher was not holding him, he made one leap right into the theater and seized the queen by her slender waist so that it went, "Snap!" It was just awful!

The poor man who directed the play was so frightened and

downhearted on account of his queen, for she was the loveliest doll he had; and now the horrid bulldog had bitten her head off. But after the people had gone away, the stranger who had come with John said that he could make her all right again, and he brought out his jar and rubbed the doll with the ointment that had cured the poor old woman when she had broken her leg. As soon as the doll had been rubbed with the ointment, it immediately became whole again. It could even move all its limbs by itself; it was no longer necessary to pull the strings. The doll was like a living person except that it couldn't talk. The man who owned the little puppet show was very pleased because now he didn't have to hold this doll, for it could dance by itself. None of the others could do that.

Later, when night fell and all the people at the inn had gone to bed, there was someone who was sighing so awfully deeply, and who kept it up so long, that everyone got up to see who it could be. The man who had directed the play went over to his little theater, for that was where the sighs were coming from. All the wooden dolls were lying in a heap, the king and all his guards; and it was they who were sighing so mournfully and staring with their big glass eyes. They wanted to be rubbed with the ointment, just like the queen, so that they too would be able to move by themselves. The queen fell right on her knees and held up her beautiful gold crown, imploring, "Please take this, but rub some ointment on my consort and my courtiers!" At that the poor man who owned the theater and the dolls could not help crying, for he felt really very sorry for them. He immediately promised to give the traveling companion all the money he would take in at the next evening's performance if only he would rub the ointment on four or five of his nicest dolls. But the traveling companion said he wanted nothing at all except the big sword that the man wore at his side. When he got it, he rubbed six of the dolls, and at once they began to dance so prettily that all the girls, the real live girls who were looking on, took to dancing too. The coachman and the cook danced together, the waiter and the chambermaid, all the guests, and the fire shovel and the fire tongs. But these last two fell over just as they took their first hop. Oh, it was a lively night!

The next morning John and his traveling companion left them all and climbed up the high mountains and through the great pine forests. They went so high that the church towers far below them looked at last like little red berries down among all the greenery; and they could see far away for many, many miles, to where they had never been! John had never before seen at one time so much of the beauty of this glorious world. The sun shone warm in the clear blue sky; far away among the mountains he heard hunters blow their horns, and so beautiful did it sound that tears of joy filled his eyes. He could not help exclaiming, "Dear Lord, I could kiss you, because you are so good to us all and have given us all the beauty that there is in the world!"

The traveling companion also stood with folded hands and looked out over the forests and towns in the warm sunshine. At that moment they heard a wonderful sound above them and, looking up, saw a great white swan hovering in the air. It was very beautiful, and it sang as they had never heard any bird sing before. But the song grew fainter and fainter, and the swan bowed its head and sank slowly down before their feet, where it lay dead, that beautiful bird.

"Two such beautiful wings," said the traveling companion. "Such big white wings as this bird has are worth a lot of money; I'll take them with me! Can you see now what a good thing it was that I got a sword?" Then with one blow he cut off both wings from the dead swan, for he meant to keep them.

They traveled many, many miles over the mountains till at last they saw before them a great town with over a hundred towers, which shone like silver in the sunshine. In the center of the town was a splendid marble castle, roofed with red gold, and there lived the king.

John and his traveling companion did not want to enter the town at once but stayed at a nearby inn to dress in their best, for they wished to make a good appearance when they walked through the streets. The innkeeper told them that the king was such a good man that he never harmed a soul, but his daughter—Heaven preserve us!—was a wicked princess! Beauty she had more than enough of; no one could be so beautiful and lovely as she was. But what good was that, when she was so evil and wicked a witch, who was responsible for the deaths of so many fine princes? She had given permission to everybody to court her. Anyone could come, prince or beggar; it was all the same to her. He only had to guess three things that she asked him. If he could do that she would marry him, and he would be king over the whole land when her father died. But if he couldn't guess the three things she asked, she either had him hanged or had his head cut off. That's how evil and wicked this beautiful princess was! Her father, the old king, was very saddened by this but he couldn't forbid her being so wicked, for he had once said that he would never have anything to do with her suitors: she could do as she liked. Every single time a prince came who wanted to guess what she asked in order to win her, he failed, and so he had either been hanged or had his head cut off. Naturally, each one had been warned in time—he could have refrained from courting her. The old king was so saddened by all the sorrow and misery that he and all his soldiers spent a whole day every year on their knees praying that the princess might become good. But that she definitely did not want to do. Old ladies, who drank brandy, dyed it black before drinking it; that was their way of mourning, and more they could not do.

"That horrible princess!" said John. "She certainly ought to be whipped; that would be the best thing for her. If only I were the old king, I would soon make her blood run."

Just then they heard the people outside shouting "Hurrah!" The princess was passing by, and she was really so beautiful that everyone forgot how wicked she was and that's why they shouted "Hurrah!" Twelve beautiful maidens, all dressed in white silk dresses with gold tulips in their hands, rode on coal-black horses by her side. The princess herself was on a snow-white horse decorated with diamonds and rubies; her riding dress was of pure gold, and the whip in her hand looked like a sunbeam. The gold crown on her head glittered like the little

stars up in heaven; and her cloak was sewn from the wings of
thousands of beautiful butterflies. Yet she herself was more
beautiful than all her clothes.

When John saw her, his face became as red as blood, and he
could hardly say a single word; the princess looked exactly like
the lovely girl with the gold crown that he had dreamed about
the night his father died. He thought she was so beautiful that
he could not help falling in love with her. Certainly it could not
be true, he said, that she was a wicked witch who had people
hanged or beheaded when they couldn't guess the riddles she
put to them. "Anybody has permission to court her, even the
poorest beggar. I will go to the castle myself, for I cannot do
otherwise!"

They all said that he shouldn't go, for he would only meet the same fate as the others. His traveling companion also advised him against it, but John was sure he would get along all right. So he brushed his shoes and his coat, washed his face and hands, combed his beautiful blond hair, and went quite alone into the town and up to the castle.

"Come in," said the old king when John knocked at the door. John opened it, and the old king, in his dressing gown and embroidered slippers, came to meet him. He had his gold crown on his head, his scepter in one hand, and his gold ball in the other. "Wait a moment!" he said, and tucked the ball under his arm so as to be able to shake hands with John. But as soon as he heard that John was a suitor, he began to cry so hard that the scepter and ball fell to the floor, and he had to dry his eyes on his dressing gown. The poor old king!

"Give it up!" he said. "You'll fail just like all the others. Take a look at this!" Then he led John out into the princess's flower garden, which was a terrifying sight to see! In every tree hung three or four princes who had courted the princess but had not been able to guess the things she asked them. Whenever there was a gust of wind, all the bones rattled so that the little birds were frightened away and never dared come into the garden. All the flowers were staked up with human bones, and in the flowerpots were grinning skulls. That was indeed a fine garden for a princess.

"Here, you see!" said the old king. "It will be the same for you as it was for all the others you find here. So please do give it up! You will make me really unhappy if you don't, because it upsets me so much!"

John kissed the hand of the good old king, and said he thought he'd do all right, for he was so fond of the beautiful princess.

Just then the princess herself and all her ladies came riding into the castle yard; so they went over to her and said, "How do you do." She looked so pretty, shook hands with John, and he loved her even more than before. She certainly couldn't be the bad, wicked witch everyone said she was. They went up into the hall, and the little pages offered them jam and gingersnaps, but the old king was so sad that he couldn't eat anything at all, and the gingersnaps were too hard for him anyway.

It was now decided that John should come to the castle again the next morning, when the judges and the entire council would be assembled to hear his attempt to answer the question. If he succeeded, he would still have to come two more times. But no one had ever succeeded in guessing the first time around, so all had lost their lives.

John was not at all worried about what would happen to him. He was actually very happy and thought only of the beautiful princess. He felt quite certain that the dear Lord would help him, but how that would come about he didn't know, nor did he want to think about it. He danced along the highway on his way back to the inn, where his traveling companion was waiting for him.

John could not say enough about how kind the princess had been toward him and how beautiful she was. He was already longing for the next day, when he was to go to the castle to try his luck at guessing.

But his traveling companion shook his head and was very sad. "I like you very much!" he said. "We might have stayed together for a long time, and now I am already going to lose you! Poor dear John, I could really cry, but I don't want to spoil your joy on what might be the last evening we are together. Let's have a good time, a very good time! Tomorrow, when you are gone, is time enough for me to weep!"

All the people in the town had heard right away that a new suitor had come for the princess; thus there was general mourning. The theater was closed; all the lady cake vendors tied black crepe around their candy pigs; the king and the clergy prayed on their knees in church. The sorrow in the town was so great because it was certain that John would do no better than any of the other suitors.

Later, that evening, the traveling companion made a big

bowl of punch and said to John that they should really have a good time now and drink a toast to the princess. But when John had drunk two glasses he became so sleepy it was impossible for him to keep his eyes open, and he couldn't help falling asleep. The traveling companion lifted him up gently from his chair and laid him on his bed. Then, as soon as it was dark, he took the two big wings he had cut off the swan and tied them tight onto his own shoulders. In his pocket he put the largest bundle of switches that he'd gotten from the old woman who had fallen and broken her leg. Then he opened the window and flew out over the town, right to the castle, where he sat down in a corner under the window that opened out from the princess's bedroom.

The whole town was quiet. As the clock struck a quarter to twelve, the window opened, and the princess, in a great white cloak and long black wings, flew away over the town and out to a great mountain. But the traveling companion made himself invisible, so that the princess couldn't see him at all, and he flew behind her, whipping her with his switches so hard that the blood flowed at every stroke. Oh, what a flight that was through the air! The wind caught her cloak, which flowed out on both sides like the large sail of a ship, and the moon shone through it.

"How it hails! How it hails!" said the princess at every blow of the switches, and that was what she deserved! At last she reached the mountain and knocked. There was a rumbling like thunder as the mountain opened and the princess went in. The traveling companion followed after her, for no one could see him, since he was invisible. They went through a great, long passage where the walls glittered in a very strange way—and up and down them ran over a thousand glowing spiders, all shining like fire. Then they reached a great hall built of silver and gold with red and blue flowers as large as sunflowers shining from the walls. But no one could pick these flowers, for the stems were hideous poisonous snakes, and the flowers were the flames that came out of their mouths. The whole ceiling was studded with shining glowworms and skyblue bats that flapped their transparent wings. It was a strange sight! In the middle of the floor was a throne, held up by the skeletons of four horses, with harnesses of red fire spiders. The throne itself was of milk-white glass, and the seat cushions were small black mice biting one another's tails. Above the throne was a canopy of rose-colored spider webs set with the prettiest little green flies, glittering like gemstones. In the middle of the throne sat an old ogre, with a crown on his ugly head and a scepter in his hand. He kissed the princess on her forehead and made her sit beside him on his costly throne; then the music began! Big black grasshoppers played on mouth organs, and the owl thumped himself on the stomach, for there wasn't any drum. What a queer concert! Little black goblins, each with a firefly on his cap, danced around in the hall. No one could see the traveling companion. He had placed himself just behind the throne, where he could see and hear everything. The courtiers, who now came in, looked very grand and distinguished, but anyone with eyes in his head could see at once what they were. They were nothing but cabbage heads stuck on broomsticks, which the ogre had conjured into life and dressed up in embroidered clothes. But that really didn't matter, because they were used only for decoration.

After the dancing had gone on awhile, the princess told the ogre that she had a new suitor and asked what she might think of to question him about the following morning, when he was to come to the castle.

"Listen!" said the ogre. "I'll tell you what to do! Choose something very simple, then it will never occur to him. You just think of one of your shoes. He'll never guess that. Then have his head chopped off, but don't forget when you come here tomorrow night to bring me his eyes. I want to eat them!"

The princess made a deep curtsy and said she would not forget the eyes. The ogre then opened the mountain and she flew back home. But the traveling companion followed her, beating her so hard with the switches that she heaved a great sigh at the severe hailstorm and hurried as fast as she could through the window into her bedroom. But the traveling companion flew back to the inn where John still slept, took off his wings, and lay down on the bed, too, for he had a right to be tired.

It was very early in the morning when John awoke. The traveling companion also got up and said that he had dreamed a very strange dream during the night about the princess and her shoe. He asked John, therefore, please to be sure to ask the princess if she wasn't thinking of her shoe! For, of course, that was what he had heard the ogre say in the mountain. But he didn't want to tell John anything about that, so he merely asked him to inquire whether she wasn't thinking of her shoe.

"I can just as well ask about one thing as another," said John. "Perhaps what you dreamed may be true, because I have always believed the Lord will help me! But I'll say goodbye to you all the same, for if I guess wrong I shall never see you again!"

So they kissed each other, and John went into town and up to the castle. The hall was full of people; the judges sat in their armchairs with their heads resting on eiderdown pillows, for they had so much to think about. The old king stood up and dried his eyes with a white handkerchief. Now the princess entered. She was even much more beautiful than the day before, and greeted them all most graciously. But to John she held out her hand, saying, "Good morning to you!"

Now John had to guess what she was thinking of. Oh, how friendlily she looked at him. But as soon as she heard him say the one word "shoe," her face turned as white as a sheet and she trembled all over, but that wasn't going to help her, because he had guessed right!

My heavens, how happy the old king was! He turned a splendid somersault, and everyone clapped his hands for him and for John, who had guessed right the first time.

The traveling companion was also very glad when he found out how happily things had turned out. But John folded his hands and thanked the dear Lord, who would surely help him again the next two times. The very next day was fixed for the second round of guessing.

That evening passed just as the previous one had. While John slept, the traveling companion flew after the princess to the mountain, beating her even more severely than the first time, for this time he had taken two bundles of switches with him. No one saw him, and he heard everything. The princess was to think of her glove, and this he told John as if it had been a dream. So John was able to guess correctly again, and there was great joy at the castle. The whole court turned somersaults, just as they had seen the king do the first time, but the princess lay on the sofa, and wouldn't say a single word! Now everything depended on whether John could guess correctly the third time. If he did, he would win the beautiful princess and inherit the whole kingdom when the old king died; if he guessed wrong, he would lose his life and the ogre would eat his beautiful blue eyes.

The evening before, John went to bed early, said his prayers, and slept very peacefully. But the traveling companion fastened the wings to his back, tied the sword at his side, took all three bundles of switches in his hand, and flew off to the castle.

It was a pitch dark night, and it was so stormy that tiles flew off the roofs of houses, and in the garden where the skeletons hung the trees bent like reeds in the wind. The lightning flashed every moment, and the thunder sounded like one continuous crash that lasted all night. Now the window burst open, and the princess flew out. She was as pale as death, but she laughed at the fearful storm and thought that it wasn't bad enough. Her white cloak whirled in the wind like the large sail of a ship, but the traveling companion whipped her with his three bundles of switches till the blood dripped down to the ground and she could hardly fly any farther. But at last she reached the mountain.

"It's stormy and hailing," she said. "Never have I been out in such weather!"

"One can even get too much of a good thing!" said the ogre. Then the princess told him that John had also guessed right the second time. If he could do the same again tomorrow, he would win and she could never again come to the mountain and never do magic tricks as before. That is why she was very sad.

"He will not be able to guess!" said the ogre. "I will think of something he never has thought of! Or else he must be a greater magician than I am. But now let's have a good time!" And he took the princess by both hands, and they danced around with all the little goblins and fireflies in the room. The red spiders dashed just as merrily up and down the walls, and it looked as if the fire flowers were giving off sparks. The owl beat his drum, the crickets piped, and the black grasshoppers played their mouth organs. That was a merry ball!

When they had danced long enough, the princess had to go home. Otherwise she might be missed at the castle. The ogre said he would accompany her, so they could be together that much longer.

Away they flew through the bad weather, and the traveling companion wore out his three bundles of switches on their backs; never had the ogre been out in such a hailstorm! Outside the castle he said goodbye to the princess and right then whispered to her, "Think of my head!" But the traveling companion heard it even so, and just as the princess slipped through the window into her bedroom and the ogre turned around to go back, he grabbed the ogre by his long black beard and with his sword chopped off his hideous head at the shoulders so fast that the ogre himself didn't see what happened. The body he threw into the sea to the fishes, but the head he merely dipped into the water and then tied it up in his silk handkerchief and took it back to the inn. Then he went to bed.

The next morning he gave John the handkerchief, but said he must not untie it until the princess asked him what it was she was thinking of.

There were so many people in the great hall of the castle that they were packed together as tightly as radishes tied in a bunch. The council sat in their chairs with their soft pillows, and the old king had a new set of clothes on, and his gold crown and scepter had been polished. Everything looked very nice! But the

princess was extremely pale and wore a coal-black dress as if she were going to a funeral.

"What have I thought about?" she asked John, and he immediately untied the handkerchief and was himself quite frightened when he saw the ogre's ugly head. Everybody shuddered, because it was such an awful thing to look at, but the princess sat as if turned to stone and couldn't say a single word. At last she got up and gave John her hand, for he had guessed right. She looked neither to the right nor to the left, but sighed deeply and said, "Now you are my master! Tonight we shall hold our wedding!"

"I like that!" said the old king. "That's just as it should be!" All the people shouted hurrah, the guard played music in the streets, the bells pealed, and the lady cake vendors took the black crepe off their candy pigs, for now all was rejoicing. Three whole roasted oxen, stuffed with ducks and hens, were set out in the middle of the market square, and everyone could cut a piece for himself. The water fountains ran with the finest wine, and anyone who bought a penny's worth of pretzels at the baker's got six big buns into the bargain, and these were buns with raisins in them!

In the evening the whole town was illuminated; soldiers fired off cannons and little boys firecrackers. Up at the castle there was eating and drinking, toasting and dancing. All the distinguished gentlemen and lovely ladies danced together, and one could hear far and wide as they sang:

> Here are many pretty girls,
> Who'd like a little swing-around.
> They love a drummer's march the best.
> Pretty girl whirl around,
> Dancing and stamping
> So the shoe soles fall-dera!

But the princess was still a witch and didn't care for John at all. The traveling companion remembered this, and gave John three feathers from the swan's wings and a little flask containing a few drops. He told him to have a large tub of water placed beside the wedding bed, and when the princess was climbing into bed, he should give her a little push so that she would fall into the water. Then he was to dunk her under three times, after first having thrown in the feathers and the drops from the flask. This would free her from the magic spell, and she would grow to love him very much.

John did everything the traveling companion had advised him to do. The princess screamed loudly as he dunked her under the water and struggled in his hands in the form of a great coal-black swan with fiery eyes. The second time she came up out of the water, the swan had turned white, except for a single black ring around its neck. John prayed piously to God and let the water cover the bird for the third time. At that very moment it changed into the most beautiful princess. She was even lovelier than before, and she thanked John with tears in her beautiful eyes, for he had released her from the spell.

The next morning the old king came with all his court, and there were constant congratulations until late in the day. Last of all came the traveling companion. He had his staff in his hand and his knapsack on his back. John kissed him many times and said that he must not go away; he should stay with him, for he was the cause of all his happiness. But the traveling companion shook his head and said gently and kindly, "No, now my time is up. I have only paid my debt. Do you remember the dead man that the evil men wanted to mistreat? You gave all you possessed so he might have peace in his grave. I am that dead man!"

Suddenly he was gone.

The wedding lasted a whole month. John and the princess loved each other very much, and the old king lived many happy days, dandling his little grandchildren on his knee and letting them play with his scepter. But John was king over the whole land.

The Little Mermaid

F ar out at sea the water is as blue as the petals of the loveliest cornflower and as clear as the purest glass. But it is very deep—deeper than any anchor rope can reach. Many church steeples would have to be placed one on top of the other to reach from the bottom up to the surface of the water. Down there live the sea folk.

Now, there is no reason to believe that there is nothing but bare white sand at the bottom of the sea! No, down there the most marvelous trees and plants grow, and they have such pliable stalks and leaves that the slightest movement of the water makes them move just as if they were alive. All the fish, big and small, slip in and out among the branches just as birds do up here in the air. At the very deepest spot lies the castle of the sea king. The walls are made of coral, and the long windows with pointed arches are of the clearest amber. The roof is made of mussel shells that open and close with the flow of the water. It is a lovely sight, for every shell contains gleaming pearls, any one of which would have done a queen's crown proud.

The sea king had been a widower for many years, and his old mother kept house for him. She was a wise old woman and proud of her noble birth, therefore she wore twelve oysters on her tail; others who were highborn were allowed to wear only six. Otherwise she deserved much praise, especially because she was so fond of the little sea princesses, her granddaughters. They were six lovely children, but the youngest was the most beautiful of all. Her skin was as clear and delicate as a rose petal, and her eyes were as blue as the deepest sea, but like all the others, she had no feet. Her body ended in a fishtail.

All day long they could play down in the castle in the great halls where living flowers grew out of the walls. When the high amber windows were opened, the fish swam in to them, just as swallows fly in to us when we open our windows. But the fish swam right over to the little princesses and ate out of their hands, and let themselves be petted.

Outside the castle was a large garden with fiery red and deep blue trees. The fruit gleamed like gold and the flowers like burning flames, for their stalks and leaves were in constant motion. The ground itself was the finest sand, but blue like a sulphur flame. A strange blue cast lay over everything down there. You would sooner have thought that you were standing high up in the air with only the sky above and below rather than at the bottom of the sea. When there was a dead calm, you could just catch a glimpse of the sun looking like a purple flower from whose center all the light streamed out.

Each of the little princesses had her own small plot in the garden where she could dig and plant as she liked. One gave her flower bed the shape of a whale, another thought it nicer to have hers like a little mermaid. But the youngest made hers perfectly round like the sun and had only flowers that shone red as the sun itself. She was a strange child, quiet and pensive, and while the other sisters decorated their gardens with all kinds of odd things they had taken from wrecked ships, the only thing she would allow in hers, besides the rosy-red flowers that looked like the sun on high, was a beautiful marble statue. It was of a handsome boy carved out of pure white stone that in a ship-wreck had sunk to the bottom of the sea. Beside the statue she planted a rose-colored weeping willow. It grew splendidly, and its fresh branches hung out over the statue and down toward the

blue sandy bottom, where its shadow appeared violet and
swayed just as the branches did. It looked as if the top and
roots were kissing each other in play.

She had no greater pleasure than to hear about the world of
human beings up above. Her old grandmother had to tell her
all she knew about ships and towns, people and animals. What
seemed especially wonderful to her was that the flowers on earth
gave off a fragrance, since they didn't do that at the bottom of
the sea, and that the woods were green and the fish that could
be seen among the branches could sing so loud and sweet that it
was a delight. Those were the little birds that her grandmother
called fish; otherwise the princesses wouldn't have understood
her, because they had never seen a bird.

"As soon as you are fifteen," said their grandmother, "you will all be allowed to rise to the surface of the sea, sit on the rocks in the moonlight, and watch the big ships sail by. You will see woods and towns, too." In the coming year the oldest sister would be fifteen, but the others—well, each one was a year younger than the other, so the youngest still had five long years left before she could come up from the bottom of the sea and see what our world looked like. But each one promised the others to tell what she had seen and what she had found to be most lovely on that first day. Their grandmother hadn't told them enough—there were so many things they wanted to know about.

No one was as full of longing as the youngest, the one who had to wait the longest and who was so quiet and pensive. Many a night she stood by the open window and looked up through the dark blue water where the fish flipped their fins and tails. She could see the moon and the stars, though they shone quite pale, but through the water they looked much bigger than they do to our eyes. Whenever it seemed as though a black cloud glided under them, then she knew it was either a whale swimming above her or a ship with many human beings on board. It certainly never occurred to them that a lovely little mermaid was standing down below stretching her white hands up toward the keel.

Now the eldest princess was fifteen and was allowed to rise above the surface of the sea.

When she came back, she had hundreds of things to tell about, but the most lovely of all, she said, was to lie in the moonlight on a sandbank in the calm sea and look at the big city close to the shore where the lights twinkled like hundreds of stars, listen to the music and the noise and clamor of carriages and human beings, see the many church towers and spires, and hear the bells pealing. Just because the little mermaid couldn't go up there, she longed for all this the most.

Oh, how eagerly the youngest sister listened; and later, in the evening, when she was standing at the open window and looking up through the dark blue water, she thought of the great city with all the noise and clamor, and it seemed to her she could hear the church bells pealing down to her.

The following year the second sister got permission to rise up through the water and swim wherever she liked. She came up just as the sun was setting and that sight was what she deemed loveliest. The whole sky looked like gold, she said, and the clouds, well, she couldn't find words to describe their beauty! Red and violet, they had sailed above her, but much faster than the clouds, like a long white veil, a flock of wild swans flew over the water toward the sun. She swam toward it, but it sank, and the rosy glow on the sea and clouds was extinguished.

The following year the third sister went up. She was the boldest of them all, so she swam up a broad river that flowed into the sea. She saw lovely green hills covered with grapevines; castles and farms peeped out from among magnificent forests. She heard how all the birds sang, and the sun shone so hot that she often had to dive under water to cool her burning face. In a little bay she came upon a whole flock of little human children. Quite naked, they ran and splashed in the water. She wanted to play with them, but they ran away terrified. And then came a little black animal—it was a dog, but she had never seen a dog before—and it barked at her so furiously that she got scared and fled to the open sea. But never could she forget the magnificent forests, the green hills, and the pretty children who could swim in the water even though they had no fishtails.

The fourth sister was not so bold. She stayed out in the middle of the stormy sea and said it was precisely this that was the most lovely thing of all. She could see all around her for many miles, and the sky above was just like a big glass bell jar. She had seen ships, but they were far away and looked like sea gulls. The funny dolphins had turned somersaults, and big whales had spouted water through their nostrils so that it looked like hundreds of fountains all around.

Now the fifth sister had her turn. Because her birthday happened to be in the winter, she saw things the others hadn't seen. The sea looked quite green, and large icebergs were floating about. Each one looked like a pearl, she said, but they were certainly much bigger than the church steeples built by human beings. They appeared in the strangest shapes and sparkled like diamonds. She had perched on one of the largest of them, and all the ships had detoured, terrified, around where she sat with her long hair floating in the wind. But late in the evening the sky was covered with clouds. The lightning flashed and the thunder rolled while the black sea lifted the large blocks of ice up high, where they glittered in the red flashes of lightning. On all the ships the sails were reefed in anxiety and fear. But she sat calmly on her floating iceberg and watched the blue flashes of lightning zigzag into the shining sea.

The first time each sister rose above the water, she was delighted with the new and beautiful things she saw. But now that they, as grown-up girls, were allowed to go up whenever they liked, they lost interest in it; they longed to be home again, and after a month had gone by they said it was most beautiful down where they lived—besides one felt so comfortable at home.

Many an evening the five sisters would rise up arm in arm, all in a row, to the surface. They had lovely voices, lovelier than those of any human being, and whenever a storm was brewing and they thought ships might be wrecked, they would swim ahead of the ships and sing so sweetly about how beautiful it was at the bottom of the sea and tell the sailors not to be afraid of going down there. But the sailors couldn't understand the words and thought it was the storm. Nor did they ever see the beauty below, for when the ship sank, the sailors drowned and only came to the castle of the sea king as corpses.

In the evenings, when the sisters rose arm in arm through the water, the little sister was left behind all alone, looking after them and about to burst into tears. But a mermaid has no tears, so she suffers all the more.

"Oh, if only I were fifteen!" she said. "I know that I shall love that world up there and the human beings who live and dwell in it."

At last she too was fifteen.

"Well, now you're ready to go off on your own!" said her

grandmother, the old Queen Mother. "Come, let me dress you up just like the rest of your sisters." And she put a wreath of white lilies on her hair, but each flower petal was half a pearl. And the old queen had eight oysters attach themselves tightly to the princess's tail to show her high rank.

"It hurts so much!" said the little mermaid.

"Well, one must suffer to look pretty!" said the old queen.

Oh, how gladly she would have shaken off all this finery and put aside the heavy wreath. The red flowers in her garden suited her much better, but she didn't dare change anything. "Goodbye," she said, and rose as light and clear as a bubble up through the water.

The sun had just gone down as she raised her head above the sea, but all the clouds still shone like roses and gold, and in the middle of the pale red sky the evening star gleamed clear and lovely. The air was mild and fresh, and the sea dead calm. There lay a big ship with three masts. Only a single sail was hoisted, not a breath of wind stirred, and the sailors were sitting around in the rigging and on the yardarms. There was music and song, and as the evening grew darker, hundreds of brightly colored lanterns were lit. They looked like the flags of every nation waving in the air. The little mermaid swam right over to the window of the cabin, and every time the water lifted her up she could look in through the clear glass panes at the many finely dressed humans. But the handsomest of them all was the young prince with big dark eyes. He was certainly not much older than sixteen; it was his birthday, and that was the reason for all these festivities. The sailors were dancing on deck, and when the young prince came out, more than a hundred rockets shot up into the air. They shone as bright as day, so the little mermaid became quite frightened and dived beneath the surface. But she soon put her head up again, and then it looked as if all the stars in the sky were falling down to her. Never before had she seen such fireworks. Great suns spun around, magnificent fire fish swung through the blue air, and everything was reflected in the clear, calm sea. The ship itself was so lit up that one could see every little rope, to say nothing of the people. Oh, how handsome the young prince was! He shook hands with the sailors and laughed and smiled while the music filled the beautiful night.

It grew late, but the little mermaid couldn't take her eyes off the ship and the handsome prince. The brightly colored lanterns were extinguished, the rockets no longer shot up into the air, and no more cannon salutes were fired. But deep down in the sea it rumbled and grumbled. During this whole time the little mermaid sat bobbing up and down on the water so that she could look into the cabin. But now the ship gained speed and one sail after the other billowed out. The waves climbed higher, great clouds gathered, and lightning flashed in the distance. Oh, there was terrible weather ahead, and the sailors reefed the sails. The big ship pitched at top speed over the wild sea. The water rose like huge black mountains that wanted to crash down over the mast, but the ship dived down like a swan among the high waves and let itself be lifted high again on the towering waters. To the little mermaid this speed seemed enjoyable, but the sailors didn't think so. The ship groaned and moaned and the thick planks buckled under the powerful blows of the heavy seas against the ship. The mast snapped in two like a reed, and the ship pitched over on its side while the water rushed into the hold. Now the little mermaid saw they were in danger. She herself had to beware of planks and bits of wreckage from the ship floating in the water. For a moment it was so pitch dark that she couldn't see a thing, but when the lightning flashed, it was again so bright that she could recognize everybody on the ship. Each one was looking out for himself the best he could. She looked for the young prince in particular, and as the ship broke apart she saw him sink into the deep sea. At first she was quite joyful, for now he would come down to her. But then she recalled that human beings could not live in the water and that he couldn't come down to her father's castle unless he was dead. No, he shouldn't die! So she swam in among beams and planks that drifted on the sea, completely forgetting that they could have crushed her. She dived deep down into the water and rose high up again among the waves, and finally reached the young prince, who could hardly swim any longer in the stormy sea. His arms and legs were growing weak; his beautiful eyes were closing. He would have died if the little mermaid had not reached him. She held his head above the water and let the waves carry her with him wherever they might.

In the morning the stormy weather had passed; of the ship not a splinter was to be seen. The sun rose red and shining out of the water; it was as if it brought life back into the prince's cheeks, but his eyes remained closed. The mermaid kissed his high, handsome forehead and stroked back his wet hair. She thought he looked like the marble statue down in her little garden. She kissed him again and wished that he would live.

Now she saw the mainland ahead of her, high blue mountains on whose peaks the white snow glistened as if swans were lying there. Down by the coast were lovely green woods, and in the foreground stood a church or a convent, she didn't know which, but it was a building. Lemon and orange trees grew in its garden, and in front of the gate stood tall palm trees. Here the sea had formed a little bay, which was quite calm but very deep all the way to the rock where the fine white sand had been washed up. Here she swam with the handsome prince and laid him on the sand, taking special care to raise his head in the warm sunshine.

Now the bells began to peal in the big white building, and many young girls came through the garden. The little mermaid swam farther out behind some large rocks sticking out of the water, covered her hair and breast with sea foam so no one could see her little face, and kept watch to see who would happen upon the poor prince.

It wasn't long before a young girl came over to him. She seemed to be quite frightened, but only for a moment. Then she fetched several humans and the mermaid saw that the prince revived and smiled at everybody around him. But he didn't smile out to her, for he didn't even know that she had saved him. She felt very sad and when they led him into the big building, she dived sorrowfully down into the water and found her way home to her father's castle.

She had always been quiet and pensive, but now she became much more so. Her sisters asked what she had seen her first time up, but she told them nothing.

Many an evening and morning she swam up to the place where she had left the prince. She saw how the fruits in the garden ripened and were picked. She saw how the snow melted on the high mountains, but she didn't see the prince, and so she always returned home even sadder than before. Her only consolation was to sit in the little garden and throw her arms around the beautiful marble statue that looked like the prince. But she didn't take care of her flowers. They grew as in a wilderness out over the paths and they intertwined their long stalks and leaves in and out among the branches of the trees so that it became quite dark.

At last she couldn't bear it any longer, and told one of her sisters. Immediately all the others knew about it, but nobody else except a few other mermaids, who didn't tell anyone except their most intimate friends. One of them knew who the prince was. She too had seen the festivities on the ship and knew where he came from and where his kingdom was.

"Come, little sister," said the other princesses, and with their arms around one another's shoulders they arose in a long row up from the sea right by the place where they knew the prince's castle stood.

It was built of a pale yellow, glittery kind of stone, with great marble stairways, one of which led right down to the sea. Splendid gilded domes rose above the roof, and between the pillars surrounding the whole building stood marble statues that looked as if they were alive. Through the clear glass of the tall windows you could see into magnificent halls, where costly silk curtains and tapestries were hung, and all of the walls were covered with large paintings that were a pleasure to look at. In the middle of the biggest hall splashed a large fountain. Its streams of water jetted high up toward the glass dome in the roof, through which the sun shone down on the water and on all the lovely plants growing in the large basin.

Now she knew where he lived, and many an evening and

night she came there through the water. She swam much closer to land than any of the others had dared. Indeed, she even went all the way up the narrow canal under the magnificent marble balcony that cast a long shadow across the water. Here she sat and looked at the young prince, who thought he was quite alone in the bright moonlight.

Many an evening she saw him sailing to the sound of music in his splendid boat from which the flags were flying. She peeped out through the green reeds, and if the wind caught her long silver-white veil, anyone who saw it thought it was a swan spreading its wings.

Many a night, when the fishermen were fishing by torchlight in the sea, she heard them tell so many good things about the young prince, and that made her happy that she had saved his life when he was drifting about half dead on the waves. And she thought of how firmly his head had rested on her breast and how lovingly she had then kissed him. He knew nothing of all this; he couldn't even dream of her.

She grew more and more fond of human beings, and wished more and more that she could rise up among them. Their world seemed to her far bigger than hers. Why, they could traverse the sea in ships and climb high mountains way above the clouds, and the lands they possessed with their woods and fields stretched farther than she could see. There was so much she wanted to know, but her sisters couldn't answer all her questions. So she asked her old grandmother, who was very knowledgeable about the upper world, as she quite correctly called the lands above the sea.

"If human beings don't drown," asked the little mermaid, "can they live forever? Don't they die as we do down here in the sea?"

"Why, yes," the old queen said, "they must also die, and their lifetime is even shorter than ours. We can live to be three hundred years old, but when we cease to exist, we become just foam on the water without even a grave down here among our loved ones. We have no immortal soul; we never have life again. We are like the green reed: once it is severed, it can never be green again. Human beings, on the contrary, have a soul, which lives on forever, lives on even after the body has turned to dust. It rises up through the clear air, up to all the shining stars! Just as we rise out of the water and see the land of the human beings, so do they rise up to unknown, beautiful places which we shall never see."

"Why didn't we get an immortal soul?" asked the little mermaid sadly. "I'd gladly give all my three hundred years just to be a human being for one single day and afterward share in the heavenly world."

"You mustn't go and think about that," said the old queen. "We live much happier and better lives than the humans do up there."

"Then I shall die, too, and float like foam upon the sea, and not hear the music of the waves or see the lovely flowers and the red sun. Isn't there anything at all I can do to win an immortal soul?"

"No," said the old queen. "Only if a human being held you so dear that you were more to him than father and mother; only if he was attached to you with all his mind and heart and let the priest place his right hand in yours with a promise of faithfulness now and for all eternity, then his soul would pass over into your body, and you would also share in the happiness of mankind. He would give you a soul and still keep his own. But that can never happen! The very thing that is so lovely here in the sea, your fishtail, they consider repulsive up there on the earth. They don't know any better! Up there one has to have two clumsy props, which they call legs, to be beautiful!"

Then the little mermaid sighed and looked sadly at her fish-tail.

"Come, let's be happy!" said the old queen. "Let's leap and jump about during the three hundred years we have to live; that's plenty of time, indeed. Afterward we can rest in our grave all the more satisfied. Tonight we're going to have a court ball!"

Now, this was a splendor never to be seen on earth. The walls and ceiling of the great ballroom were made of thick but clear glass. Several hundred gigantic mussel shells, rosy red and grass green, stood in rows on each side filled with a blue flame, which lit up the whole hall and shone out through the walls so the sea outside was brightly illuminated. You could see all the countless fish, great and small, swimming toward the glass wall. On some the scales shone red violet; on others they seemed to be silver and gold. Through the middle of the hall flowed a broad stream on which the mermen and mermaids danced to their own lovely singing. No human beings on earth have such beautiful voices. The little mermaid sang more beautifully than anyone else, and they clapped their hands for her, and for a moment her heart was filled with joy, because she knew that she had the loveliest voice of all on earth or in the sea! But soon she began thinking again of the world above her. She couldn't forget the handsome prince and her sorrow that she did not possess, like him, an immortal soul. So she stole out of her father's castle, and while everything inside was song and merriment, she sat sadly in her little garden. Then she heard a bugle sounding down through the water, and she thought, "Now, he must be sailing up there, the one I love more than father and mother, the one to whom my thoughts are attached, and in whose hand I would place my life's happiness. I would risk everything to win him and an immortal soul. While my sisters are dancing in my father's castle I'll go to the sea witch. I've always been so afraid of her, but perhaps she can advise and help me."

Now the little mermaid left her garden and set out toward the roaring whirlpools behind which the sea witch lived. She had never been that direction before. No flowers grew there, no sea grass, only the bare, gray, sandy bottom stretched on toward the whirlpools, in which the water, like roaring mill wheels, swirled around and pulled everything within reach down into the depths. In between these crushing whirlpools she had to go to enter the realm of the sea witch, and for a long way the only road went over hot bubbling mire that the witch called her peat bog. Behind it lay her house, right in the middle of an eerie wood. All the trees and bushes were polyps—half animal and half plant. They looked like snakes with a hundred heads growing out of the ground. All the branches were long slimy arms with fingers like wriggling worms, and joint by joint they moved from the roots to the outermost tips. Whatever they could grab in the sea, they twined their arms around and never let go. Terrified, the little mermaid remained standing outside the wood. Her heart was pounding with fear; she almost turned back, but then she thought of the prince and the human soul, and that gave her courage. She bound her long, flowing hair tightly around her head so the polyps couldn't seize her by it. She crossed her hands over her breast and darted off through the water like a fish, in among the hideous polyps that stretched out their wriggling arms and fingers after her. She saw how each of them held something it had caught; hundreds of small arms held onto it like strong iron bands. Humans who had perished at sea and sunk all the way to the bottom peered forth as white skeletons from the polyps' arms. Also held tightly were ships' rudders and sea chests, skeletons of land animals, and— most horrible of all—a little mermaid they had caught and strangled.

Now she came to a large slimy clearing in the woods where big fat water snakes gamboled, showing their ugly yellow-white bellies. In the center of the clearing was a house built of the white bones of shipwrecked humans. There sat the sea witch letting a toad eat from her mouth, just the way human beings let a little canary eat sugar. She called the hideous, fat water snakes her little chickens and let them writhe on her big spongy breasts.

"I know what you want, all right," said the sea witch. "It's very foolish of you, but all the same you shall have your way, for it will bring you misery, my pretty princess! You want to get rid of your fishtail and have two stumps to walk on instead, just like human beings, so the young prince can fall in love with you, and you can win him and an immortal soul." At this the sea witch let out a laugh so loud and hideous that the toad and the snakes fell to the ground where they lay writhing. "You've come just in time," said the witch. "Tomorrow, after the sun rises, I couldn't help you until another year had passed. I shall make you a potion, and before the sun rises you must swim to land with it, seat yourself on the shore there, and drink it. Then your tail will split in two and shrink into what humans call pretty legs. But it will hurt! It will feel as if a sharp sword were cutting through you! Everybody who sees you will say that you are the loveliest living creature they have ever seen. You will keep your flowing movements; no dancer will be able to match you in grace, but every step you take will be like walking on a sharp knife so that your blood flows! If you want to suffer all this, then I'll help you."

"Yes," said the little mermaid in a trembling voice, and she thought of the prince and of winning an immortal soul.

"But remember," said the witch, "once you have taken on a human shape, you can never become a mermaid again! You can never descend down through the water to your sisters and to your father's castle. And if you do not win the prince's love, so that for your sake he forgets his father and mother and becomes attached to you with his whole mind and lets the priest place your hand in his and you become man and wife, you will not win an immortal soul! On the first morning after he has married someone else, your heart will break and you will become foam on the water."

"This is what I want!" said the little mermaid, and turned pale as death.

"But you must also pay me," said the witch, "and it is no small thing that I demand! You have the most beautiful voice of all down here at the bottom of the sea, and you probably think that you'll be able to enchant him with it. But that voice you must give to me! I want the best thing you possess in return for my precious potion. Why, I must put some of my own blood into it so that the potion will be as sharp as a two-edged sword."

"But if you take my voice," said the little mermaid, "what will I have left?"

"Your lovely figure," said the witch, "your flowing movements, and your eloquent eyes. With them you can easily enchant a human heart. Well, have you lost your courage? Stick out your little tongue so that I can cut it off as payment, and you shall have the potent potion."

"So be it!" said the little mermaid, and the witch put her kettle on to brew the magic potion. "Cleanliness is a good thing," she said and scoured her kettle with the snakes, which she had tied up into a knot. Then she cut herself in the breast and let her black blood drip into the kettle. The steam made the strangest shapes that were frightening and dreadful to see. The witch kept putting new things into the kettle, and when it all was cooking properly, it sounded like a crocodile weeping. At last the potion was ready, and it looked like the clearest water.

"Here you have it!" said the witch, and cut out the tongue of the little mermaid, who was now mute and could neither sing nor speak.

"If any of the polyps should grab you when you go back through my wood," said the witch, "just throw a single drop of this potion on them and their arms and fingers will burst into a thousand pieces." But the little mermaid didn't have to do that. The polyps drew back in terror when they saw the shining potion that gleamed in her hand like a glowing star. And so she soon came through the forest, the bog, and the roaring whirlpools.

She could see her father's castle. The torches had been extinguished in the great ballroom. They were probably all asleep, but she dared not go to them now that she was mute and was going to leave them forever. It was as if her heart would break with grief. She stole into the garden, picked a flower from each of her sisters' flower beds, blew a thousand kisses toward the castle, and rose up through the dark blue sea.

The sun had not yet risen when she saw the prince's castle and went up the magnificent marble stairway. The moon was shining bright and clear. The little mermaid drank the burning, sharp potion, and it was as if a two-edged sword were cutting through her delicate body. She fainted from the pain and lay as if dead. When the sun was shining on the sea, she awoke

and felt a stinging pain, but right in front of her stood the handsome young prince. He fixed his coal-black eyes upon her so that she had to lower her own, and then she saw that her fishtail was gone and she had the prettiest little white legs that any little girl could have. But she was quite naked, so she veiled herself with her thick, long hair. The prince asked who she was and how she had come there, and she looked at him gently and yet so sadly with her dark blue eyes, for she could not speak. Then he took her by the hand and led her into the castle. Each step she took, as the witch had predicted, was like stepping on pointed awls and sharp knives, but she gladly endured it. Led by the prince she rose light as a bubble, and he and everyone else marveled at her graceful, flowing movements.

She was given precious robes of silk and muslin to wear. In the castle she was the loveliest of all. But she was mute and could neither sing nor speak. Beautiful slave girls, dressed in silk and gold, came to sing before the prince and his royal parents. One of them sang more sweetly than all the others, and when the prince clapped his hands and smiled at her, the little mermaid felt very unhappy. She knew that she herself had sung far more beautifully, and she thought, "Oh, if only he knew that I have given away my voice for all eternity to be with him!"

Now the slave girls danced in graceful, flowing movements to the most splendid music. Then the little mermaid lifted her beautiful white arms, and rising on the tips of her toes, glided across the floor, dancing as no one had ever danced before. With each movement, her beauty became more and more apparent, and her eyes spoke more deeply to the heart than the slave girl's song.

Everyone was enchanted, especially the prince, who called her his little foundling, and she danced on and on even though each time her foot touched the ground it was like stepping on sharp knives. The prince said she was to stay with him forever, and she was allowed to sleep outside his door on a velvet cushion.

He had men's clothes made for her so that she could accompany him on horseback. They rode through the fragrant woods, where green branches brushed her shoulders and little birds sang among the fresh leaves. She climbed up the high mountains with the prince, and even though her delicate feet bled so the others could see it, she only laughed at this and followed him until they could see the clouds sailing far below them like a flock of birds on their way to far-off lands.

Back in the prince's castle, while at night the others slept, she would go out onto the broad marble steps and cool her burning feet by standing in the cold sea water. Then she would think of those who were down there in the depths.

One night her sisters came arm in arm, singing mournfully

as they swam across the water, and she waved to them. They recognized her and told her how unhappy she had made them all. They visited her every night after that, and one night in the far distance she saw her old grandmother, who had not been to the surface of the sea for many years, and the sea king with his crown upon his head. They stretched out their hands toward her but dared not come so close to the land as her sisters.

Day by day she grew dearer to the prince. He loved her as one would love a dear, good child, but it did not occur at all to him to make her his queen. Yet she had to become his wife, or else she would never win an immortal soul and on the morning after his wedding would turn into foam on the sea.

"Don't you love me most of all?" the eyes of the little mermaid seemed to ask when he took her in his arms and kissed her beautiful forehead.

"Yes, I love you best," said the prince, "for you have the kindest heart of all. You are more devoted to me than anyone else, and you look like a young girl I once saw but shall certainly never find again. I was on a ship that was wrecked; the waves carried me ashore near a holy temple where several young girls were serving. The youngest of them found me on the shore and saved my life. I only saw her twice. She was the only one I could love in this world, but you look like her and you have almost replaced her image in my soul. She belongs to the holy temple, and therefore good fortune has sent you to me. We shall never part!"

"Alas! He doesn't know that I saved his life!" thought the little mermaid. "It was I who carried him over the sea to the wood where the temple stands. I hid behind the foam and watched to see if any human beings would come. I saw the beautiful girl, whom he loves more than me!" And the mermaid sighed deeply, for she couldn't cry. "The girl belongs to the holy temple, as the prince has told me. She will never come out into the world, so they will never meet again. I am with him, I see him every day. I will take care of him, love him, give all my life to him!"

But now people were saying that the prince was going to

marry the beautiful daughter of the neighboring king, and that was why he was equipping such a splendid ship. The rumor was that the prince was to travel to see the country of the neighboring king, but the real reason was to see his daughter. He was to have a large retinue with him. But the little mermaid shook her head and laughed. She knew the prince's thoughts far better than anyone else. "I must go away," he had told her. "I must go and see the beautiful princess. My parents insist on it, but they won't force me to bring her home as my bride! I cannot love her! She doesn't look like the beautiful girl in the temple, as you do. If I should ever choose a bride, I would sooner choose you, my mute foundling with the eloquent eyes!" And he kissed her red mouth, played with her long hair, and laid his head on her heart, so that it was filled with dreams of human happiness and an immortal soul.

"I hope you're not afraid of the sea, my mute child!" he said when they stood on the deck of the splendid ship that was to carry him to the country of the neighboring king. And he told her of storms and calms at sea and of strange fish in the depths and of what the diver had seen down there. And she smiled at his words, for of course she knew about the bottom of the sea far better than anyone else.

In the moonlit night, when all were asleep—except the man at the helm—she sat by the railing of the ship and stared down through the clear water, and it seemed to her that she could see her father's castle. Up on the very top stood her old grandmother, with her silver crown on her head, gazing up through the strong currents at the keel of the ship. Then her sisters came up above the water. They looked at her with deep sorrow in their eyes and wrung their white hands. She waved and smiled at them and was going to tell them that she was well and happy, but the ship's boy came along and her sisters dived down, so he felt certain that the white he had seen was foam on the sea.

The next morning the ship sailed into the harbor of the neighboring king's magnificent city. All the church bells were pealing, and from the tall towers trumpets were sounded, while the soldiers stood with flying banners and glittering bayonets. Every day there was a feast. Balls and parties followed one after the other, but the princess had yet to appear. People said she had been brought up far away in a holy temple, where she learned all the royal virtues. At last she arrived.

The little mermaid waited eagerly to see her beauty, and she had to admit that she had never seen a more exquisite creature. Her skin was fine and delicate, and behind her long dark eyelashes smiled a pair of dark blue, loyal eyes.

"It is you!" said the prince. "You, who saved me when I lay like a dead man on the shore!" And he clasped his blushing bride in his arms. "Oh, I am far too happy!" he said to the little mermaid. "The best I could ever dare hope for has come true! You will share in my happiness, for you love me best of all." And the little mermaid kissed his hand, and already she seemed to feel her heart breaking. The morning after his wedding would indeed bring her death and turn her into foam upon the sea.

All the church bells were pealing. Heralds rode through the streets and announced the betrothal. On every altar burned fragrant oils in costly silver lamps. Priests swung censers, and bride and bridegroom gave each other their hands and received the blessing of the bishop. The little mermaid, dressed in silk and gold, was holding the bride's train, but her ears heard nothing of the festive music, her eyes saw none of the holy ceremony. She thought of the last night before her death, of all she had lost in this world.

That very evening the bride and bridegroom went on board the ship. Cannons were fired, all the flags were flying, and in the middle of the ship a sumptuous tent of purple and gold had been set up with the most luxurious cushions on which the wedded couple was to sleep in the calm, cool night. The sails swelled in the breeze, and the ship glided lightly and smoothly over the clear sea.

When it grew dark, brightly colored lanterns were lighted, and the sailors danced lively dances on the deck. The little mermaid couldn't help thinking of the first time she had risen above the sea and had seen the same splendor and gaiety. And she whirled along in the dance, soared as a swallow soars when it is being pursued, and everyone cheered in admiration. Never had she danced so wonderfully. It was as though sharp knives were cutting into her delicate feet, but she didn't feel it; the pain in her heart was even sharper. She knew this was the last evening she would see the one for whom she had left her family and her home, sacrificed her lovely voice, and daily suffered endless torment without his ever realizing it. It was the last night she would breathe the same air as he, see the deep sea and the starry blue sky. A never-ending night without thoughts or dreams awaited her who had no soul and had no way to win one. And there was gaiety and merriment on the ship until long past midnight, and she laughed and danced, with the thought of death in her heart. The prince kissed his beautiful bride and she played with his dark hair, and arm in arm they went to rest in the magnificent tent.

Silence and hush fell on the ship. Only the helmsman stood at the tiller. The little mermaid laid her white arms on the railing and looked toward the east for the dawn, for she knew that the first rays of the sun would kill her. Then she saw her sisters rising out of the sea. They were pale like herself. Their long beautiful hair no longer floated in the breeze—it had all been cut off.

"We have given it to the sea witch so that she may bring you help and save you from dying tonight! She has given us a knife! Here is it! See how sharp it is! Before the sun comes up, you must plunge it into the prince's heart, and when his warm blood splashes over your feet, they will grow together into a fishtail, and you will become a mermaid again and able to come down into the water to us and live your three hundred years before you turn into lifeless, salty sea foam. Hurry! Either he or you must die before the sun rises! Our old grandmother has been mourning so much that her white hair has fallen out, as ours fell under the witch's scissors. Kill the prince and come back! Hurry! Do you see that red streak in the sky? In a few minutes the sun will rise, and then you must die!" And they uttered a strange, deep sigh and disappeared in the waves.

The little mermaid drew back the purple curtain from the tent, and she looked at the lovely bride sleeping with her head on the prince's breast. She bent down and kissed his handsome forehead, then looked at the sky, where the dawn became brighter and brighter; she looked at the sharp knife, and again fastened her eyes on the prince, who in his dreams murmured the name of his bride. She alone was in his thoughts. The knife trembled in the mermaid's hand—but then she threw it far out into the waves. They gleamed red where it fell and it seemed as if drops of blood bubbled up through the water. Once more she looked at the prince with dimming eyes, then threw herself from the ship down into the sea, and she felt her body dissolve into foam.

Now the sun rose out of the sea. Its rays fell mild and warm on the death-cold sea foam, and the little mermaid did not feel death. She saw the bright sun, and above her floated hundreds of beautiful, transparent beings. Through them she could see the white sails of the ship and the red clouds in the sky. Their voices were music but so ethereal that no human ear could hear it, just as no earthly eye could see them. Without wings, they floated by their own lightness through the air. The little mermaid saw that she had a body like theirs and that it rose higher and higher out of the foam.

"To whom do I come?" she said, and her voice sounded like that of the other beings, so ethereal that no earthly music could possibly render it.

"To the daughters of the air!" answered the others. "A mermaid has no immortal soul and can never gain one unless she wins the love of a human being; her eternal life depends on the power of someone else! The daughters of the air have no immortal soul either, but by good deeds they can create one for themselves. We fly to the hot countries, where the sultry air of pestilence kills human beings. There we waft cooling breezes. We spread the fragrance of flowers through the air and send freshness and healing. When we have striven for three hundred years to do all the good we can, we receive an immortal soul and share in the eternal happiness of human beings. You, poor little mermaid, have striven with all your heart for the same goal. You have suffered and endured and have risen to the world of the spirits of the air. Now by good deeds you can create an immortal soul for yourself after three hundred years."

And the little mermaid raised her bright arms up toward God's sun, and for the first time she felt tears. On the ship there was again life and bustle. She saw the prince with his beautiful bride searching for her. Sorrowfully they gazed at the bubbling foam, as if they knew she had thrown herself into the waves. Invisible, she kissed the bride's forehead, smiled at the prince, and rose with the other children of the air up onto the rose-red cloud that sailed through the air.

"In three hundred years we will float like this into the kingdom of God!"

"We might even come there sooner," whispered one. "We float unseen into the houses of human beings where there are children, and for each day that we find a good child who makes

his parents happy and deserves their love, our period of trial is shortened by God. The child does not know when we fly through the room; and when we smile at him in our joy, one year is taken from the three hundred. But if we see a naughty and nasty child, we must weep tears of sorrow, and each tear adds a day to our period of trial!"

The Swineherd

Once upon a time there was a penniless prince. He had a kingdom that was very small but still it was big enough to get married on, and get married is what he wanted to do.

Still, it was quite spunky of him to dare to say to the emperor's daughter, "Will you have me?" But he dared all right because his name was famous far and wide, and there were a hundred princesses who would have been glad to have him. But do you think she was?

Now, let's listen.

On the grave of the prince's father grew a rosebush, such a lovely rosebush! It bloomed only once every five years and then only a single rose, but that rose smelled so sweet that anyone who smelled it forgot all his troubles and woes. He also had a nightingale that could sing as if all the lovely tunes in the world were in its little throat. Now, it was this rose and this nightingale that the princess was to have, therefore they were put into two large silver cases and sent to her.

The emperor had them brought before him in the great hall where the princess was playing "Company's Coming" with her ladies in waiting—that's all they ever did—and when she saw the large cases with the presents in them, she clapped her hands for joy.

"If only it's a little pussy cat," she said. But out came the lovely rose.

"My, how beautifully it's made!" said all the ladies in waiting.

"It's more than beautiful," said the emperor, "it's nice!"

But the princess touched it, and she nearly burst into tears. "Ugh! Daddy!" she said. "It's not artificial, it's *real!*"

"Ugh!" said all the courtiers. "It's real!"

"Let's first see what's in the other case before we get angry," suggested the emperor. Then out came the nightingale. It sang so sweetly that at first they couldn't find fault with it.

"*Superbe! Charmant!*" said the ladies in waiting, for they all spoke French, each one worse than the other.

"My, how that bird reminds me of the late empress's music box!" said an old courtier. "Ah, yes! Exactly the same tone, the same delivery!"

"Yes!" said the emperor, and he cried like a little child. "I can hardly believe it is real!" said the princess.

"Why, yes! It is a real bird," said the ones who brought it.

"Well, then, let that bird fly away!" said the princess, and she would in no way permit the prince to come.

But he didn't lose heart. He smeared his face brown and black, pulled a cap down over his eyes, and knocked at the door.

"Hello, Emperor," he said. "Can't I be hired at the castle?"

"Oh, there are so many who apply for work here," said the emperor. "But let me see. I need someone to take care of the pigs because we have so many of them."

And so the prince was hired as the Imperial Swineherd. He was given a wretched little room down by the pigsty, and there he had to stay. But all day long he sat and worked, and by the time it was evening he had made a pretty little pot with bells all around it, and as soon as the pot began to boil they tinkled merrily, playing that old tune:

> Oh, my dearest Augustine,
> All this is gone, gone, gone!

But most remarkable of all, when anyone stuck a finger into the steam from the pot, he could immediately smell what food was being cooked on every stove in town. See, that was certainly something better than a rose!

Just then the princess came along with all her ladies in waiting. When she heard the tune, she stood still and looked very pleased for she, too, could play "Oh, My Dearest Augustine." It was the only piece she knew, but she could play it with one finger!

"Why, that's the one I know!" she said. "Then he must be a cultivated swineherd! Listen! Go in and ask him what that instrument costs." And so one of the ladies in waiting had to run in, but first she changed her shoes.

"How much do you want for that pot?" said the lady in waiting.

"I want ten kisses from the princess!" said the swineherd.

"Good gracious!" said the lady in waiting.

"Well, it's not worth less!" said the swineherd.

"Well, what does he say?" asked the princess.

"I really couldn't repeat it!" said the lady in waiting. "It's so awful!"

"Then you can whisper!" And so she whispered.

"Why, he's naughty!" said the princess, and off she went. But when she had gone a little way, the bells began to tinkle so merrily:

> Oh, my dearest Augustine,
> All this is gone, gone, gone!

"Listen!" said the princess. "Ask him if he'll take ten kisses from my ladies in waiting!"

"No, thanks," said the swineherd, "ten kisses from the princess or else I keep the pot."

"What a bore!" said the princess. "But all of you will have to stand around me so nobody sees it."

And the ladies in waiting positioned themselves around her, holding out their skirts, and then the swineherd got his ten kisses, and she got the pot.

My, what fun they had! All evening and all the next day the pot was made to boil. There wasn't a single stove in the whole town that they didn't know what was cooked there, whether at the chamberlain's or at the shoemaker's. The ladies in waiting danced and clapped their hands.

"We know who's going to have fruit soup and pancakes! We know who's going to have porridge and meatballs! How interesting it is!"

"Highly interesting," said the chief lady in waiting.

"Yes, but keep it to yourselves, for I'm the emperor's daughter!"

"Good gracious, yes!" they all said.

The swineherd—that is to say the prince, but they didn't know, of course, that he was anything but a real swineherd—didn't let a day go by without accomplishing something, and so he made a rattle. When it was swung around, it played all the waltzes, jigs, and polkas that have been known since the world began.

"But that is *superbe!*" said the princess as she passed by. "I've never heard a lovelier composition! Listen, go in and ask him what that instrument costs, but no kisses!"

"He wants a hundred kisses from the princess!" said the lady in waiting who'd been in to ask.

"He must be crazy!" said the princess, and then she left. But after going a short way, she stopped. "One should encourage the arts," she said. "After all, I'm the emperor's daughter. Tell him he can have ten kisses, just like yesterday, the rest he can get from my ladies in waiting!"

"Oh, but we'd really rather not!" said the ladies in waiting.

"Nonsense!" said the princess. "If I can kiss him, you can,

too! Remember, I give you board and wages." And so the lady in waiting had to go in to him again.

"One hundred kisses from the princess," he said, "or else each keeps what he has!"

"Stand around!" she said, and all the ladies in waiting positioned themselves around them, and he began kissing.

"What can all that commotion be down there by the pigsty?" said the emperor, who had just stepped out on the balcony. He rubbed his eyes and put on his glasses. "Why, it's the ladies in waiting up to their pranks! I'd better go down there." So he pulled up his slippers at the back, for they were shoes that he had worn out.

Goodness, how he hurried!

As soon as he entered the courtyard he walked very softly, and the ladies in waiting were so busy counting kisses to make sure the swineherd didn't get too many, but not too few either, that they didn't notice the emperor at all. He stood on tiptoe.

"What on earth!" he said when he saw them kissing, and then he hit them on the head with his slipper just as the swineherd got his eighty-sixth kiss. "Get out!" said the emperor, for he was angry, and both princess and swineherd were put out of his empire.

There she stood now and cried, and the swineherd cursed, and the rain poured down.

"Oh, poor, miserable me!" said the princess. "If only I'd taken the handsome prince. Oh, how unhappy I am!"

And the swineherd stepped behind a tree; he wiped the black and brown off his face and threw away his ugly clothes, and then he stepped forth in his prince's clothing looking so handsome that the princess had to make a curtsy.

"I've come to loathe you!" he said. "You wouldn't have an honest prince! You couldn't appreciate the rose and the nightin-

gale! But the swineherd you could kiss for a music box! It's served you right!"

And with that he went into his kingdom, shut the door, and bolted it. So now all she could do was stand outside and sing:

> Oh my dearest Augustine,
> All this is gone, gone, gone!

The Buckwheat

Time and again, if you happen, after a thunderstorm, to walk past a field where buckwheat is growing, you may observe that it is burnt entirely black; it's as though a pillar of fire had passed over it. And the farmer will tell you, "It got that way from lightning." But why did it get that way? I'll tell you what the sparrow told me, and the sparrow heard it from an old willow tree that stood close by a field of buckwheat, and it stands there still. It is such a respectable and tall willow tree, but old and wrinkled. Its trunk has been split right down the middle, and grass and brambles are growing out of the cleft! The tree bends forward, and the branches hang down to the ground as if they were long green strands of hair.

In the surrounding fields, grains of all sorts grew—rye and barley and oats. How beautiful the oats are; when ripe, they look like a whole lot of little yellow canaries sitting on a branch. The grains stood there full of grace, and the fuller they became, the lower they bowed their heads in pious humility.

But there was also a field of buckwheat, and that field lay right by the old willow tree. The buckwheat did not bow its head like the other grains; it stood stiff and proud.

"I am quite as rich as the other heads of grain," it said. "And besides, I am so much more handsome; my flowers are as beautiful as apple blossoms; it's a pleasure to look at me and my fellows. Do you know anything more magnificent than we are, you old willow tree?"

And the willow tree nodded its head as if to say, "Yes, of course!" But the buckwheat strutted with pride and said, "That stupid tree! It's so old it has grass growing in its navel."

Now a terrible storm came up. All the flowers of the field folded their leaves or bent their lovely heads as the storm passed over them, but the buckwheat, in its pride, still stood erect.

"Bow your head as we do!" said the flowers.

"I don't have to," said the buckwheat.

"Bow your head as we do!" said the grain. "Now the angel of the storm comes flying hither; he has wings that reach all the way from the clouds to the earth; he will cut you down before you can beg him for mercy!"

"No, I don't want to bow!" said the buckwheat.

"Close your blossoms and bow your blades," said the old willow tree. "Don't look at the lightning when the cloud breaks. Even humans don't dare do that, for through the lightning you can see right into God's heaven, and that sight can blind even human eyes! What then would happen to us plants of the earth if we should dare look into it—we, who are much more inferior?"

"Much more inferior?" said the buckwheat. "Well, now I really want to look right into God's heaven!" And so it did in its pride and arrogance. The whole world seemed to be aflame, so bright was the lightning.

When the storm was over, the flowers and the grains stood high in the still, pure air, refreshed by the rain. But the buckwheat had been burnt as black as coal by the lightning; it was now a dead and useless plant on the field.

And the old willow tree moved its branches in the wind, and

large drops of water fell from the green leaves, as though the tree were weeping. And the sparrows asked, "Why are you weeping? It is so beautiful here! See how the sun is shining, how the clouds are drifting! Smell the fragrance of the flowers and the bushes! Why are you weeping, old willow tree?"

And the willow tree told of the buckwheat's pride and arrogance and punishment. It always follows! I, who am telling the story, heard it from the sparrows! They told it to me one evening when I asked them for a story.

The Nightingale

In China, you know of course, the emperor is Chinese, and everybody he has around him is Chinese. Now, many years have gone by, but that is just why the story is worth listening to before it is forgotten! The emperor's castle was the most magnificent in the world, completely and entirely of fine porcelain, so precious but so fragile that one had to be really careful about touching it. In the garden the most wonderful flowers were to be seen, and fastened to the most magnificent of them were silver bells that tinkled so that no one could walk past without noticing the flower. Indeed, everything had been well thought out in the emperor's garden, and it reached so far that even the gardener didn't know where it ended. If one kept on walking, there was the loveliest forest with high trees and deep lakes. The forest went right down to the sea, which was deep and blue. Great ships could sail right in under the branches, and in these branches lived a nightingale that sang so gloriously that even the poor fisherman who had so many other things to keep him busy would lie still and listen when he was out at night drawing in his net and happened to hear the nightingale. "Dear God, how beautiful it is!" he said, but then he had to attend to his work and forgot the bird. Yet the next night when it sang again, and the fisherman was there, he said the same thing, "Dear God, how beautiful it is!"

From all the countries of the world travelers came to the emperor's city, and they admired it, the castle and the garden, but when they got to hear the nightingale, they all said, "That is really the best!"

And the travelers told all about it when they came home, and learned men wrote many books about the city, the castle, and the garden, but they didn't forget the nightingale. That was given the highest place of all, and those who could write poetry wrote the loveliest poems—all of them about the nightingale in the forest by the deep sea.

These books went around the world, and of course some of them at last reached the emperor. He sat in his gold chair; he read and read, and nodded his head continually because it pleased him to hear the magnificent descriptions of the city, the castle, and the garden. "But the nightingale is really the best of all!" was also written there.

"What in the world?" said the emperor. "The nightingale! I don't know anything at all about that! Is there such a bird here in my empire, even in my own garden? I've never heard of it! I have to read about it in a book!"

And then he called his chamberlain, who was so grand that when anyone of lower rank dared to speak to him or ask about anything, his only answer was "P," and that doesn't mean anything.

"There is supposed to be a highly remarkable bird here called a nightingale!" said the emperor. "It is said to be the very best thing in my great empire! Why hasn't anyone said anything to me about it?"

"I've never before heard it mentioned!" said the chamberlain. "It has never been presented at court!"

"I want it to come here this evening and sing for me!" said the emperor. "The whole world knows what I have, and I do not!"

"I have never before heard it mentioned!" said the chamberlain. "I shall search for it—I shall find it!"

But where was it to be found? The chamberlain ran up and down all the stairs, through halls and corridors. None of the many people he met had heard tell of the nightingale, so the chamberlain ran back again to the emperor and said that it was probably a fable made up by those who wrote books. "Your Imperial Majesty should not believe what is written in a book! It is invention and something called sorcery!"

"But the book in which I read it," said the emperor, "was sent to me from the mighty emperor of Japan, and so it can't be false. I want to hear the nightingale! It shall be here this evening! It has my highest favor! And if it doesn't come, the whole court will be thumped on their tummies after they have eaten their dinner."

"Tsing-pe!" said the chamberlain and ran back up and down all the stairs, through all the halls and corridors, and half of the court ran along with him because they didn't want to be thumped on the tummy. There was a lot of asking about the remarkable nightingale that the whole world knew about except the people at court.

Finally they met a poor little girl in the kitchen. She said, "Oh heavens, the nightingale! I know it well! Yes, how it can sing! Every evening I have permission to bring a few of the scraps from the table home to my poor sick mother. She lives down by the shore, and on my way back when I'm tired and stop to rest in the forest, I hear the nightingale sing. It brings tears to my eyes. It's just as though my mother kissed me!"

"Little kitchen maid," said the chamberlain, "I shall get you a permanent position in the kitchen and permission to watch the emperor eating if you can lead us to the nightingale. It has been summoned to appear this evening!"

And so they all set out for the forest where the nightingale usually sang. Half the court went too. As they were going along, a cow started mooing.

"Oh!" said the courtiers. "There we have it! There is certainly a remarkable force in such a tiny animal. I'm quite sure I've heard it before!"

"No, those are the cows mooing!" said the little kitchen maid. "We're still a long way from the place!"

Now the frogs started croaking in the pond.

"Delightful!" said the Chinese imperial chaplain. "Now I hear her! It's just like tiny church bells."

"No, those are the frogs!" said the little kitchen maid. "But now I think we'll soon hear it!"

Then the nightingale started to sing.

"That's it!" said the little girl. "Listen! Listen! And there it sits!" And she pointed to a little gray bird up in the branches.

"Is it possible?" said the chamberlain. "I never imagined it like this! How ordinary it looks! It has probably lost its color from the sight of so many distinguished personages!"

"Little nightingale!" shouted the little kitchen maid quite loudly. "Our gracious emperor would so like you to sing for him!"

"With the greatest pleasure!" said the nightingale, and sang so that it was a delight.

"It is just like glass bells!" said the chamberlain. "And look at that tiny throat. How it vibrates! It's remarkable that we've never heard it before! It will be a great success at court!"

"Shall I sing once more for the emperor?" asked the nightingale, who thought the emperor was there.

"My fine little nightingale," said the chamberlain, "it gives me the greatest pleasure to summon you to a court celebration this evening, where you will enchant his High Imperial Grace with your *charmante* song!"

"It sounds best out in nature!" said the nightingale, but it followed them gladly when it heard it was the emperor's wish.

The palace had been properly polished up! Walls and floors, which were of porcelain, shone from many thousands of gold lamps! The loveliest flowers, which could tinkle like bells, were arranged in the halls. There was such a draft and so much running around that the bells tinkled and drowned out everything else.

In the middle of the great hall, where the emperor sat, a gold perch had been placed for the nightingale to sit on. The whole court was there, and the little kitchen maid had been given permission to stand behind the door, for now she had the title of Real Kitchen Maid. They all were wearing their most splendid attire, and they all looked at the little gray bird to which the emperor was nodding.

And the nightingale sang so delightfully that tears came to the emperor's eyes, tears rolled down his cheeks. Then the nightingale sang even more beautifully. It went straight to the heart. And the emperor was so happy that he said the nightingale was to have his gold slipper to wear around its neck. But the nightingale said no, thank you, it had already been rewarded enough.

"I have seen tears in the emperor's eyes! For me, that is the richest treasure! An emperor's tears have a wondrous power! God knows I have been rewarded enough!" And then it sang again with its sweet and glorious voice.

"That is the most adorable coquetry I know of!" said the ladies standing around. And they put water in their mouths so they could gurgle whenever anyone spoke to them. They thought they were nightingales, too. Even the lackeys and chambermaids let it be known that they were also satisfied, and that is saying a lot, for they're the hardest of all to please. Yes, indeed, the nightingale had really been a success!

It was now to remain at court and have its own cage as well as freedom to take a walk outside twice each day and once at night. It was given twelve servants to go along with it; each one held a silken ribbon that was attached to its leg, and they held on good and tight. That kind of walk was no pleasure at all!

The whole city talked about the remarkable bird, and whenever two people met, the first merely said "Night!" and the other said "Gale!" And then they sighed and understood each other! Yes, eleven grocers' children were named after it, but not one of them could sing a note.

One day a big package came to the emperor. On the outside was written "Nightingale."

"Here's a new book about our famous bird!" said the emperor. But it was no book, it was a little *objet d'art* which lay in a box—an artificial nightingale made to resemble the real one, except that it was encrusted with diamonds, rubies, and sapphires. When the artificial bird was wound up, it could sing one of the tunes the real one sang, and its tail bobbed up and down and glittered with silver and gold. Around its neck hung a little ribbon and on it was written, "The Emperor of Japan's nightingale is poor compared to the Emperor of China's."

"It is lovely!" they all said. And the person who had brought the artificial bird was immediately granted the title of Chief Imperial Nightingale Bringer.

"Now they must sing together! What a duet that will be!"

And so they had to sing together, but it didn't go really well, because the real nightingale sang its own way and the artificial bird worked with mechanical wheels. "It's not to be blamed," said the music master. "It keeps time perfectly and quite according to my school of music!" Then the artificial bird had to sing alone. It was as much of a success as the real one; besides that, it was so much nicer to look at. It glittered like bracelets and brooches.

Thirty-three times it sang one and the same tune, and still it wasn't tired. The people would have liked to hear it again, but the emperor thought the living nightingale should also sing a little. But where was it? No one had noticed that it had flown out of the open window, away to its green forests.

"What is this all about?" said the emperor. And the courtiers used harsh words and said that the nightingale was a most ungrateful bird. "But we have the best bird!" they said, and then the artificial bird had to sing again. That was the thirty-fourth time they had heard the same tune, but they still didn't know all of it, because it was so hard. And the music master praised the bird inordinately—yes, he even assured them that it was better than the real nightingale, not only with regard to its clothes and the many beautiful diamonds, but within as well.

"For you see, my lords and ladies, and Your Emperorship above all, with the real nightingale you can never be sure what to expect, but with the artificial bird everything is definite! That is how it will be, and no other way! You can account for it. It can be split open to show human ingenuity, how the wheels are arranged, how they operate, and how one thing leads to another!"

"Those are my thoughts precisely!" they all said. And on the following Sunday the music master was allowed to show the bird to the people. They were also going to hear it sing, said the emperor. And they heard it, and they were as pleased as if they had all gotten high on tea, for that's so very Chinese. They all said "Oh!" and held their index fingers in the air and then nodded. But the poor fishermen who had heard the real nightingale said, "It sounds pretty enough, and it looks all right, too. But something is missing. I don't know what it is."

The real nightingale was banished from land and empire.

The artificial bird had its place on a silk cushion close to the emperor's bed. All the gifts it had received, gold and precious stones, lay around it. In title it had risen to High Imperial Bedside Table Singer, and in rank to number one on the left, for the emperor considered the side where the heart is to be the most distinguished. And even the heart of an emperor is on the left side. The music master wrote a twenty-five-volume work about the artificial bird. It was so learned and so long and had the most difficult Chinese words, so all the people said they had read and understood it, for otherwise they would have been thought stupid and thumped on the tummy.

It went like this for a whole year. The emperor, the court, and all the other Chinese knew by heart every little cluck in the song of the artificial bird. But this is exactly why they liked it best of all—they could sing along with it themselves, and that they did! The street kids sang "Zizizi! Klukklukkluk!" And the emperor sang it! Yes, it was certainly lovely!

But one evening, as the artificial bird was singing away and the emperor was lying in bed listening to it, something went "snap" inside the bird. Something had broken. "Whirrrrrrrrr!" All the wheels spun around, and then the music stopped.

The emperor sprang out of bed right away and had his personal physician summoned. But how could he help? Then they fetched the watchmaker, and after much talk and many look-see's he put the bird more or less in order. But he said it must be used very sparingly because the cogs were so worn it wasn't possible to put in new ones that would produce music reliably. What a great woe! Only once a year did they dare let the artificial bird sing, and even that was hard on it. But then the music master made a little speech using difficult words, and said it was just as good as before, and so it was just as good as before.

Now five years passed and a great sorrow fell upon the land—because, actually, they were all fond of their emperor—and he was sick and wouldn't live, it was said. A new emperor had already been chosen, and people stood out in the street and asked the chamberlain how their emperor was.

"P!" he said and shook his head.

Cold and pale, the emperor lay in his great magnificent bed. The whole court thought he was dead, and each one of them ran off to greet the new emperor. The lackeys ran out to talk about it, and the chambermaids had a big coffee klatch. In all the halls and corridors cloths had been put down to deaden the sound of footsteps, and so it was so still, so still. But the emperor was not dead yet. Stiff and pale, he lay in the magnificent bed with the long velvet curtains and the heavy gold tassels. High above him a window stood open, and the moon shone in on the emperor and the artificial bird.

The poor emperor could hardly breathe. It was as though something sat on his chest. He opened his eyes, and then he saw that it was Death who was sitting on his chest and had put on his gold crown and held in one hand the imperial gold sword and in the other his magnificent banner. And from among all the folds of the long velvet curtains around the bed,

strange heads were sticking out. Some were quite hideous, and others so blessed and mild—these were all the emperor's good and wicked deeds looking at him now that Death was sitting on his heart.

"Do you remember this?" whispered one after the other. "Do you remember that?" And then they told him so much that the sweat stood on his brow.

"I never knew that!" said the emperor. "Music! Music! The big Chinese drum!" he shouted. "So I don't have to hear all the things they're saying!"

And they kept at it, and Death nodded, just the way the Chinese do at everything that is said.

"Music! Music!" shrieked the emperor. "You blessed little gold bird, sing! Oh, sing! I've given you gold and precious things. I myself hung my gold slipper around your neck. Sing! Oh, sing!"

But the bird stood still. There was no one to wind it up, and it couldn't sing otherwise. But Death kept on looking at the emperor out of his big empty eye sockets. And it was so still, so frighteningly still.

Just at that moment close by the window the loveliest song could be heard. It was the little living nightingale, sitting on the branch outside. It had heard of the emperor's need and had come to sing him comfort and hope. And as it sang, the shapes became paler and paler, and the blood started to flow faster and faster in the emperor's weak limbs, and Death himself listened and said, "Keep on, little nightingale, keep on!"

"Yes, if you'll give me the magnificent gold sword! Yes, if you'll give me the rich banner! If you'll give me the emperor's crown!"

And Death gave each treasure for a song, and the nightingale kept on singing. And it sang about the quiet churchyard where the white roses grow and where the elder tree scents the air, and where the fresh grass is watered by the tears of the bereaved. Then Death was filled with longing for his garden and drifted like a cold, white mist out of the window.

"Thank you, thank you!" said the emperor. "You heavenly little bird, I know you, all right! I have driven you out of my land and empire, and still you have sung the evil visions away from my bed and removed Death from my heart! How can I reward you?"

"You have rewarded me!" said the nightingale. "I received the tears from your eyes the first time I sang. I'll never forget that. Those are the jewels that do a singer's heart good. But sleep now, and get well and strong! I shall sing for you!"

And it sang, and the emperor fell into a sweet sleep, such a mild and beneficial sleep.

The sun was shining in on him through the windows when he awoke, strengthened and well. None of his servants had returned yet, for they thought he was dead, but the nightingale still sat there and sang.

"You must always stay with me!" said the emperor. "You shall sing only when you want to, and I shall break the artificial bird into a thousand pieces."

"Don't do that!" said the nightingale. "It has done what good it could! Keep it as before! I cannot settle and live at the palace, but let me come when I want to myself. Then in the evening I'll sit on the branch there by the window and sing for you, so that you can be happy and thoughtful as well! I shall sing about the happy and about those who suffer! I shall sing of good and evil which all around you is kept hidden! The little songbird flies far off to the poor fisherman, to the farmer's roof, to everyone who is far from you and your court! I love your heart better than your crown, and yet your crown has a scent of sanctity about it! I will come. I will sing for you! But you must promise me one thing!"

"Everything!" said the emperor, standing there in his imperial robe, which he himself had put on, and holding the sword, heavy with gold, up to his heart.

"One thing I beg of you! Tell no one that you have a little bird that tells you everything! Then it will go even better!"

And then the nightingale flew away.

The servants came in to see to their dead emperor. Yes, there they stood. And the emperor said, "Good morning!"

The Sweethearts

A top and a ball were lying in a drawer together with some other toys, when the top said to the ball, "Shouldn't we be sweethearts, since we are lying in the same drawer together anyway?" But the ball, who was made of morocco leather and put on just as many airs as a snobbish young lady, would not hear of such a thing.

The little boy who owned the toys came the next day. He painted the top red and yellow and drove a brass nail right through the middle. It was splendid to see the top spin around!

"Look at me now!" he said to the ball. "What do you say now! Shouldn't we be sweethearts? We go so well together. You can hop and I can dance! No one could ever be happier than we two would be!"

"That's what you think!" said the ball. "You don't seem to realize that my father and mother were morocco slippers, and that I have a cork inside!"

"Yes, but I am made of mahogany!" said the top. "And the judge turned me out himself. He has his own lathe, and it was a great pleasure for him to do it!"

"Oh, is that so?" said the ball.

"May I never be whipped, if I'm lying!" answered the top.

"You speak well for yourself!" said the ball. "But I have to say no. I am as good as half engaged to a swallow. Every time I hop up in the air, he sticks his head out of his nest and says, "Will you, will you?" And I have inwardly said yes, and that is as good as a half engagement! But I promise that I shall never forget you!"

"That's a big help!" said the top. After that they didn't talk to each other anymore.

The next day the ball was taken out. The top saw how she flew high up in the air like a bird, so high that she disappeared from sight. She came back every time, but she always made a big hop when she touched the ground. This came either from longing or because she had a cork inside. The ninth time she stayed away and didn't come back again. The boy searched and searched, but she was gone.

"I know where she is, all right!" sighed the top. "She is in the swallow's nest married to the swallow!"

The more the top thought about it, the more infatuated with the ball he became. Just because he could not have her, his love grew. She had taken another, and that was what was so special about it! And the top danced and spun around, but he was always thinking about the ball, who grew more and more beautiful in his thoughts. So it went for many years—until it became an old love affair.

And the top was no longer young! But then one day he was covered all over with gilt. Never before had he looked so handsome! Now he was a golden top, and he whirled until he hummed. Yes, this was really something! But all of a sudden he whirled too high—and was gone!

They searched and searched, even in the cellar, but he was nowhere to be found.

Where was he?

He had hopped into the garbage where all sorts of rubbish was lying: cabbage stalks, sweepings, and rubble that had fallen out of the gutters.

"Oh, this is a fine place to be! My new gilding will be

spoiled in no time! And what kind of rabble have I fallen in with!" He peered at a rangy cabbage stalk that had been over-plucked and at a strange round thing that looked like an old apple. But it wasn't an apple. It was an old ball, which had lain in the gutter for many years and through which water had been oozing.

"Thank heavens! Here is finally one of my own kind that I can talk to!" said the ball, looking at the gilded top. "I am actually made of morocco leather sewn by the hands of a fine young lady, and I have a cork inside! But no one could tell that by looking at me! I was just about to marry a swallow when I fell into the gutter, and there I've lain for five years oozing water! Believe me, that's a long time for a fine young lady!"

But the top said nothing. He was thinking about his old sweetheart, and the more he heard, the more sure he was that this was she.

Then the maid came to empty the trash. "Hey, there's the gold top!" she said.

And the top was brought back to the playroom to high esteem and honor, but nothing more was heard of the ball, and the top never spoke of his old love affair again. That sort of thing passes when your lover has lain for five years oozing in the gutter. Indeed, you don't even recognize her, when you meet her in the garbage.

The Ugly Duckling

It was so lovely out in the country—it was summer! The grain stood yellow, the oats green, the hay had been stacked down in the green meadows, and there the stork went about on his long, red legs and spoke Egyptian, for that was the language he had learned from his mother. The fields and meadows were surrounded by great forests, and there were deep lakes in the middle of the forests. Yes, indeed, it certainly was lovely out in the country! There in the midst of the sunshine stood an old manor house surrounded by a deep moat, and from the wall down to the water grew the great leaves of the dock plant, and they were so high that little children could stand upright under the biggest of them. It was just as rank under them as in the deepest forest, and here it was that a duck sat on her nest. She was hatching her little ducklings, but she'd almost had enough of that because it took so long, and she seldom had a visitor. The other ducks would rather go swimming about in the moat than run up to sit under a dock leaf and quack with her.

At last one eggshell after another started cracking. "Peep! Peep!" they said. All the egg yolks had come to life and were sticking out their heads.

"Quack! Quack!" she said, and they hurried out as quickly as they could, looking all around them under the green leaves; and their mother let them look as much as they liked because green is good for the eyes.

"My, how big the world is!" said all the ducklings, for now they certainly had much more room than when they lay inside the eggs.

"Do you think this is the whole world?" said the mother. "It stretches far beyond the other side of the garden, right into the parson's field! But I've never been there! You're all here now, aren't you?" Then she got up. "No, I don't have them all! The largest egg is still there! How long will it take? Now, I'm getting tired of this!" And she sat down again.

"Well, how's it going?" asked an old duck who had come to pay her a call.

"It's taking so long for the one egg," said the duck who was lying on it. "It won't crack open! But now take a look at the others! They're the loveliest ducklings I've ever seen! They all look like their father—the wretch! He never comes to visit me."

"Let me see the egg that won't crack!" said the old duck. "You can be certain it's a turkey egg! That's how I, too, was fooled once, and had my troubles and worries with those young ones because they're afraid of the water, let me tell you! I couldn't get them out in it! I quacked and snapped, but it didn't help! Let me see the egg! Yes, that's a turkey egg! You just let it lie there, and teach the other children how to swim!"

"I'll just sit on it a little longer," said the duck. "I've been sitting here so long now, I may as well sit until the amusement park closes down for the winter."

"Have it your own way," said the old duck, and off she went.

At last the large egg cracked. "Peep! Peep!" said the little one and tumbled out. He was so big and ugly. The duck looked at him. "That's certainly a terribly big duckling, that one!" she said. "None of the others look like that! Could it really be a turkey chick? Well, we'll soon find out! It's into the water with him, even if I have to kick him out myself!"

The next day there was such glorious, fine weather. The sun shone on all the green dock leaves, and the mother duck came down to the moat with her whole family. Splash! Into the water she jumped. "Quack! Quack!" she said, and one duckling after another plopped in. They went under, but they came up at once and floated beautifully. Their legs paddled all on their own, and they were all in the water. Even the ugly gray duckling was swimming with them.

"No, that's no turkey!" said the mother. "See how beautifully it uses its legs, how straight it holds itself! That's my own child! Actually, on the whole it's quite pretty, when one takes a good look at it! Quack! Quack! Now, come with me, I'll take you out into the world, and introduce you to the duck yard. But always keep close to me so that no one steps on you, and watch out for the cats!"

And so they came out into the duck yard. There was a frightful commotion there, for two families were fighting over an eel's head, and then the cat got it anyway.

"See, that's the way it goes out in the world!" said the mother duck and licked her bill, for she, too, wanted the eel's head. "Now shake a leg!" she said. "Move right along, and bow your heads to the old duck over there. She's the most distinguished of them all here! She has Spanish blood—that's why she's so fat. And do you see? She has a red rag around her leg! That's something especially fine and the greatest distinction any duck can receive. It means that nobody wants to get rid of her and that she shall be known by animals and men! Be quick! Don't keep your legs together! A well brought-up duckling keeps its legs far apart, just like father and mother! Now then! Bow your heads and say 'Quack!' "

And this they did. But the other ducks round about looked at them and said quite loudly, "Just look at that! Now we're going to have to put up with that rabble, as if there weren't enough of us already! And fie! How that one duckling looks!

We won't have him here!" And at once one duck flew over and bit him in the neck.

"Leave him alone," said the mother. "He's not bothering anyone!"

"Yes, but he's too big and too different," said the duck that had bitten him, "so he should be given what for!"

"Those are pretty children mother has," said the old duck with the rag around her leg. "All pretty except that one; that one hasn't turned out so well! I do wish she could do him over again!"

"That cannot be done, Your Grace," said the duckling's mother. "He's not pretty, but he has a very good disposition and swims as beautifully as any of the others—yes, I could even say better! I think he'll grow prettier or he'll get a little smaller in time! He's lain too long in the egg, and that's why he hasn't got the right shape!" And then she ruffled the feathers on his neck and smoothed him here and there. "Besides, he's a drake," she said, "and so it doesn't matter so much! I think he'll grow very strong. He'll make his way, all right!"

"The other ducklings are lovely," said the old duck. "Just make yourselves at home, and if you find an eel's head, you may bring it to me."

And so they felt at home.

But the poor duckling who had come out of the egg last and looked so ugly was bitten, pushed, and jeered at by both the ducks and the hens. "He's too big!" they all said, and the turkey cock, who had been born with spurs and therefore thought himself an emperor, puffed himself up like a ship in full sail. He went right up to him, and then he gobbled and grew quite red in the face. The poor duckling didn't know what to do! He was so miserable because he looked so ugly and was scorned by the whole duck yard.

That's how the first day passed, and after that things grew worse and worse. The poor duckling was chased by everyone; even his brothers and sisters were mean to him and were always saying, "If only the cat would get you, you ugly thing!" And his mother said, "If only you were far away!" And the ducks bit him and the hens pecked him and the girl who had to feed the animals kicked at him with her foot.

Then he ran and flew over the hedge. The little birds in the bushes started up in fear. "That's because I'm so ugly!" thought the duckling and shut his eyes, but he kept on running. Then he came out into the great marsh where the wild ducks lived. Here he lay all night; he was so tired and unhappy.

In the morning the wild ducks flew up and looked at their new companion. "What kind of duck are you?" they asked, and the duckling turned in every direction and greeted them as well as he could.

"You are thoroughly ugly!" said the wild ducks. "But actually it doesn't matter to us as long as you don't marry into our family!" Poor thing! He certainly wasn't thinking of marrying—if he could only have permission to lie among the reeds and drink a little bog water.

There he lay for two whole days. Then along came two wild geese, or rather wild ganders, for they were two he's. It hadn't been long since they'd been hatched; that's why they were so fresh!

"Listen, pal!" they said. "You're so ugly we like you! Do you want to come along and be a bird of passage? Nearby, in another marsh, are some sweet, lovely wild geese, all unattached ladies who know how to say 'Quack!' You'll be able to make your fortune, ugly as you are!"

"Bang! Bang!" resounded above them. Both ganders fell dead in the reeds, and the water became blood red. "Bang! Bang!" came the sounds again, and whole flocks of wild geese flew up from the reeds. Then the guns cracked again. A great hunt was on. The hunters lay all around the marsh. Yes, some were sitting up in the branches of the trees which stretched far out over the reeds. The blue smoke drifted like clouds in among the dark trees and hung low over the water. Into the mud came the hunting dogs—splash! splash! Reeds and rushes swayed on all sides. It was terrifying for the poor duckling. He turned his head to put it under his wing, and at that very moment a huge dog stood close beside him! The dog's tongue hung way out of his mouth and his eyes gleamed dreadfully! He came right at the duckling with gaping jaws, showed his sharp teeth, and—splash! splash!—he went on without seizing it.

"Oh, thank God!" sighed the duckling. "I'm so ugly even the dog doesn't want to bite me!"

And so it lay quite still while the buckshot whizzed through the reeds, and shot after shot sounded.

Not until late in the day did it grow quiet, but the poor duckling didn't dare get up. He waited several hours more before he looked about, and then he hurried away from the marsh as fast as he could. He ran over field and meadow. It was windy, so he had trouble making any headway.

Toward evening he came to a poor little farmhouse. It was so wretched that it didn't know itself on which side to fall, so it remained standing. The wind blew so hard around the duckling that he had to sit on his tail to keep from being blown away—and it grew worse and worse. Then he noticed that the door had come off one of the hinges and was hanging so crookedly that he could slip through the opening into the room; and this he did.

Here lived an old woman with her cat and her hen. The cat, whom she called Sonny, could arch his back and purr; he could even give off sparks, but then one had to stroke him the wrong way. The hen had very short little legs, and so she was called Chicky Short Legs. She laid eggs well, and the woman loved her as if she were her own child.

In the morning the strange duckling was noticed at once, and the cat began to purr and the hen to cluck.

"What's that?" said the woman and looked all around, but she couldn't see very well, so she thought the duckling was a fat duck that had lost its way. "Well, this is a fine catch!" she said. "Now I can have duck eggs, if only it's not a drake! I'll have to find out about that!"

And so the duckling was accepted on probation for three weeks, but no eggs came. And the cat was master of the house, and the hen the lady, and they always said, "We and the world!" for they thought they were half of it, and by far the better

half. The duckling thought there might be another way of looking at that, but the hen wouldn't hear of it.

"Can you lay eggs?" she asked.

"No!"

"Then keep your mouth shut!"

And the cat said, "Can you arch your back, purr, and give off sparks?"

"No!"

"Well, then, keep your opinion to yourself when sensible people are talking!"

And the duckling sat in the corner and was in a bad mood. Then he happened to think of the fresh air and the sunshine. He was seized with such a strange desire to float on the water that at last he couldn't help it—he had to tell the hen about it.

"What's the matter with you?" she asked. "You don't have anything to do. That's why you get such strange ideas! Lay eggs or purr, then it'll pass!"

"But it's so wonderful to float on the water," said the duckling, "so lovely to dunk your head and dive down to the bottom!"

"Oh, that's a great pleasure!" said the hen. "You must be crazy! Ask the cat—he's the wisest one I know—if he likes to float on the water or to dive! Never mind what I think. Ask our mistress, the old woman; nobody in the world is wiser than she! Do you think she wants to float and dunk her head?"

"You don't understand me!" said the duckling.

"Well, if we don't understand you, who is going to understand you? You'll surely never be wiser than the cat and the woman, not to mention myself! Don't be conceited, my child! And thank your Creator for all the kindness that has been shown to you! Don't you have a warm room, and haven't you acquaintances you can learn something from? But you're a jerk, and it's no fun to associate with you! You can believe me, it's for your own good! I tell you unpleasant things, and that's how you can always tell your true friends! See to it now that you lay eggs and learn to purr or give off sparks!"

"I think I'll go out into the wide world!" said the duckling.

"Yes, you do that," said the hen.

And then the duckling went. He floated on the water and he dived, but he was ignored by every animal because of his ugliness.

Now it was autumn. The leaves in the forest turned yellow and brown. The wind took hold of them so that they danced about, and the sky looked cold. The clouds hung heavy with hail and snowflakes, and on the fence stood the raven, screeching, "Aw! Aw!" because of the cold. Yes, it was enough to make one freeze just thinking about it. The poor duckling certainly had a hard time.

One evening the sun was setting so gloriously. A whole flock of beautiful, large birds came out of the bushes. The duckling had never seen anything so beautiful. They were all shining white with long, graceful necks—they were swans. They uttered a very strange call, spread out their splendid long wings, and flew away from the cold regions to warmer lands, to open lakes! They rose so high, so high, and the ugly little duckling had such a strange feeling. He turned round and round in the water like a wheel, stretched his neck high in the air toward them, and uttered such a strange, loud cry that he frightened himself. Oh! He couldn't forget those beautiful birds, those happy birds! And when he could no longer see them, he dove right down to the bottom, and when he came up again, he was quite beside himself. He didn't know what the birds were called, or where they were flying, yet he loved them as he had never loved anyone before. He didn't envy them at all. How could he think of wishing for such loveliness for himself? He would have been glad if the ducks had only put up with him in their midst—the poor ugly thing!

And the winter grew so cold, so cold! The duckling had to swim about in the water to keep it from freezing over. But every night the hole in which he swam became smaller and smaller. It froze so hard that the crust of the ice creaked. The duckling had to use his legs all the time so the water wouldn't be covered over. At last he was exhausted, lay quite still, and froze fast in the ice.

Early in the morning a farmer came by and saw him. He went out and broke the ice into pieces with his wooden shoe and carried the duckling home to his wife. There he was revived.

The children wanted to play with him, but the duckling thought they wanted to hurt him and in his fright flew right into the milk pot, and the milk splashed all over the room. The woman shrieked and threw up her hands, and he flew into the trough where the butter was and then down into the flour barrel and out again. My, how he looked now! And the woman shrieked and struck at him with the fire tongs, and the children fell over each other trying to catch the duckling, and they laughed and shouted! Fortunately the door stood open. Out he flew among the bushes into the newly fallen snow, and there he lay as if unconscious.

But it would be much too sad to tell about all the suffering and misery he had to endure that hard winter. He was lying in the marsh among the reeds when the sun began to shine warmly again. The larks sang—it was wonderful springtime.

Then all at once the duckling lifted his wings. They beat the air more strongly than before and carried him powerfully away. And before he knew it, he was in a great garden where the apple trees were in bloom, where the lilacs sent forth their fragrance and hung on their long green branches right down toward the winding canals. Oh, how beautiful it was here, so spring fresh! And straight ahead from the thicket came three beautiful white swans. They ruffled their feathers and floated so lightly on the water. The duckling recognized the magnificent birds and was filled with a strange melancholy.

"I'll fly over to them, those royal birds! And they will peck me to death because I, who am so ugly, dare approach them. But that doesn't matter! Better to be killed by them than to be nipped by the ducks, pecked by the hens, kicked by the girl who takes care of the poultry yard, and to suffer so much during the winter!" And he flew out into the water and swam toward the magnificent swans. They saw him and hurried toward him with rustling feathers. "Just kill me!" said the poor bird and bent his head down to the water, expecting death. But what did he see in the clear water? He saw beneath him his own image, but he was no longer a clumsy, dark gray bird, ugly and repulsive—he was a swan himself!

It doesn't matter if one is born in a duck yard, when one has lain in a swan's egg!

The duckling felt quite happy about all the misery and hardship he had suffered, for now he could really appreciate his happiness and all the splendor that greeted him. And the big swans swam all around him and stroked him with their bills.

Some little children came into the garden. They threw bread and seeds out into the water and the youngest cried, "There's a new one!" And the other children joined in shouting jubilantly, "Yes, a new one has come!" And they clapped their hands and danced about and ran to get father and mother. Bread and cake were thrown into the water, and they all said, "The new one is the prettiest! So young and so beautiful!" And the old swans bowed before him.

Then he felt very shy and hid his head under his wings—he didn't know what to do! He was much too happy, but not at all proud, for a good heart is never proud! He thought how he had been persecuted and ridiculed, and now he heard everyone saying that he was the most beautiful of all beautiful birds. And the lilacs bent their branches right down into the water before him, and the sun shone so warm and so mild. Then he shook his feathers, lifted his slender neck, and with all his heart rejoiced, "I never dreamed of so much happiness when I was the ugly duckling!"

The Fir Tree

Out in the forest grew such a pretty fir tree. It stood in a good spot—it got sun, there was plenty of air, and all around it grew many bigger comrades—both pines and firs. But the little fir tree was so eager to grow; it didn't give a thought to the warm sun and the fresh air, it wasn't interested in the farmer's children who ran about and chattered while they were out picking strawberries or raspberries. Often they came with a whole jarful or had strawberries strung on straws; then they would sit down by the little tree and say, "Oh, how neat and tiny it is!" The tree didn't want to hear that at all.

The next year it was taller by a shoot, and the year after that by another much longer—for on a fir tree you can always tell how many years it has grown by the number of spaces between the branches.

"Oh, if only I were a great, big tree, like the others!" the little tree sighed. "Then I could spread my branches far out and from my crown I could gaze out into the wide world! The birds would build nests in my branches, and when the wind blew, I could nod so grandly, just like the others!"

It got no pleasure at all from the sunshine, from the birds or the reddish clouds that sailed over it morning and evening.

When it was winter, and the snow lay sparkling white all around, a hare would come hopping along and jump right over the little tree. Oh it was so annoying! But then two winters passed, and when the third came, the tree was so big that the hare had to go around it. "Oh, let me grow, let me grow, let me become tall and old; that's the only worthwhile thing in the world!" thought the tree.

In the autumn the woodcutters always came and felled some of the biggest trees. It happened every year, and each time the young fir tree, which was now quite grown up, shuddered because the great, magnificent trees fell groaning and crashing to the ground. Their branches were chopped off, and they looked so naked, so long and thin; they could hardly be recognized. Then they were loaded on wagons, and horses drew them out of the forest.

Where were they going? What was in store for them?

In the spring when the swallows and the storks came, the tree asked them, "Don't you know where they were taken? Haven't you come across them?"

The swallows didn't know anything. But the stork looked pensive, nodded his head, and said, "Yes, I think so. I passed many new ships when I flew from Egypt. On the ships were splendid masts; I dare say that they were the ones—they smelled of fir. They send their greetings; they stand proud, they do!"

"Oh, if only I were big enough to fly out over the sea, too! What is the sea, anyway, and what does it look like?"

"Oh, it is much too vast to explain," said the stork and went on its way.

"Rejoice in your youth!" said the sunbeams. "Rejoice in your fine growth and in the young life within you!"

And the wind kissed the tree, and the dew wept tears over it, but the fir tree didn't understand any of it.

When it was almost Christmas, quite young trees were chopped down, often trees which were not even as big or as old as the fir who was always restless and wanted to get away. These young trees—they were precisely the very handsomest ones—

always kept their branches. They, too, were put on wagons, and horses drew them out of the forest.

"Where are they going?" asked the fir tree. "They're no bigger than I am; there was even one that was much smaller. Why did they keep all their branches? Where are they rolling off to?"

"We know! We know!" twittered the sparrows. "We peeped in through the windows down in the town. We know where they're being taken. Oh, they will come into the greatest glory and splendor imaginable! We peeped in through the windows and saw that they were planted right in the middle of the warm room and decorated with the most beautiful things: gilded apples, gingerbread, cakes, toys, and many hundreds of candles!"

"And then—?" asked the fir tree and trembled in all its branches. "And then—? What happens then?"

"Well, we didn't see any more. But there has never been anything like it!"

"Perhaps I was born to go that glorious way!" rejoiced the tree. "That would be even better than going across the sea! How sick I am with longing! If only it were Christmas! Now I'm as tall and outstretched as those that were taken away last year. Oh, if only I were already on the wagon! If only I were in the warm room with all that pomp and splendor! And then—! Then something still better, still more beautiful will come, otherwise why would they decorate me so? There must be something still grander coming, still more glorious! But what? Oh, I'm suffering! I'm longing! I don't even know myself what is going on with me!"

"Rejoice in us!" said the air and the sunlight. "Rejoice in your happy youth out here in nature."

But the tree didn't rejoice at all. It grew and grew, winter and summer it stood green, dark green it stood. People who saw it said, "What a lovely tree!"

And at Christmas it was cut down first of all. The ax chopped right through its marrow. The tree fell with a sigh to the ground. It felt a pain, a faintness. It was impossible for it to think about its good fortune now—it was sad to be parted from its home, from the spot where it had sprouted up. It realized that it would never again see its dear old comrades, the little bushes and flowers all around, maybe not even the birds. The departure wasn't pleasant at all.

The tree first came to itself in a courtyard where it had been unloaded with the other trees. It heard a man say, "This one's great! It's perfect for us!"

Then two servants in full uniform came and carried the fir tree into a beautiful, big room. Portraits hung on all the walls, and on either side of the great tiled stove stood large Chinese vases with lions on the lids. There were rocking chairs, silk-upholstered sofas, and large tables piled with picture books and toys worth a hundred times a hundred dollars—at least that's what the children said. And the fir tree was set up in a big wooden tub filled with sand, but no one could see that it was a tub because a green cloth covered it, and it stood on a large, many-colored rug. Oh, how the tree trembled! What was going to happen? Servants and housemaids began to trim it. On one branch they hung small baskets cut out of colored paper; each basket was filled with candy, gilded apples, and walnuts hung as if they grew there, and more than a hundred small red, blue, and white candles were fastened onto the branches. Dolls that looked exactly like real people—the tree had never seen anything like it before—dangled from the green branches, and all the way up at the very top a large tinsel star was placed. It was magnificent, simply unbelievably magnificent!

"Tonight," they all said, "tonight it will shine!"

"Oh," thought the tree, "if only it were evening! If only the candles would soon be lit! And what will happen then? Will the trees come from the forest to see me? Will the sparrows look in at the windows? Will I take root and stand here all decorated winter and summer?"

That's how much the tree knew! But it got a regular bark-ache from just longing, and barkaches are just as painful for trees as headaches are for the rest of us.

Now the candles were lit. What radiance, what glory! The

tree quivered in all its branches so that one of the candles set fire to some needles. It really scorched!

"Heaven help us!" screamed the maids, and they hastened to put it out.

Now the tree didn't even dare to tremble. Oh, it was awful! It was so afraid of dropping some of its decorations; it was completely bewildered by all the splendor. And now the double doors were thrown open and a flock of children rushed in as if they were going to overturn the whole tree. The grownups followed more sedately after them. The children stood completely still but only for a moment; then they started shouting again so that the room resounded. They danced around the tree, and one present after another was plucked from its branches.

"What's that they're doing?" thought the tree. "What's going to happen now?" And the candles burned right down to the branches, and as they burned down they were put out, and then the children got permission to plunder the tree. Oh, they rushed at it so that it creaked in every branch. If it hadn't been fastened to the ceiling by the topmost shoot and the gold star, it would have fallen over.

The children danced around with their fine toys. No one paid any attention to the tree except the old nursemaid who went and peered among the branches, but that was only to see if there wasn't a fig or an apple that had been forgotten.

"A story! A story!" shouted the children, and they pulled a little, fat man over to the tree, and he sat down right under it—"because it's just like being in the green out-of-doors," he said. "And it'll do the tree good to listen, too! But I'm only going to tell one story. Do you want the one about 'Ivede-Avede' or the one about 'Clumpy-Dumpy Who Fell Down the Stairs and Yet Rose High in the World and Won the Princess?'"

"'Ivede-Avede,'" shouted some. "'Clumpy-Dumpy,'" shouted others. There was an awful shrieking and clamoring; only the fir tree kept entirely silent, thinking, "Aren't I to take part, to do anything at all?" But it had already played its part and done what it was supposed to do.

And the man told about "Clumpy-Dumpy Who Fell Down the Stairs and Yet Rose High in the World and Won the Princess." And the children clapped their hands and cried, "Tell some more! Tell some more!" They also wanted to hear "Ivede-Avede," but they only got the story about "Clumpy-Dumpy." The fir tree stood perfectly still, full of thoughts. "The birds out in the forest had never told anything like that. Clumpy-Dumpy fell down the stairs and yet won the princess! Yes, that's the way it goes in the world," thought the fir tree, and it believed the story was true because such a nice man had told it. "Yes, who knows! Perhaps I'll fall down the stairs, too, and win a princess!" And it looked forward to being decorated again the next day with candles and toys, tinsel and fruit.

"Tomorrow I won't quiver," it thought. "I'll really enjoy all my splendor. Tomorrow I'll hear the story about Clumpy-Dumpy again and maybe the one about Ivede-Avede, too." And the tree stood silent and pensive the whole night long.

In the morning a stable boy and a servant girl came in.

"Now it's all beginning again," thought the tree, but they dragged it out of the room, up the stairs, into the attic, and there in a dark corner where no daylight ever reached, it was put away.

"What does this mean?" thought the tree. "What am I supposed to do now? What will I hear about up here?" And it leaned against the wall and stood thinking and thinking. And it had plenty of time because days and nights passed. No one came up, and when somebody finally did come, it was only to put away some large boxes in a corner. The tree was entirely hidden—you'd think it had been completely forgotten.

"Now it's winter outside!" thought the tree. "The ground is hard and covered with snow, so the people couldn't plant me. Therefore I'm supposed to stand here out of the cold until spring. How very thoughtful! How good people are! If only it weren't so dark and so terribly lonely. Not even a little hare! After all, it was so nice out there in the forest when there was snow all over, and the hare came hopping past. Yes, even when it jumped over me, though I didn't like it at the time. Up here it's so terribly lonely."

"Squeak, squeak!" said a little mouse just then and scurried across the floor. And then another little one came. They sniffed at the fir tree and crept about among its branches.

"It's so terribly cold," said the small mice, "otherwise it's a heavenly place to be, isn't that so, old fir tree?"

"I'm not at all old!" said the fir tree. "There are many that are much older than I!"

"Where do you come from?" asked the mice. "And what do you know?" They were so terribly curious. "Tell us about the loveliest spot on earth. Have you been there? Have you been in the pantry where cheeses lie on the shelves and hams hang from the ceiling, where you dance on tallow candles, and go in thin and come out fat?"

"I don't know that place," said the tree, "but I know the forest where the sun shines and the birds sing." And then it told them all about its youth, and the small mice had never heard anything like it before, so they really listened and said, "What a lot you've seen! How happy you must have been!"

"I?" said the fir tree, and thought about what it had itself just been telling. "Yes, those were actually happy times." But then it told about Christmas Eve, when it had been trimmed with cakes and candles.

"Oh!" said the little mice. "How lucky you've been, you old fir tree!"

"I'm not old at all!" said the tree. "It was only this winter I came from the forest. I'm still in the prime of life. I've just stopped growing."

"What wonderful stories you tell!" said the little mice, and the next night they came with four other little mice, so they too could hear the tree tell stories. And the more it told, the more clearly it remembered everything itself, and it thought, "Those were really happy times! But they can come again, they can come again! Clumpy-Dumpy fell down the stairs and still he won the princess, maybe I can win a princess, too!" And the fir tree thought about a pretty little birch that grew out in the forest; for to the fir tree it was a real, beautiful princess.

"Who's Clumpy-Dumpy?" asked the little mice. And then the fir tree told the whole story. It could remember every single word, and the little mice were ready to jump into the top of the tree from pure joy. The next night many more mice came and on Sunday even two rats. But they said that the story wasn't funny, and that made the little mice sad because now they thought less of it, too.

"Do you only know that one story?" asked the rats.

"Only the one," answered the tree. "I heard it on the happiest evening of my life, but at the time I didn't realize how happy I was."

"It's an extremely bad story! Don't you know any with bacon and tallow candles in them? No pantry stories?"

"No!" said the tree.

"Well, thanks, but no thanks," replied the rats, and they went off to where they had come from.

Finally the little mice stayed away, too, and then the tree sighed. "It was really quite pleasant when those perky little mice sat around me and listened to what I had to tell. Now that's over, too. But I'll remember to enjoy myself the next time I'm brought down.

But when did that happen?—

Yes, it was early one morning. Some people came and rummaged around in the attic. The boxes were moved and the tree brought out. True enough, they threw it rather roughly down on the floor, but a moment later a stable boy dragged it over toward the stairs where the sun shone.

"Now life's beginning again!" thought the tree. It felt the fresh air, the first sunbeam—then it was out in the yard. Everything happened so quickly that the tree completely forgot to look at itself, there was so much to see all around. The yard was right next to a garden, and everything was in bloom. Roses hung so fresh and fragrant over the low fence, the linden trees were in flower, and the swallows flew about and said, "Chirp,

chirp, my husband's come!" But it wasn't the fir tree they meant.

"Now I'm really going to enjoy life!" it rejoiced, and spread its branches out wide—alas, they were all withered and yellow. It lay in a corner among nettles and weeds. The gold star was still at the top and glittered in the bright sunshine.

Out in the yard several of the lively children were playing who had danced around the tree on Christmas Eve and been so delighted with it. One of the smallest ran over and pulled off the gold star.

"Look what's still on the awful old Christmas tree!" he said, trampling on the branches so that they cracked under his boots.

And the tree looked at the splendor and freshness of the flowers in the garden, and then looked at itself, and it wished it had stayed in the dark corner of the attic. It thought about its fresh youth in the forest, of the merry Christmas Eve, and of the little mice who had listened so happily to the story about Clumpy-Dumpy.

"It's over, it's over!" said the poor tree. "If I had only enjoyed myself while I could! It's over, it's all over!"

And the stable boy came and chopped the tree into kindling; a whole bundle lay there. It blazed up nicely under the big cop-

per kettle, and it sighed so deeply, and each sigh was a little retort. And that's why the children who were playing ran in and
sat down in front of the fire, peering into it and shouting,
"Bang! Bang!" But with each retort, which was a deep sigh, the
tree thought about a summer day in the forest, a winter night
out there when the stars shone, it thought about Christmas Eve
and about "Clumpy-Dumpy," the only story it had ever heard
or knew how to tell. And then the tree was burnt up.

The boys played in the yard, and the smallest had on his
chest the gold star the tree had worn on its happiest evening.
Now that was gone, and the tree was gone and the story, too.

It's over! It's all over! And that's how it is with all stories!

The Snow Queen

A TALE IN SEVEN STORIES

The First Story

Which Is About the Looking Glass and the Splinters

Look here! Now we're going to begin. When we've come to the end of the story, we'll know more than we do now, for it has to do with an evil troll! One of the worst of all, the Devil himself! One day he was in very good spirits, for he had made a looking glass with the peculiarity that everything good and beautiful reflected in it shrank to almost nothing but everything useless and ugly stood right out and became even worse. In it the loveliest scenery looked like boiled spinach and the nicest people turned hideous or stood on their heads and had no stomachs. Faces became so distorted that they couldn't be recognized, and if you had a single freckle, you could be certain it would spread over nose and mouth. "That was great fun," said the Devil. If a good, pious thought occurred to someone, a leer appeared in the looking glass, so that the troll-devil had to laugh at his clever invention. Everyone who went to the troll school—for he ran a troll school—went around saying that there had been a miracle. For now, they thought, one could see for the first time how the world and the people in it really looked. They ran all over with the looking glass until at last there wasn't a country or a person that hadn't been distorted in it. Now they also wanted to fly up to heaven itself to make fun of the angels and the Lord. The higher they flew with the looking glass the more it leered; they could hardly hold on to it. Higher and higher they flew—closer to God and the angels. Then the looking glass shook so terribly because of its leering that it flew out of their hands and fell down to earth, where it broke into a hundred million billion, and even more, pieces. And then it did much more harm than before, because some of the pieces were scarcely as big as a grain of sand, and these flew about in the wide world. And whenever they got into anyone's eye, they stuck there, and these people saw everything wrong or had only eyes for what was bad about a thing, for every little piece of the looking glass had retained the same power as the whole looking glass. Some people even got a little splinter in their hearts, and that was terrible indeed—the heart became just like a lump of ice. Some pieces of the looking glass were so large that they were used as windowpanes, but it wasn't a good idea to look at one's friends through these panes. Other pieces were used in spectacles, and when people put on these spectacles to see well and see straight, things went badly; the Devil split his sides laughing, that tickled him so. But little splinters of glass were still flying about in the air—and now we shall hear!

The Second Story

A Little Boy and a Little Girl

In the great city, where there are so many houses and people that there is not enough room for everyone to have a little garden, and where most of them have to be content with flowers in pots, there were, however, two poor children who had a garden somewhat larger than a flowerpot. They weren't brother and sister, but they were just as fond of each other as if they had been. Their parents lived right next to each other; they lived in two garrets. Where the roof of one house almost touched the other, and the gutter ran along the eaves, a little window in each house faced toward the other. You had only to straddle the gutter to get from one window to the one opposite.

Outside, the parents each had a big wooden box, and in it grew kitchen herbs that they used and a little rosebush; there was one in each box, and they grew gloriously. Now the parents got the idea of placing the boxes across the gutter so that they almost reached from one window to the other and looked exactly like two beds of flowers. The sweet pea vines hung down over the boxes, and the rosebushes shot out long branches, twining around the windows and bending toward each other—

it was almost like a triumphal arch of greenery and flowers. Since the boxes were very high, and the children knew they mustn't climb on them, they were often allowed to step out to each other and sit on their little stools under the roses; and there they played splendidly together.

In the winter this pleasure, of course, came to an end. The windows were often completely frosted over, but then the children warmed copper coins on the stove and held the hot coin against the frozen pane. This made a fine peephole, as round as could be. Behind it peeped a gentle, loving eye, one from each window—it was the little boy and the little girl. He was called Kay and she was called Gerda. In the summer they could reach each other with one jump, but in the winter they first had to go down a lot of stairs and then up a lot of stairs. Outside the snow was falling heavily.

"Those are white bees that are swarming," said the old grandmother.

"Do they also have a queen bee?" asked the little boy, for he knew that among real bees there is such a thing.

"Yes, they have!" said the grandmother. "She always flies where the swarm is thickest! She's the largest of them all, and she never stays still on the ground. She flies up again into the black cloud. Many a winter's night she flies through the streets of the city and looks in at the windows, and then they freeze over so strangely as if covered with flowers."

"Yes, I've seen that!" said both of the children, and so they knew it was true.

"Can the Snow Queen come in here?" asked the little girl.

"Just let her come," said the boy. "I'll put her on the hot stove, and then she'll melt."

But the grandmother smoothed his hair and told some other stories.

In the evening, when little Kay was at home and half undressed, he clambered up on the chair by the window and peeped out through the little hole. A few snowflakes were falling outside, and one of them, the largest of all, remained lying on the edge of one of the flower boxes. The snowflake grew bigger and bigger; it became at last a whole lady dressed in the finest white gauze that seemed to be made up of millions of starlike flakes. She was so beautiful and delicate, but of ice—glaring, glittering ice. Yet she was alive. Her eyes stared like two bright stars, but there was no peace or rest in them. She nodded to the window and beckoned with her hand. The little boy grew frightened and jumped down from the chair. Just then it seemed as if a great bird flew outside past the window.

The next day there was a clear frost—and then spring arrived. The sun shone, bits of green peeped forth, the swallows built nests, the windows were opened, and the children again sat in their little garden high up by the gutter above all the rest of the house.

The roses bloomed so wonderfully that summer! The little girl had learned a hymn, and in it there was something about roses, and these roses made her think of her own. She sang it for the little boy, and he sang it with her:

> The roses grow in the dale,
> Where the Holy Child we shall hail.

And the little ones held each other by the hand, kissed the roses, looked into God's bright sunshine, and spoke to it as if the Holy Child were there. How wonderful these summer days were, how beautiful it was to be out among the fresh rose-bushes, which never seemed to want to stop blooming.

Kay and Gerda sat looking at a picture book of animals and birds. Then it was—the clock on the great church tower had just struck five—that Kay said, "Ouch! Something stuck me in the heart! And now I've got something in my eye!"

The little girl put her arms around his neck; he blinked his eyes. No, there was nothing to be seen.

"I think it's gone!" he said, but it wasn't gone. It happened to be one of those glass splinters that had flown from the looking glass, the troll mirror—we certainly all remember that—the evil glass that made everything great and good that was mirrored in it small and hideous, while everything evil and wicked stood out sharply and every fault showed up at once.

Poor Kay had also received a splinter right in his heart. Soon it would become like a lump of ice. It didn't hurt now, but it was there.

"Why are you crying?" he asked. "You look ugly! There's nothing wrong with me! Ugh!" he shouted suddenly. "That rose is being eaten by a worm! And look, that one there is all crooked! Those are really ugly roses! They look just like the boxes they're standing in!" And he gave the box a hard kick with his foot and broke off the two roses.

"Kay, what are you doing?" cried the little girl. When he saw how frightened she was, he broke off another rose and ran in through his window away from dear little Gerda.

When she came later with the picture book, he said it was for babies, and when his grandmother told stories, he always put in a "but." And when he got a chance, he would walk behind her, put on glasses, and talk just like her. It was such a perfect imitation, he made people laugh. Soon he could mimic how everyone in the whole street talked and walked. Everything peculiar and not nice about them Kay knew how to imitate. People said, "He certainly must have a good head, that boy!" But it was the glass he had gotten in his eye, the glass that stuck in his heart; that was why he teased even little Gerda, who loved him with all her heart.

His games now were quite different from the old ones—they were so rational. One winter's day when the snowflakes were drifting down, he came with a big magnifying glass, held out a corner of his blue coat, and let the snowflakes fall on it.

"Now look through the glass, Gerda!" he said, and every snowflake became much bigger and looked like a magnificent flower or a ten-pointed star. It was wonderful to look at.

"See how complicated they are!" said Kay. "This is much more interesting than real flowers! And there's not a single flaw in them; they're completely perfect as long as they don't melt!"

A little later Kay came wearing big gloves and had his sled on his back. He shouted right into Gerda's ears, "I have permission to go sledding in the big square where the others play!" And off he went.

Over in the square the most daring of the boys often tied their sleds to the farmer's wagon and rode a good distance with it. That was great fun! Just as they were having the most fun, a great sleigh came along. It was painted all white, and in it sat a person wrapped in a fleecy white fur and wearing a white fur cap. The sleigh drove twice around the square, and in a flash Kay got his little sled tied to it, and now he was driving away with it. It went faster and faster into the next street. With a turn of the head the one who was driving nodded in such a friendly way to Kay, it was just as if they knew each other. Each time Kay wanted to untie his little sled, the person nodded again, and Kay remained where he was. They drove right out through the town gate. The snow began falling so thickly that the little boy couldn't see his hand in front of his face as he rushed along, and then he quickly let go of the rope in order to get loose from the great sleigh, but it was no use. His little vehicle hung on, and away they went as fast as the wind. Then he shouted very loudly, but nobody heard him, and the snow drifted down, and the sleigh rushed on. Every now and then it gave a jolt—it seemed as if he were rushing over ditches and fences. He was terrified. He wanted to say the Lord's Prayer, but he could only remember the multiplication table.

The snowflakes grew bigger and bigger, at last they looked like huge white hens. Suddenly they flew to one side, the great sleigh stopped, and the person who was riding in it stood up. Coat and cap were all of snow. It was a woman so tall and straight, so shining white—it was the Snow Queen.

"We've made good progress!" she said. "But if you're freezing, creep into my bearskin!" And she put him beside her in the sleigh and wrapped the fur around him. It was as if he were sinking into a snowdrift. "Are you still cold?" she asked, and she kissed him on the forehead. Oh! it was colder than ice, it went right to his heart, which was halfway a lump of ice anyhow. It was as if he were going to die—but only for a moment, then it felt quite good; he no longer noticed the cold around him.

"My sled! Don't forget my sled!" That was the first thing he thought of, and it was tied to one of the white hens, which flew along behind with the sled on its back. The Snow Queen kissed Kay once again, and then he had forgotten little Gerda, and Grandmother, and all the others at home.

"Now you won't get any more kisses!" she said. "For I might kiss you to death!"

Kay looked at her. She was so beautiful. A more intelligent, lovelier face he couldn't imagine; now she didn't seem to be of ice, as she had that time she had sat outside the window and beckoned to him. In his eyes she was perfect; he didn't feel at all afraid. He told her that he could do arithmetic in his head, even with fractions, that he knew the square mileage of different countries and how many inhabitants they had. And she kept smiling at him. Then it seemed to him that what he knew still wasn't enough, and he looked up into the great, great sky, and she flew with him, flew high up on the black cloud; and the storm whistled and roared as if it sang old songs. They flew over woods and lakes, over sea and land. Down below the cold wind whistled, the wolves howled, the snow glittered and over it flew black crows screaming. But up above, the moon shone so big and bright, and Kay looked at it through the long, long winter night. By day he slept at the Snow Queen's feet.

The Third Story

The Flower Garden of the Woman Who Could Do Magic

But how did little Gerda get on when Kay didn't come back? Where could he be? Nobody knew, nobody could offer any news of him. The boys simply said they had seen him tie his little sled to a magnificent big one which had driven down the street and out through the town gate. Nobody knew where he was; many tears flowed, little Gerda wept so hard and so long. Then they said he was dead, that he had drowned in the river that ran near the town. Oh, they were certainly long, dark winter days!

Now spring came with warmer sunshine.

"Kay is dead and gone!" said little Gerda.

"I don't believe it!" said the sunshine.

"He's dead and gone!" she said to the swallows.

"We don't believe it!" they replied, and finally little Gerda didn't believe it either.

"I'll put on my new red shoes," she said one morning, "those that Kay has never seen, and I'll go down to the river and ask it!"

It was quite early. She kissed her old grandmother, who was

asleep, put on her red shoes, and walked all alone out through the town gate to the river.

"Is it true that you've taken my little playmate? I'll give you my red shoes if you'll give him back to me!"

And it seemed to her that the waves nodded so strangely. Then she took her red shoes, her dearest possession, and threw them both out into the river; but they fell close to the shore, and the little waves carried them right back toward land to her. It was as if the river didn't want to take from her the dearest things she had, since it didn't have little Kay after all. But she thought she hadn't thrown the shoes out far enough, and so she climbed into a boat that was lying among the reeds, went all the way to the farthest end, and threw the shoes. But the boat hadn't been made fast, and her movement made it glide from land. She noticed it and hurried to get back, but before she could make it, the boat was more than a yard from shore, and was gliding away faster.

Little Gerda became quite frightened and began to cry. But nobody heard her except the sparrows, and they couldn't carry her to land. But they flew along the shore and sang as if to comfort her, "Here we are! Here we are!" The boat drifted with the stream, and little Gerda sat quite still in just her stockings. Her little red shoes floated along behind, but they couldn't catch up with the boat, which picked up more speed.

It was lovely on both shores—beautiful flowers, old trees, and slopes with sheep and cows—but not a person was to be seen.

"Perhaps the river is carrying me to little Kay," thought Gerda, and then she was in better spirits, stood up, and watched the beautiful green shores for many hours. She came to a big cherry orchard where there was a little house with strange red and blue windows as well as a straw-thatched roof and two wooden soldiers outside, who presented arms to those who sailed by.

Gerda shouted to them—she thought they were alive—but of course they didn't answer. She came quite close to them; the river carried the boat right in toward shore.

Gerda shouted even louder, and out of the house came an old, old woman leaning on a crook-handled cane; she was wearing a large sun hat with the loveliest flowers painted on it.

"You poor little child!" said the old woman. "However did you get out on the great strong stream and drift so far out into the wide world?" And the old woman went all the way out into the water, hooked the boat with her cane, pulled it to land, and lifted little Gerda out.

And Gerda was glad to be on dry land, but, all the same, she felt a little afraid of the strange old woman.

"Come now, and tell me who you are and how you came here!" she said.

And Gerda told her everything, and the old woman shook her head and said, "Humm! Humm!" And when Gerda had told her everything and asked if she hadn't seen little Kay, the woman said that he hadn't passed by, but that he'd probably come. She shouldn't be downhearted, but should taste her cherries, look at her flowers—they were prettier than any picture book, and each could tell a whole story. Then she took Gerda by the hand, they went into the little house, and the old woman locked the door.

The windows were so high up, and the glass in them was red, blue, and yellow. Inside the daylight shone so strangely in many colors, but on the table stood the loveliest cherries, and Gerda ate as many as she wanted, for this she dared to do. And while she was eating, the old woman combed her hair with a golden comb, and her hair curled and shone so delightfully yellow all around her little, friendly face, which was so round and looked like a rose.

"I've really been looking for such a sweet little girl," said the old woman. "Now you shall see how well we two shall get on together!" And as she combed little Gerda's hair, Gerda forgot more and more her foster brother Kay, for the old woman could do magic. But she wasn't a wicked witch, she only practiced a little magic for her own pleasure, and now she very much wanted to keep little Gerda. So she went into the garden, stretched out her crooked cane toward all the rosebushes, and, no matter how beautifully they were blooming, they all sank down into the black earth, and no one could see where they had been. The old woman was afraid that when Gerda saw the roses, she would think of her own and remember little Kay, and then she would run away.

Now she took Gerda out into the flower garden. My, how fragrant and lovely it was here! Every conceivable flower, for every season of the year, stood here in the most magnificent bloom. No picture book could have been more colorful and attractive. Gerda jumped for joy and played till the sun went down behind the high cherry trees. Then she was given a lovely bed with red silk comforters; they were stuffed with blue violets, and she slept and dreamed as delightfully as any queen on her wedding day.

The next day she was able to play again with the flowers in the warm sunshine—and in this way many days went by. Gerda knew every flower, but as many as there were of them, it still seemed to her that one was missing, but which one she didn't know. Then one day she was sitting, looking at the old woman's sun hat with the painted flowers, and indeed the prettiest of them was a rose. The old woman had forgotten to take it off the hat when she had made the others sink down into the earth. But that's how it is, if you're forgetful!

"What!" said Gerda. "There aren't any roses here!" And she ran in among the flower beds and searched and searched, but there were none to be found. Then she sat down and wept, but her hot tears fell just where a rosebush had sunk, and when the warm tears moistened the ground, the bush shot up all at once, as full of blossoms as when it had sunk down. And Gerda threw her arms around it and kissed the roses, and she thought of the beautiful roses at home and along with them of little Kay.

"Oh, how I've been delayed!" said the little girl. "I was going to find Kay! Don't you know where he is?" she asked the roses. "Do you think he is dead and gone?"

"He's not dead!" said the roses. "We've been down in the ground, of course, where all the dead are, but Kay wasn't there!"

"Thank you!" said little Gerda, and she went over to the other flowers and looked into their cups and asked, "Don't you know where little Kay is?"

But each flower stood in the sun and dreamed of its own tale or story. Little Gerda was told so awfully many of these, but no one knew anything about Kay.

And so what did the tiger lily say?

"Do you hear the drum? Boom! Boom! There are only two notes, always Boom! Boom! Hear the women's dirge! Hear the cries of the priests! In her long red mantle the Hindu woman stands on the pyre, the flames rise up around her and her dead husband. But the Hindu woman is thinking of the one alive here in the circle, the one whose eyes burn hotter than the flames, the one whose burning eyes reach deeper into her heart than the flames which will soon burn her body to ashes. Can the flame of the heart die in the flames of the pyre?"

"I don't understand that at all!" said little Gerda.

"That's my tale!" said the tiger lily.

What does the convolvulus say?

"Overhanging the narrow mountain path is an old feudal castle; thick periwinkle grows leaf by leaf up over the ancient red walls around the balcony, and there stands a beautiful girl; she leans out over the balustrade and gazes down the road. No rose hangs fresher from the branches than she; no apple blossom when borne from the tree by the wind sways more lightly than she. How the magnificent silk kirtle rustles! Isn't he coming?"

"Is it Kay you mean?" asked little Gerda.

"I'm speaking only about my tale, my dream," answered the convolvulus.

What does the little snowdrop say?

"Between the trees the long board is hanging by ropes; it's a swing. Two pretty little girls—their dresses are as white as snow, long green silk ribbons are fluttering from their hats—sit swinging. Their brother, who is bigger than they, is standing up in the swing. He has his arm around the rope to hold on with, for in one hand he has a little bowl and in the other a clay pipe; he is blowing soap bubbles. The swing is swinging, and the bubbles are floating with beautiful changing colors; the last still clings to the pipe swaying in the wind; the swing is moving. The little black dog, light as the bubbles, stands on its hind legs and wants to get on the swing; the swing sweeps past, the dog tumbles down and yelps angrily, it is being teased. The bubbles burst—a swinging board, a leaping soap picture, that's my song!"

"What you tell about may be pretty, but you tell it so mournfully, and you haven't mentioned little Kay at all."

What do the hyacinths say?

"There were three lovely sisters, so ethereal and delicate. One's dress was red, the second's was blue, the third's was all white; hand in hand they danced by the quiet lake in the bright moonlight. They were not elfin girls, they were humans. There was such a sweet fragrance, and the girls disappeared in the forest. The fragrance became stronger; three coffins, in which lay the three lovely girls, glided from the dense forest across the lake; fireflies flew twinkling about like little hovering flames. Are the dancing girls asleep, or are they dead? The flower fragrance says they are corpses; the evening bell is tolling for the dead!"

"You make me quite sad," said little Gerda. "Your fragrance is so strong; I have to think of the dead girls! Oh! is little Kay really dead? The roses have been down in the ground and they say no!"

"Ding dong!" tolled the hyacinth bells. "We're not ringing for little Kay—we don't know him! We're just singing our song, the only one we know!"

And Gerda went over to the buttercup, which shone out from among its glistening green leaves.

"You're a bright little sun!" said Gerda. "Tell me if you know where I may find my playmate?"

And the buttercup shone so prettily and looked back at Gerda. What song could the buttercup sing? It wasn't about Kay either.

"In a small yard Our Lord's sun was shining so warmly on

the first day of spring. The beams glided down along the neighbor's white wall; close by grew the first yellow flowers, shining like gold in the warm sunbeams. The old grandmother was out in her chair, her granddaughter, the poor, pretty servant girl, came home for a short visit. She kissed her grandmother. There was gold, gold from the heart, in that blessed kiss—gold on the lips, gold in the earth, gold in the morning hour. See, that's my little story!" said the buttercup.

"My poor old grandmother!" sighed Gerda. "Yes, she's probably longing for me and grieving for me, just as she did for little Kay. But I'm coming home soon and then I'll bring Kay with me. It's no use asking the flowers; they know only their own song, they're not telling me anything!" And she tied her little dress up, so that she could run faster. But the narcissus hit her on the leg as she jumped over it. Then she stopped, looked at the tall yellow flower, and asked, "Do you perhaps know something?" And she bent right down to the narcissus. And what did it say?

"I can see myself! I can see myself!" said the narcissus. "Oh! Oh! How fragrant I am! Up in the little garret stands a little dancer half dressed. Now she is standing on one leg, now on both; she kicks out at the whole world; she's nothing but an illusion. She is pouring water from the teapot on a piece of cloth she's holding—it's her corset. Cleanliness is a good thing! The white dress is hanging on the peg; it has also been washed in the teapot and dried on the roof. She puts it on and the saffron-yellow handkerchief around her neck, then the dress shines even whiter. Leg in the air! See how she stands tall on one stalk! I can see myself! I can see myself!"

"I don't care at all about that!" said Gerda. "That's nothing to tell me!" And then she ran to the edge of the garden.

The door was closed, but she wiggled the rusty hook so that it came loose and the door flew open, and little Gerda ran barefoot out into the wide world. She looked back three times, but no one came after her. At last she couldn't run anymore and sat down on a big stone. And when she looked around her, summer was over—it was late autumn. One couldn't tell this at all inside the beautiful garden where there was always sunshine and flowers from every season.

"Oh, God! How I've slowed myself down!" said little Gerda. "Why, autumn has come! So I don't dare rest!" and she got up to go.

Oh! How sore and tired her little feet were, and all around it looked cold and raw. The long willow leaves were all yellow, and they were dripping from the mist. One leaf fell after the other; only the sloe bore fruit but so sour that it puckered the mouth. Oh! How gray and gloomy it was in the wide world.

The Fourth Story

Prince and Princess

Gerda had to rest again. Then a crow hopped on the snow, right across from where she sat. For a long time he had been sitting looking at her and wagging his head. Now he said, "Caw! Caw! How do! How do!" He couldn't say it any better, but he meant the little girl well and asked where she was going all alone out in the wide world. The word "alone" Gerda understood very well and really felt all that it meant. And so she told the crow the story of her whole life and asked if he hadn't seen Kay.

And the crow nodded quite thoughtfully and said, "Could be! Could be!"

"What? Do you think so?" cried the little girl and nearly squeezed the crow to death, she kissed him so.

"Take it easy, take it easy!" said the crow. "I think I know —I think it could be little Kay, but now he has probably forgotten you for the princess!"

"Does he live with a princess?" asked Gerda.

"Yes, listen!" said the crow. "But it's so hard for me to speak your language. If you understand crow language, then I can tell it better!"

"No, I never learned it!" said Gerda. "But Grandmother understood it, and she knew pig latin. If only I had learned it!"

"No matter!" said the crow. "I'll tell you as well as I can, but it'll be bad all the same." And then he told what he knew.

"In this kingdom where we're sitting now, there lives a princess who is immensely smart. She has even read all the newspapers in the world and forgotten them again—that's how smart she is. The other day she was sitting on the throne—and that's not really so much fun, people say—when she happened to hum a song, the very one that goes: 'Why shouldn't I marry?' 'Listen! There's something to that!' she said, and then she wanted to get married. But she wanted a husband who could speak up for himself when spoken to, not one who just stood there looking distinguished, because that's so boring. Now she had all the ladies in waiting drummed up, and when they heard what she wanted, they were so pleased. 'I like that!' they said. 'I was just thinking that the other day!' You may be sure that every word I say is true!" said the crow. "I have a tame sweetheart who walks freely around in the castle, and she has told me everything!"

Of course his sweetheart was also a crow, for birds of a feather flock together, so one crow always picks another.

"The newspapers came out right away with a border of hearts

and the princess's monogram. One could read that every young man who was good-looking was free to come up to the castle and speak with the princess, and the one who talked so that it was clear he was at home there and who sounded the best, he was the one the princess would take for her husband! Well, well!" said the crow. "You can believe me, it's as true as I'm sitting here. People came in droves; there was jostling and running but no one succeeded, neither on the first day nor the second. They were all good talkers when they were out in the street, but when they came in through the castle gate and saw the guards in silver, and up along the staircase the lackeys in gold, and the great illuminated halls, they became flustered. And when they stood before the throne where the princess was sitting, they didn't know what to say except the last word she had spoken, and that she didn't care to hear again. It was just as if people in there had taken some snuff on a full stomach and fallen into a doze until they came back out in the street again— yes, then they could talk! There was a line all the way from the city gate to the castle. I went inside myself to see it!" said the crow, "They got both hungry and thirsty, but from the castle they didn't get so much as a glass of lukewarm water. To be sure, some of the smartest had brought along sandwiches, but they didn't share with their neighbors. They thought like this, 'Just let him look hungry, then the princess won't take him!'"

"But Kay, little Kay!" asked Gerda. "When did he get there? Was he among all those people?"

"Give me time! Give me time! Now we're just coming to him! It was on the third day when a little person, without horse or carriage, came marching boldly right up to the castle; his eyes sparkled like yours; he had beautiful long hair, but apart from that he had shabby clothes!"

"That was Kay!" Gerda cried jubilantly. "Oh, so I have found him!" And she clapped her hands.

"He had a little knapsack on his back!" said the Crow.

"No, that was probably his sled," said Gerda, "because he went away with his sled!"

"That's quite possible!" said the crow. "I didn't get a close look! But this much I know from my tame sweetheart, that when he came in through the castle gate and saw the bodyguard in silver, and up along the staircase the lackeys in gold, he wasn't in the least intimidated. He nodded and said to them, 'It must be boring to stand on the stairs; I'd rather go inside!' There the halls blazed with light; Privy Councilors and Excellencies walked in their bare feet and bore gold platters. One could certainly get solemn! His boots creaked so loudly, but still he didn't get frightened!"

"That has to be Kay!" said Gerda. "I know he had new boots: I've heard them creak in Grandmother's room!"

"Yes, they certainly did creak!" said the crow. "And he walked boldly straight in to the princess, who was sitting on a pearl as big as a spinning wheel; and all the ladies in waiting with their maids and their maids' maids, and all the cavaliers with their servants and their servants' servants, who themselves have pages, were standing around; and the nearer they stood to the door, the prouder they looked. The servants' servants' page, who always wears slippers, was standing in the doorway so proudly that one could hardly bear to look at him!"

"That must be dreadful!" said little Gerda. "And yet Kay has won the princess?"

"If I hadn't been a crow, I'd have taken her myself, even though I'm engaged. They say he spoke as well as I speak when I speak crow language; I heard that from my tame sweetheart. He was bold and charming; he hadn't come to court the princess at all, but only to hear her wisdom; and he liked it, and she liked him, too."

"Yes, surely! That was Kay!" said Gerda. "He was so smart he could do arithmetic in his head with fractions. Oh! Won't you take me inside the castle?"

"Well, that's easily said," said the crow, "but how are we going to do it? I'll talk it over with my tame sweetheart; she can probably advise us, for this I must tell you—a little girl like you will never be allowed in."

"Indeed, I will!" said Gerda. "When Kay hears that I'm here, he'll come right out and get me!"

"Wait for me by the stile there!" said the crow wagging his head, and he flew away.

Not until late in the evening did the crow return. "Caw! Caw!" he said. "I've lots of greetings for you from her! And here's a little loaf of bread for you. She took it from the kitchen. There's bread enough there, and you're probably hungry! It's impossible for you to get into the castle, for you're barefoot. The guards in silver and the lackeys in gold wouldn't allow it. But don't cry, you'll get up there. My sweetheart knows a little back stairway that leads up to the bedroom, and she knows where she can get the key!"

And they went into the garden, into the great avenue where the leaves were falling one after the other; and when the lights went out in the castle one by one, the crow led little Gerda over to a back door, which stood ajar.

Oh, how Gerda's heart was pounding with fear and longing! It was just as if she was going to do something wicked, yet she only wanted to know whether it was little Kay. Indeed, it had to be! She could imagine so vividly his clever eyes, his long hair. She could clearly see him smile, just as he had when they sat at home under the roses. Of course, he would be glad to see her, to hear how far she had walked for his sake, to know how unhappy everyone at home had been when he hadn't come back. She was both frightened and glad!

Now they were in the stairway; there was a little lamp burning on a cupboard. In the middle of the floor stood the tame crow, turning its head in every direction and looking at Gerda, who curtsied as Grandmother had taught her.

"My fiancé has spoken so nicely of you, my little lady," said the tame crow. "Your biography, as it is called, is also very touching! If you'll take the lamp, I'll lead the way. We will go straight there, then we won't meet anybody!"

"I feel that someone is coming right behind!" said Gerda, and something went rushing past her—it was just like shadows along the wall, horses with flowing manes and thin legs, pages, ladies and gentlemen on horseback.

"Those are only dreams!" said the crow. "They come to fetch

Their Highnesses' thoughts out to the hunt. That's a good thing, for then you can look more closely at them in bed. But I expect if you come into favor and receive honors that you will show a grateful heart!"

"Why, that's nothing to talk about!" said the crow from the forest.

Now they entered the first hall. The walls were covered with rose-red satin and artificial flowers. Here the dreams were already sweeping past them, but they went so fast that Gerda couldn't see Their Highnesses. Each hall was more magnificent than the last; indeed, you could really be dazzled—and now they were in the bedroom. The ceiling in here was like a great palm tree with fronds of glass, costly glass, and in the middle of the floor, hanging from a thick stalk of gold, were two beds, and each looked like a lily. One was white, and in that lay the princess; the other was red, and it was in this one that Gerda was to look for little Kay. She bent one of the red leaves aside, and she saw the nape of a brown neck. Oh, it was Kay! She called out his name quite loudly and held the lamp toward him. The dreams rushed on horseback into the room again. He awoke, turned his head, and—it was not little Kay!

Only the prince's neck was like Kay's, but young and handsome he was. And from the white lily-bed the princess peeped out and asked what was going on. Then little Gerda wept and told her whole story and all that the crows had done for her.

"You poor little thing!" said the prince and princess, and they praised the crows and said that they weren't angry at them at all but they shouldn't do it again. As it was, they were to be rewarded.

"Would you like to fly away free?" asked the princess. "Or do you want a permanent position as court crows—with all the scraps from the kitchen?"

And both crows curtsied and asked for permanent positions, for they thought of their old age and said, "It is so good to have something set aside for 'a rainy day,' as it is called."

And the prince got out of his bed and let Gerda sleep in it, and more than that he couldn't do. She folded her little hands and thought, "Indeed, how good people and animals are!" and then she closed her eyes and slept so peacefully. All the dreams came flying in again, now looking like God's angels, and they pulled a little sled, and on it Kay sat and nodded. But all this was only a dream, and therefore it was gone as soon as she woke up.

The next day she was dressed from top to toe in silk and velvet. She was invited to stay at the castle and have a good time, but all she asked for was a little carriage with a horse to draw it and a pair of little boots; then she wanted to drive out into the wide world and find Kay.

And she got both boots and a muff. She was nicely dressed, and when she was ready to leave, a new coach of pure gold stood at the door. The coat of arms of the prince and princess shone from it like a star. Coachmen, footmen, and outriders—for there were outriders, too—sat wearing golden crowns. The prince and princess themselves helped her into the carriage and wished her good luck. The crow from the woods, who was now married, followed along the first fifteen miles. He sat beside her, for he couldn't stand to drive backward; the other crow stood in the gate and flapped her wings. She didn't go with them, because she had suffered from headaches ever since she had been given a permanent position and too much to eat. The carriage was lined inside with sugar twists and packed under the seat with fruit and ginger cookies.

"Farewell! Farewell!" cried the prince and princess, and little Gerda wept, and the crow wept. Thus the first miles passed. Then the crow also said farewell, and that was the hardest parting. He flew up into a tree and flapped his black wings as long as he could see the carriage, which shone like the bright sunshine.

The Fifth Story

The Little Robber Girl

They drove through the dark forest, but the carriage shone like a flame. It dazzled the eyes of the robbers so that they couldn't stand it.

"It's gold! It's gold!" they shouted. They rushed forward, grabbed hold of the horses, killed the little outriders, the coachman, and the footmen, and then pulled little Gerda out of the carriage.

"She's plump! She's pretty! She's been fattened on nutmeats!" said the old robber woman who had a long bristly beard and eyebrows that hung down over her eyes. "She's just like a fat little lamb! Oh, how good she'll taste!" And she pulled out her shining knife, and it gleamed so that it was horrible.

"Ouch!" said the old woman at that very moment; she had been bitten in the ear by her own little daughter, who hung on her back and was so wild and naughty that it was fun to see. "You nasty brat!" said the mother and didn't have time to slaughter Gerda.

"She shall play with me!" said the little robber girl. "She

shall give me her muff, her pretty dress, sleep with me in my bed!" And then she bit her again, so that the robber woman jumped in the air and turned around, and all the robbers laughed and said, "Look how she dances with her brat!"

"I want to get in the carriage!" said the little robber girl, and she simply had to have her way, for she was so spoiled and so obstinate. She and Gerda sat in the carriage, and they drove over stubble and brier deeper into the forest. The little robber girl was as big as Gerda but stronger, with broader shoulders and dark skin. Her eyes were completely black, and they looked almost mournful. She put her arms around little Gerda's waist and said, "They're not going to slaughter you as long as I don't get angry with you! I suppose you're a princess?"

"No," said little Gerda, and then she told everything she had been through, and how fond she was of little Kay.

The robber girl looked quite seriously at her, nodded her head a little, and said, "They're not going to slaughter you even if I do get angry with you, for then I'll do it myself!" And she dried Gerda's eyes and put both her hands in the beautiful muff that was so soft and warm.

Now the carriage stopped. They were in the middle of the courtyard in a robber castle. It had split from top to bottom; ravens and crows flew out of the open cracks, and great bulldogs—each one looking as if it could swallow a man—jumped high into the air. But they didn't bark, for that was forbidden.

In the big, old sooty hall a huge fire burned in the middle of the stone floor; the smoke trailed along under the ceiling and had to find a way out itself. A great kettle of soup was boiling, and hares and rabbits were turning on a spit.

"You shall sleep tonight with me and all my little pets!" said the robber girl. They got something to eat and drink and then went over to a corner where straw and blankets lay. Over their heads roosting on sticks and perches were nearly a hundred pigeons, all of which seemed to be asleep, but they stirred a bit when the two little girls approached.

"They're all mine!" said the little robber girl and suddenly grabbed one of the nearest, held it by the legs, and shook it so that it flapped its wings. "Kiss it!" she cried and flapped Gerda in the face with it. "There sit the wood rascals!" she went on, pointing behind a lot of bars that had been nailed up in front of a hole in the wall high above. "Those are wood rascals, those two! They fly right away if you don't keep them well locked up. And here's my old sweetheart 'Baa'!" And she tugged at the horn of a reindeer that had a bright copper ring around its neck and was tied up. "Him we've always kept tied up, otherwise he'd run away from us. Every single evening I tickle his neck with my sharp knife—he's so afraid of it!" And the little girl drew a long knife out of a crack in the wall and let it slide over the reindeer's neck; the poor animal kicked out with his legs, and the robber girl laughed and then pulled Gerda down into the bed with her.

"Do you take the knife along even when you're going to sleep?" asked Gerda, and looked at it a little frightened.

"I always sleep with a knife!" said the little robber girl. "You never know what can happen. But tell me again now what you told before about little Kay and why you went out into the wide world." And Gerda told from the beginning, and the wood pigeons cooed up in the cage; the other pigeons slept. The little robber girl put her arm around Gerda's neck, held the knife in the other hand, and slept so that one could hear her. But Gerda couldn't close her eyes at all; she didn't know whether she was going to live or die. The robbers sat around the fire singing and drinking, and the old robber woman turned somersaults. Oh! It was just horrible for the little girl to watch.

Then the wood pigeons said, "Coo! Coo! We have seen little Kay. A white hen was carrying his sled, he was sitting in the Snow Queen's carriage as it rushed close over the forest when we were lying in our nests. She blew upon us young pigeons and all died except the two of us. Coo! Coo!"

"What are you saying up there?" cried Gerda. "Where was the Snow Queen traveling? Do you know anything about that?"

"She was probably traveling to Lapland, for there's always ice and snow there! Just ask the reindeer who stands tied with the rope."

"There it's all ice and snow! There it's a glorious and grand place!" said the reindeer. "That's where you can spring about free in the vast glittering valleys! That's where the Snow Queen has her summer tent, but her permanent castle is up near the North Pole on the island called Spitzbergen!"

"Oh, Kay, little Kay!" sighed Gerda.

"Now, you must lie still!" said the robber girl. "Or else you'll get the knife in your stomach!"

In the morning Gerda told her everything the wood pigeons had said, and the little robber girl looked quite serious, but nodded her head and said, "Never mind! Never mind!" She asked the reindeer, "Do you know where Lapland is?"

'Who should know better than I?" said the animal, and his eyes danced in his head. "That's where I was born and bred, that's where I leapt about on the fields of snow!"

"Listen!" said the robber girl to Gerda. "You see, all our men are away, but Mother is still here, and she'll stay; but later in the morning she'll drink from the big bottle and afterward take a little nap; then I'll do something for you!" Now she jumped out of the bed, flung herself on her mother's neck, pulled her mustache, and said, "My own sweet billy goat, good morning!" And her mother snapped her under her nose so it turned red and blue, but it was all out of pure love.

Then, when the mother had taken a drink from her bottle and was taking a little nap, the robber girl went over to the reindeer and said, "I should especially like to tickle you many more times with my sharp knife, because you're so funny then, but never mind! I'm going to untie your rope and help you outside, so that you can run to Lapland. But you must shake a leg and bring this little girl for me to the Snow Queen's castle, where her playmate is. You've certainly heard what she told about, for she talked loud enough and you eavesdrop!"

The reindeer jumped for joy. The robber girl lifted little Gerda up and was cautious enough to tie her fast, yes, even to give her a little pillow to sit on. "Never mind," she said, "there are your fur boots, for it'll be cold; but I'm keeping the muff, it's much too pretty! Still, you won't freeze. Here are my mother's big mittens; they'll reach up to your elbows. Stick your hands in! Now your hands look just like my hideous mother's!"

And Gerda wept for joy.

"I can't stand your sniveling!" said the little robber girl. "Now you really should look pleased! And here you have two loaves and a ham so you can't starve." It all was tied behind on the reindeer's back. The little robber girl opened the door, coaxed all the big dogs inside, and then she cut the rope with her knife and said to the reindeer, "Now run! But take good care of the little girl!"

And Gerda stretched out her hands in the big mittens toward the robber girl and said farewell, and the reindeer took off over bushes and stubble, through the great forest, over marshes and steppes, as fast as he could. The wolves howled and the ravens screeched. "Whoosh! Whoosh!" came from the sky. It was just as if it sneezed red.

"Those are my old Northern Lights!" said the reindeer. "See how they shine!" And then he ran on ever farther, night and day. The loaves were eaten up, the ham too, and then they were in Lapland.

The Sixth Story

The Lapp Woman and the Finn Woman

They came to a stop at a little house; it was so miserable. The roof reached down to the ground, and the door was so low that the family had to crawl on their stomachs when they wanted to go in or out. There was nobody at home except an old Lapp woman, who stood frying fish over an oil lamp. And the reindeer told all of Gerda's story—but first all about his own, for he thought it was far more important, and Gerda was so overcome by the cold that she couldn't talk anyway.

"Oh, you poor thing!" said the Lapp woman. "Then you still have a long way to run! You have to travel more than five hundred miles into Finmark, for there the Snow Queen stays in her country place and burns blue lights every single evening. I'll write a few words on a dried cod, I don't have any paper! I'll give it to you to take to the Finn woman up there; she can give you better information than I."

So when Gerda had gotten warmed and had something to eat and drink, the Lapp woman wrote a few words on a dried cod, told Gerda to take good care of it, tied her again firmly onto the reindeer, and away he sprang. "Whoosh! Whoosh!" it said up in the sky; all night the loveliest blue Northern Lights burned—

and then they came to Finmark and knocked at the Finn woman's chimney, for she didn't even have a door.

It was so hot inside that the Finn woman herself went around almost naked. She was small and quite swarthy. She loosened little Gerda's clothes at once and took off her mittens and boots, for otherwise she would have gotten too warm. After putting a piece of ice on the reindeer's head, she read what was written on the cod. She read it three times, then she knew it by heart and put the fish in the stewpot, for it could be eaten, of course, and she never wasted anything.

Now the reindeer told first his story and then little Gerda's, and the Finn woman blinked her clever eyes but didn't say anything.

"You are so clever," said the reindeer. "I know you can tie up all the winds of the world with a cotton thread. When the skipper unties one knot, he gets a good wind; when he loosens the second, it blows hard; and when he unties the third and fourth, then there is such a storm that the forests fall flat. Won't you give the little girl a potion so that she can have the strength of twelve men and overcome the Snow Queen?"

"The strength of twelve men!" said the Finn woman. "Indeed, that might be enough!" And she went over to a shelf, brought out a big, rolled-up hide, and this she unrolled. Strange letters were written on it, and the Finn woman read until the perspiration poured down from her forehead.

But the reindeer again begged so hard for little Gerda, and Gerda looked with such tearful, beseeching eyes at the Finn woman, that she began to blink her eyes again and drew the reindeer over to a corner where she whispered to it while she put fresh ice on its head.

"Little Kay is with the Snow Queen all right and finds everything there to his liking, and he thinks it's the best place in the world; but that's because he's got a splinter of glass in his heart and a tiny speck of glass in his eye. They must come out first or he'll never become a decent human being, and the Snow Queen will keep her power over him."

"But can't you give little Gerda something to take, so she can gain power over everything?"

"I can't give her greater power than she already has! Don't you see how great it is? Don't you see how human beings and animals must serve her, how—barefoot—she has come so far in the world? She must not be told of her power by us. It's in her heart, it's in the fact that she's a sweet, innocent child. If she can't come to the Snow Queen by herself and get the glass out of little Kay, then we can't help! Ten miles from here the Snow Queen's garden begins; you can carry the little girl that far. Put her down by the big bush with red berries that's standing in the snow. Don't stand gossiping, and hurry back here!" And the Finn woman lifted little Gerda up onto the reindeer, who ran as fast as he could.

"Oh, I didn't get my boots! I didn't get my mittens!" cried little Gerda. She could feel that in the piercing cold, but the reindeer didn't dare stop. He ran until he came to the big bush with the red berries. There he put Gerda down and kissed her on the mouth. Big shining tears ran down the animal's cheeks. Then he ran back again as fast as he could. There stood poor Gerda without shoes and without gloves in the middle of the terrible, ice-cold Finmark.

She ran forward as fast as she could. Then came a whole regiment of snowflakes. But they didn't fall from the sky, for it was quite clear and shone with the Northern Lights. The snowflakes ran right along the ground, and the nearer they came the larger they grew. Gerda remembered well how large and complicated the snowflakes had looked the time she had seen them through the magnifying glass. But here, to be sure, they were much larger and more terrible—they were alive! They were the Snow Queen's advance guards, and they had the strangest shapes. Some looked like big, ugly porcupines, others like whole knots of snakes that stuck forth their heads, and others like fat little bears with bristly fur all shining white—they were all living snowflakes.

Then little Gerda said the Lord's Prayer, and the cold was so intense that she could see her own breath; it came out of her mouth like smoke. Her breath grew thicker and thicker, and it took the shape of bright little angels, which grew bigger and bigger as they touched the ground. And they all had helmets on their heads and spears and shields in their hands. They became more and more numerous, and when Gerda had finished the Lord's Prayer, a whole legion surrounded her. They struck with their spears at the dreadful snowflakes, which flew into hundreds of pieces, and little Gerda walked on quite safely and fearlessly. The angels patted her feet and hands so she didn't feel the cold so much, and she walked quickly on toward the Snow Queen's castle.

But now we should see how Kay is getting along. He certainly wasn't thinking of little Gerda, least of all that she was standing outside the castle.

The Seventh Story

What Happened in the Snow Queen's Castle and What Happened Afterward

The walls of the castle were made of the drifting snow, and the windows and doors of the piercing winds. There were over a hundred halls, depending on the way the snow drifted; the largest of these stretched for many miles, all illuminated by the glaring Northern Lights, and they were so large, so empty, so icy cold, and so glittering. There was never merriment here, not even so much as a little ball for bears, where the storm could trumpet and the polar bears walk on their hind legs and show their good manners; never any little party games with muzzle-slapping and paw-tapping; never a little coffee bash with the white lady-foxes. It was empty, vast, and cold in the halls of the Snow Queen. The Northern Lights flared up so punctually that one could calculate when they were at their highest and when at their lowest. In the middle of this empty, unending snow hall was a frozen lake. It had cracked into a thousand pieces, but each piece was so exactly like the next that it was quite a work of art. And in the middle of it sat the Snow Queen when she was at home, and she then said that she was sitting on the Looking Glass of Reason and that this was the only one and the best one in the world.

Little Kay was all blue with cold—yes, almost black—but he didn't feel it. For after all, she had kissed the icy shivers out of him, and his heart was practically a lump of ice. He went around dragging some sharp, flat pieces of ice which he arranged in every possible way, for he wanted to make something out of them. It was just like when the rest of us have little pieces of wood, and arrange them in patterns—what we call a Chinese puzzle. Kay was also making patterns, the most complicated ones; this was the Ice Puzzle of Reason. To his eyes these patterns were quite remarkable and of the highest importance. That was because of the speck of glass sitting in his eye! He arranged whole patterns that made up a written word, but he could never figure out how to form the word he really wanted—the word Eternity. And the Snow Queen had said, "If you can find this pattern for me, then you shall be your own master, and I will give you the whole world and a pair of new skates." But he wasn't able to do that.

"Now I'm going to rush off to the warm countries!" said the

Snow Queen. "I want to go and have a look down into the sooty kettles!" These were the fire-spouting mountains, Etna and Vesuvius, as they are called. "I'm going to whitewash them a bit. That's the thing to do! It's good on top of lemons and grapes!" And then the Snow Queen flew off, and Kay sat quite alone in the vast, empty ice hall, which was many miles long, and looked at the pieces of ice, and thought and thought until it creaked in him. He sat quite stiff and still—one would think that he had frozen to death.

It was then that little Gerda stepped into the castle through the great gate of the piercing winds. But she said an evening prayer, and then the winds quieted down as if they were going to sleep, and she stepped into the great, empty, cold halls. Then she saw Kay and recognized him, flung her arms around his neck, and held him so tight, crying, "Kay! Sweet little Kay! At last I've found you!"

But he sat quite still—stiff and cold. Then little Gerda wept hot tears. They fell on his breast, they penetrated to his heart, they thawed the lump of ice and dissolved the little glass splinter in it. He looked at her, and she sang the hymn:

> The roses grow in the dale,
> Where the Holy Child we shall hail.

Then Kay burst into tears; he wept so that the speck of glass trickled out of his eye. He recognized her and shouted jubilantly, "Gerda! Sweet little Gerda! Wherever have you been all this time? And where have I been?" And he looked about him. "How cold it is here! How empty and big!" And he clung to Gerda, and she laughed and wept for joy. It was so wonderful that even the pieces of ice danced for joy all around. And when they were tired and lay down, they arranged themselves into just the letters the Snow Queen had said he had to find if he was to become his own master, and then she would give him the whole world and a pair of new skates.

And Gerda kissed his cheeks, and they bloomed; she kissed his eyes, and they shone like hers; she kissed his hands and feet, and he became well and strong. The Snow Queen could come home anytime—his release stood written there in shining pieces of ice.

And they took each other by the hand and wandered out of the big castle. They talked about Grandmother and the roses up on the roof, and wherever they walked the winds were quite still, and the sun came forth. And when they came to the bush with the red berries, the reindeer stood there waiting. He had with him another young reindeer, a doe whose udder was full, and she gave the little ones her warm milk and kissed them on the mouth. Then they carried Kay and Gerda first to the Finn woman, where they warmed themselves in the hot room and got instructions for their journey home, then to the Lapp woman, who had sewn new clothes for them and gotten her sled ready.

And the reindeer and the young doe sprang alongside and accompanied them right to the border of the country. There the first green leaves peeped forth, there they said goodbye to the reindeer and the Lapp woman. "Farewell!" they all said. And the first little birds began to twitter, the forest had green buds, and out of it came a young girl riding a magnificent horse which Gerda remembered. It had been harnessed to the golden coach. She had a shining red cap on her head and pistols in her belt. It was the little robber girl, who had gotten bored staying at home and now wanted to go first to the north and later in another direction if that didn't please her. She recognized Gerda at once, and Gerda recognized her! They were overjoyed.

"You're a fine one for tramping off!" she said to little Kay. "I'd like to know whether you deserve someone running to the end of the world for your sake!"

But Gerda patted her on the cheek and asked about the prince and princess.

"They've gone abroad!" said the robber girl.

"But the crow?" asked little Gerda.

"Well, the crow is dead!" she answered. "His tame sweetheart has become a widow and goes about with a piece of black woolen yarn around her leg. She feels awfully sorry for herself, but it's all rubbish! But tell me now how you've fared, and how you got hold of him!"

And Gerda and Kay both told her.

"And snip-snap-snurre-basselurre!" said the robber girl, and she took them both by the hand and promised that if she ever came through their town, she would come up and pay them a visit. Then she rode out into the wide world, but Gerda and Kay walked hand in hand, and wherever they went it was lovely spring with flowers and greenery. The church bells rang, and they recognized the high towers, the big town. It was the one in which they lived, and they went into it and over to Grandmother's door, up the stairs into the room where everything stood in the same place as before, and the clock said "Tick! Tock!" and the hands turned. But as they went through the door, they noticed that they had become grown-up people. The roses from the roof gutter were blooming in through the open windows, and there stood the little baby chairs. And Kay and Gerda sat down on their own chairs and held each other by the hand. They had forgotten the cold, empty splendor at the Snow Queen's like a bad dream. Grandmother was sitting in God's bright sunshine reading aloud from the Bible, "Unless you become like children, you will never enter the Kingdom of God!"

And Kay and Gerda looked into each other's eyes, and all at once they understood the old hymn,

> The roses grow in the dale,
> Where the Holy Child we shall hail.

There they both sat, grown up and yet children—children at heart. And it was summer—warm, glorious summer.

The Shadow

In hot countries the sun's rays can really burn! People become a mahogany color, and in the very hottest countries they are scorched into Negroes, and it was to one of these hot countries that a learned man had come from the cold north. Now, he thought that he could run around freely just as he had at home, but soon he learned otherwise; he and all sensible people had to stay inside. Shutters and doors were kept closed all day long; it looked as though the whole house was asleep or there was no one at home. The narrow street of high-built houses where he lived was situated so that it got full sun from morning to evening. It was really unbearable! The learned man from the cold countries—he was a young man, an intelligent man—felt as if he were sitting in a red-hot oven. It took its toll; he became very thin. Even his shadow shrank; it became much smaller than at home—the sun took its toll of it as well. Neither of them revived until evening after the sun had gone down.

That was really a pleasure to see. As soon as light was brought into the room, the shadow stretched itself all the way up the wall, yes, even along the ceiling, that's how long it made itself. It had to stretch in order to regain its strength. The learned man went out on the balcony to do his stretching there, and as the stars appeared in the lovely, clear air, it seemed to him that he came to life again. On all the balconies along the street—and each window has a balcony in the hot countries—people appeared, because people must have fresh air even if they are used to being mahogany! Everything became so lively both above and below! Shoemakers and tailors, everyone moved out onto the streets. Tables and chairs were brought out, lamps burned. Over a thousand lamps burned, and one person talked and another sang, and people strolled about, carts rolled through, donkeys passed—dingalingaling! They have bells on. There were bodies buried to the sound of hymns, street urchins set off firecrackers, and church bells pealed. Yes, it was really lively down on the street! Only in that one house, which lay right across the street from where the foreign, learned man lived, was there complete silence. And yet someone lived there because there were flowers on the balcony; they grew so well in the heat of the sun, and they couldn't do that without being watered, and someone had to be there to water them. Someone had to live there. The door over there was also ajar later on in the evening; but it was dark inside, at least in the front room. From deeper within came the sound of music. The foreign, learned man thought that it was magnificent, but it could easily be that he just imagined it, because he thought that everything was magnificent there in the hot countries—if there just had not been so much sun! The stranger's landlord said that he didn't know who had rented the neighbor's house, no one was to be seen, and regarding the music, he thought that it was dreadfully dull. "It's just as if someone sat and practiced a piece he couldn't find the end to, always the same piece: 'I'll finish it!' he probably says, but he doesn't finish it no matter how long he plays."

One night the stranger awakened; he was sleeping by the open balcony door. The curtain was lifted by the wind, and he thought that a strange radiance came from the neighbor's balcony. All the flowers shone like flames in the most beautiful colors, and in the midst of the flowers stood a slender, lovely maiden. It was as though she also was glowing. The sight dazzled his eyes, his eyes widened so much that he awoke. With one leap he was on the floor; very softly he moved behind the curtain, but the maiden was gone, the radiance was gone. The flowers didn't glow at all but were doing very well as always. The door was open a crack, and from deep within the music sounded so soft and lovely that one could give oneself over to beautiful thoughts because of it. It was just like sorcery, and who lived there anyway? Where was the real entrance? The whole ground floor consisted of one store after another, and people couldn't always be running in and out through them.

One evening the stranger sat out on his balcony. In the room behind him a lamp burned, so it was quite natural that his shadow fell on the neighbor's wall. Yes, there it sat on the other side of the street in the midst of the flowers on the balcony, and when the stranger moved, the shadow also moved because that's what it's supposed to do.

"I do believe my shadow is the only living thing to be seen over there!" said the learned man. "Look how nicely it is sitting among the flowers. The door is standing half open. Now the shadow should be smart and go inside, look around, and then come and tell me what it has seen! Yes, you should do something useful!" he said in jest. "Be so kind as to enter! Well, are you going?" and then he nodded to the shadow, and the shadow nodded back. "All right, go ahead, but don't forget to come back!" and the stranger got up, and his shadow over on the neighbor's balcony got up also, and the stranger turned, and the shadow turned, too. Yes, if someone had been paying close attention, he would have been able to see clearly that the shadow went through the half-open balcony door at the neighbor's at the very same moment that the stranger went into his living room and let the long curtain close behind him.

The next morning the learned man went out to drink coffee and read the papers. "What's this?" he said when he came out into the sunshine, "I don't have any shadow! So, it really must have gone yesterday evening and hasn't come back! This is embarrassing!"

And it annoyed him, but not so much because the shadow was gone as because he knew there was a story about a man without a shadow. Everyone in the cold countries knew that story, and if the learned man were to go there now and tell his story, they would say that he was just imitating the other one, and there was really no need to do that. Therefore, he didn't want to talk about it at all, and that was certainly a sensible plan.

That evening he went out on his balcony again, first placing the lamp so that it was behind him, because he knew that the shadow insisted on having his master as shield, but he couldn't lure it out. He curled himself up; he stretched himself out. But the shadow wasn't there, nobody came. He said, "humph, humph!" but it was of no avail.

It was annoying. But in the hot countries everything grows so fast, and after a week had gone by, he noticed to his great delight that a new shadow grew out from under his feet whenever he went out into the sunshine. The root must have been left behind. After three weeks he had quite a respectable shadow, which, when he went home to the northern countries, grew more and more during the course of the journey so that at last it was so long and so big that half of it would have been enough.

Then the learned man arrived home, and he wrote books about what was true in the world and what was good and what was beautiful. Days went by, and years went by—yes, many years went by.

One evening when he was sitting in his living room, there was a very soft knocking on his door.

"Come in!" he said, but no one came in. Then he opened the door, and there stood before him a man so terribly thin that he felt quite uncomfortable. By the way, the man was extremely well dressed—it had to be a very distinguished person.

"With whom have I the honor of speaking?" inquired the learned man.

"Yes, exactly as I thought!" said the distinguished man. "You don't recognize me! I have gained so much body lately, I have really put on flesh and clothes. You probably never thought that you would see me in such fine shape. Don't you recognize your old shadow? Yes, you likely didn't think that I would come back again. Things have gone extremely well for me since I was last with you. I have become very wealthy in every respect! If I decide to purchase my freedom from bondage, then I can!" And he jangled a whole bunch of expensive fobs that hung from his watch chain, and he fingered the thick gold chain that he wore around his neck. How his fingers sparkled with diamond rings! And all of it was real.

"Am I dreaming?" said the learned man. "What is this all about?"

"No, it is not quite ordinary!" said the shadow. "But you yourself are not ordinary either, and I, as you well know, have walked in your footsteps since childhood. As soon as you thought I was ready to go alone out into the world, I went my own way. My circumstances are superb, but a kind of longing came over me to see you once more before you die. After all, you must die, you know! Besides, I also wanted to see these countries again. Naturally, one always has a feeling for the fatherland. I know that you now have another shadow. Do I owe it or you anything? If you would only be so kind as to tell me."

"Oh, is it really you!" said the learned man. "This is remarkable! I would never have believed that one's old shadow could return as a person!"

"Tell me what I owe," said the shadow, "because I don't want to stand in anybody's debt on any account!"

"Don't talk that way!" said the learned man. "What debt is there to be discussed? Be as free as anybody! I am overjoyed at your good luck! Sit down old friend, and tell me a bit about how it all happened, and what you saw over at the neighbor's house down there in the hot countries!"

"Well, I'll tell you all about it," said the shadow, and he sat down, "but then you must also promise me that no matter where you meet me you will never say to anyone here in town that I was once your shadow! I am thinking about getting engaged. I can afford more than one family!"

"You can rest easy," said the learned man, "I will never tell anyone who you really are. Here's my hand! I promise, on my honor as a gentleman."

"On my honor as a shadow!" said the shadow. Naturally, it had to talk that way.

It was really remarkable how much it had become a person. It was dressed entirely in black with the finest black cloth, patent leather boots, and a hat that could be compressed so that it was just the crown and brim, not to mention what we already know about—the watch fobs, golden chain, and diamond rings. Yes, the shadow was extremely well dressed, and that's precisely what it was that made it a person.

"I'll tell you all about it!" said the shadow, and he put his feet with the patent leather boots down as hard as he could on the sleeve of the learned man's new shadow, which lay like a poodle at his master's feet. Now this was either out of arrogance or perhaps to make sure that it would follow him; and the prone shadow kept quiet and still in order to listen properly. It wanted to hear, of course, how it might free itself and work its way up to being its own master.

"Do you know who lived in the neighbor's house?" said the shadow. "It was Poetry—the most wonderful of all! I was there for three weeks, and that's as good as if I had lived there for three thousand years and had read all that has been composed and written. That's what I'm saying, and it's true. I have seen all, and I know all!"

"Poetry!" cried the learned man. "Oh, yes! She often lives as a hermit in the big cities. Poetry! Yes, I have seen her for a single, short moment, but my eyes were heavy with sleep. She stood at the balcony and shone like the Northern Lights—tell me, tell me! You were on the balcony, you went through the door, and then—"

"Why, then—I was in the antechamber," said the shadow. "You remember how you always used to sit looking across into the antechamber. There was no light there. It was in a kind of twilight, but one door after the next stood open leading through a long series of rooms and chambers, and there was plenty of light. I would surely have perished from all that light if I had proceeded on until I reached the lady. But I was cautious, I took my time, and that's what one should do!"

"And what did you see?" asked the learned man.

"I saw everything, and I'd tell you all about it, only—it's not at all pride on my part, but as a free man with my accomplishments, not to mention my high position and superb circumstances—I do wish you would call me by my last name."

"I beg your pardon," said the learned man. "It's an old habit that is very stubborn. You're quite right, and I'll try to remember. But now tell me about everything you saw."

"Everything," said the shadow, "for I have seen all, and I know all." "What were the innermost rooms like?" asked the learned man. "Was it like being in a cool forest? Was it like being in a holy church? Were those rooms like the bright, starlit heavens when seen from a high mountain?"

"Everything beautiful was there," said the shadow. "I did not exactly go in all the way. I stayed in the twilight of the outermost room, but there I was in an excellent position! I saw everything, and I know everything! I've been at Poetry's court, in the antechamber."

"But what did you see? Did the ancient gods walk through the high halls? Did the heroes of yore do battle there? Were sweet children playing there, and did they tell about their dreams?"

"I'm telling you, I was there, and you should realize that I saw everything there was to see! If you had gone across the street, you wouldn't have turned into a person, but that's what I did! And furthermore, I gained the knowledge of my innermost nature, my innate kinship with Poetry. When I was with you, I didn't think about it at all, but whenever the sun rose or set, you know, I became curiously tall. By moonlight, I was almost more distinct than you yourself. But at that time, I didn't understand my nature. In the antechamber, it was all made clear to me. I became a person! I left there changed, but you were no longer in the hot countries, and I was, as a person, ashamed to walk around as I was. I needed boots and clothes—

in short, all the trappings that characterize a person. I went on my way.—Yes, I can trust you. You're certainly not going to put it in a book.—I went on my way beneath the skirts of the woman who sold cakes at the market. That's where I hid myself, and she had no idea just what she had there. It was evening when I first came out. I ran in the moonlight along the street. I stretched myself up along the wall. That tickles one's back so nicely! I ran up, and I ran down. I peeked through the highest windows into the room beyond and up on the roof. I peeked where nobody else could peek, and I saw what nobody else could see, what nobody else should see! This is, after all, a base world. I did not want to be a person unless it was considered to be something. I saw the most incredible things among wives, among husbands, among parents, and among sweet, lovely children. I saw," said the shadow, "what no one should know, but which everyone would so much like to know—his neighbor's faults! If I had written for a newspaper, wouldn't that have been read! But I wrote to the individuals themselves, and there was a great furor in every town I visited. They were so afraid of me! And they doted on me! Professors made me a professor! Tailors gave me new clothes—I'm well stocked! The mintmaster turned out coins for me! And women said I was so handsome! Thus I became the person I am! And now I will say goodbye. Here is my card. I live on the sunny side and am always at home in rainy weather."

And the shadow left.

"That was strange!" said the learned man.

Days and years passed until the shadow came again.

"How is it going?" he asked.

"Oh!" said the learned man, "I write about what is true and good and beautiful, but no one seems to care to hear about such things. I'm in despair because I take it so much to heart."

"But I never do that," said the shadow. "I'm growing fat, as everyone should try to do. You don't understand the world— you let it get to you. You should travel! I'm going on a trip this summer. Do you want to go along? I'd like to have a traveling companion. Will you travel with me as my shadow? It would be a great pleasure to have you along. I'll pay your expenses."

"That's going pretty far!" said the learned man.

"It depends on how you take it!" said the shadow. "It would be awfully good for you to travel! If you'll be my shadow, then you can travel for free!"

"That's going too far!" said the learned man.

"But that's the way the world is," said the shadow, "and that's the way it'll always be." And then the shadow went on his way.

The learned man was not doing very well at all. Trouble and sorrow followed him, and what he said about the true and the good and the beautiful, that was for most people like casting roses at the feet of a cow. At last he became very ill.

"You look like a shadow!" people said to him, and a shiver went through the learned man because he gave thought to these words.

"You must go to a spa," said the shadow, who came and visited him. "There's nothing else to be done. Since we've known each other for so long, I'll take you along. I'll pay the expenses of the trip, and you write descriptions and entertain me on the way. I want to go to a spa myself. My beard doesn't grow as it should, and that's also a disease because it won't do not to have a beard. Now, be reasonable and accept my offer; we shall travel as companions."

And so they traveled: the shadow was now the master, and the master was now the shadow. They drove with each other, they rode, they walked together side by side or before or behind, according to the position of the sun. The shadow always took care to take the best for himself, but it didn't matter to the learned man. He was really a kindhearted man, and extremely gentle and friendly. One day he said to the shadow, "Since we're now traveling companions, and we've likewise grown up together from childhood, why shouldn't we use each other's first names? It sounds so much more familiar."

"There's something to what you say," said the shadow, who now was the real master. "Your intentions are forthright and good, and I'd like mine to be just as forthright and good. You, as a learned man, must know well how strange nature can be. Some people cannot stand to touch sacking—it makes them quite ill; others shiver all over when anyone scratches a pane of glass with a nail. I get exactly the same feeling when I hear you use my first name. I feel as if I were pressed down to the ground—reduced to my former position with you. You see, it's a question of feeling, not pride. I can't let you use my first name with me, but I could easily call you by yours, so half of your wish will be fulfilled."

And so, the shadow called its former master by his first name.

"This is absurd!" thought the learned man. "I must call him by his last name, and he calls me by my first name," but he had to put up with it.

Then they arrived at a spa where there were many strangers and among them a beautiful princess whose malady was such that she saw much too clearly, and that was quite alarming.

Just as soon as the shadow arrived there, she noticed that he was a very different sort of person from all the others. "They say that he's here because his beard won't grow, but I can see the real reason—he can't cast a shadow."

She was very curious, and so a little later, while on a walk, she started a conversation with the strange gentleman. Being a princess, she could dispense with ceremony, and so she said, "Your sickness is that you can't cast a shadow."

"Your Royal Highness must be significantly better!" said the shadow. "I know that your problem is that you see much too well, but it must have disappeared. You're cured! Indeed, I have a very unusual shadow! Don't you see the person who always walks close to me? Other people have ordinary shadows, but I don't care for the ordinary. People often give their servants finer clothes for their uniforms than they wear themselves, and, similarly, I've allowed my shadow to be done up like a real person. In fact, you can see, I've even given *him* a shadow of his own. This has been very expensive, but I do like to be different!"

"What!" thought the princess. "Am I actually recovered? There is nothing like these baths. Of late, the waters have had almost miraculous powers. But I'm not going to leave, because now it's getting interesting. I like this stranger very much. If only his beard doesn't grow, because then he'll leave."

That evening in the grand ballroom the princess danced with the shadow. She was light, but he was still lighter. She'd never had such a partner before. She told him what country she came from, and he knew that country; he had been there, though at a time when she was not at home. He had peeked in through the upper and lower windows; he had seen both this and that, thus he could answer the princess's questions and make intimations so that she was absolutely amazed. He had to be the wisest man in the whole world! She had a very high opinion of what he knew, and when they danced again, she fell in love. The shadow picked up on this because she looked at him with such a penetrating glance. Then they danced once more, and she was just about to tell him, but she held back. She thought about her country and about the many people she would come to rule over. "He is a wise man," she said to herself. "That's all right! And he dances well. That's all right, too. But does he have the necessary knowledge. That is just as important. He must be tested." And she began to ask him very difficult questions that she herself didn't know the answers to, and the shadow made a strange face.

"Then you don't know the answer!" said the princess.

"Oh, I learned that in kindergarten," said the shadow. "I believe even my shadow over there by the door could answer that!"

"Your shadow!" said the princess. "That would be rather re-markable!"

"Now, I'm not saying that he can for sure," said the shadow. "But I believe he can. He's followed me for so many years and listened to what I've said. I believe he can. But your Royal Highness must permit me to point out to you that he is so proud of passing for a person that if he is to be kept in a good mood—and he must be in order to give good answers—he must be treated exactly like a person."

"Oh, this sounds like fun!" said the princess.

So she went up to the learned man standing by the door and began conversing with him about the sun and the moon, and about people both inside and out, and he answered wisely and well.

"How wonderful that man must be who has such a wise shadow!" she thought. "It would be an absolute blessing for my people and my country if I were to choose him for my husband. I'll do it!"

And they were soon agreed, the princess and the shadow, but no one was to know anything about it before she returned to her own country.

"No one, not even my own shadow!" said the shadow, and he had his own reasons for that!

Then they came to the country where the princess ruled when she was at home.

"Listen to me, my good friend!" said the shadow to the learned man. "I am now as happy and as powerful as anyone can be! I want to do something special for you! You shall always live with me at the castle, drive out with me in my royal carriage, and receive a hundred thousand dollars each year, but then you must let yourself be called a shadow by everybody. You must never tell anyone that you have ever been a person, and once every year when I sit on the balcony in the sunshine and let myself be seen, you must lie at my feet, as a shadow should. I can tell you, I'm going to marry the princess! This evening the wedding will be celebrated."

"No, this is too absurd!" said the learned man. "I don't want to do it! I won't do it! It would be deceiving the whole country and the princess, too. I am going to tell everything—that I am the man and you are the shadow! You are only dressed like a man!"

"No one will believe you," said the shadow. "Be reasonable, or I'll call the guard!"

"I'm going straight to the princess!" said the learned man.

"But I'm going first," said the shadow, "and you're going to jail!" And to the jail he went because, of course, the guards obeyed the one they knew their princess wanted to marry.

"You're trembling!" said the princess when the shadow came to her. "Has anything happened? You mustn't get sick this evening. We're holding our wedding!"

"I've experienced the most horrible thing that could ever be experienced!" said the shadow. "Imagine! A poor shadow's brain can't bear much! Imagine! My shadow has gone crazy! He actually believes that he is a person, and that I—just imagine—that I am his shadow!"

"This is terrible!" said the princess. "He's been locked up, hasn't he?"

"That he has! I'm afraid he'll never recover."

"Poor shadow!" said the princess. "He must be very unhappy. It would be a real act of charity to free him from the little life that he has left! And when I think about it, it seems to me that it's necessary to do away with him without fanfare."

"That's a bit harsh," said the shadow, "because he's been a faithful servant!" and he heaved what sounded like a sigh.

"You're of noble character!" said the princess.

That evening the whole city was alight. Cannons were fired—boom! And soldiers presented arms. What a wedding it was! The princess and the shadow went out on the balcony to show themselves and to receive another round of cheers, "Hurrah!"

The learned man heard nothing about any of this, for they had already done away with him.

The Drop of Water

Certainly you know what a magnifying glass is—a round lens that makes everything appear a hundred times larger than it really is. If you take a magnifying glass and hold it up to your eye and look at a drop of water from a pond, you will see more than a thousand strange creatures, which you ordinarily would never see in water, but they are there, that's for sure. It looks almost like a whole plateful of shrimp, all darting and crowding each other; and they're so voracious that they tear arms and legs, pieces and chunks, from each other. And yet they seem quite happy and content in their own way.

Now there was once an old man that everybody called Creepley Crawley because that was his name. He always wanted to get the best out of everything, and when he couldn't do it any other way, he used sorcery.

So one day he was sitting and holding his magnifying glass up to his eye looking at a drop of water that had been taken from a puddle in the ditch outside. How it was alive with thousands of creeping and crawling creatures all leaping and darting, tugging at each other and gnawing on each other!

"Oh, this is horrible!" said old Creepley Crawley. "There

must be some way of getting them to live in peace and quiet so that each one minds his own business." He thought and thought, but he couldn't figure out how to do it, so he took to conjuring. "I will give them color so that they can be seen more clearly!" he said. Then he poured into the water a tiny drop of something that looked like red wine, but it was really witches' blood, the very finest that sold for a dime; and then all the strange creatures turned rosy-red all over. It looked like a whole cityful of naked barbarians.

"What do you have there?" asked another old sorcerer, who had no name at all, and that was what made him so remarkable.

"Well, if you can guess what it is," said Creepley Crawley, "I will make you a present of it, but it isn't easy to figure out if you don't already know what it is."

So the sorcerer without a name looked through the magnifying glass. It looked exactly like a whole city where everybody was running around without any clothes on! It was horrible, but it was even more horrible to see how each one pushed and bumped the others, how they quibbled and squabbled, bit each other and knocked each other around. The ones on the bottom strove to get to the top, and those on the top struggled to get to the bottom! "Look, look! His leg is longer than mine! Bah! Off with it! And there is one with a little bump behind his ear, an innocent little bump, but it's hurting him, and it will come

to hurt him more!" So they hacked at it, and they grabbed him, and they ate him all on account of the little bump. One of the creatures sat there as still as a nice little girl and wished only for peace and serenity. But the others wouldn't have it, so they pulled her forth, and they tugged at her and tore at her and devoured her!

"That is extremely funny!" said the other sorcerer.

"Yes, but what do you think it is?" asked Creepley Crawley. "Can you figure it out?"

"That's easy!" said the other. "It's Copenhagen, of course, or some other big city. They're all alike, you know! It's a big city, that's what it is!"

"It's ditchwater!" said Creepley Crawley.

The Little Match Girl

It was so dreadfully cold. Snow was falling, and the evening was growing dark. It was also the last evening of the old year, New Year's Eve. In all that cold and darkness, a poor little girl walked the streets with bare feet and nothing to cover her head. To be sure, she had been wearing slippers when she left home, but what good was that! The slippers were very large—her mother had used them last, that's how big they were! And the little girl had lost them when she scurried across the street just as two wagons went rushing by. One of the slippers couldn't be found, and a boy ran off with the other. He said that he could use it as a cradle when he had children of his own.

Now the little girl walked along on her tiny bare feet, which were all red and blue from the cold. In an old apron she had a lot of matches, and she held a bunch in her hand. No one had bought any from her all day long. No one had given her a single cent. She walked along hungry and cold and looked so very miserable, the poor thing! Snowflakes fell on her long golden hair that curled so prettily about her neck. But she had no thought for this finery. From all the windows, lights were shining, and in the street there was a delicious aroma of roast goose. It was New Year's Eve! And that was what she thought about.

In a corner between two houses—one of them jutted farther

out into the street than the other—she sat down and huddled up. She drew her little legs under her, but froze even more, and she didn't dare go home. She hadn't sold any matches, hadn't gotten a single cent. Her father would beat her, and it was cold at home as well. They had only the roof over their heads, and the wind whistled in, even though straw and rags had been stuffed into the largest cracks. Her tiny hands were almost numb with cold. One little match would help so much! If only she dared to pull one out of the bundle, strike it on the wall, and warm her fingers. She drew one out, "ra-a-atch" how it sputtered, how it blazed! It was a warm, clear flame just like a tiny candle when she cupped it in her hand. It was a strange candle! It seemed to the little girl that she sat in front of a big iron stove with shiny brass knobs and a brass top. The fire burned so cheerily and warmed so well! Oh no, what was that! The little girl had just stretched out her feet to warm them as well—then the flame went out! The stove disappeared, and she sat with a little stump of a burnt-out match in her hand.

She struck another, it burned, it shone, and where the light fell on the wall, the wall became transparent like gauze. She could see right into the room where the table was set with a gleaming white tablecloth and fine china, and the roast goose stuffed with apples and prunes steamed deliciously. What was even more wonderful, the goose hopped off its platter and waddled across the floor with a fork and knife stuck in its back. It came right up to the poor girl. Then the match went out, and there was just a thick, cold wall to be seen.

She lit a new one. Then she was sitting under the loveliest Christmas tree. It was even bigger and more beautiful than the one she had seen through the glass door of the wealthy merchant's house this past Christmas. A thousand candles burned amid the green branches, and brightly colored pictures like those in shop windows looked down upon her. The little girl reached out with both her hands—then the match went out. The many Christmas candles rose higher and higher. She saw now that they were bright stars. One of them fell and left a long fiery streak across the sky.

"Now someone's dying!" said the little girl, because her old grandmother, the only one who had ever been good to her but now was dead, had said: when a star falls, a soul goes up to God.

She struck another match on the wall. It shone all around her, and in its radiance stood the old grandmother, so bright, so shining, so gentle and good.

"Grandma!" cried the little girl. "Oh, take me with you! I know you'll be gone when the match goes out just like the warm stove and the wonderful roast goose and the beautiful, big Christmas tree!" And she quickly struck all the rest of the matches in the bunch. She wanted to keep her grandmother with her. And the matches blazed with such a radiance that it was brighter than the light of day. Grandmother had never been so beautiful, so grand. She took the little girl up on her arm, and they flew in joy and splendor so high, so high, and there was no cold, no hunger, no fear—they were with God!

But in the corner by the house, the little girl sat in the cold morning hours with red cheeks, and with a smile on her lips— dead, frozen to death on the last night of the year. New Year's morning dawned over the little body that sat with the matches, and one bunch was almost burned up. She just wanted to get warm, they said. No one knew what beauty she had beheld, in what radiance she and her old grandmother had entered into the joy of the New Year!

The Story of a Mother

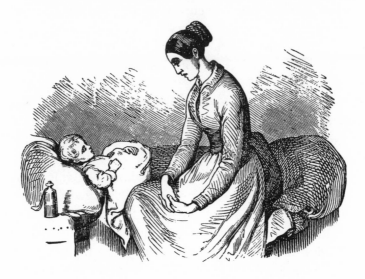

There sat a mother by her little child; she was so sorrowful, so afraid it might die. It was very pale. Its tiny eyes had closed, its breathing was faint, and every now and then it breathed deeply as if it were sighing, and the mother looked even more sorrowfully at the little soul.

Then there was a knock at the door, and a poor old man came in all wrapped up in a large horse blanket; it was warm and that's what he needed, for it was a cold winter. Everything outside was covered with ice and snow, and the wind blew sharply into the traveler's face.

And since the old man was shivering with cold and the little child was sleeping for a moment, the mother went over and set some beer in a little pot over the stove to warm it for him. The old man sat rocking; and the mother sat down on a chair close to him and looked at her sick child who was breathing so hard, and she lifted its tiny hand.

"Don't you think I'll get to keep him?" she said. "The Lord won't take him away from me!"

And the old man—it was Death himself—nodded so

strangely. It could just as well have meant "yes" as "no." And the mother looked down into her lap, and tears streamed down her cheeks. Her head grew so heavy; for three days and nights she had not closed her eyes, and now she slept, but only for a moment, then she started up and shivered with cold. "What is that?" she said, and she looked all around. But the old man was gone, and her little child was gone; he had taken it with him. Over in the corner, the old clock ticked and ticked; the heavy pendulum swung slower and slower, until with a final shudder, it stopped.

But the poor mother rushed out of the house and called after her child.

Outside in the snow sat a woman in long black robes, and she said, "Death has been in your room; I saw him hurry away with your little child. He travels faster than the wind; he never brings back what he has taken away."

"Just tell me which way he went!" said the mother. "Tell me the way, and I will find him."

"I know the way," said the woman in the black robes. "But before I tell you, you must first sing to me all the songs you've ever sung to your child. I like them. I've heard them before. I am Night; I saw your tears while you sang them."

"I'll sing them all, every one!" said the mother. "But don't stop me. I must catch him; I must find my child!"

But Night sat mute and motionless. Then the mother wrung her hands, singing and weeping, and there were many songs, but even more tears! And at last Night said, "Turn to the right into the dark fir forest. That's where I saw Death go with your little child."

Deep in the forest the paths crossed, and she didn't know which way to go. A thornbush grew there, with neither leaf nor flower on it. It was of course cold wintertime, and ice coated all the branches.

"Have you seen Death pass by with my little child?"

"Yes, I have," said the thornbush, "but I won't tell you which way he went unless you first warm me at your bosom. I'm freezing to death, I'm turning all into ice."

And she pressed the thornbush to her breast very hard to warm it up thoroughly. And the thorns pierced right into her flesh, and her blood flowed in large drops. But the thornbush sprouted fresh, green leaves, and it began to bloom in the cold winter night—so warm is the heart of a sorrowful mother! And the thornbush told her the way she should go.

Then she came to a large lake where there was neither ship nor boat. The lake was not frozen hard enough to bear her, nor was it ice-free and shallow enough to be waded, yet cross it she must if she wanted to find her child. So she lay down to drink the lake dry. That was of course impossible for a human being to do, but the sorrowful mother thought perhaps a miracle might happen.

"No, that won't do!" said the lake. "Let us rather try to come to an agreement. I love to collect pearls; your eyes are the brightest I've ever seen. If you'll cry them out for me, then I'll carry you over to the vast greenhouse where Death lives and tends his flowers and trees—each one of them is a human life!"

"Oh, what wouldn't I give to get to my child!" said the weeping mother. And she wept even more, and her eyes sank down to the bottom of the lake and became two precious pearls. But the lake lifted her as if she sat in a swing, and she flew in an arc to the opposite shore where a strange house stood that was many miles long. It was hard to decide whether it was a mountain with forests and caves or really a building. But the poor mother couldn't see it at all—she had cried her eyes out.

"Where can I find Death, who took away my little child?" she asked.

"He has not come back yet," said the old woman who was supposed to take care of Death's vast greenhouse. "How did you find your way here? Who has helped you?"

"The Lord has helped me," she said. "He is merciful, and you will be merciful, too. Where will I find my little child?"

"Well, I do not know your child," said the woman, "and you can't even see. Many flowers and trees have withered during the night; soon Death will come to transplant them. You must know that every human being has a tree or flower of life, according to the nature of each. They look like any other plants, but they have heartbeats; a child's heart can also beat! Look around, maybe you'll recognize your child's heartbeat. But what will you give me if I tell you what else you must do?"

"I have nothing to give," said the sorrowful mother. "But I'll go to the end of the world for you."

"I have nothing for you to do there," said the woman, "but you can give me your long, black hair. You must know that it is beautiful, and I like it very much! You can have my white hair instead; that's better than nothing."

"Aren't you going to demand anything else?" said the mother. "I'll gladly give it to you." And she gave away her beautiful hair and received in its place the snow-white hair of the old woman.

And then they entered Death's vast greenhouse, where flowers and trees grew together so strangely. There were delicate hyacinths under bell jars and big vigorous peonies. There were water plants, some very fresh, other sickly; water snakes lay on them, and black crabs were clamped onto the stalks. There were beautiful palm trees, oaks and plantains. There was parsley and flowering thyme. Each tree and flower had its own name; each was a human life; the people still lived, one in China, one in Greenland, all around the world. There were large trees in little pots so they stood misshapen and ready to burst out of them. In many places there were little, puny flowers in rich loam with moss laid over their roots, and they were petted and cared for. But the sorrowful mother bent down over all the tiniest plants and could hear a human heart beating within them, and out of millions she recognized her child's.

"There it is!" she cried and stretched her hand over a little blue crocus which was very sick and drooped to one side.

"Don't touch the flower!" said the old woman. "But stand here, and when Death comes—I expect him any minute—don't let him pull up the plant, but you threaten to do the same to the other flowers. That will scare him! For he will have to answer to the Lord for them; no plant may be pulled up before the Lord has given permission."

Suddenly there was an icy-cold draft through the hall, and the blind mother could feel that Death had arrived.

"How have you been able to find the way here?" he asked. "How could you get here faster than I?"

"I'm a mother!" she said.

And Death reached his long hand toward the tiny delicate crocus, but she held hands firmly around it so tightly; yet she was afraid that she might touch one of the petals. Then Death blew upon her hands, and she felt that it was colder than the cold wind, and her hands sank down, benumbed.

"You can't do anything against me!" said Death.

"But the Lord can!" she said.

"I only do what he wants!" said Death. "I am His gardener. I take up all His flowers and trees and transplant them into the vast Garden of Paradise in the unknown land, but how they grow there, and how it is there, I don't dare tell you!"

"Give me back my child!" said the mother, and wept and implored. All at once she seized a beautiful flower in each hand, exclaiming, "I will break off all your flowers—I'm desperate!"

"Don't touch them!" said Death. "You say that you are so unhappy, and now you want to make another mother just as unhappy!"

"Another mother!" said the poor woman, and immediately she let go of both flowers.

"Here are your eyes again," said Death. "I fished them out of the lake, they glistened so brightly. I didn't know they were yours. Take them back; they're brighter now than before. Now look down into this deep well close to you. I'll tell you the names of the two flowers you wanted to pull up, and you'll see their whole future, the entire course of their human lives. You'll see all that you wanted to disrupt and destroy."

And she looked down into the well. It was uplifting to see how one of these lives turned out to be a blessing to the world, to see how much joy and happiness were spread all around. And she saw the life of the other, and it was full of sorrow and want, fear and misery.

"Both are God's will!" said Death.

"Which of them is misery's flower, and which the blessed one?" she asked.

"That I won't tell you," said Death. "But this I will tell you: one flower was your child's. It was your own child's destiny that you saw, your own child's future!"

The mother shrieked in terror, "Which of them was my child? Tell me! Save the innocent one! Save my child from all that misery! Take it away—take it into God's kingdom! Forget my tears! Forget my prayers, and all that I have said and done!"

"I don't understand you," said Death. "Do you want your child back again, or shall I take it in there to the unknown?"

And the mother wrung her hands, fell upon her knees, and prayed to the Lord, "Hear me not when I pray for what is not Thy will. Thy will is always best. Hear me not! Hear me not!"

And she buried her face in her lap.

And Death went with her child into the unknown land.

The Bell

In the evening in the narrow streets of the big city, when the
sun went down and the clouds shone like gold among the
chimneys, one or another person would hear a strange sound,
just like the pealing of a church bell. But it was only for a
moment that it could be heard, for there was such a rumbling
of carts and shouting, and that's always distracting. "Now the
evening bell is ringing!" people would say. "Now the sun is
going down!"

Those who walked outside the city, where the houses stood
farther apart and there were gardens and small fields, saw a still
more glorious evening sky and heard far louder the ringing of
the bell. It was as if the sound came from a church deep within
the still, fragrant forest. And people would look in that direction and feel quite solemn.

Time went on, and people began to say to one another, "I
wonder if there's a church out there in the forest? That bell has
such a strange, beautiful sound. Shouldn't we go there and take
a closer look at it." And the rich people drove and the poor people walked, but the road was so strangely long for them, and

when they reached a large grove of willows growing at the edge of the forest, they set themselves down and looked into the long branches and thought that they were really out in the heart of nature. The owner of a coffeehouse from the city came and put up a refreshment stand there; then another coffeehouse owner arrived, and he hung right over his stand a bell that was covered with tar to withstand the rain, and it was without a clapper. When people went home again, they said that it had been so romantic—and that means something different from just a cup of tea. Three persons maintained that they had made their way into the forest to where it ended, and had heard the strange ringing of the bell the whole time, but when they got there, the sound seemed to be coming from the city. One of them wrote a long lyric about it and said that the bell sounded like the voice of a mother to a dear, bright child. No melody was more beautiful than the ringing of the bell.

The emperor of the land also heard of it, and promised that whoever could discover just where the sound came from would receive the title of World's Bell Ringer, even if it turned out not to be a bell at all.

Now, a lot of people went to the woods for the sake of that fine position, but only one returned home with any kind of explanation. None of them had gone deep enough into the forest, and neither had he, but he said anyway that the ringing sound came from a very large owl in a hollow tree. It was a sort of owl of wisdom that knocked its head constantly against the tree, but whether the sound came from its head or from the hollow trunk, he could not as yet say with any certainty. And so he was appointed World's Bell Ringer, and every year he wrote a little treatise about the owl. But that didn't make anyone the wiser.

Now, it happened to be confirmation day. The minister had spoken so beautifully and sincerely. The young people to be confirmed had been deeply moved. It was an important day for them; all at once they were to turn from children into grown people. The child's soul was, as it were, to fly over into a more sensible person. There was the brightest sunshine. The young people walked out from the city, and from the forest with a strange loudness came the ringing of the great, unknown bell. At once they felt a strong desire to go there—all but three. One of them had to go home to try on her ball gown, for it was really because of that gown and that ball that she had been confirmed this year; otherwise she wouldn't have been allowed to go! The second was a poor boy who had borrowed his confirmation clothes and dress boots from the landlord's son, and he had to return them at a specific time. The third said that he never went to any strange place unless his parents went along, and that he had always been a good child and would continue to be so even though he had been confirmed, and nobody should make fun of that—but they did anyway!

So these three did not go along. The others started off. The sun shone and the birds sang, and the young people sang with them and took each other by the hand, for they had not yet received any positions and were all newly confirmed before our Lord.

But soon two of the smallest grew tired and turned back toward the city. Two little girls sat down and made wreaths— they didn't go along either. And when the others reached the willows where the coffeehouse owner lived, they said, "See now, here we are! The bell does not really exist at all! It's only something people imagine!"

Just at that moment, from deep within the forest, the bell sounded so sweetly and solemnly that four or five decided to go a little farther into the forest. It was so dense and the foliage so abundant that it was really hard to make any progress. Woodruff and anemones grew almost too high; flowering convolvulus and blackberry vines hung in long garlands from tree to tree where the nightingale sang and the sunbeams played. Oh, it was so heavenly! But it was no place for the girls to go walking. They would have gotten their clothes torn to shreds. Great boulders lay scattered about, overgrown with moss of all colors. Fresh spring water trickled forth, and it said something curious like "kluk, kluk!"

"That couldn't be the bell!" said one of the young people,

lying down to listen. "This must be studied thoroughly!" So he stayed and let the others go on.

They came to a house built of bark and branches. A large tree heavy with wild apples leaned over it as if about to shake all its blessings on the roof, which was abloom with roses. The long branches lay right along the gable, where a little bell was hung. Could this be the bell they had heard? Yes, all agreed that it was, with the exception of one. He said that this bell was too small and delicate to be heard so far away, as they had heard it, and that its tones were completely different from those that had moved the hearts of men. Because the one who spoke was a king's son, the others said, "A fellow like that always wants to be smarter than anybody else."

So they let him go on alone, and as he walked the forest filled his breast with its solitude more and more. But he still could hear the little bell that the others were so pleased with. At times when the wind came from the direction of the refreshment stand, he could also hear someone calling that the tea was ready. But the deep tones of the bell sounded stronger, and it was almost as if an organ were playing with it. The sound came from the left, from the side where the heart is.

Suddenly, there was a rustling in the bushes, and a little boy stood in front of the king's son—a boy wearing wooden shoes and a jacket so short that you could see how long his wrists were. They knew each other. The boy was one of the three who had not been able to go with the others because he'd had to go home to return the coat and dress boots to the landlord's son. He had done this, and then, in his wooden shoes and shabby clothes, had started off alone, for the bell rang so loud, so deep, that he had to go.

"Then we can go together!" said the king's son. But the poor boy in the wooden shoes was too bashful. He tugged at his short coat sleeves and said that he was afraid he couldn't walk fast enough. Besides, he thought that the bell was to be found to the right, for everything great and splendid had a place to the right.

"Well then, we won't meet at all!" said the king's son, nodding to the poor boy, who walked into the darkest densest part of the forest, where the thorns tore his shabby clothes to shreds and scratched his face and hands and feet till they bled. The king's son also got some deep scratches, but the sun shone along his path, and he's the one we will follow, for he was a bright lad.

"I will and must find the bell!" he said. "Even if I have to go to the end of the world!"

The ugly monkeys sat up in the treetops, grinning and showing all their teeth.

"Let's pelt him!" they said. "Let's pelt him! He's a king's son!"

But undismayed he went on deeper and deeper into the forest, where the most marvelous flowers were growing. There were white starlike lilies with blood red stamens, sky blue tulips that sparkled in the wind, and apple trees whose apples looked like great shining soap bubbles. Just think how those trees would glisten in the sunshine! Around the edges of the most beautiful green meadows, where stags and does gamboled in the grass, grew splendid oaks and beech trees, and if any of the trees had a split in its bark, grass and long vines were growing there. There were also large forest glades with placid lakes where white swans swam and stretched their wings. The king's son often stood still and listened. Many times he thought that the sound of the bell came up to him from one of these deep lakes. But then he realized that it wasn't from there but from deeper within the forest that the bell rang.

Now the sun was sinking, the sky shone red as fire. It became so still, so very still in the forest, and he sank to his knees, sang his evening hymn, and said, "Never will I find what I'm seeking! The sun is going down. Now night is coming, the dark night. But perhaps I can still see the round red sun once more before it sinks below the earth. I will climb up those cliffs there. They rise as high as the highest trees!"

He grabbed at the vines and roots and clambered up the wet stones, where water snakes crawled and toads seemed to bark at him. But he reached the top before the sun was all the way down. Seen from that height, oh, what splendor! The sea, the vast, magnificent sea that rolled its long waves against the shore, was stretched out before him. And the sun stood like a great, shining altar far out where sea and sky met. Everything melted together into glowing colors, the forest sang, and the ocean sang, and his heart sang with them. All of nature was a great holy church in which trees and drifting clouds were the pillars, flowers and grass the woven velvet cloth, and the sky itself the great dome. Up there the red colors were extinguished when the sun went down, but millions of stars were ignited, millions of diamond lamps shone then, and the king's son stretched his arms toward the sky, toward the sea and the forest—and at that moment, from a path off to the right, came the poor boy with the short sleeves and the wooden shoes. He had gotten there just as soon, going his own way, and they ran to meet each other and held each other's hands in the great church of nature and poetry. And over them sounded the invisible, holy bell. Blessed spirits moved in dance around it to a joyous hallelujah!

The Flax

The flax was in full bloom. It has such pretty blue flowers as soft as the wings of a moth, and even more delicate. The sun shone on the flax, and the rain clouds watered it, and that was as good for the flax as it is for little children to be washed and then kissed by their mother—they look so much prettier afterward. Thus it was with the flax.

"People say I am thriving," said the flax, "and that I am growing so delightfully tall, a splendid piece of linen will be made from me. Oh, how happy I am! I am certainly the happiest of anybody. I feel so good, and I know something will become of me. How the sun cheers one up, and how good and fresh the rain tastes! I'm incomparably happy, I'm the happiest of anybody!"

"Yeah! Yeah!" jeered the stakes in the fence. "You don't know the world, but we know it! We have knots in us!" And then they creaked miserably:

> "Snip, snap, snurre
> Basselurre
> The song is over."

"No, it is not over," replied the flax, "the sun will shine to-morrow; the rain does me so much good, I can hear myself growing. I can feel that I am in bloom—I am the happiest of anybody!"

But one day people came, took hold of the flax, and pulled it up by the roots. That hurt! And then it was thrown into water as if to drown it and, after that, put over the fire as though it were to be roasted. It was dreadful!

"One cannot always have what one wishes!" said the flax. "It is just as well to try something new, it gives one experience."

But it seemed to get worse. The flax was bruised and broken, scutched and hackled or whatever it was called, and at last put on the spinning wheel—whirr! It wasn't possible to keep one's thoughts collected.

"I've been extraordinarily happy," thought the flax in all its pain. "One ought to be grateful for the good things one has enjoyed! Grateful, grateful, oh, yes!" and still the flax said the same when taken to the loom. And here it was made into a large, handsome piece of linen. All the flax, every single plant, was made into that one piece.

"Yes, but can you beat this! I never would have expected this. Look how lucky I've been! The stakes really knew what they were talking about with their

'Snip, snap, snurre,
Basselurre.'

The song isn't ended at all! It's just beginning. Can you beat this! Yes, even though I have suffered, I've turned out to be something! I am the happiest of anybody! I am so strong and so soft, so white and so long! This is far better than being a plant—even if one does have flowers, nobody attends to one, and one only gets water when it rains. Now, I am getting attention! The girl turns me over every morning, and I have a showerbath from the sprinkling can every evening. Say, the parson's wife herself came and talked about me and said I was the finest piece of linen in the parish. I couldn't be happier!"

Now, the linen was taken into the house and cut up with

scissors. Oh, how it was cut and clipped, how it was pierced and stuck through with needles, because that's the way it was done! It wasn't at all pleasant. It was at last made up into twelve articles of clothing, the kind that's unmentionable, although people can't do without them. There were twelve of them.

"So now I have really become something! So this was my fate! This is grand! Now I shall be of use in the world, and there is really no pleasure like that of being useful. We are now twelve pieces, but we are still one and the same—we are a dozen! Now this can't be beaten!"

The years passed—and the linen couldn't last any longer.

"All things must pass away some time or other," said each piece. "I'd like very much to last a little longer, but one should not expect the impossible." And so the linen was torn into bits and shreds—they believed it was all over for them because they were hacked and mashed and boiled, indeed they didn't know what all, and then they became beautiful, fine, white paper!

"Now, my word, this is a surprise! And a most delightful surprise, too!" said the paper. "Why, now I'm finer than ever, and I shall be written upon! What one couldn't write on me! This can't be beaten!" And the most charming stories in the world were written on it, and people heard what was written, and it was so right and good that it made them much wiser and better. Truly, a great blessing was given to the world in the words written on that paper.

"Certainly, this is more than I could ever have dreamed of when I was a little blue flower in the field! How could I have imagined I was to bring knowledge and happiness to mankind? I still cannot understand it even now. Yet, that's the way it is! The Lord knows, I've never done anything more than just try to exist, and yet the Lord carries me from glory to glory; and every time that I think to myself, 'The song is over,' that's when it changes into something far higher and better. Now, I suppose I'll be sent on a journey, around the whole world, so that everyone can read me. That would be most sensible. Once I had blue flowers, now in place of every single flower I have a most beautiful thought—I am the happiest of anybody!"

But the paper was not sent on its journey, it went to the printer's instead, and there all that was written on it was printed in a book, yes, in many hundreds of books, and this way an infinitely greater number of people could receive benefit and pleasure than if that one piece of paper that had been written on had itself been sent around the world. It would have been worn to shreds before it had gone halfway.

"Yes, this is much more sensible," thought the paper all covered with writing. "That never occurred to me. I should stay at home and be revered just like an old grandfather. It's me that has been written on—the ink flowed out of the pen right onto me. I'll stay at home, and the books will do all the running around. Now, something will really get done! How glad I am! How happy I am!"

So the paper was gathered up and put on the shelf. "It is good to rest upon one's just deserts," said the paper. "It is quite right that one should collect oneself and reflect on what one is all about. Now, for the first time, I really know what is in me! And to know oneself, that is true progress. I wonder what is coming now? It'll be something better, it's always getting better!"

One day the paper was placed by the stove. It was to be burned because it mustn't be sold to the grocer to wrap up butter and brown sugar. And all the children in the house gathered around. They wanted to see the blaze, they wanted to see all the red sparks that seem to dart to and fro in the ashes, dying out one after another so quickly. These are "the children going home from school," and the last spark of all is the teacher; often he seems to have gone, but then he comes along a little behind all the others.

And now the paper lay on the fire. "Oh!" How it burst into flame! "Oh!" it said, and at that very moment it blazed up. The flame reached higher than the flax could ever have lifted its little blue flower, and it shone brighter than the white linen could ever have shone. All the letters written on the paper turned fiery red for one moment, and all the words and thoughts went up in flame.

"Now, I am going straight up to the sun," it said from within the flame. It was as though a thousand voices had said it as one; and the flame burst through the chimney, and rose high. And finer than the flame, entirely invisible to mortal eyes, hovered little tiny beings, just as many as there had been flowers on the flax. They were even lighter than the flame that had given birth to them. When it had quite died out, and nothing remained of the paper but the black ashes, they once again danced over them, and wherever they touched, their footprints could be seen—they were the red sparks: "the children went home from school, and the teacher was the last!" It was a pleasure to watch this, and the children of the house stood and sang by the dead ashes:

> "Snip, snap, snurre,
> Basselurre,
> The song is over."

But the tiny invisible beings each replied, "The song is never over! That is the best of everything! I know that, and therefore I am the happiest of anybody!"

But that the little children could neither hear nor understand, and they weren't supposed to anyway, for children should not know everything.

In a Thousand
Years' Time

Yes, in a thousand years' time they'll come on wings of
steam, through the air, across the sea! America's youth
will visit old Europe. They'll come to the ancient monuments
here and to the cities falling to ruin, just as we in our day travel
to the crumbling splendors of southern Asia.

In a thousand years' time they'll come!

The Thames, the Danube, the Rhine are flowing still. Mont
Blanc is standing with a snowcap, the Northern Lights are
shining over the Nordic countries, but generation after generation has gone to dust, ranks of the powerful of the moment are

forgotten, like those who already sleep in the burial mound, where the well-to-do flour merchant, on whose property it is, puts together a bench for himself so that he can sit and look out over the flat, waving fields of grain.

"To Europe!" is the cry of America's young generation. "To the land of our forefathers, the beautiful land of reminiscence and fantasy, Europe!"

The airship comes. It is overcrowded with travelers, for the trip is faster than by sea. The electromagnetic cable under the sea has already telegraphed how large the air caravan is. Europe has already been sighted—it is the coast of Ireland that can be seen—but the passengers are still asleep. They don't want to be awakened until they are over England. There they'll set foot on European soil in the Land of Shakespeare, as it is called by the cultured; there are others who call it the Land of Politics, the Land of Machines.

The stopover here lasts a whole day; that's how much time the busy generation has to spend on great England and Scotland.

The journey goes through the Channel Tunnel to France, the land of Charlemagne and Napoleon. Molière is named, the learned speak of Classical and Romantic schools in the distant past, and there is rejoicing over heroes, skalds, and scientists that our age has never known, but who will be born in the crater of Europe, Paris.

The airship flies over the land from where Columbus set out, where Cortez was born, and where Calderón sang dramas in flowing verse. Beautiful, dark-eyed women still live in the flowering valleys, and in ancient songs El Cid and Alhambra are named.

Through the air, across the sea to Italy, where ancient, eternal Rome lay. It has been razed, the Campagna is a wilderness. Of Saint Peter's Church, only the solitary remains of a wall can be shown, but there is doubt about its authenticity.

To Greece, in order to sleep for one night at the luxurious hotel high atop Mount Olympus—then one has been there! The journey continues to the Bosporus, to rest there for a few hours and see the place where Byzantium lay. Poor fishermen spread their nets where the legend tells of the Garden of Harems in the time of the Turks.

Ruins of mighty cities by the surging Danube, cities unknown to our age, are flown over. But here and there—cities rich in memories, those yet to come, those yet unborn—here and there the air caravan descends and arises again.

Down there lies Germany, once girdled by the tightest network of railways and canals, the land where Luther spoke and Goethe sang, and where Mozart in his day bore the scepter of music! Great names shone out in science and art, names we do not know. A one-day stop in Germany, and one day in Scandinavia, Ørsted's and Linnaeus's fatherland, and Norway, the land of ancient heroes and young Norwegians. Iceland is sampled on the homeward journey; geysers no longer boil, Hekla is extinguished, but, as an eternal stone monument to the Sagas, the great craggy island stands in the turbulent sea!

"There's a lot to be seen in Europe!" says the young American. "And we've seen it in eight days. And it can be done, as the great traveler"—a name is mentioned belonging to one of their contemporaries—"has shown in his famous work: *Europe in Eight Days.*"

Clod-Hans

AN OLD STORY RETOLD

Out in the country there was an old manor, and in it lived an old squire with two sons who were so sharp-witted that half would have been enough! They decided to propose to the king's daughter, and that was all right to do because she had let it be proclaimed that she would marry the man she thought could best speak up for himself.

Now the two spent a week in preparation. That was all the time they had, but it was enough because they already knew a lot, and that's always a help. One of them had memorized the entire Latin dictionary as well as the local newspaper for the last three years, and both forward and backward at that. The other had studied all the guild articles and what every alderman should know, and therefore he thought he would be able to discuss affairs of state. Furthermore, he knew how to embroider suspenders, for he had style and was clever with his fingers.

"I'm going to win the king's daughter!" they both said, and

so their father gave them each a fine horse. The one who had memorized the dictionary and newspapers got a coal-black horse, and the one who was as smart as an alderman and did embroidery got a milk-white one. And then they greased the corners of their mouths with cod-liver oil so they could talk more smoothly. All the servants were down in the yard to see them mount their horses, and just then the third brother came along—for there were three of them—but no one counted the third for much because he wasn't a scholar like the other two, and they called him Clod-Hans.

"Where are you headed for in your Sunday best?" he asked.

"To court, to talk ourselves into a marriage with the king's daughter. Haven't you heard what is being proclaimed throughout the land?" And they told him all about it.

"Good gracious, then I'd better go, too!" said Clod-Hans, and his brothers laughed at him and rode away.

"Father, let me have a horse," Clod-Hans shouted. "I've a yen to get married. If she'll take me, she'll take me. And if she won't, then I'll take her all the same."

"Nonsense!" said his father. "I'll give no horse to you. Why, you're not well spoken at all. Your brothers, now, they're capable young men."

"If I can't have a horse," said Clod-Hans, "I'll take the billy goat—it's my own and can easily carry me." So he sat astride the billy goat, dug his heels into its flanks, and dashed off down the road. Whee! How he galloped! "Here I come!" said Clod-Hans, and he sang so the echoes rang.

Ahead of him, his brothers rode along in complete silence; they didn't say a word. They had to memorize all the clever things they were going to say, because it all had to be so well thought out.

"Hey, hey! Here I come!" shouted Clod-Hans. "Look what I found on the road!" And he showed them a dead crow that he had come across.

"Clod!" they said. "What are you going to do with that?"

"Make the king's daughter a present of it!"

"Yes, you just do that!" they said, laughing, and rode on.

"Hey, hey! Here I come! Look what I've found now! You don't find this sort of thing on the road every day."

The brothers turned around again to see what it was.

"Clod!" they said. "That's just an old wooden shoe that has lost its upper. Is that also for the king's daughter?"

"It certainly is!" said Clod-Hans, and the brothers laughed and rode on until they were far ahead of him.

"Hey, hey! Here I am!" shouted Clod-Hans. "My, now it's getting worse and worse! Hey, hey! This can't be beat!"

"What have you found now?" said the brothers.

"Oh," said Clod-Hans, "nothing to speak of! How happy the king's daughter will be!"

"Ugh!" said the brothers. "That's just mud that's been thrown up out of the ditch!"

"Yes, that it is!" said Clod-Hans. "And it's the finest kind— you can hardly hold it!" and he filled his pockets with it.

But the brothers rode on as hard as they could, and they came to the city gates a whole hour before him. There the suitors were given numbers as they arrived and were placed in rows six abreast—so close together that they couldn't move their arms. And it was just as well, for otherwise they would have knifed each other in the back just because one was standing ahead of the other.

All the people of the country were standing around the castle, right up to the windows in order to see the king's daughter receive her suitors. But just as each one came into the hall, his eloquence failed him.

"Won't do!" said the king's daughter. "Out!"

Now came the brother who had memorized the dictionary. But he had clean forgotten it from standing in line. And the floor creaked, and because the ceiling was of mirrors he saw himself upside down on his head, and at each window stood three secretaries and an alderman who wrote down everything that was said so it could go right into the newspaper and be sold on the corner for a dime. It was terrible! And then they had made such a roaring fire in the stove that the sides glowed red hot.

"It's awfully warm in here!" said the suitor.

"That's because my father's roasting cockerels today!" said the king's daughter.

Duh! There he stood. He hadn't expected to hear that. He couldn't find a word to say because he had wanted to say something amusing. Duh!

"Won't do!" said the king's daughter. "Out!" And so he had to leave. Now the second brother came.

"It's terribly hot here!" he said.

"Yes, we're roasting cockerels today!" said the king's daughter.

"I beg your . . . What? . . ." he said, and all the secretaries wrote: "I beg your . . . What? . . ."

"Won't do!" said the king's daughter. "Out!"

Now Clod-Hans came along. He rode the billy goat straight into the hall.

"Well, this is a scorcher!" he said.

"That's because I'm roasting cockerels!" said the king's daughter.

"Well, how handy!" said Clod-Hans. "Then maybe I can have a crow roasted!"

"Of course, you can!" said the king's daughter. "But do you have anything to roast it in? I have neither a pot nor a pan!"

"Oh, but I have!" said Clod-Hans. "Here's a cooker with a handle!" And he pulled out the old wooden shoe and put the crow right in the middle of it.

"Why that's enough for a whole meal," said the king's daughter, "but where will we get the drippings from?"

"Well, I have some in my pocket!" said Clod-Hans. "I've so much that I can afford to slop some around." And then he poured a little mud out of his pocket.

"Now you're talking!" said the king's daughter. "Why, you've got the answers! And you are well spoken! You're the one I'm going to marry! But do you know that every word we're saying and have said is being written down and will appear in the newspaper tomorrow? At each window you can see three secretaries and an old alderman. And the alderman is the worst of all, because he can't understand a thing." Now, she said this just to frighten him. And all the secretaries snickered and spattered ink on the floor.

"So those are my betters!" said Clod-Hans. "Then I'll give the best to the alderman." And he emptied his pockets and threw mud right in the alderman's face!

"That was well done!" said the king's daughter. "I couldn't have done it, but I'm certainly going to learn how!"

And so Clod-Hans became king and got a wife and a crown and sat on a throne. And we got it straight from the alderman's newspaper—and you can't believe a word in it.

"She Was No Good"

The mayor was standing by the open window; he had on a dress shirt with a stickpin in its frill. He was extremely well shaven, his own work. However, he had accidentally given himself a little nick, and a scrap of newspaper was stuck over the cut.

"Hey, you, youngster!" he called.

The youngster was none other than the washerwoman's son, who was just passing by and doffed his cap respectfully. The cap was folded over at the rim so it could be put into a pocket. In his poor but clean and very well-patched clothes and his heavy wooden shoes, the boy stood respectfully, as if he were standing before the king himself.

"You're a good boy," said the mayor. "You're a polite boy! Your mother is probably washing clothes down at the river, and that's where you are going with what you have in your pocket. That's an awful thing with your mother! How much do you have there?"

"A half cup," said the boy in a low, frightened voice.

"And this morning she had the same?" continued the man.

"No, that was yesterday!" answered the boy.

"Two halves make a whole! She is no good! It's a pity about that class of people! Tell your mother she should be ashamed of herself! And don't you ever become a drunkard—but you probably will anyhow! Poor child! Run along now!"

And the boy went. He was still holding his cap in his hand, and the wind blew his blond hair so that it stood up in long tufts. He went down the street, into an alley, and down to the river, where his mother stood out in the water by her washing stool, beating the heavy linen with a paddle. There was a strong current in the river, for the mill's sluices were open; the bed sheet was carried along by the current and nearly overturned her washing stool. The washerwoman had to stand up against it.

"I'm about to sail away," she said. "It's a good thing you've come, because I need something to pick up my strength. It's cold out here in the water. For six hours I've been standing here. Have you brought me something?"

The boy held out the flask, and his mother put it to her lips and took a swallow.

"Oh, that does me good! How it warms me up! It's just as good as hot food, and it isn't so expensive! Drink, my boy! You look so pale; you're freezing in those thin clothes! After all, it's autumn. Ooh, the water is cold! If only I don't get sick! But I won't! Give me another sip, and drink some yourself, but only a little drop, for you mustn't get used to it, my poor, penniless child!"

And she walked around the bridge, where the boy was standing, and up onto land. Water streamed from the straw mat that she had around her waist; water ran from her skirt.

"I moil and toil till my fingers bleed, but it doesn't matter, if only I can give you an honest start in life, my sweet child!"

At that moment a somewhat older woman came along who was poorly clad and scruffy. She was lame in one leg and had a great, big false curl hanging down to hide one eye, but this only made the defect more conspicuous. She was a friend of the washerwoman's; the neighbors called her "Gimpy-Maren with the curl."

"Poor thing," she cried, "how you moil and toil in the cold water! You could certainly use a little something to warm you up, and yet some people grudge you the few drops you do take!" And soon everything the mayor had said to the boy was repeated to the washerwoman, for Maren had overheard it all, and it had annoyed her to hear him talk like that to the child about his own mother and the few drops she took, especially since the mayor himself was in the midst of preparing a big dinner party with wine by the case! "Good wines, strong wines! Many will drink a drop too much, but they don't call that drinking! They are good enough, but you are no good!"

"Did he talk like that to you, child?" asked the washerwoman, her lips trembling. "You have a mother who is no good! Maybe he's right! But he shouldn't say it to the child. I have put up with a lot from that house!"

"That's right, you used to work there when the mayor's parents were alive and lived there. That was many years ago! Many bushels of salt have been eaten since then, so people have a right to be thirsty!" and Maren laughed. "There is a big dinner today at the mayor's—they were going to cancel it, but it was too late, and the food was all made. I heard about it from the fellow who does odd jobs there. A letter came an hour ago, saying that the mayor's younger brother had died in Copenhagen!"

"Died!" cried the washerwoman, turning as white as a corpse.

"Oh, goodness gracious," said Maren, "you're taking it so hard! Of course, you must have known him from when you were working there in the house."

"Is he really dead? He was the best, the very finest person. The Lord won't get many like him!" Tears ran down her cheeks. "Oh, my God! Everything is spinning around! It's because I emptied the bottle. I couldn't take it. I don't feel so well!" And she supported herself against the fence.

"Good Lord, you really are ill, my dear!" said the woman. "See if it won't go away! No, you are really sick! I'd better get you home!"

"But the wash!"

"I'll take care of that! Take me by the arm! The boy can stay here and watch it for the time being, and then I'll come back and wash the rest. It's only a little bit!"

The poor washerwoman's legs were wobbling beneath her.

"I've stood too long in the cold water! I haven't had anything to eat or drink since this morning! I have a fever all over! Oh, dear Jesus, help me get home! My poor child!" And she wept.

The boy cried and was soon alone beside the river with the wet linen. The two women walked slowly—the washerwoman was unsteady on her feet—up the alley and along the street past the mayor's. Right opposite his house, she collapsed on the cobblestones, and a crowd gathered.

Gimpy-Maren ran to the mayor's house for help. He and his guests were looking out the windows.

"It's the washerwoman!" he said. "She's had a drop too much! She's no good! It's a pity for that handsome boy of hers; I really have taken a fancy to that child. His mother is no good!"

And the washerwoman was brought to her senses and led to her poor home, where she was put to bed. The goodhearted Maren went to prepare a bowl of warm beer with butter and sugar—that was her idea of good medicine. And then she returned to the river, where she did a very poor, though well-intentioned job with the washing; she really only pulled the wet laundry up on shore and put it into a crate.

That evening she was sitting in the washerwoman's poor room. She had gotten from the mayor's cook a couple of candied potatoes and a lovely fat piece of ham for the patient. Maren and the boy feasted on these; the patient enjoyed the aroma. "It is so nourishing," she said.

The boy went to bed, in the very same one in which his mother was lying, but he slept crosswise at the foot of the bed with an old rug over him that had been made of blue and red strips of material sewn together.

The washerwoman was feeling a little better; the warm beer had given her strength, and the aroma of the fine food had done her good.

"Thank you, you kind soul!" she said to Maren. "I'll tell you all about it, when the boy is asleep! I think he's asleep already! See how sweet he looks with his eyes closed. He has no idea what his mother is going through. May the Lord never let him experience anything like it. Well, I worked for the councilor and his wife, the mayor's parents, when it happened that their youngest son came home, the one that was away at the university. That was back when I was young, wild, and carefree, but I was a good girl—as God is my witness!" said the washerwoman. "And the student was so lighthearted and happy; he was so wonderful! Every drop of blood in his veins was honest and true; a better person has never walked the earth. He was a son of the house, and I was only a servant girl, but we became sweethearts—chastely and honorably. A kiss is no sin, after all, if two people really love each other. Then he told his mother about us. She was like the dear Lord on earth for him; she was so wise, kind, and loving. He went away and put his gold ring on my finger. After he was well away, my mistress called for me; she stood there so grave and yet so mild and spoke as the Lord might well have. She made clear the distance, in spirit and in truth, between him and me. 'Now he sees how attractive you are, but good looks will fade in time! You haven't been educated as he; you can never be spiritual equals, and that is the problem. I respect the poor,' she said, 'and I know that in heaven a poor man could be seated closer to God than many rich men, but in this world if one is driving along and tries to switch traces, the cart will overturn! And you two would overturn! Now I know that an honest man, a good artisan, has been courting you—Erik the glovemaker. He is a widower with no children and is doing very well. Think it over!' Every word she spoke was like a knife in my heart, but the lady was right, and that weighed me down and oppressed me! I kissed her hand and wept my bitter tears. Even more so when I was in my own room, lying on my bed. It was an awful night that followed—

the Lord knows how I suffered and struggled! I went to Church on Sunday and took holy communion to see things in God's light. Then it was like an act of providence; when I was leaving the church, I met Erik the glovemaker. There were no longer any doubts in my mind. We were suited to each other, both in rank and in means; indeed, he was even a well-to-do man. And so I went right over to him, took his hand, and said, 'Am I still in your thoughts?' 'Yes, forever and always,' he said. 'Do you want to marry a girl who respects and honors you but does not love you, though that may well come!' 'It will come,' he said, and then we took each other by the hand. I went home to my mistress. The gold ring that her son had given me I had been wearing next to my bare breast, for I couldn't wear it on my finger by day, but only at night when I went to bed. I kissed the ring until my lips bled, then gave it to my mistress and told her that the following week the banns would be read for me and the glovemaker. Then my mistress took me in her arms and kissed me; she didn't say I was no good, but in those days I was perhaps better than now, even though I had not yet suffered so many of the misfortunes of the world. The wedding was held at Candlemas, and the first year went well. We employed a journeyman and an apprentice, and you, Maren, took care of the house for us."

"Oh, you were a good mistress!" said Maren. "Never shall I forget how kind you and your husband were!"

"That was during the good years that you were with us! We had no children then. I never saw the student again. Well, I did see him once, but he didn't see me. He came here to his mother's funeral, and I saw him standing by the grave, looking so pale and so sad, but that was on account of his mother. When his father died later, he was abroad and didn't come and hasn't been here since. He never married, I know. He was a lawyer, to be sure—he didn't remember me, and if he had seen me he would never have recognized me, as ugly as I am. And that's all right, too, I suppose!"

She spoke of the bitter days of hardship, how misfortune

seemed to overwhelm them. They had five hundred dollars, and since there was a house on their street for sale for two hundred, they considered it a good investment to buy it and have it torn down and a new one built. And so the house was bought. The bricklayer and carpenter estimated that the new house would cost twelve hundred dollars. Erik the glovemaker had good credit and got the money as a loan from Copenhagen, but the captain who was to have brought the money was lost at sea, and the money along with him.

"That was when I gave birth to my darling boy, who lies sleeping here. His father fell into a long and severe illness; for nine months I had to dress and undress him every day. Things went downhill for us. We borrowed and borrowed. Even our clothes went to pay bills, and then my husband died, leaving us all alone! I have worked and moiled, slaved and toiled, for the boy's sake, washing stairways and washing linen, all kinds of linen. But my lot won't change; it is the dear Lord's will! But he will surely release me and take care of the boy."

And then she fell asleep.

Toward morning she felt stronger, strong enough, she thought, to go back to her work. She had no sooner stepped into the cold water, when a shivering, a faintness, seized her; she reached out desperately with her hands, took one step toward the bank, and collapsed. Her head lay on dry land, but her feet were in the river; the wooden shoes she wore while standing in the water—there was a handful of straw in each of them—were carried away by the current. Here she was found by Maren, who had come with coffee.

A message from the mayor had arrived for her at home that she was to appear before him immediately because he had something to say to her. It was too late. A barber was fetched to let her blood, but the washerwoman was dead.

"She has drunk herself to death," said the mayor.

In the letter that had brought the news of death of the mayor's brother there was word of his will, and it was mentioned that he had left six hundred dollars to the glovemaker's widow, who had once served his parents! The money was to be paid out in large or small sums to her and her child, according to their need.

"There was some nonsense between my brother and her," said the mayor. "It's a good thing that she's out of the way. Now the boy will get it all, and I'll place him with some honest people. He'll turn out to be a good craftsman." And on these words the Lord laid his blessing.

And the mayor sent for the boy, promised to take care of him, and told him what a good thing it was that his mother was dead—she was no good!

They carried her to the churchyard, to the pauper's cemetery. Maren planted a little rose bush on her grave. The boy stood beside her.

"My darling mother!" he said, as his tears welled up. "Is it true that she was no good?:"

"Oh, she was good!" said the old lady, looking up to heaven. "I know that from the experience of many years, and from the last night, too. I tell you she was good, and the Lord in heaven says so, too. So just let the world say, 'She was no good!'"

The Old Oak Tree's Last Dream

A CHRISTMAS TALE

In the forest, high on a slope above the open beach, there stood
a very old oak tree that was exactly three hundred and sixty-
five years old, but for the tree that long period of time was no
more than the same number of days and nights for us humans.
We are awake during the day and sleep at night, when we then
dream our dreams. With the tree it is different—the tree is
awake for three seasons. Only when winter approaches does it
get sleep; winter is its time for sleeping. That is its night after
the long day which is called spring, summer, and fall.

On many a warm summer's day mayflies have danced around
its crown, lived and soared and been happy. And if, then,
one such little creature rested on a broad oak leaf for a moment
in silent ecstasy, the tree always said, "Poor little thing! Just
one single day is your whole life! How short! It's so sad!"

"Sad!" the mayfly always answered. "What do you mean by

that? Everything is so wonderfully light, so warm and beautiful, and I'm so happy."

"But only one day, and then it's all over!"

"Over!" said the mayfly. "What is over? Are you also over?"

"No, I live for perhaps thousands of your days, and my day is made up of whole seasons! That is something so long that you couldn't even comprehend it!"

"No, because I don't understand you! You have thousands of my days, but I have thousands of moments to be happy and joyous in! Will all beauty in the world die when you die?"

"No," said the tree. "It will last longer, infinitely longer, than I can imagine!"

"But then we are even. It's just that we figure things differently!"

And the mayfly danced and soared in the air, rejoicing over its delicate, elaborate wings, their gauze and velvet, rejoicing in the warm air that was spiced with the scent from the clover field and from the hedge of wild roses, the elder and the honeysuckle, to say nothing of the woodruff, primroses, and wild mint. There was a scent so strong that the mayfly felt itself a little intoxicated from it all. The day was long and beautiful, full of joy and sweet sensation, and when in time the sun sank, the little fly always felt itself so pleasantly tired from all that gaiety. Its wings wouldn't carry it any longer, and it glided very gently down onto the soft, swaying blades of grass, nodded its head as it was able, and fell so cheerfully asleep. That was death.

"Poor little mayfly!" said the oak tree. "That was certainly much too short a life."

And every summer day the same dance was repeated, the same speech and response and deep sleep. It was repeated down through whole generations of mayflies, and they were all just as happy, just as joyous. The oak tree stayed awake through its spring morning, summer afternoon, and autumn evening. Now it would soon be time to sleep, its night—winter—was coming.

Already the storms were singing, "Good night! Good night! There fell a leaf! There fell a leaf! We pluck! We pluck! See about falling asleep! We sing you to sleep, we shake you to sleep, but isn't it true that it feels good in the old branches! They creak from pure pleasure! Sleep deep! Sleep deep! It is your three hundred and sixty-fifth night; you are really only an infant. Sleep deep! The clouds dust down snow; it becomes a whole sheet, a warm blanket around your feet! Sleep deep, and sweet dreams!"

And the oak tree stood disrobed of all its foliage, ready to rest all the long winter and during it to dream many a dream, always something it had experienced, just as in the dreams of humans.

It, too, had once been small. An acorn had been its cradle. According to human reckoning, it was in its fourth century of life. It was the biggest and most splendid tree in the forest; with its crown it rose high above all the other trees and could be seen from far out at sea, serving sailors as a landmark. It thought not at all about how many eyes sought it out. High up in its green crown settled wood pigeons, and the cuckoo warbled there. In the fall when the leaves looked like hammered copper plates, migrating birds came to rest in its branches before they traversed the sea. But now it was winter; the tree stood leafless. One could clearly see how bent and gnarled the branches were as they stretched out. Crows and jackdaws came and alighted there in shifts to discuss the hard times that were coming and how difficult it was to find food during the winter.

It was just at the holy time of Christmas that the tree dreamed its most beautiful dream. We shall hear about it.

The tree felt distinctly that it was a time of celebration. It seemed to hear from all around church bells pealing; moreover, the weather was mild and warm, like a beautiful summer day. It spread out its mighty crown, so fresh and green; sunbeams played among leaves and branches; the air was filled with the scent of herbs and bushes; many-colored butterflies played tag; and the mayflies danced as if everything only existed so that they might dance and enjoy themselves. Everything that the tree had experienced through the ages and seen going on around it passed by like a festive parade. From days of yore it saw riding through the forest knights and ladies on horseback, with feathers in their hats and falcons on their hands. The hunting horn sounded, and the hounds gave voice. It saw enemy soldiers, with shiny weapons and colorful uniforms, spears and halberds, put up their tents and take them down again; sentry fires flickered, and the soldiers sang and slept under the tree's outspread branches. It saw lovers in quiet bliss meet here in the moonlight and carve their names, only the first initial, into the gray-green bark. Once a zither and an aeolian harp had hung there—yes, years had passed in the meantime—hung up in the branches of the oak by merry, itinerant journeymen. Now they were hanging there again; now, again, they sounded so lovely. The wood pigeons cooed as if they wanted to tell what the tree was feeling about all this, and the cuckoo warbled how many summer days the tree would live.

Then it was as if a new vital force rustled all the way down into the tiniest roots and up into the highest branches, right out into the leaves. The tree sensed that it was stretching. Yes, it felt with its roots how there was also life and warmth down in the ground. It felt its strength increase. It grew higher and higher. The trunk shot upward. There was nothing that wasn't in motion; it grew more and ever more. The crown became fuller, spread out, rose up—and as the tree grew, so grew its sense of well-being, its blissful longing ever to reach higher, right up to the warm, glowing sun.

It had already grown up above the clouds, where dark hordes of migratory birds or great white flocks of swans flew beneath it.

And each one of the tree's leaves could see, as if it had eyes to see with. The stars became visible by day; they looked so big and bright. Each of them winked like a pair of clear, mild eyes; they were reminiscent of the eyes of near ones and dear ones, the eyes of children, of sweethearts when they met under the tree.

It was a moment of bliss, so joyful! And yet in all that joy it longed and desired that all the other trees of the forest down below, all the bushes, herbs, and flowers, could also rise up to experience and feel this joy and glory. The mighty oak tree in its dream of splendor was not completely happy unless they were all there, great and small; and that feeling trembled through limbs and leaves, as deep and fervent as in any human breast.

The crown of the tree moved as if it were searching and seeking. It looked back and caught the scent of woodruff and the even stronger scent of honeysuckle and violets. It thought it could hear the cuckoo answering it.

Yes, the forest's green treetops peeped through the clouds. Down below it could see the other trees grow and rise up around itself. Bushes and plants shot high up into the air; several wrenched themselves loose, roots and all, and flew up more quickly. The birch was the quickest; like a white streak of lightning, its slender trunk flashed upward, its boughs billowed like green gauze and banners. The whole forest world, even the brown plumed reeds, grew along with the trees, and the birds joined in and sang, and on a straw that fluttered loose and flew up like a long green silk ribbon, there sat a grasshopper, playing with its wing on its shinbone. June beetles hummed and bees buzzed; every bird sang with its beak. Everything was song and joy right up into heaven.

"But the little blue flower by the water; it must come, too!" said the oak tree. "And the Canterbury bells! And the little daisy!" Indeed, the oak wanted to have them all along.

"We're coming, too! We're coming, too!" echoed singing voices.

"But the pretty woodruff of last summer! And the year before that, the great abundance of lilies of the valley! And the wild apple tree, how beautiful it stood! And all that forest splendor for years, for many, many years! If it had only lived and still existed, then it could have come along!"

"We're coming, too! We're coming, too!" echoed singing

voices from even higher up—they must have flown on ahead.

"Oh, this is much too unbelievably beautiful!" exulted the old oak. "I have them all here! Great and small! Not one of them has been forgotten! How can all this joy be possible, even conceivable?"

"In God's heaven it is possible and conceivable!" came the echo.

And the tree, ever growing, sensed its roots loosening from the earth.

"This is the best of all!" said the tree. "Now no bonds hold me! I can fly up to the Highest One of All in splendor and ever-lasting light! And I have all my dear ones along. Great and small, all are coming with me!"

"All!"

That was the oak tree's dream, and as it dreamed, a violent storm passed over the sea and the land during that holy night of Christmas. The sea churned heavy waves onto the shore; the tree creaked and cracked and was pulled from the ground, just when it was dreaming that its roots were freeing themselves. It fell. Its three hundred and sixty-five years were now as one day had been for the mayfly.

When the sun rose on Christmas morning, the storm had quieted. All the church bells were pealing joyfully, and from each chimney, even from the chimney of the poor sharecropper, rose smoke, bluish as if from the altar at a druid feast, the sacrificial smoke of thanksgiving. The sea became more and more still, and out there, on a large vessel that had survived the bad weather during the night, many flags were hoisted in happy and beautiful celebration of Christmas.

"The tree is gone! The old oak tree, our landmark on the shore!" said the sailors. "It fell during the storm last night! What can replace it! Nothing can!"

That was the eulogy, short but sincere, for the tree, which lay outstretched on the blanket of snow by the shore. And from the ship came the sound of a hymn, a song about the joy of Christmas and of Christ the saviour of souls and of eternal life:

Sing high to the sky, God's churchgoing men!
Halleluja, now we're content!
This joy is a joy without equal!
Halleluja! Amen! Amen!

So sounded the old hymn, and each person out on the ship was raised up in his own way by it and by the prayer, just as the old tree rose up in its last, most beautiful dream on the night of Christmas.

The Butterfly

T he butterfly wanted to have a sweetheart; naturally he wanted one of the pretty little flowers. He looked at them; each one was sitting so quiet and serious on its stalk, the way a maiden is supposed to sit when she isn't engaged. But here were so many to choose from that it turned out to be difficult. The butterfly couldn't be bothered, so he flew to the daisy. The French call her Marguerite; they know she can prophesy the future, and she does it when sweethearts pluck petal after petal from her, and with each one they ask a question about the loved one: "Loves me? Loves me not? Loves a lot? A teeny bit? Not at all?" Or something like that. Each one asks in his own language. The butterfly also came to ask. He didn't pick off the petals, but placed a kiss on each one—it was his opinion that one gets farthest by being friendly.

"Sweet Marguerite Daisy!" he said. "You are the wisest lady of all the flowers! You understand how to foretell the future! Tell me, will I marry this one or that one? Who will I marry? When I find out, I can fly right over and propose!"

But Marguerite did not answer. She didn't like his calling her a lady, for after all she was a maiden, and then one is not a lady. He asked a second time, and asked a third, and when he didn't get a single word out of her, he couldn't be bothered with asking her anymore but flew right off to go courting.

It was in the early spring. There were great numbers of snowdrops and crocuses. "You are very nice!" said the butterfly.

"Lovely little candidates for confirmation! But somewhat green!" Like all young men, he had an eye out for older girls. Then he flew to the anemones. They were a little too tart for him, the violets a little too romantic, the tulips too flashy, the white narcissus too bourgeois, the linden blossoms too small—and they had so many relatives. True enough, the apple blossoms looked like roses, but they bloomed today and fell off tomorrow, all depending on how the wind blew. That was too short a marriage, he thought. The sweet pea was most pleasing; it was white and red, pure and delicate—one of those home-loving maidens who look good and yet are handy in the kitchen. He was just about to propose to her, but at that instant he saw a pea pod hanging nearby with a withered flower at the tip. "Who's that?" he asked. "That's my sister," said the sweet pea.

"Well, so that's how you're going to look later on!" That frightened the butterfly, and so he flew away.

The honeysuckles hung over the fence. There were lots of those maidens with long faces and sallow complexions. They weren't his type at all. Well, what was his type? Ask him!

Spring passed, summer passed, and then it was autumn. He had made no progress. And the flowers came in the loveliest garments. But what use was it? The fresh, fragrant lightness of youth was missing. Fragrance is exactly what the heart craves in old age, and there is not much fragrance to dahlias and hollyhocks. So the butterfly flew down to the mint.

"Now, it has no flowers at all. But all of it is a flower, giving off a fragrance from root to tip, with a flower scent in every leaf. I will take her!"

And so he proposed at last.

But the mint stood stiff and still, and at last it said, "Friendship, but no more! I'm old, and you're old! We could live for each other very well, but get married—no! Let's not make fools of ourselves in our old age!"

And so the butterfly got no one at all. He had searched too long, and that is something one shouldn't do. The butterfly became a bachelor, as it is called.

It was late autumn with rain and drizzle. The wind sent

shivers down the backs of the old willow trees so that they creaked. It wasn't good flying outside in summer clothes—you'd be in for an unpleasant surprise, as they say. But the butterfly didn't fly outside, either. He had accidentally gotten inside, where there was a fire in the stove, yes, just as hot as summer. He could live. But "living isn't enough!" he said. "One must have sunshine, freedom, and a little flower!"

And he flew against the windowpane, was seen, admired, and stuck on a pin in the curio chest. More could not be done for him.

"Now I, too, am sitting on a stalk, just like the flowers!" said the butterfly. "But it isn't very pleasant! It's probably like being married—you're stuck!" And he comforted himself with that.

"That's poor comfort," said the potted plants in the living room.

"But potted plants can't be quite trusted," thought the butterfly. "They have too much to do with people!"

The Snail and the Rosebush

Around the garden was a fence of hazel bushes, and beyond that were fields and meadows with cows and sheep, but in the middle of the garden stood a rosebush in bloom. Under it sat a snail that was full of itself—it was everything unto itself.

"Wait until my time comes!" it said. "I'll accomplish something more than yielding roses, or bearing nuts, or giving milk like cows and sheep!"

"I expect a great deal from you!" said the rosebush. "Dare I ask when it will come about?"

"I'm taking my time!" said the snail. "Now, you're always in such a rush! That doesn't raise anybody's expectations!"

The next year the snail lay in about the same spot in the sunshine under the rosebush, which set buds and unfolded its roses, always fresh, always new. And the snail crept half out of its shell, stretched out its feelers, and drew them back again.

"Everything looks just like last year! There hasn't been any progress. The rosebush keeps to its roses, it won't get any further!"

Summer passed, autumn passed. The rosebush still yielded roses and buds until the snow fell. The weather became cold and wet; the rosebush bowed down to the ground, the snail crept into the ground.

Then a new year began; and the roses came forth, and the snail came forth.

"You're an old rose cane now!" it said. "It's about time for you to die out. You've given the world everything you had. Whether that meant anything is a question I didn't have any time to think about. But after all it's clear, you haven't done the least for your inner development; otherwise something different would have come of you. Can you defend what you've done? You'll soon be nothing but a bare stick! Can you understand what I'm saying?"

"You frighten me!" said the rosebush. "I've never thought about that!"

"No, you've probably never bothered much with thinking! Have you ever figured out for yourself why you bloomed, and how the blooming came about? Why in that way, and why not in some other way?"

"No!" said the rosebush. "I bloomed in joy, because I couldn't do otherwise. The sun was so warm, the air so refresh-

ing, I drank the clear dew, and the heavy rain. I breathed, I lived! From the ground a strength came up into me; from above there also came a strength. I felt a happiness, always new, always great, and that's why I always had to bloom. That was my life. I couldn't do otherwise!"

"You've led a very easy life!" said the snail.

"To be sure! Everything was given to me!" said the rosebush. "But still more was given to you! You have one of those deep-thinking natures; you are one of the highly gifted who will surprise the world!"

"I've no such intention at all!" said the snail. "I don't care about the world! What have I to do with the world? I have enough with myself, and I am enough for myself!"

"But shouldn't we all here on earth give the best that is in us to others, bring them what we can! Yes, I've only given roses! But you? You, who received so much, what did you give the world? What will you give it?"

"What did I give? What will I give? I spit on it! It's worthless! I don't care about it. Bear your roses! You'll never get any further! Let the hazel bush bear nuts. Let cows and sheep give milk. They have each of them their admirers—I have mine inside myself! I'm going into myself, and there I'll stay. I don't care about the world!"

And then the snail went into its house, and closed it up.

"It's so sad!" said the rosebush. "Even if I wanted to, I can't creep into myself. I must always spring out, spring out into roses. The petals fall, and the wind carries them away! But I saw one of my roses being put into the housewife's hymnbook. One of my roses found a place on the breast of a beautiful young girl, and one was kissed in blissful joy by a child's lips. It did so much good; it was a true blessing. That is my memory, my life!"

And the rosebush bloomed in innocence, and the snail languished in its house. He didn't care about the world.

And years passed.

The snail was as dust to dust; the rosebush was as dust to dust. The dried rose in the hymnbook had also vanished—but in the garden new rosebushes were blooming, in the garden new snails were growing. They crept into their houses and spat— they didn't care about the world.

Shall we read the story again from the beginning? It will never be any different.

What People Do Think Up

There was once a young man who was studying to become a poet. He wanted to be one by Easter and then get married and earn his living from poetizing, and he knew that was just a matter of thinking things up. But he was unable to think things up. He had been born too late. Everything had been used up before he came into the world. Everything had already been composed and written about.

"Those lucky people who were born a thousand years ago!" he said. "It was easy for them to become immortal! Even those who were born a hundred years ago were lucky; there were still things left to write about. But now everything in the world has been written up. What can I ever find to write down?"

He studied the matter until he got sick and feeble, the poor fellow. No doctor could help him, but maybe the wise old woman could. She lived in a little house by the tollgate. She opened the toll bar for people in carriages and on horseback, but she certainly knew more than how to open a bar. She was smarter than the doctor, who drives his own carriage and pays rich man's taxes.

"I must go to her!" said the young man.

The house she lived in was small and tidy but not very interesting to look at. There wasn't a tree or flower to be seen anywhere. There was a beehive by her door—very practical! There was a small potato patch—very practical! And there was a ditch with blackthorn bushes that had lost their flowers and were now setting berries that puckered your mouth if you tasted them before they had been nipped by frost.

"I'm looking at the very picture of our prosaic times," thought the young man. And that was, after all, a thought—a pearl that he had found by the wise old woman's door.

"Write it down," she told him. "Crumbs are bread, too! I know why you've come here. You can't think things up, yet you want to be a poet by Easter!"

"Everything has already been written!" he said. "Our times are not like the old days!"

"No!" the old woman said. "In the old days, wise old women were burned alive, and poets went around with hollow bellies and their elbows sticking out of their sleeves. The times are in fact good; they are the best times of all! But you don't have the right way of looking at them. You don't use your ears, and you're probably not saying the Lord's Prayer at night. There are plenty of things to write and tell about, if only you know how. You can draw it out of the plants and fruits of the earth, ladle it from running and still waters. But you must know how—know how to capture a sunbeam. Just try on my spectacles and put my ear trumpet to your ear, then pray to the Lord, and do stop thinking about yourself!"

That last request was very difficult—indeed, more than a wise old woman should ever demand.

He was given the spectacles and the ear trumpet and positioned in the middle of the potato patch, where she put a big potato in his hand. A sound could be heard in it; it was a song with words, the story of the potato. It was very interesting—an everyday story in ten parts. Ten lines sufficed.

And what did the potato sing about?

It sang about itself and its family, about the coming of potatoes to Europe, about the disparagement they had suffered and endured before they came to be recognized—as they are today—as of greater benefit than any gold nugget.

"By the king's command, we were distributed from the town hall of every town. A proclamation was issued concerning our great importance, but nobody believed it. No one even knew how to plant us. One man dug a hole and emptied his whole bushel of potatoes into it. Another stuck one potato in the ground here, one there, and waited for them to sprout into a whole tree, so he could shake the potatoes down like fruit. We did grow, too, and flowered and set water-filled fruit, but it all withered away. No one thought about what might be beneath the ground—blessed potatoes. Yes, we have suffered and endured—that is to say, our fathers did. We and they, it's all the same. Such interesting stories!"

"That's enough, now!" the old woman said. "Take a look at the blackthorn bushes!"

"We, too," said the blackthorns, "have close relatives in the homeland of the potato, but farther north than where they grow. Norsemen came from Norway; they steered westward through fogs and storms to an unknown land, where beneath ice and snow they found herbs and grass and bushes with blue-black berries like wine grapes. They were blackthorn berries—they ripened in the frost, and we do that, too. So the country was called 'Vineland' or 'Greenland' or 'Blackthorn Land.'"

"That is quite a romantic story!" the young man said.

"Now come along with me," said the wise old woman, and she led him to the beehive. He peered inside. What life and activity! Bees were stationed in all the passages, fanning with their wings to keep the air fresh throughout the entire factory. That was their job. Now other bees, born with baskets on their legs, arrived from outside. They brought flower dust, which was emptied, sorted, and made into honey and wax. They came and they flew off. The queen also wanted to fly off, but if she did they would all have to follow her! Even though the time for this hadn't arrived, she was determined to fly. So the bees bit off Her Majesty's wings, and she had to stay.

"Now climb up on top of the ditch," said the wise old woman. "Come and have a look at the highway, where there are so many fine people to be seen!"

"Oh, my! That is certainly a milling throng!" said the young man. "Story after story—it's all whirring and whirling! It's too much for me! Oh, I'm falling backward!"

"No!" said the old woman. "Go forward instead. Go right into the middle of the crowd. Open your eyes to it, your ears, and your heart as well. Soon you will be able to think things up! But before you go, I must have back my spectacles and ear trumpet." And she took both of them away from him.

"Now I can't see anything at all!" the young man said. "Now I can't hear anything!"

"Well then, you won't be a poet by Easter!" said the wise old woman.

"But when?" he asked.

"Neither by Easter nor by Whitsuntide. You will never learn to think things up!"

"But how can I earn my living from poetry?"

"You can manage that even before Lent! Write about poets! Criticize their writings—that's like criticizing them! Just don't let that worry you. Criticize as harshly as you can, and you'll be rewarded enough to support both yourself and your wife!"

"What people do think up!" said the young man, and then he criticized every poet, since he couldn't become one himself.

We got this story from the wise old woman. She knows what people do think up.

The Gardener
and the Lord and Lady

About five miles from the capital stood an old manor house
with thick walls, towers, and stepped gables.

Living here—but only in the summer—was a rich, aristocratic family. This manor was the best and the most beautiful of
all the manors it owned. On the outside it looked newly built,
and inside it was cozy and comfortable. The family's arms were
carved in stone above the gate. Lovely roses twined about the
coat of arms and the bay, and a whole grass carpet was spread
out in front of the manor. There were red hawthornes and white
hawthornes; there were rare flowers even outside the greenhouse.

The lord and lady also had a skillful gardener. It was a joy to
see the flower garden, the orchard, and the vegetable garden.
Adjoining this was what was left of the original old garden of
the estate with some hedges trimmed in the shape of crowns

and pyramids. Behind these stood two immense old trees. They were always nearly leafless, and you might well think that a gale or a waterspout had spattered them with big lumps of dung; but each lump was a bird's nest.

Here, from time immemorial, a swarm of screeching rooks and crows had dwelled. It was a whole community of birds, and the birds were the aristocrats, the property owners, the oldest family on the estate, the real lords of the manor. None of the people down below meant anything to them, but they put up with these low-walking creatures even though they occasionally banged away with guns, sending chills up the birds' spines so that each bird flew up in fright, screeching, "Riff! Raff! Raff!"

The gardener often spoke to his lord and lady about having the old trees felled. They didn't look good, and once they were gone, one would most likely be rid of those screeching birds; they would go somewhere else. But the lord and lady wanted to be rid of neither the trees nor the swarm of birds. They were something the estate couldn't do without; they were something from the old days, and they shouldn't be entirely wiped out.

"Those trees are the hereditary estate of the birds. Let them keep it, my dear Larsen!"

The gardener's name was Larsen, but that's of no real importance here.

"My dear Larsen, don't you have enough to take care of already? The entire flower garden, the greenhouses, the orchard, and the vegetable garden?"

He did have those—he tended them, looking after and cultivating them with zeal and skill. And the lord and lady admitted this, but they didn't conceal from him that they, when visiting other people, often ate fruit or saw flowers that surpassed those they had in their own garden. And that saddened the gardener, for he wanted the best and did his best. He was good at heart and good at his job.

One day the lord and lady sent for him and said benignly and aristocratically that on the previous day, at the home of distinguished friends, they had been served a variety of apples and pears so juicy and flavorful that they and all the guests had expressed their admiration. The fruits were, to be sure, not domestic, but they ought to be imported and made to grow here if our climate permitted. It was known that they had been purchased in the city from the leading fruit dealer. The gardener was to ride in and find out where these apples and pears had come from and then send for cuttings.

The gardener knew the fruit dealer well, for it was precisely to him that he, on behalf of the lord and lady, sold the overabundance of fruit that grew in the estate garden.

And the gardener went to the city and asked the fruit dealer where he had obtained these highly celebrated apples and pears.

"They're from your own garden!" said the fruit dealer, and showed him both an apple and a pear, which he recognized.

Well, how happy this made the gardener. He hurried back to the lord and lady and told them that both the apples and the pears were from their own garden.

The lord and lady couldn't believe this at all. "It's not possible, Larsen! Can you get a written declaration from the fruit dealer?"

And this he could. He brought a written attestation.

"How very odd!" said the lord and lady.

Every day now big bowls of these magnificent apples and pears from their own garden appeared on the table of the lord and lady. Bushels and barrels of these fruits were sent to friends in the city and outside the city—yes, even abroad. It was a great pleasure! Yet they had to add that, after all, the past two summers had been remarkably good for orchard fruits. These had turned out well everywhere in the land.

Some time passed. The lord and lady dined at court. On the following day the gardener was summoned to his lord and lady. At the royal table they had been served such juicy, flavorful melons from their majesties' greenhouse.

"You must go to the castle gardener, my good Larsen, and get us some of the seeds from these priceless melons!"

"But the castle gardener got the seeds from us!" said the gardener, quite pleased.

"Then that man has known how to bring the fruit to a higher

stage of development," replied the lord and lady. "Each melon was excellent!"

"Well, then I can be proud!" said the gardener. "I must tell my gracious lord and lady, this year the castle gardener hasn't had any luck with his melons, and when he saw how splendidly ours were doing and tasted them, he ordered three to be sent up to the castle!"

"Larsen! Don't delude yourself that they were the melons from our garden!"

"I think so!" said the gardener and went to the castle gardener and got from him written proof that the melons on the royal table had come from the manor.

This was really a surprise to the lord and lady, and they made no secret of the story. They showed the attestation—indeed, melon seeds were sent far and wide, just as previously the cuttings had been.

Concerning these, news was received that they took and set fruit quite well, and the fruit was named after the lord and lady's manor—thus the name was now to be read in English, German, and French.

No one had ever anticipated this!

"If only the gardener doesn't get too many big ideas about himself!" said the lord and lady.

He reacted in a different way. Now he was eager to strive to establish his name as one of the best gardeners in the land, to try each year to produce something outstanding from every garden variety; and this he did. Yet he was often told that the very first fruit he had brought, the apples and the pears, were really the best; all later varieties were vastly inferior. The melons, to be sure, had been very good, but after all they were something quite different. The strawberries could be called excellent, but still they were no better than those on the other estates. And when one year the radishes failed, they talked only about the unsuccessful radishes and not about the other good things that had been brought up to the manor.

It was almost as if the lord and lady found relief in saying, "Well, it didn't go well, this year, my dear Larsen!" They were quite happy in being able to say, "It didn't go well this year."

A couple of times a week the gardener brought fresh flowers up to the parlor, always so tastefully arranged. In the arrangement the colors showed up as if they stood in a brighter light.

"You have taste, Larsen!" said the lord and lady. "That is a gift that comes from Our Lord, not from yourself!"

One day the gardener brought a large crystal bowl. In it lay the leaf of a water lily. On this had been placed, with its long thick stalk down in the water, a brilliant, blue flower as big as a sunflower.

"Hindustani lotus!" exclaimed the lord and lady.

They had never seen such a flower before, and by day it was placed in the sunshine and in the evening in reflected light. Everyone who looked at it found it remarkably beautiful and unusual. Indeed, even the most distinguished of the land's young ladies said so, and she was a princess. She was wise and goodhearted.

The lord and lady took pride in presenting her with the flower, and it went with the princess up to the castle.

Now the lord and lady went down into the garden to pick a similar flower themselves, if such a one could still be found, but it was not to be found. So they summoned the gardener and asked where he had gotten the blue lotus from.

"We have searched in vain!" they said. "We have been in the greenhouses and all around the flower garden!"

"No, that's not where it is!" said the gardener. "It's only a humble flower from the vegetable garden! But, isn't it true how beautiful it is! It looks like a blue cactus, but it's only an artichoke blossom!"

"You should have told us that right away!" said the lord and lady. "We couldn't help thinking that it was an unusual foreign flower. You've disgraced us before the young princess! She saw the flower here and found it so beautiful. She didn't recognize it, and she's well informed on botany, but that science has nothing to do with vegetables. How would it occur to you, my good Larsen, to put such a flower in the parlor? It makes us look ridiculous!"

And the magnificent blue flower, which had been brought from the vegetable garden, was removed from the manor's parlor, where it didn't belong. Indeed, the lord and lady apologized to the princess and told her that the flower was only a vegetable which the gardener had taken into his head to display, but for that reason he had been severely reprimanded.

"That's a shame and an injustice!" said the princess. "Why, he has opened our eyes to a magnificent flower that we never noticed before. He has shown us beauty where it never occurred to us to look! Every day, as long as the artichokes are in bloom, the castle gardener shall bring one up to me in my parlor!"

And this was done.

The lord and lady informed the gardener that he could again bring them a fresh artichoke blossom.

"It is basically pretty," they said. "Highly remarkable!" And the gardener was praised.

"That's what Larsen likes!" said the lord and lady. "He's a spoiled child!"

In the autumn there was a terrible storm. It grew worse during the night, so violent that many big trees on the edge of the forest were torn up by the roots. And to the great sorrow of the lord and lady—they regarded it as sorrow—but to the gardener's delight, the two big trees with all the birds' nests blew down. The screeching of the rooks and crows could be heard through the storm. They beat their wings on the windowpanes said the servants at the manor.

"Well, now you're happy, Larsen!" said the lord and lady. "The storm has felled the trees, and the birds have taken to the forest. Now there isn't a glimpse of the old days; every trace and every hint are gone! For us, it has been distressing!"

The gardener said nothing, but he thought about what he had been pondering a long time—the best way to use the splendid sunny spot that had never been at his disposal before. It was going to be the pride of the garden and the joy of the lord and lady.

The big, blown-down trees had smashed and crushed the ancient box hedges with all their cut-out shapes. Here he raised a thicket of plants, domestic plants from field and forest.

What no other gardener had thought of planting in such rich abundance in the garden of an estate he planted here in the kind of soil each one needed, and in shade or sunshine, as each species required. He tended them lovingly, and they grew gloriously.

The juniper bush from the heath of Jutland rose, in shape and color, like the Italian cypress. The shiny, prickly holly, always green in the cold of winter and in the summer sun, was a delight to the eye. In front grew ferns, many different varieties, some looking as if they were children of the palm tree, and others as if they were parents of that delicate, lovely plant we call maidenhair. Here stood the despised burdock, which, in its freshness, is so beautiful that it would make a good showing in a bouquet. The burdock was in dry soil. But lower down in the moist soil grew the dock plant, also a despised plant, yet with its height and immense leaf, so beautifully picturesque. Waist-high, with flower upon flower like a huge many-armed candelabrum, rose the great mullein, transplanted from the field. Here stood woodruff, primroses, lilies of the valley, the wild calla lily, and the delicate three-leaved wood sorrel. It was a delight to see.

In front, supported by strings of steel wire, grew rows of dwarf pear trees from French soil. They received sunshine and good care, and soon bore big, juicy fruit, as in their country of origin.

In place of the two old leafless trees, a tall flagpole was put up, from which the Danish flag flew. And close by was another pole, around which, in summer and at harvest time, the hop twined with its fragrant clusters of flowers. But in winter—according to ancient custom—a sheaf of oats was hung from it so the birds of the sky might have their meal at the joyous Christmas time.

"Our good Larsen is getting sentimental in his old age!" said the lord and lady. "But he's faithful and devoted to us!"

Around New Year's, in one of the capital's illustrated papers, a picture of the old manor house appeared. One could see the flagpole and the sheaf of oats for the birds of the sky at the joyous Christmas time. And it was mentioned and emphasized as a lovely thought that an old custom had been restored to honor and respect, and this was so characteristic of precisely this old manor.

"Everything that Larsen does," said the lord and lady, "they beat a drum for! That is a happy man! Why, we should almost be proud of having him!"

But they weren't proud at all! They felt that they were the lord and lady. They could give Larsen notice, but they didn't do it. They were good people, and there are so many good people of their kind, and that is gratifying for every Larsen.

Well, that's the story of "The Gardener and the Lord and Lady."

Now you can think about it!

The Cripple

There was an old manor house where a fine, young family lived. They had riches and many blessings; they liked to enjoy themselves, and they were very charitable. They wanted to make everybody as happy as they were themselves.

On Christmas Eve a beautifully decorated Christmas tree stood in the old banquet hall, where fires burned in the fireplaces and fir branches were hung around the old paintings. Here the manor family and their guests gathered, and there was singing and dancing.

Earlier in the evening, Christmas had already been celebrated in the servants' quarters. Here also there was a large fir tree, with lighted red and white candles, small Danish flags, paper cutouts of swans, and fishnets made of colored paper and filled with goodies. The poor children from the parish had been invited, and each one had its mother along. She didn't look very long at the Christmas tree; she looked over at the Christmas tables laid out with woolens and linens, cloth for dresses and pants. Yes, this is where the mothers and the older children were looking. Only the tiny children stretched out their hands toward the candles, the tinsel, and the flags.

This whole group had come early in the afternoon and been served Christmas pudding and roast goose with red cabbage. Then when the Christmas tree had been looked at and the gifts handed out, each one got a small glass of punch and apple fritters filled with lots of apples.

Afterward they returned to their own poor homes and talked about the "fine manner of life," which was to say the good food, and the presents were once again thoroughly inspected.

Now, we have Garden-Kirsten and Garden-Ole. They were married to each other and earned their lodging and their daily bread by weeding and digging in the manor garden. At every Christmas party they received their goodly portion of the presents. They had five children, and all five were clothed by the manor family.

"They are charitable people, our employers," they said. "But they can afford it, and they enjoy doing it."

"There are some good clothes here for the four children to wear," said Garden-Ole, "but why is there nothing for the Cripple? They usually remember him, too, even if he isn't at the party."

It was the eldest of the children they called the Cripple. Otherwise, his name was Hans.

When little, he had been the most able and liveliest child, but all of a sudden he had become "wobbly in the legs," as they put it. He could neither stand nor walk, and now he had been bedridden for close to five years.

"Yes, I received something for him, too," said his mother. "But it's nothing much. It's only a book for him to read!"

"He won't get fat on that!" said his father.

But Hans was pleased with the book. He was a very bright boy who enjoyed reading but also used his time for working, insofar as he, who always had to lie in bed, could be of some benefit. He was good with his hands. Indeed, he put them to use knitting woolen socks—even entire bedspreads. The lady of the manor had praised them and bought them.

It was a book of fairy tales that Hans had received. In it was much to read and much to think about.

"That's of no use in this house," said his parents, "but let him read. It passes the time, and he can't always be knitting socks."

Spring came. Green things and flowers began to sprout, and weeds, too, which nettles are often called, even if there is such a pretty verse about them in a hymn:

> If all the kings marched in a row,
> In their finest fettle,
> They couldn't get the smallest leaf
> To grow upon a nettle.

There was a lot to do in the manor garden, not just for the gardener and his apprentices, but also for Garden-Kirsten and Garden-Ole.

"It's a real grind," they said. "And as soon as we've raked the paths and made them really nice, they get walked on all over again. There's a flood of visitors at the manor. That must cost a lot! But the owners are rich people!"

"Things are strangely divided," said Ole. "The minister says we are all the Lord's children. Why, then, is there such a difference?"

"It comes from man's original sin!" said Kirsten.

In the evening they talked about it again, with Cripple-Hans lying in bed with his book of fairy tales.

Hardships, work, and toil had put calluses on their hands and calluses on their opinions and judgments, too. They couldn't cope with things; they couldn't manage, and talking about it made them more sulky and angry.

"Some people have wealth and happiness, others only poverty! Why should we suffer for our first parents' curiosity and disobedience? We wouldn't have behaved as those two did!"

"Yes, we would!" said Cripple-Hans suddenly. "It's all right here in this book!"

"What's in the book?" asked his parents.

And Hans read for them the old fairy tale about the woodcutter and his wife. They, too, bickered about Adam's and Eve's curiosity, which was the cause of their misfortune. Then the king of the land came by. "Follow me home," he said, "and you shall have everything that I do—a seven-course dinner and one extra course just for display. It's in a closed tureen, and you

mustn't touch it, because then it's all over with living like a
king!" "What could there be in the tureen?" said the woman.
"That's none of our business," said the man. "Well, I'm not
curious," said the woman, "but I'd just like to know why we
don't dare lift the lid. It must be some delicacy!" "If only
there's no mechanical trick about it," said the man, "like a pis-
tol shot that goes bang and wakes up the whole house!" "Eeek!"
said the woman, and she didn't touch the tureen. But during
the night she dreamed that the lid lifted itself, and there was an
aroma of the most wonderful punch, like the kind served at
weddings and funerals. In it lay a large silver coin with an
inscription, "If you drink of this punch, you will become the
two richest people in the world, and everyone else will become
paupers!" And just then the woman woke up and told her husband about her dream. "You think too much about that thing,"
he said. "We could lift it gently," said the woman. "Very
gently," said the man. And the woman lifted the lid with great
care. Then two small, nimble mice hopped out and disappeared
at once into a mousehole. "Good night!" said the king. "Now
you can go home and lie in your own bed. Don't blame Adam
and Eve anymore. You yourselves have been just as inquisitive
and ungrateful!"

"Where did that story in the book come from?" said Garden-
Ole. "It's just as if it were meant for us. It's really something to
think about!"

The next day they went to work again. They were roasted by

the sun and soaked to the skin by the rain. Within them were sulky thoughts that they brooded over.

It was still light that evening at home. They had just eaten their milk porridge.

"Read the story about the woodcutter to us again," said Garden-Ole.

"But there are so many lovely stories in this book," said Hans, "so many that you don't know."

"Yes, but those I don't care about!" said Garden-Ole. "I want to hear the one I know!"

And he and his wife heard it again.

More than one evening they came back to that story.

"Actually, I can't quite make sense out of it," said Garden-Ole. "It's the same with people as it is with milk—it turns sour and separates. Part of it becomes curd cheese, and the rest the thin, watery whey. Some people are lucky in everything, enjoy all that life has to offer, and never know sorrow or want."

All this Cripple-Hans heard. His legs were feeble but there was nothing wrong with his head. He read aloud for them from his book of fairy tales, read about "The Man without Sorrow and Want." Yes, where could he be found, for found he must be:

The king lay sick in bed and could not be cured unless he was dressed in a shirt that had been borne and worn on the body of a man who could truthfully say he had never known sorrow or want. A message was sent to every country in the world, to all the castles and manors, to all the prosperous and happy people. But when they were questioned very closely, every one of them had actually suffered sorrow and want. "I haven't!" said the swineherd, who sat on the edge of the ditch, laughing and singing. "I'm the happiest person!" "Give us your shirt, then," said the emissaries. "You will be paid for it with half a kingdom." But he had no shirt at all, yet he called himself the happiest person!

"Now, he was a fine fellow!" shouted Garden-Ole, and he and his wife laughed as they hadn't laughed for years.

Then the schoolmaster came by.

"How happy you are!" he said. "That is a rare thing here in this house. Have you won a prize in the lottery?"

"No, nothing like that!" said Garden-Ole. "It's because Hans was reading to us from his book of fairy tales. He read about 'The Man without Sorrow and Want,' and that fellow had no shirt. It certainly cheers you up to hear such things, and from a printed book at that! Everyone has his load to bear; one is not alone. There's always comfort in that!"

"Where did you get the book?" asked the schoolmaster.

"Our Hans got it at Christmas time over a year ago. The manor family gave it to him. They know he likes to read and of course that he is a cripple. At the time, we would rather have seen him get two serviceable shirts. But the book is remarkable—it can almost answer one's thoughts!"

The schoolmaster took the book and opened it.

"Let's have the same story again," said Garden-Ole. "I don't quite get it yet. And then he must also read the other one about the woodcutter."

These two stories were, indeed, enough for Ole. They were like two sunbeams shining into that humble room, into the downtrodden thoughts that had made them cross and sulky.

Hans had read the whole book, read it many times. The fairy tales carried him out into the world, where he of course couldn't go because his legs would not carry him.

The schoolmaster sat beside his bed. They talked together, and it was a pleasure for both of them.

From that day on, the schoolmaster visited Hans more often, when his parents were at work. It was like a party for the boy each time he came. How he listened to what the old man told him about the size of the world and its many lands, and that the sun was almost half a million times larger than the earth and so far away that a cannonball traveling at its usual speed would take all of twenty-five years to get from the sun to the earth, while rays of light could reach the earth in eight minutes.

All this is well known to any smart school boy, of course, but to Hans it was all new, and even more wonderful than what was in the book of fairy tales.

Two or three times a year the schoolmaster dined with the manor family, and on one such occasion he told about how important the book of fairy tales was in that poor house, how just two stories had brought about spiritual awakening and blessing. The bright, sickly little boy had, through his reading, brought reflection and joy into the house.

When the schoolmaster set off from the manor house for home, the lady pressed a couple of shiny silver dollars into his hand for little Hans.

"Father and Mother must have them," said the boy, when the schoolmaster brought him the coins.

And Garden-Ole and Garden-Kirsten both said, "Cripple-Hans, after all, is also a great help and a blessing to us!"

A few days later, when his parents were away at work at the manor house, the manor family's carriage stopped outside. It was the kindhearted lady who came, happy that her Christmas gift had been such comfort and pleasure to the boy and his parents.

She brought fine bread, fruit, and a bottle of sweet syrup, but what was still more delightful, she brought him a gilded cage containing a little black bird that could whistle very prettily. The cage with the bird in it was placed on the old chest of drawers a little way from the boy's bed. There he could see and hear the bird, and, yes, people all the way out on the highway could hear its song.

Garden-Ole and Garden-Kirsten didn't return home until after the lady had driven away. They sensed how happy Hans was, though they thought the present he had received would only bring trouble.

"Rich people don't think things through," they said. "Now we have that to take care of, too. Cripple-Hans can't do it, of course. The cat will end up with it!"

A week went by, and still another week. During that time

the cat had often been in the room without frightening the bird, much less harming it. Then a great event occurred. It was in the afternoon, while his parents and the other children were at work, and Hans was quite alone. He had the book of fairy tales in his hand and was reading about the fisherman's wife who got all her wishes fulfilled. She wished to be king, and she became one; she wished to be emperor, and she became one; but next she wished to be the dear Lord—and there she was, sitting in the muddy ditch she had come from.

Now that story had nothing to do with the bird or the cat, but it just happened to be the story he was reading when this event took place. He always remembered that afterward.

The cage stood on the chest of drawers, and the cat stood on the floor staring fixedly, with its yellow-green eyes, up at the bird. There was something in the cat's look that seemed to say to the bird, "How pretty you are! I wouldn't mind eating you!" That Hans understood—he could read it in the cat's face.

"Get away, cat!" he shouted. "You just get out of this room!"

The cat seemed to be getting ready to spring.

Hans couldn't reach it and had nothing to throw at it but his dearest treasure, the book of fairy tales. This he threw, but the cover was loose and flew one way, while the book itself, with all its pages, flew the other. With slow steps the cat retreated

slightly and looked at Hans as if to say, "Don't get yourself mixed up in this affair, little Hans! I can walk and I can spring. You can't do any of these things!"

Hans was very upset and kept his eyes on the cat. The bird also became uneasy. There wasn't anybody he could call. The cat seemed to know that, and it made ready to spring again. Hans shook his bedspread at it—he had no trouble using his hands—but the cat paid no attention to the bedspread. And after that, too, had been thrown at it to no avail, the cat sprang up onto the chair and then onto the windowsill. There it was closer to the bird.

Hans could feel the blood racing through his veins, but he didn't think about it. He thought only about the cat and the bird. The boy couldn't get out of bed without help, nor could he stand on his legs, much less walk. It was as if his heart turned over when he saw the cat leap from the window onto the chest and bump the cage so that it overturned. The bird fluttered about in bewilderment inside the cage.

Hans screamed; a spasm went through him. And without thinking about it, he sprang out of bed, went toward the chest, threw the cat down, and got hold of the cage, where the bird was in great terror. He held the cage in his hand and ran through the door onto the road.

Then tears streamed down his cheeks, and he rejoiced and shouted, "I can walk! I can walk!"

He had recovered the use of his legs. Such a thing can happen, and it happened to Hans.

The schoolmaster lived close by, and he ran to him in his bare feet with only his shirt and bed jacket on, holding the cage with the bird in it.

"I can walk!" he shouted. "Oh, Lord, my Lord!" And he sobbed out of sheer joy.

And there was joy in the house of Garden-Ole and Garden-Kirsten. "We will never live to see a happier day," they both said.

Hans was called up to the manor house. He had not walked

that road for many years. It was as if the trees and the nut bushes that he knew so well nodded to him and said, "Hello, Hans! Welcome back out here!" The sun shone on his face and right into his heart.

The manor family, the young, blessed couple, let him sit with them and looked as happy as if he were one of their own family.

But the happiest was the lady, for she had given him the book of fairy tales and the little songbird. The bird was now dead, to be sure, having died of fright, but it had in a way been the means of his recovery. And the book had brought him and his parents to an awakening. He still had it, and he wanted to keep it and read it, no matter how old he became. Now he could also be a help to his family at home. He wanted to learn a trade—most of all he wanted to be a bookbinder, "because," he said, "then I can get all the new books to read!"

Later in the afternoon the manor lady called both his parents up to her. She and her husband had talked together about Hans—he was a devout and intelligent boy, with a love of reading and a facility for learning. The Lord always champions a worthy cause.

That evening his parents were really happy when they returned home from the manor house, especially Kirsten. But a week later she cried, for then little Hans went away. He was dressed in good clothes. He was a good boy, but now he was to travel far across the salty sea to go to a grammar school far away, and many years would pass before they might see him again.

He did not take the book of fairy tales with him—his parents wanted to keep it to remember him by. And his father often read from it, but never anything but those two stories, for those he knew so well.

And they received letters from Hans, each one happier than the last. He lived with nice people, in good circumstances. But most fun of all was going to school—there was so much to learn and to know. He wished now only to live to be a hundred years old and eventually become a schoolmaster.

"If we could only live to see it!" said his parents, and they held each other by the hand, as if at communion.

"Just think of what has happened to Hans!" said Ole. "The Lord also thinks of the poor man's child! That this could happen to the Cripple! Isn't it just as if Hans had read it to us out of the book of fairy tales!"

Auntie Toothache

Where did we get this story? Do you want to know? We got it from the barrel—the one filled with wastepaper.

Many a good and rare book has ended up at the butcher's and the grocer's, not to be read but to fill a practical need. They must have paper as containers for cornstarch and coffee beans, as wrapping for salted herring, butter, and cheese. Written material can also be useful.

Often things that shouldn't go into the barrel do go into the barrel.

I know a grocer's helper, the son of a butcher. He has worked his way up from the basement storeroom to the shop at street level—a person of great learning, wrapping-paper learning, of both the printed and handwritten variety. He has an interesting collection, and in it are a number of important documents from the wastepaper baskets of one or another busy, absent-minded official, one or another confidential letter from girlfriend to girlfriend—reports of scandals which were not to go further, not to be mentioned by anyone. He is a living rescue operation for no small part of our literature, and he collects from a wide field—he has his parents' store and that of his present employer, and there he has rescued many a book, or pages of a book, well worth reading twice.

He has shown me his collection of printed and handwritten materials from the barrel, the richest of them from the butcher's. There lay a couple of leaves from a largish composition book. The especially beautiful and clear handwriting attracted my attention at once.

"That was written by the student!" he said. "The student who lived right across the street and died a month ago. One can see that he suffered terribly from toothaches. It's a lot of fun to read! There is just a little left of what was written. It was a whole book and a bit more. My parents gave the student's landlady a half pound of green soap for it. Here is what I managed to save."

I borrowed it, I read it, and now I pass it on.

The title was:

Auntie Toothache

I

Auntie gave me candy when I was little. My teeth could stand it then and weren't ruined. Now I am older and have become a university student; she still spoils me with sweets. She says that I am a poet.

I have something of the poet in me, but not enough. Often when I walk through the city streets, it seems to me as if I am walking in a great library: the houses are the bookcases, and each floor a shelf with books. Over there is a story of everyday life; there, a good old comedy and scientific works from every field; over here smutty literature and good reading. I can fantasize and philosophize about that whole library.

There is something of the poet in me, but not enough. Many people no doubt have just as much of it in them as I do without wearing a sign or a badge with the name "poet" on it.

There has been given to them and to me a divine gift, a blessing great enough for oneself but much too little to be portioned out to others. It comes like a ray of sunlight and fills one's thought and soul. It comes like a fragrance of flowers, like a melody one knows and remembers, though not where it is from.

The other evening I was sitting in my room and felt a need for something to read, but had nary a book, not a leaf. At that moment a leaf fell, fresh and green, from the linden tree, and the breeze carried it in through the window to me.

I examined its many branching veins. A little bug was moving across them, as if making a thorough study of the leaf. This made me think of human wisdom. We too crawl around on a leaf; we know only it, but we immediately deliver a lecture on the whole great tree—the root, the trunk, and the crown; the great tree: God, the world, and immortality—and all we know about it is one little leaf!

As I was sitting there, I received a visit from Auntie Millie.

I showed her the leaf with the bug and told her my thoughts about them, and her eyes shone.

"You are a poet!" she said. "Perhaps the greatest we have! If I should live to see it, I would go gladly to my grave. Ever since the brewer Rasmussen's funeral you have amazed me with your powerful imagination!"

Auntie Millie said this and kissed me.

Who was Auntie Millie, and who was Rasmussen the brewer?

II

My mother's aunt was called "Auntie" by us children; we had no other name for her.

She gave us jam and sugar, even though it was damaging to our teeth; but she said that she had a weakness for sweet children. It was cruel to deny them a little something sweet when they liked it so much.

And that's why we liked Auntie so much.

She was an old maid, as far back as I can remember, always old! She never changed in age.

In earlier years she suffered a great deal from toothaches and was always talking about it; and so it was that her friend, Rasmussen the brewer, made a joke and called her Auntie Toothache.

He hadn't done any brewing in recent years, and lived off the interest on his savings. He visited Auntie often, and was older than she. He had no teeth at all—only some black stumps.

As a child he had eaten too much sugar, he told us children, and that's how a person gets to look like that.

Auntie had surely never eaten sugar in her childhood; she had the most beautiful white teeth.

She took good care of them and didn't sleep with them at night!—said Rasmussen the brewer. We children knew that he said it just to be mean, but Auntie said he didn't mean anything by it.

One morning at brunch she told about a horrible dream she had had the night before—one of her teeth had fallen out.

"That means," she said, "that I will lose a true friend!"

"If it was a false tooth," the brewer said with a chuckle, "then it can only mean that you will lose a false friend!"

"You are a rude old man!" Auntie said and was angry—a state I have never seen her in before or since.

Later she said that her old friend had only been teasing her. He was the finest person on earth, and when he should happen to die, he would become one of God's little angels in heaven.

I thought a lot about that transformation and whether I would be able to recognize him in his new form.

When Auntie was young, and he was young too, he had proposed to her. She took too long to think it over, did nothing, went on doing nothing, and remained always an old maid, but always a true friend.

And then the brewer Rasmussen died.

He was taken to his grave in the most expensive hearse and had a large procession of people in uniform, wearing medals.

Auntie stood by the window dressed in mourning, together with all of us children, except for our little brother, who had been brought by the stork the week before. When the hearse and the procession had passed and the street was empty, Auntie wanted to go, but I didn't—I was waiting for the angel, Brewer Rasmussen. He must by now have become one of God's little winged children and would surely appear.

"Auntie," I said, "don't you think he'll come now? Or that when the stork brings us a little brother again, he'll bring us Angel Rasmussen?"

Auntie was completely overwhelmed by my imagination and

said, "That child will become a great poet!" And she kept repeating this all through my school years, after my confirmation, and even now that I am a student at the university.

She was, and is, to me the most sympathetic of friends, both in my poet's agony and in my dental agony. I have attacks of both.

"Just write all your thoughts down," she said, "and put them in the desk drawer! That's what Jean Paul did—he became a great poet, even though I don't particularly like him. He isn't thrilling! You must be thrilling! And you will be thrilling!"

The night after that talk I lay full of longing and anguish, need and desire to become the great poet Auntie saw and sensed in me. I suffered the agony of a poet, but there is a worse agony—the agony of *toothache!* It squeezed and squashed me. I became a writhing worm with an herb bag and a mustard plaster.

"I know all about it!" said Auntie.

There was a sorrowful smile on her lips, and her teeth gleamed so white.

But I must begin a new chapter in my and Auntie's story.

III

I had moved into a new apartment and lived there a month. I was talking about it with Auntie.

"I live with a quiet family. They don't pay me any heed, even if I ring three times. Besides, it is a real hubbub-house, full of clamor and din from wind and weather and people. I live just above the entrance gate; every carriage that drives in or out makes the pictures on the walls dance. The gate slams and shakes the house as if there were an earthquake. If I'm lying in bed, the jolts go right through all my limbs, but that's supposed to be good for the nerves. If it's windy, and it's always windy in this country, the long window hooks outside swing back and forth and hit against the wall, and the bell on the gate to the neighbor's yard rings with each gust of wind.

The people who live in the building straggle home from late in the evening until far into the night. The lodger just above me, who gives trombone lessons during the day, comes home the latest of all and doesn't go to bed until he has taken a short midnight walk with heavy tread and iron-heeled boots.

There are no storm windows, but there is a broken window-pane that the landlady has pasted over with some paper. The wind blows in through the crack anyway and produces a sound like the buzzing of a hornet. That is music to sleep by. If I do finally fall asleep, I am soon awakened by the crowing of cocks—hen and rooster announce from the chicken coop of the man in the basement that it will soon be morning. The small Norwegian ponies—they don't have any stable—are tied up in the storeroom under the stairs and kick against the door and the paneling for exercise.

The day dawns. The janitor, who lives with his family in the attic, comes thundering down the stairs. The wooden shoes clatter, the gate slams, and the house shakes. And when this is over, the lodger above begins to do his exercises. He lifts a heavy iron ball in each hand, but he can't hold onto them, and they fall on the floor again and again, while at the same time the building's younger generation, which has to go to school, rushes off screaming. I go to the window and open it to get some fresh air, and it is refreshing—when I can get it, and when the young woman in the rear of the building is not cleaning gloves with chemical stain remover—it's her livelihood. Otherwise, it is a pleasant building, and I live with a quiet family."

This was the account I gave Auntie about my apartment, although my delivery was livelier, for an oral presentation is more vivid than anything written.

"You are a poet!" cried Auntie. "Just write down what you have said, and you'll be as good as Dickens! Indeed, to me you are much more interesting! You paint when you speak! You describe your building so that one can see it! It gives me the shivers! Keep on with your poetry! Put some life into it—people, beautiful people, especially unhappy ones!"

I wrote down my description of the house as it stands, with its noise and noisesomeness, but put only myself into it, without any plot. That came later!

IV

It was in the wintertime, late at night after the theater was usually closed. It was terrible weather, a snowstorm that was almost impossible to make any headway through.

Auntie was at the theater, and I showed up to accompany her home, but it was difficult to get anywhere, to say nothing of accompanying someone else. All the cabs were engaged. Auntie lived way off in another part of town, while my dwelling was close to the theater. If this had not been the case, we would have had to seek shelter in a sentry box for a while.

We stumbled along in the deep snow, engulfed by whirling snowflakes. I variously lifted her, supported her, and propelled her. Only twice did we fall, but we fell softly.

We reached my gate, where we shook ourselves off. On the stairs, too, we shook ourselves again, and yet there was still enough snow on us to cover the floor of the vestibule.

We wrestled off our overcoats and our sweaters, and whatever other clothing could be removed. The landlady lent Auntie dry stockings and a robe. These things she would need, said the landlady, and added that it would be impossible for my aunt to get home that night, which was true. She asked Auntie to make do with her parlor, where she would make up a bed for her on the sofa, in front of the permanently locked-off door to my room.

And so she stayed.

The fire burned in my stove, the tea urn was brought to the table, and it came to be cozy in the little room, if not as cozy as in Auntie's own room, where in the wintertime there are heavy draperies before the door, heavy draperies before the windows, and double carpets on the floor, with three layers of thick paper underneath. One sits there as if in a well-corked bottle full of warm air, but, as I have said, it also came to be cozy in my place. Outside the wind was whistling.

Auntie talked and reminisced. The days of her youth came back; the brewer came back, and other old memories.

She could remember when I got my first tooth, and the family's delight over it.

My first tooth! That innocent tooth, shining like a tiny drop of white milk—indeed, a milk tooth!

One came and then more came, a whole rank of them, side by side, both above and below—the loveliest of baby teeth, and yet these were only the vanguard, not the real ones that have to last a whole lifetime.

They, too, came, and the wisdom teeth as well, the flankers for each rank, born in great trouble and pain.

They also go, every single one of them! They go before their term of service is up. Even the last tooth goes, and that is not a happy day. That is a day for mourning.

Then you are old, even if you feel young.

Such thoughts and talk are not pleasant, and yet we came to talk about all this. We went back to my childhood years and talked and talked. It was twelve o'clock before Auntie went to settle down for the night in the next room.

"Good night, my sweet child," she called. "Now I'm going to sleep as if I were lying in my own trundle bed."

And she slept peacefully, but there was no peace, either in the house or outside. The storm rattled the windows, banged the long, dangling iron hooks against the house, and rang the neighbor's bell in the backyard. The lodger upstairs had come home, and he was still taking his little nightly tour back and forth. He kicked his boots off and went to bed and to sleep, but he snores so that anyone with good ears can hear him through the ceiling.

I found no sleep; I couldn't settle down. Nor did the weather settle down. It was extremely lively. The wind whistled and sang in its way. My teeth also began to be lively, and they whistled and sang in their way. They were striking up a terrible toothache.

There was a draft from the window. The moon shone in upon the floor; the light came and went as the clouds came and went in the stormy weather. There was a restlessness in the shadow and light, but eventually the shadow on the floor looked like something. I looked at the moving shape and felt an icy blast.

On the floor sat a thin, long figure, such as a child might draw with a piece of chalk on a slate, something supposed to look like a person—a single thin line forms the body, and one line and then another are the arms; each of the legs is also just a line, and the head a polygon.

Soon the figure became more distinct. It turned out to have some sort of cloth robe, very thin and very fine, but it revealed that the figure was a female.

I heard a humming sound. Was it she or the wind that was droning like a hornet through the crack in the pane?

No, it was she, Madame Toothache herself! Her Most High Terribleness, Satania Infernalis! God deliver and preserve us from her visits!

"It is good to be here!" she hummed. "These are nice quarters—water-logged ground, swampy ground! Here have been mosquitoes humming around, with poison in their stings, and now I have the sting. It must be honed on human teeth. Those in the mouth of the fellow in bed here shine so white. They have defied sweet and sour, heat and cold, nutshells and plum pits; but I shall rock them, knock them, mulch their roots with drafts, and give them cold feet!"

That was a terrifying speech, a terrifying visitor!

"So, now you're a poet!" she said. "Well, I'll make a poem of you in all the rhythms of agony! I'll work iron and steel into your body, restring your nerves with wire!"

It was as if a glowing-hot awl went jabbing into my jawbone. I writhed and I twisted.

"An excellent set of teeth," she said, "like an organ to play upon! We'll have a magnificent mouth-organ concert, with

kettledrums and trumpets, piccolo and trombone in the wisdom
tooth! A great poet, great music!"

And then she started up; she looked terrifying, even though
not more of her than her hand could be seen, the shadowy gray,
ice-cold hand, with the long, needle-thin fingers. Each of them
was an implement of torture: the thumb and the forefinger were
pincers and wrench; the middle finger ended in a pointed awl;
the ring finger was a gimlet, and the little finger, a syringe containing mosquito poison.

"I am going to teach you meter!" she said. "A great poet
must have a great toothache, a little poet a little toothache!"

"Oh, let me be a little poet!" I begged. "Let me be nothing
at all! And I'm not a poet; I only have fits of poetry, like fits of
toothache! Go away! Go away!"

"Will you acknowledge, then, that I am mightier than poetry, philosophy, mathematics, and the whole of music?" she
said. "Mightier than all those feelings that are painted on
canvas or carved in marble? I am older than any of them. I was
born near the Garden of Eden, just outside, where the wind

blew and the sodden toadstools grew. It was I who got Eve to wear clothes in the cold weather, and Adam, too. You had better believe there was power in the first toothache."

"I believe it all!" I said. "Go away! Go away!"

"Well, if you will give up being a poet, never put a verse on paper, slate, or any kind of writing material, then I will let you go, but I'll come again if you write any poetry!"

"I swear!" I said. "Only let me never see or feel you any more!"

"See me you shall, but in a fuller figure, one dearer to you than I am now. You will see me as Auntie Millie, and I will say, 'Write poetry, my sweet boy! You are a great poet, perhaps the greatest we have!' But if you believe me and start to write poetry, then I will set your verses to music and play them on your ivories! You sweet child! Remember me when you see Auntie Millie!"

Then she disappeared.

At our parting I received something like the searing jab of an awl through my jaw, but soon it subsided, and then I sort of floated off on gentle waters, gazed at white water lilies, with their broad green leaves yielding and sinking down under me, withering and dissolving. I sank with them and dissolved into peace and rest—

"To die and melt away like snow!" resounded in the water. "To vaporize into clouds, to drift away like clouds!"

There shone down to me through the water great, glowing names and inscriptions on waving victory banners—certificates of immortality written on mayfly wings.

The sleep was a deep, dreamless sleep. I didn't hear the whistling wind, the banging gate, the ringing of the neighbor's gate bell, or the lodger's strenuous gymnastics.

What bliss!

Then came a gust of wind so strong that the locked door to Auntie's room sprang open. Auntie sprang up, put on her shoes, got dressed, and came into my room.

I was sleeping like one of God's angels, she said, and she hadn't the heart to wake me.

I later woke up by myself and opened my eyes. I had totally forgotten that Auntie was here in the building, but I remembered it right away and remembered my toothache vision. Dream and reality were blended together.

"I suppose you didn't write anything last night after we said good night?" she said. "If you only had! You are my poet, and you will always be!"

It seemed to me that she smiled so insidiously. I didn't know if she was the good-natured Auntie Millie, who loved me, or the terrifying one I had made the promise to the night before.

"Have you written any poetry, my sweet child?"

"No, no!" I shouted. "You are Auntie Millie, aren't you?"

"Who else?" she said. And it was Auntie Millie.

She kissed me, got into a cab, and drove home.

I wrote down what is written here. It isn't in verse, and it will never be printed.

Indeed, this is where the manuscript ended.

My young friend, the grocer's assistant in-training, couldn't turn up the missing sheets. They had gone out into the world as wrapping paper around salted herring, butter, and green soap. They had fulfilled their destiny!

The brewer is dead; Auntie is dead; the student is dead, the one whose flashes of inspiration ended up in the barrel.

This is the end of the story—the story of Auntie Toothache.

Notes

The Tinderbox

Andersen used "The Tinderbox" ("Fyrtøiet") as the lead piece in his first slender fascicle of tales, *Eventyr, fortalte for Børn. Første Samling. Første Hefte* (*Tales, Told for Children. First Installment. First Part*), which was published in May 1835, a scant month after the appearance of his first critical success, the novel *Improvisatoren* (*The Improvisatore*).

Andersen himself was very excited about his new undertaking. In a letter written New Year's Day he announced to his Odense friend Henriette Hanck: "Now I am beginning some 'children's tales.' I'm aiming to conquer the coming generation, you know." Later, in the preface to the fascicle of tales published in 1837, he described in some detail how he came to write his *Tales, Told for Children:* "During my childhood I loved to hear tales and stories; many of these are still quite living in my mind. Some seem to be Danish in origin, emanating from the folk. I have never found these among other peoples. I have retold them in my own way, permitted myself to make any change I thought fitting, let my fantasy refresh the faded hues in the images. That is how these four tales came into being: 'The Tinderbox,' 'Little Claus and Big Claus,' 'The Princess on the Pea,' and 'The Traveling Companion.'"

However, reviewers greeted Andersen's *Tales, Told for Children,* with a mixed response—in particular, they saw no moral lesson fit for impressionable young children in "The Tinderbox," a tale about a soldier who without a second thought repays an old lady by killing her and abducts a sleeping princess, who rather enjoys the experience! Andersen, as always, took the criticism very much to heart, as can be seen in the petulant remarks with which he opened his preface of 1837: "None of my works has been evaluated so diversely as *Tales, Told for Children.* While individuals whose judgment I value highly have declared them the most valuable of anything I have written, others have thought that these tales were quite insignificant and advised me not to write more. An evaluation so diverse and the apparent silence with which the public press has disregarded them has diminished my desire to produce any more of this genre."

The Round Tower (*Rundetaarn*), to which the witch compared the eyes of the third dog, was an astronomical observatory that dominated the skyline of nineteenth-century Copenhagen.

The Princess on the Pea

"The Princess on the Pea" ("Prindsessen paa Ærten") was published in Andersen's first fascicle of tales, *Eventyr, fortalte for Børn. Første Samling. Første Hefte,* in 1835.

Andersen says in the preface to his installment of tales published in 1837 that "The Princess on the Pea" is based on a tale he heard as a child. This folktale is unrecorded in Denmark, but that it is a part of Swedish tradition has been pointed out by Georg Christensen in his essay "H. C. Andersen og de danske Folkeeventyr" ("H. C. Andersen and Danish Folk Tales") in *Danske Studier* (1906). The tale as recorded in Sweden has the title "Prinsessa' som lå' på sju ärter" ("The Princess Who Lay on Seven Peas") and is about a poor girl who, hoping to make her way in the world, takes the advice of her pet dog and poses as a princess. The suspicious queen subjects the girl to several tests, in the last of which she puts seven peas under as many mattresses for the girl to sleep on. The dog tells the girl about it so in the morning she can claim to have slept badly, as a true princess would. Elias Bredsdorff in *Hans Christian Andersen: The Story of His Life and Work 1805–75* (1975) points out, "In the Swedish version, therefore, the heroine wins by cheating, whereas in Andersen's version the heroine proves herself to be a real princess by actually being hypersensitive."

It has been claimed that the literary source for "The Princess on the Pea" is Ludwig Tieck's *Puss in Boots* (*Der gestiefelte Kater*), 1797, which in turn may stem from a story in an even older work, Charles Perrault's *Histoires ou contes du temps passé avec des moralités* (*Stories or Tales of Olden Times, with Some Moral Lessons*), 1697; but neither Perrault nor Tieck uses the pea and the mattress—only the motif of the cat as adviser is present in their versions. It seems better to take Andersen's word for it and consider "The Princess on the Pea" a retelling of a Danish variant of this ancient folktale.

The Traveling Companion

"The Traveling Companion" ("Reisekammeraten") was published in Andersen's second slender volume of tales, *Eventyr, fortalte for Børn. Første Samling. Andet Hefte (Tales, Told for Children. First Installment. Second Part)*, in 1835.

This tale is a revised version of "The Dead Man: A Folk Tale from Fyn," which had appeared as the final text of Andersen's first poetry collection, *Digte (Poems)*, in 1830. It was accompanied by the following note: "As a child it was my greatest pleasure to listen to tales; a great number of these are still alive in my memory, and some of them are not very well—or not at all—known. I have retold one here, and if I see it accepted with applause, I shall retell more in the same manner and publish a cycle of Danish folktales."

"The Dead Man" displays two of the most striking aspects of Andersen's early authorship: in style it copies the mannered and ornate work of the eighteenth-century Romantic author J. K. A. Musäus, and in subject it is a retelling of a story already known to him, in this instance the Danish folktale "The Help of the Dead" ("Den dødes hjælp"). For a detailed examination of the revision that turned the unsuccessful early "Dead Man" into "The Traveling Companion," see the Introduction to this volume.

According to Danish folk belief, small elves called *nisser,* such as the one that John saw on the church tower, inhabit all rural buildings, especially those not in constant, daily use.

The Little Mermaid

"The Little Mermaid" was published as "Den lille Havfrue" in *Eventyr, fortalte for Børn. Første Samling. Tredie Hefte (Tales, Told for Children. First Installment. Third Part)*, in 1837.

In the preface, entitled "To the Older Readers," for this volume, Andersen admits that "The Little Mermaid" is not primarily for children: "If I were to have it published separately as a little book, then people might make greater demands on it, so I decided it would be best to have it included in the in-progress cycle of fairy tales. Any one of the others is perhaps more suited to children than this one whose deeper meaning only adults understand, but I nonetheless hope that children will enjoy it, and the dissolution scene itself, taken literally, will engage them."

Indeed, the end of this tale has proved fascinating for adults as well. During the 1960s in Denmark a critical battle arose between those who thought the happy ending had been added to a work which otherwise pointed toward a tragic conclusion and those who thought the ending was an integral part of the tale. Evidence suggesting that the latter critics are correct comes from Andersen himself. The tale was planned early in 1836, and in a letter of February 1836, Andersen calls it by the title "Luftens Døttre" ("Daughters of the Air"); by May he had changed the title to "Havets Døttre" ("Daughters of the Sea"). As was later the case with "The Ugly Duckling" and "The Cripple," Andersen began with a title that almost gave away the theme of the story and moved toward one more noncommital. The variation in title, however, shows that the idea for the end of "The Little Mermaid" was with Andersen from the very first stages of its composition.

A letter to B. S. Ingemann dated 11 February 1837 contains some interesting observations not only about the theme of "The Little Mermaid" but about the depth of Andersen's commitment to it (and presumably to its ending):

At the earliest opportunity you shall receive a new installment of children's tales—which of course you don't care for. Heiberg says they are the best I have written. The latest tale, "The Little Mermaid," you will like; it is better than "Thumbelina" ["Tommelise"] and is, except for "The Little Abbess's Story" ["Den lille Abbedisses Historie"] in *The Improvisatore* [*Improvisatoren*], the only one of my works that has affected me while I was writing it. You smile, perhaps? Well, I don't know how other writers feel! *I* suffer with my characters; I share their humors, whether good or bad; and I can be nice or nasty according to the scene on which I happen to be working. This latest, third installment of tales for children is probably the best, and you're going to like it! Yes, your wife will like it very much! I have not, like de la Motte-Fouqué in "Undine," allowed the mermaid's acquiring of an immortal soul to depend upon an alien creature, upon the love of a human being. I'm sure that's wrong! It would depend rather a lot on chance, wouldn't it? I *won't* accept that sort of thing in this world. I have permitted my mermaid to follow a more natural, more divine path. No other writer, I believe, has indicated it yet, and that's why I am glad to have it in my tale. You'll see for yourself!"

The chief proponent of the view that Andersen merely tacked on a happy ending is Eigil Nyborg, in *Den indre linie i H. C. Andersens eventyr* (*The Underlying Thread in H. C. Andersen's Tales*), 1962. His main opponent is Søren Baggesen in an article, "Individuation eller Frelse" ("Individuation or Redemption"), which appeared in *Kritik* (1967).

Literary sources for this tale are the German Romantic work *Undine* (1811) by Friedrich de la Motte-Fouqué and B. S. Ingemann's own story, published in 1817, *De Underjordiske* (*The Creatures from the Underworld*).

Although Andersen took great pains with his tales, writing and rewriting them until he was finally satisfied, occasionally he did err, as when the grandmother (p. 45) says they can "rest in our grave" ("hvile sig ud i sin Grav"), contradicting her earlier statement that "merfolk" have no graves but turn into foam on the water when they cease to exist.

The famous bronze statue of the little mermaid by Edvard Eriksen was set up on Langelinie, the harbor promenade of Copenhagen, in 1913.

The Swineherd

Andersen published "The Swineherd" ("Svinedrengen") in *Eventyr, fortalte for Børn. Ny Samling. Tredie Hefte* (*Tales, Told for Children. New Installment. Third Part*) in 1842.

In his notes to the collected edition *Eventyr og Historier* (*Tales and Stories*), 1862, Andersen indicates the source for this tale: "'The Swineherd' has a few features from an old Danish folktale, which, in the manner it was told to me as a child, could not be decently repeated." The folktale in question, known as "Den stolte jomfru" ("The Proud Maiden"), has a happy ending, which Andersen saw fit to discard in his quite radical reworking of the tale.

When he wrote to Henriette Hanck on 10 June 1840, Andersen bragged to his friend about "The Swineherd": "When I get to town, a new installment of tales will be published, containing 'The Swineherd,' 'The Rose Elf,' and 'The Sandman.' You know 'The Swineherd,' don't you? In Copenhagen it has become one of my best-known tales, since Phister [one of the leading actors of his day] has recited it four or five times on the stage. People regard it as the most entertaining of all my tales." However, Andersen's plans to publish a new installment languished until 1842, when he was able to add a fourth tale, "The Buckwheat," to the three that had been lying in a drawer since the spring of 1840.

The Buckwheat

"The Buckwheat" ("Boghveden") was originally written in 1839 for a Danish "folk calendar," a new yearly publication with stories and poems designed for a popular audience—an imitation of Germany's well-known *Deutscher Volkskalender*. However, it did not find its way into any of this publication's four issues, but was finally used to flesh out Andersen's own otherwise too slender collection of tales *Eventyr, fortalte for Børn. Ny Samling. Tredie Hefte* in 1842.

In his doctoral dissertation, *H. C. Andersen og hans Eventyr (H. C. Andersen and His Tales,* 1907), Hans Brix has suggested that Andersen's intention in this parable was to pillory the Heibergs for their arrogant treatment of him concerning the staging of his play *The Moorish Maid.* First, Mrs. Heiberg, the leading actress of her day, demanded that Andersen rewrite the title role so that it would better display her talent; then, after Andersen had made the changes, her husband Johan Ludvig Heiberg, a prominent literary figure and censor for the Royal Theater, informed the playwright that he was opposed to accepting the play. However, as H. Topsøe-Jensen has pointed out in his notes to *Tommelise. Boghveden (Thumbelina. The Buckwheat,* 1968), there is no real evidence to support Brix's assertion, and it seems better simply to accept Andersen's own words concerning his inspiration for this parable: "The story about the buckwheat is based on a folk belief that lightning chars buckwheat black."

The Nightingale

"The Nightingale" was published as "Nattergalen" in *Nye Eventyr. Første Bind. Første Samling (New Tales. First Volume. First Installment)* in 1844. The volume was dedicated to Carl Bagger "as humble thanks for the fresh thoughts and warm feelings his rich poetic compositions have given me." Bagger, a poet, came from an even more humble background than Andersen's, and the two men had been friends since Andersen's student days. In this volume's title the words "told for children" were deleted.

Andersen's date book for 1843 shows that three of the four tales for *Nye Eventyr* were brought to completion within a six-day period:

7 October—finished "The Young Swan."
10 October—composed "The Angel."
11 October—at Tivoli, an evening with Carstensens. Began the Chinese tale ["The Nightingale"].
12 October—ate at home, visited around, ended the Chinese tale.

The speed of composition suggests that the concerns dealt with in these tales not told for children must have lain ready at hand for Andersen when he decided to change his concept of the kind of tale he was writing. In a letter to B. S. Ingemann on 20 November 1843, Andersen exclaimed, "I believe—and I would be so glad if I were right—that I have figured out how to compose tales!" In each story Andersen has dealt with an aspect of his own situation, but in disguise. The dedication to Bagger and the new form of the title of the volume both indicate that he was well aware of the new level of meaning in these tales.

The public responded with enthusiasm to *Nye Eventyr*. Although the date on the title page is 1844, the book actually appeared on 11 November 1843, in time for the Christmas rush. On 18 December, Andersen's publisher informed him that the first printing of 850 copies had been sold out and a second printing had been ordered.

The idea of writing about a real nightingale and a music box can be traced back to a comment in Andersen's date book on 12 July 1838: "Wrote 'The Nightingale and the Music Box'"; but there is no trace of a draft from this period. The theme also appears in "The Swineherd," where the prince's nightingale is compared to the queen mother's music box.

The Sweethearts

"The Sweethearts" ("Kjærestefolkene") was published in *Nye Eventyr. Første Bind. Første Samling* in 1844.

In 1830, Andersen, twenty-five, fell in love with Riborg Voigt, the sister of a fellow student, who lived in Faaborg on the island of Fyn. Andersen proposed to her, but she was already engaged to the man she later married. For several years after this he avoided the Voigt family, but in 1840 he met them at a concert, along with Riborg's husband, though she herself was not there. He wrote to Edvard Collin's wife, Henriette, on 3 August 1840: "I saw her husband. . . . The memory is actually like amber beads; if you rub them, the old fragrance comes forth." Andersen's resistance to meeting the Voigts—and particularly Riborg—seems to have diminished after the concert, and in 1843 he saw Riborg, her husband, and children at a country fair and later drove to Faaborg with her family. It was shortly after this that he wrote "The Sweethearts."

The Ugly Duckling

"The Ugly Duckling" ("Den grimme Ælling") appeared as the last tale in the 1844 collection, *Nye Eventyr. Første Bind. Første Samling.*

The tale was begun in July 1842, when Andersen was visiting the Gisselfeldt estate. An entry in his journal for 5 July 1842 reads: "Wandered around in the forest and fields, felt listless. —Got the idea of writing a 'Story about a duck'; that helped my mood a bit." On 7 October 1843, he wrote in his date book: "Finished 'Svaneungen' [The young swan]." But when he sent the tale to the printer on 19 October, Andersen had changed the title to "The Ugly Duckling."

In his notes to the collected edition of 1862, *Eventyr og Historier* (*Tales and Stories*), Andersen wrote of the four tales that comprised *Nye Eventyr* (1844): "The first half of 'The Ugly Duckling' was written during a brief summer stay at Gisselfeldt, and the end first found its way to paper half a year later, whereas the three others ["The Angel," "The Sweethearts," and "The Nightingale"] were produced in an outpouring." It has slipped his mind here that he had attempted a first version of "The Nightingale" some five years before he wrote the story that appeared in *Nye Eventyr*. Andersen is also mistaken in remembering only a six-month interval between beginning to write "The Ugly Duckling" and finishing the tale. He did, however, remember it as being hardest to compose, perhaps because it was the most directly autobiographical. In a letter to Georg Brandes on 21 July 1869, Andersen admitted, "In 'The Ugly Duckling' there is a reflection of my own life." The tale is an allegorical treatment of the same themes that figure in his autobiographical novels *The Improvisatore* (1835) and *Only a Fiddler* (1837).

When *Nye Eventyr* was published on 10 November 1843, copies were sent to Carl Bagger, Carsten Hauch, and B. S. Ingemann. Replies from the last two indicated that "The Ugly Duckling" was their favorite among the four tales. Since its publication it has been one of the most beloved of Andersen's tales both in Denmark and abroad.

The Fir Tree

"The Fir Tree" ("Grantræet") was originally published in 1845 in *Nye Eventyr. Første Bind. Anden Samling* (*New Tales. First Volume. Second Installment*).

In notes to the collected edition of tales and stories, *Eventyr og Historier* (1862), Andersen remarks that the idea for "The Fir Tree" came to him while he was attending a performance of *Don Giovanni* at the Royal Theater in Copenhagen during the winter of 1844–45. However, as is sometimes the case in his notes to the collected edition, Andersen's memory is at fault, for *Don Giovanni* was not performed in Copenhagen during that winter season. Thus we must rely entirely on Andersen's journal and date book for any knowledge of the genesis of "The Fir Tree," and what they have to yield is very slight indeed: in his date book for 4 December 1844 he merely wrote "Eventyret Grantræet." Since he had recorded on the previous day that he had just finished another tale, it seems likely that this entry indicates the completion of a first draft.

According to a letter written 3 November 1845 to one of his German translators, Heinrich Zeise, Andersen counted "The Fir Tree" among the best tales he had written thus far. In it he has reworked many of the themes that he developed earlier in "The Daisy" ("Gaaseurten") but has focused the story more completely on the hopes of the tree and its fate, creating a more coherent allegory.

Of the two stories that the old man is asked to tell on Christmas Eve, the first, "Clumpy-Dumpy," is a folktale very similar to Andersen's own "Clod-Hans" ("Klods-Hans," 1855); the irony is that the fate of the main character in this tale that the fir tree tells and retells to his audience in the attic is exactly the opposite of that of the fir tree itself. The second story, "Ivede-Avede," is not a story at all, but a nursery rhyme that begins:

> Ivede, avede
> Kivede, kavede
>
> Drunk is our councilman,
> After him comes Numskull-Jack.

Later Andersen attempted to write a tale entitled "Ivede-Avede," but he never finished it. The fragment is to be found among his papers in the Collin Collection at the Royal Library in Copenhagen.

The Snow Queen

"The Snow Queen" ("Sneedronningen") was published in *Nye Eventyr. Første Bind. Anden Samling* in 1845.

Andersen's date book shows that "The Fir Tree" was written on 4 December 1844 and "The Snow Queen," begun the next day, was completed by 12 December. Two of the finest works in Danish literature were written within eight days. "A number of tales flowed into my soul," wrote Andersen to the Grand Duke of Weimar in January 1845: "I felt almost ill until I had them put down on paper." In a letter to B. S. Ingemann during the same month, Andersen said: "My last tale, 'The Snow Queen,' has been a great delight to write; it permeated my mind to such an extent that it came out dancing over the paper."

Two passages from Andersen's autobiography, *Mit Livs Eventyr* (*The Fairy Tale of My Life*), 1855, show that some of the images used in "The Snow Queen" had been with him since childhood. He writes of the time when his father died: "His corpse lay in the bed . . . and a cricket chirped the whole night through. 'He's dead,' my mother said to the cricket, 'you don't need to call to him. The ice maiden has fetched him.' And I understood what she meant. I remembered from the winter before, when our window panes had been frozen over, that my father had shown us a figure in the frost like that of a maiden with her arms outstretched. 'She is probably after me,' he had said in jest. And now, when he lay dead on the bed, my mother remembered this, and it occupied my thoughts also." Andersen writes of his home at that time: "The little kitchen was full of shining plates and metal pans; and by means of a ladder it was possible to go out on the roof, where, in the gutters between our house and the neighbor's, there stood a big box filled with soil and kitchen herbs—my mother's entire garden. In my tale 'The Snow Queen' that garden still blooms."

Quoted in "The Snow Queen" are a nursery rhyme (see the endnote to "The Flax") and a couplet from the hymn "Den yndigste Rose er funden" ("The Fairest of Roses Is Found"), by the Danish pietistic poet Hans Adolph Brorson (1694–1764). The theme of the hymn, which celebrates the saving mission of the child Jesus, is reflected in the story, when the humble and childlike Gerda becomes Kay's salvation. In his letter to the Grand Duke of Weimar, Andersen commented that "The Snow Queen" was about "the victory of the heart over cold intellect."

"The Snow Queen" has inspired one of the finest essays ever written on Andersen, Paul V. Rubow's "Et Vintereventyr" ("A Winter's Tale") in the volume *Reminiscenser* (*Reminiscences*), 1940.

The Shadow

"The Shadow" first appeared in *Nye Eventyr. Andet Bind. Første Samling* (*New Tales. Second Volume. First Installment*) in 1847. Later the same year Andersen published it in English translation along with "The Drop of Water," "The Story of a Mother," and three other tales in *A Christmas Greeting to My English Friends*, dedicated to Charles Dickens, whom he had met for the first time while visiting England earlier that year.

In notes to the collected edition of tales and stories, *Eventyr og Historier* (1862), Andersen recollected that he had spent part of the summer of 1846 in Naples and that it was there in Naples that he had gotten the idea to write "The Shadow." However, he is mistaken when he recalls in these notes that he waited until returning to Copenhagen to begin writing his new tale, because his journal entry for 8 and 9 June 1846 says that it was so hot he stayed inside and on the evening of the second day began writing the "story of my shadow." The opening of the tale reflects how the searing climate of Naples served as a source of inspiration for "The Shadow," and, indeed, many impressions recorded in his journal during this period have been incorporated into the "Neapolitan" part of the story.

Another autobiographical episode in "The Shadow" is the witty scene in which the learned young man asks his former shadow whether they might not use each other's first names. In the original Danish the learned man's request really concerns the use of the familiar form of the pronoun "you," which is *du* in Danish, rather than the formal *De,* which is used chiefly with strangers, persons one knows only slightly, and members of the older generation. In a letter written in May 1831 Andersen had himself made this request of Edvard Collin, whom he had known for almost ten years and regarded as a brother. He was bitterly disappointed when Collin said no.

In this tale Andersen takes a sly dig at his critics at home in Denmark, who were ever ready to point out when he was "decorating himself with borrowed feathers" by retelling a story composed by someone else; indeed, they did seem unwilling to appreciate Andersen's original contributions to these retellings. When the learned man discovers that his shadow is gone, he is annoyed, because if he tells anyone back home what has happened, they will only say he is imitating a well-known story about a man without a shadow. Here, Andersen is acknowledging his debt to Adelbert von Chamisso's widely read tale *Peter Schlemihl* (1814), which in turn may well have been inspired by E. T. A. Hoffmann's "Abenteur einer Sylvesternacht" ("A Sylvester-Night Tale").

It was Andersen's custom to read drafts of his tales aloud to friends and acquaintances, occasionally making use of their reactions and suggestions in resolving compositional problems. And so it was with "The Shadow." The original ending to the story read: "The learned man heard nothing about any of this, *for they had already done away with him, and that he could be happy about."* A later draft shows that Andersen had crossed out the italicized words and substituted instead: "for he had been decapitated." After having read the tale aloud several times with the new ending, he received a note from a friend, Ernst Weis, who had heard the tale twice and suggested that by specifying the mode of execution the author in fact distracted his audience from the more philosophical aspects of the tale. Weis had his own solution to the problem: "But the learned man didn't see anything of the festivities. He died one night in the prison. People spoke about how the arm of justice had finally reached him, but no one knew what crime he had committed; and, in fact, it was probably just as well that he had departed from this world." Andersen must have agreed with Weis's point about "decapitated," but otherwise ignored his friend's moralizing and wordy counterproposal. Instead, Andersen returned to a slightly modified version of his own original ending, "for they had already done away with him."

Reviewers of the installment of tales in which "The Shadow" appeared called this tale one of Andersen's better efforts, but it was not until 1869, when the highly respected literary critic Georg Brandes singled it out for high praise in his essay about Andersen in *Illustreret Tidende* (*Illustrated Times*), that "The Shadow" came to be acknowledged as one of Andersen's greatest masterpieces.

The Drop of Water

"The Drop of Water" was first published in English along with five other stories in *A Christmas Greeting to My English Friends* (1847), dedicated to Charles Dickens. It was first published in Danish as "Vanddraaben" in *Nye Eventyr. Andet Bind. Anden Samling* (*New Tales. Second Volume. Second Installment*) in 1848.

According to Andersen's date book entry for 8 November 1847, he had just finished writing four tales in a remarkably short period— three days. Among these was "The Drop of Water." Later in his notes to the collected edition of tales and stories, *Eventyr og Historier* (1862), he remarked that this tale was created for H. C. Ørsted, the leading Danish scientist of his day and Andersen's dear friend. The genesis of "The Drop of Water" can perhaps be traced back to 1830, when he vacationed at Hofmansgave, the country place of a botanist, Niels Hofman Bang, and wrote the following on 15 July in a letter to his young friend Ludvig Læssøe: "the last day I was at Hofmansgave I had a pleasurable experience—namely, I saw microorganisms. Think, just a little drop of water on a glass slide, and there was a whole world of creatures in which the largest were as big as grasshoppers, the smallest like pinheads. Some really did look like grasshoppers, others had the most monstrous shapes, and all of them scrambled around among each other, and the larger ones ate the smaller."

In a newspaper article in 1935, Paul Læssøe Müller discussed another possible formative influence on "The Drop of Water"— namely, *Night and Morning* (1841), a novel by the English author Bulwer-Lytton. Apparently Andersen read this work in order to practice his English just before leaving for England in 1847. The beginning of book 4 bears an interesting resemblance to Andersen's tale:

If, reader, you have ever looked through a solar microscope at the monsters in a drop of water, perhaps you have wondered to yourself how things so terrible have been hitherto unknown to you—you have felt a loathing at the limpid element you hitherto deemed so pure—you have half fancied that you would cease to be a water-drinker; yet, the next day you have forgotten the grim life that started before you, with its countless shapes, in that teeming globule; and, if so tempted by your thirst, you have not shrunk from the lying crystal, although myriads of the horrible Unseen are mangling, devouring, gorging each other, in the liquid you so tranquilly imbibe; so is it with that ancestral and master element called Life. Lapped in your sleek comforts, and lolling on the sofa of your patent conscience—when, perhaps for the first time, you look through the glass of science upon one ghastly globule in the waters that heave around, that fill up, with their succulence, the pores of earth, that moisten every atom subject to your eyes, or handled by your touch—you are startled and dismayed; you say, mentally, 'Can such things be? I never dreamed of this before! I thought what was invisible to me was non-existent in itself—I will remember this dread experiment.' The next day the experiment is forgotten.—The Chemist may rarefy the Globule—can Science make pure the World?

The Little Match Girl

"The Little Match Girl" ("Den lille Pige med Svovlstikkerne") was originally written in 1846 for *Dansk Folkekalender* (*Danish Folk Calendar*). Andersen later included it in *Nye Eventyr. Andet Bind. Anden Samling* in 1848.

In notes to his collected tales and stories, *Eventyr og Historier* (1862), Andersen tells us that he composed "The Little Match Girl" at Graasten Castle in southern Jutland when he received a letter from a Mr. Flinch, the publisher of an almanac, requesting him to write a tale about one of three pictures enclosed with the letter and promising to publish the resulting tale in the next issue of the almanac. Andersen selected the now familiar picture of a little match girl that had originally appeared in Flinch's almanac of 1843 as the illustration for an article entitled "Do Well When You Give." Notations in Andersen's date book indicate that he received the letter from Flinch on 18 November 1845 and started that very day to work on his tale. The next day he made a fair copy and sent it off to his good friend Mrs. Ingeborg Drewsen, née Collin, who was apparently to read it and then send it on to the publisher.

How was it that Andersen was able to write this tale so quickly? In *H. C. Andersen og hans Eventyr* (1907), Hans Brix suggested that "The Little Match Girl" contains a reminiscence of a story that Andersen's mother told about the cold and hunger she herself had suffered as a child when she was required by her parents to go out begging.

The Story of a Mother

Andersen's parable "The Story of a Mother" was first published in English along with "The Drop of Water," "The Shadow," and three other tales in a volume entitled *A Christmas Greeting to My English Friends* (1847), dedicated to Charles Dickens. The following year it was made available to the Danish reading public as "Historien om en Moder" in *Nye Eventyr. Andet Bind. Anden Samling.*

Concerning this story Andersen remarked in his notes to the collected edition of his tales and stories, *Eventyr og Historier* (1862): "'The Story of a Mother' sprang forth without any cause. The idea came to me as I was walking in the street and unfolded itself for me to write down. This tale is supposed to be especially popular among the Hindus, to whom it has been made available in translation."

The popularity abroad of "The Story of a Mother" is attested by the fact that in 1875 a commemorative volume in honor of Andersen's seventieth birthday was published, containing this tale in fifteen different languages—Danish, Swedish, Icelandic, German, Low German, Dutch, English, French, Spanish, Modern Greek, Russian, Polish, Czechoslovakian, Hungarian, and Finnish. This tribute to Andersen appeared only five months before he died of cancer at Rolighed, the home of his close friends the Melchiors.

The Bell

"The Bell" ("Klokken") first appeared in the children's magazine *Maanedsskrift for Børn* in May 1845, but was not published in book form until 1850, when it was included in the illustrated volume of Andersen's collected tales, *Eventyr* (*Tales*).

In his note to the collected edition of tales and stories, *Eventyr og Historier* (1862), Andersen wrote about "The Bell": "This tale and almost all the following tales and stories were of my own invention.

They lay like a little seed, needing only a current, a ray of sunshine, a drop of elixir for them to germinate." It is interesting to know that Andersen felt that this story was not suggested by an experience or a circumstance outside himself, but stemmed from his own preoccupations, for it embodies ideas that he thought about frequently, though not always in the same way. Elias Bredsdorff in *Hans Christian Andersen: The Story of His Life and Work 1805–75* (1975) makes this observation: "Anybody who tries to analyse the philosophy of his tales will find that there is in them a deep dualism. 'The Bell' and 'The Shadow,' for instance, have themes which are basically very similar, and yet they express two contrasting philosophies."

The Flax

Andersen first published "The Flax" ("Hørren") in the newspaper *Fædrelandet (The Fatherland)* on 3 April 1849. After the outbreak of war with Germany in early 1848, Andersen was deeply concerned about the fate of his country and the sufferings of its soldiers. "The Flax," an optimistic story about success found through trial and tribulation, is perhaps an attempt by Andersen to cope with his depression. It is interesting to note that he never commented on this tale.

Quoted in "The Flax" is an adaptation of a nursery rhyme often used by Danish tellers of folktales to end their stories: "Snip snap snude / Nu er eventyret ude" (Snip snap snude, now the tale is over). Andersen employs this nursery rhyme as it is recited in a game of cards called "Kørente Margrete," in which the first player says "snip" as he plays his card, after which the others in turn finish out the rhyme by saying "snap" and "snurre." "Basselure" is said as the player who wins the game plays his last card.

Andersen included "The Flax" in the first Danish illustrated edition of his collected tales, *Eventyr,* in 1850. He himself selected the young artist Vilhelm Pedersen as illustrator for this and subsequent volumes of his tales and stories.

In a Thousand Years' Time

"In a Thousand Years' Time" ("Om Aartusinder") was first published in the newspaper *Fædrelandet* on 26 January 1852 and later included in *Historier. Anden Samling (Stories. Second Installment)* in 1853.

In the year and a half before the story appeared in *Fædrelandet*, Andersen in playful correspondence with a dear friend, Henriette Wulff, who was visiting in the West Indies, had toyed first with the idea of air mail (via stork wing in a letter of late September 1850) and then with the idea of air travel as an alternative for persons, such as himself, who were subject to seasickness (in a letter of 18 December 1851). His travel book *In Sweden* (*I Sverrig*), which appeared in May 1851, contains a final chapter, "Poetry's California," eulogizing the telegraph and the railroad and exhorting the poet to make use of the Eldorado of technology: "It is our time! Poet, you possess it! Sing of it in spirit and in truth!" Andersen's attitude toward science was no doubt influenced by his affection for his friend H. C. Ørsted, the discoverer of electromagnetism.

In "In a Thousand Years' Time," however, Andersen points out that technical advancement without corresponding spiritual progress is a shallow achievement. This is a somewhat unusual stand for him to take, and we may speculate that he was influenced by the ongoing debate on the subject which he conducted with his friend the poet B. S. Ingemann and which he described to Henriette Wulff in a letter of 5 June 1853: "I carry on daily a little debate with Ingemann about the meaning of invention, since he places poetry high above science, but I do not. He admits that our age is the age of invention, but that it is only in mechanical, in material things that advances have been made. I regard these as the necessary means for spiritual advancement, the sturdy branches upon which poetry then can set its flowers. The fact that people are brought closer together, that lands and cities are changed by the steam [engine] and electromagnetism into one great congregation seems to me to be so spiritually great and magnificent, that I am uplifted by this thought as high as any poet's song has ever been able to uplift me."

Clod-Hans

Andersen first published "Clod-Hans: An Old Story Retold" ("Klods-Hans: En gammel Historie fortalt igjen") in 1855 in the collected edition of his stories, *Historier,* which was illustrated by Vilhelm Pedersen.

Andersen's earliest tales were based mainly on folktales he had heard as a child in Odense. After 1843, however, most of the tales he wrote were of his own creation; in his notes to the collected edition of his tales and stories, *Eventyr og Historier* (1862), he identifies his first three original tales as "Little Ida's Flowers" ("Den lille Idas Blomster"), "Thumbelina" ("Tommelise"), and "The Little Mermaid" ("Den lille Havfrue"). It might be recalled that in the case of "The Little Mermaid," at least, "original" means inspired by German *Kunstmärchen* rather than by a Danish folktale.

"Clod-Hans," then, represents a return by a more mature Andersen to the sources of his first inspiration, this time to the Danish folktale known as "The Princess Has Her Mouth Shut" ("Munden stoppet paa prinsessen").

"She Was No Good"

"'She Was No Good'" ("'Hun duede ikke'") was first published in *Folkekalender for Danmark* (*A Folk Calendar for Denmark*) for the year 1853. Later Andersen included it in *Historier* (*Stories*) in 1855, a collected edition drawn from two slender volumes, also entitled *Historier,* 1852 and 1853, and supplemented with a number of stories which, like "'She Was No Good,'" had first seen the light of day in various issues of *Folkekalender for Danmark.*

In notes to the collected edition of his tales and stories, *Eventyr og Historier* (1862), Andersen describes how this story was conceived:

"'She Was No Good'" had its real beginning in a few words that I heard my mother say when I was a child. One day on the street I saw a boy hurrying down to the washing place by Odense River, where his mother stood out in the water rinsing linen. I heard a widow lady well known for her severity scolding the boy from a window: "Are you going again now down to the river with hard liquor for your mother! That is horrible! Ugh! Just let me see that you never turn out to be like your mother! She is no good!" I went home and told what I had heard. Everyone said, "Yes, the washerwoman drinks! She is no good!" Only my mother defended her. "Don't judge her so harshly!" she said. "That poor woman works and slaves, stands in that cold water, and often for days at a time doesn't taste warm food. She has to have something to sustain her. What she takes probably isn't the right thing, but she doesn't have anything better! She has endured a lot; she is upstanding; she keeps her little boy clean and healthy!" My mother's mild words made a deep impression on me, since I myself along with everyone else had judged the washerwoman harshly. Many years later, another minor incident made me think about how quickly and harshly people often judge others, when a merciful heart might perceive things quite differently. Then that whole incident and my mother's words came so freshly to mind that I wrote the story "'She Was No Good.'"

In *H. C. Andersen og hans Eventyr* (1907) Hans Brix has discussed at length the autobiographical aspects of this story about a poor washerwoman, arguing that it is Andersen's impassioned defense of his mother. Brix posits that both the washerwoman and her old friend "Gimpy-Maren with the curl" are drawn from Andersen's mother Anne Marie: the washerwoman reflects the experiences of Anne Marie during her youth and middle age, and the kind Maren, especially with regard to her appearance, is his mother as she was in her later years—lame and with a cataract in one eye. In his recent monograph *H. C. Andersen & Herskabet* (*H. C. Andersen and the Lord and Lady*), 1973, Peer E. Sørensen has noted that in concluding "'She Was No Good'" with an unexpected bequest, Andersen has vitiated the position of antagonism toward the unfeeling upper classes that he has maintained throughout the rest of the story.

The Old Oak Tree's Last Dream

Andersen published "The Old Oak Tree's Last Dream: A Christmas Tale" ("Det gamle Egetræs sidste Drøm: Et Jule-Eventyr") in *Nye Eventyr og Historier. Første Række. Første Samling* (*New Tales and Stories. First Series. First Installment*) in 1858.

In a bread-and-butter letter written 23 February 1858 to Mrs. Scavenius, his hostess during his Christmas stay at the Basnæs estate, Andersen mentions that "The Old Oak Tree's Last Dream" had been written while he was her guest: "The reason I haven't corresponded in a long while, indeed, have even entirely ceased sending letters to friends abroad, lies in the fact that since I returned home from Basnæs I have been more productive than I have been in a long time. I have written no less than seven new tales. . . . The two that appeal the most originated at dear Basnæs—they are 'The Oak Tree's Last Dream' and, in particular, 'Something' ['Noget']. . . . In a week the tales will be published, and I will send a copy immediately to the dear house by Store Belt." Indeed, "The Old Oak Tree's Last Dream" evokes the setting of Basnæs, where estate lands extended down to the waters of Store Belt, which separates the island of Sjælland from Fyn.

The Butterfly

Andersen first published "The Butterfly" ("Sommerfuglen") in *Folke-kalender for Danmark* for the year 1861. He then later included it in *Nye Eventyr og Historier. Anden Række. Anden Samling (New Tales and Stories. Second Series. Second Installment)* in 1862.

According to his notes to the collected edition *Eventyr og Historier* in 1874, Andersen composed "The Butterfly" in 1860 while on a walking tour in Switzerland that took him from Montreux to Chillon. In these notes Andersen also voices his dissatisfaction about the critical response to his later tales:

> In recent years it has been said by some people that it is especially my very first tales that are of importance; all the later ones are inferior to these. . . . Those people who read my first tales as children have grown older and have lost the freshness of mind with which they once read and responded to literature. Perhaps one or another person has even thought that my tales have achieved such wide distribution and recognition in the world that this must be too great a joy for any living author to experience. So, since the oldest tales have undergone their trial by fire, those have been left alone, and the newer ones have been tackled, for something must be depreciated! Often people throw out comments without sorting out for themselves which tales and stories are among the recent ones and which among the earlier. Several times I have heard it said: "Yes, I like best your really old tales," and should I then ask, "which are those?" I usually get by way of answer, "'The Butterfly,' 'It Is Perfectly True,' 'The Snowman,'" and these are precisely the ones that are among the recent ones, a couple of them among the most recent of all.

The Snail and the Rosebush

"The Snail and the Rosebush" ("Sneglen og Rosenhækken") was published in 1862 in the volume *Nye Eventyr og Historier. Anden Række. Anden Samling,* dedicated to the Norwegian writer Bjørnstjerne Bjørnson.

Andersen wrote this tale while traveling in Italy in 1861. On 14

May 1861 Andersen recorded in his journal a conversation with his traveling companion, the young Jonas, Edvard Collin's son. They were discussing Jonas's cousin the philosopher Viggo Drewsen, whom Jonas claimed to be of far greater merit than someone such as the extroverted, productive Bjørnson. In praise of his reticent cousin, Jonas said that Drewsen was "preoccupied with his own development, not concerning himself with other people." Andersen apparently took issue with Jonas, for, as he noted in his journal: "This [conversation] made me write the story about 'The Snail and the Rosebush.'" After he read his latest composition to Jonas some ten days later, Andersen duly recorded Jonas's reaction in the following journal entry: "Jonas found great malice toward Viggo, who—even if he were never to show any results to the world, even if he were to lie naked in the street like Lazarus—would rank as an *excellent* human being."

It has been suggested that Andersen may also have had Søren Kierkegaard in mind when sketching the character of the snail in "The Snail and the Rosebush," taking somewhat belated revenge for Kierkegaard's *From the Papers of a Person Still Alive, Published Against His Will: On Andersen as a Novelist* (1838), a devastating book-length criticism of Andersen's novel *Only a Fiddler*.

What People Do Think Up

The first publication of "What People Do Think Up" was in America, in Horace E. Scudder's *Riverside Monthly Magazine for Young People* (July 1869), where it appeared in a translation entitled "What One Can Invent." Scudder's interest in Andersen was of long standing. In 1861 he had written an article, "The Fairy Legends of Hans Christian Andersen," for the *National Quarterly Review,* volume 3 (1861), and in subsequent years had tried several times to correspond with Andersen himself, without success. In 1868, however, Andersen did reply, and an extensive and friendly correspondence ensued. (See *The Andersen-Scudder Letters,* edited by Jean Hersholt and Waldemar Westergaard, 1949.) With Scudder, who became his American editor and publisher, Andersen worked out an agreement to submit translations of his work to the *Riverside Monthly Magazine* before they appeared anywhere else and to allow at least three months to elapse after their publication in the American magazine before attempting to publish them elsewhere. This arrangement allowed Andersen to be paid by Scudder at the rate for original work (translations being less profitable for the author). Thus, "What People Do Think Up" was published in Denmark (a year after its appearance in the *Riverside Monthly Magazine*) as "Hvad man kan hitte paa" in *Tre nye Eventyr og Historier (Three New Tales and Stories)* in 1870. It was dedicated to Edvard Collin, "my faithful friend during difficult times and good."

Indeed, the circumstances of this tale's composition may have recalled Collin to him, for in his journal entry for 7 February 1869 Andersen wrote: "Went from the Collins' to the theater and saw 'Jeppe on the Hill' [a comedy by Holberg]; there I composed the tale 'What People Do Think Up' and wrote it down later in the evening." The following day he wrote: "Spent the entire morning revising and making a fair copy of the tale I composed last night. Read it first to Mrs. Jette [Henriette] Collin; she was enthusiastic and said it was the best of the last three." (According to H. Topsøe-Jensen, the other two probably were "The Comet" ["Kometen"] and "Sunshine Stories" ["Solskinshistorier"].)

In his notes to *Eventyr og Historier,* 1874, Andersen mentions that "What People Do Think Up" belongs among "the tales written from personal experience." Whenever Andersen says this about a tale, he means that in it he has worked off a personal animus against someone.

Helge Topsøe-Jensen, in *Anderseniana* (1953), traces the inserted story of the potato—another variation on one of Andersen's favorite themes, the lack of appreciation for something plain but worthy—back to a sketch entitled "The Potatoes" ("Kartoflerne"), 1855, quoting a letter from Andersen to Henriette Wulff, dated 16 February: "Tonight for the first time I felt an urge to write something new, a little piece about 'Potatoes.'" Topsøe-Jensen reproduces in his study two versions of this sketch, which Andersen himself never published.

The Gardener and the Lord and Lady

"The Gardener and the Lord and Lady" was published twice in 1872—in Danish in the volume *Nye Eventyr og Historier. Tredie Række. Første Samling (New Tales and Stories. Third Series. First Installment)* and in an English translation revised by Horace E. Scudder and entitled "The Gardener and the Manor" in the August issue of *Scribner's Monthly.*

In a letter written 28 May 1871 to Mrs. Dorothea Melchior, Andersen described the huge old trees with their enormous flocks of birds which he saw at the Basnæs estate, where he was staying: "You enter an avenue lined with tall old trees. . . . Here is a whole world of birds; rooks, crows, and jackdaws fly around the tall trees, which are set all over with nests, as if gobs of manure had been dropped onto all the branches; this is not a very pretty picture, but a true one." Andersen describes an estate surrounded by old trees crowded with birds in another, earlier story, "Hønse-Grethes Familie" ("Chicken-Grethe's Family"), published in 1869. Evidently the image had special meaning for him.

Another aspect of "The Gardener and the Lord and Lady" is explored by the Marxist critic Peer E. Sørensen, who alludes to the title of the story in the title of his own book about Andersen, *H. C. Andersen & Herskabet* (*H. C. Andersen and the Lord and Lady*), 1973. Sørensen writes: "The opposition between the gardener and the lord and lady is the major structural principle of the text, which was written from a point of view sympathetic toward the lower class—from which in this story all fruitfulness and virtue stem—and critical toward the upper class—from which stems all that is artificial and unauthentic."

Knowledge of the circumstances of Andersen's childhood and of his behavior as an adult, however, leads one to suspect that Sørensen's views do not reflect the complexity of the author's feelings about the relation between social standing and virtue.

The Cripple

Andersen published "The Cripple" ("Krøblingen") as the third of four stories in what turned out to be his last volume of tales, *Nye Eventyr og Historier. Tredie Række. Anden Samling* (*New Tales and Stories. Third Series. Second Installment*) in 1872.

Work on "The Cripple" began 12 July 1872, the day after he had completed "Auntie Toothache" ("Tante Tandpine"), over which he had fussed for a good two years. His journal entry for that day reads: "Beautiful warm weather; thought a lot last night about the story of the woodcutter and his wife and got the idea to use it, so stayed home and wrote industriously." The following day his journal entry records that he had "written away all day on 'The Book of Fairy Tales'; felt very tired; read it to the Melchiors." What Andersen has not told us in these entries is that he based part of this tale on an experience that he had previously recorded in his journal on 2 January 1867, while staying at the Holsteinborg estate on Sjælland:

Yesterday Pastor Berg told me that when he saw me for the first time a couple of years ago it was right at Christmas time and I had told a story about the sick king who would regain his health if someone were to bring him a shirt owned by the happiest person of all—and when the happiest person was found, he didn't own a shirt! That story made an impression on the pastor, because he had just heard the story the day before in exactly the opposite situation, namely in the home of a poor couple who were complaining to each other about their hard life. Then their son, a half idiot who was lying in bed, told them the story about the happiest person of all who didn't own a shirt, and that cheered them up. Pastor Berg told of the coincidence regarding the story that he had heard here and the day before there, and the Countess gave him five dollars for the poor couple, who were happily surprised at the gift that had been occasioned by the poor idiot boy's story and attempt at comforting them. It was thus from him that the help had come.

In the weeks following its composition Andersen read the story aloud while visiting friends, as was his custom; but by the time he delivered a fair copy to the printer on 7 October 1872, he had changed the title to a less obvious one, "The Cripple." One more interesting text change was made by Andersen, probably when he was going over the galley proofs: his manuscript read, "He wished now only to live to be a hundred years old and eventually become a schoolmaster. *He became an archdeacon!*" Andersen crossed out the italicized sentence, thereby muting the strident moralism of the story.

In his description of the advent of spring, heralding both the spiring of flowering plants and the sprouting of noxious weeds, Andersen has quoted a verse from a well-known pietistic hymn, "Op! al den ting som Gud har giort" ("Arise! Each Thing That God Has Made"), in Hans Adolph Brorson's collection of religious songs, *Troens Rare Klenodie* (*The Rare Treasure of Faith*), 1739.

"The Cripple" was well received by contemporary readers and critics alike, perhaps in part because, with its message that people should be satisfied with their lot in life rather than brooding about what they do not have, it appealed to a conservative reaction against Socialist unrest and riots in Copenhagen earlier that year. Andersen himself echoes some of his reviewers, who had called "The Cripple" an "apotheosis of the art of tale-writing," when in his own notes to the collected edition of tales and stories, *Eventyr og Historier* (1874), he comments that this tale "as a kind of glorification of the art of tale writing might suitably have served to conclude the entire collection."

Auntie Toothache

Andersen used "Auntie Toothache" ("Tante Tandpine") to close what turned out to be his last volume of tales, *Nye Eventyr og Historier. Tredie Række. Anden Samling,* in 1872.

As with many of his finest tales, Andersen worked over "Auntie Toothache" for a number of years. In 1870 he mentioned his project for the first time to Henriette Collin in a letter dated 24 June 1870: "Yesterday I began a tale 'Auntie Toothache'; afterward I changed the title to 'Auntie Mikke's Teeth.' It has to do with toothaches and false teeth. I must certainly try somehow to profit from the torment that is my lot. In the meantime, I noticed while I was writing that it wasn't so easy to render the story, if I wanted to stay within the bounds of poetic expression."

One year later, on 30 May 1871, he again wrote to Henriette Collin about his bothersome project: "You might remember that when I was here last year I had begun to compose a tale about 'false teeth,' but I found that it was so ill-favored that I abandoned it. This year, since nothing yet seems to flourish in my poetic garden . . . that little monster has returned to torment me, though in a different, less displeasing form. So I am now writing away at 'Auntie Toothache's Dream,' but only time will tell whether it will turn out to be anything."

Unmentioned by Andersen in this second letter to Mrs. Collin is the fact that he had lived near the Royal Theater during the preceding winter and was working a description of these lodgings, as well as his new idea of the dream, into his slowly evolving tale. His journal for that winter, especially the entries for 15 and 16 February 1871, has preserved his complaints about his neighbors and their noise, and it all sounds much like the student's account to his Auntie Millie. In his article "Om H. C. Andersens Eventyr Tante Tandpine" ("About H. C. Andersen's tale 'Auntie Toothache,'" *Tandlægebladet,* 1944), Kai O. Mehlsen has pointed out that the description of the dream figure, the personification of toothache, incorporates the most common tools used by nineteenth-century dentists. Particularly gruesome is the awl, which was driven into the root canal of a decayed tooth in order to kill the nerve.

Andersen altered the original ending of "Auntie Toothache" as it was first published in 1872 when he was reading galley proofs for the fifth volume of the collected edition of 1874. The original 1872 text read as follows:

The brewer is dead; Auntie is dead; the student is dead, the one whose flashes of inspiration ended up in the barrel.
Everything ends up in the barrel.

In 1874 Andersen crossed out the italicized sentence and substituted a new one that served to mitigate the black pessimism of this story: "This is the end of the story—the story of Auntie Toothache."

Contemporary reviewers of the volume in which "Auntie Toothache" appeared in 1872 were deaf to the tone struck in this tale and expressed their gratitude to the author whose "plain and simple childlike words describe life's light and bright side."

Bibliography

The standard critical edition of Hans Christian Andersen's tales and stories is *H. C. Andersens Eventyr: Kritisk udgivet efter de originale Eventyrhæfter med Varianter,* edited by Erik Dal and Erling Nielsen (Copenhagen: Hans Reitzel, 1963–; volumes 1–5 have appeared; 6 and 7 are forthcoming). The illustrations accompanying the editions, both foreign and Danish, of Andersen's tales and stories are discussed in detail by Erik Dal in *Udenlandske H. C. Andersen–illustrationer 1838–1968* (Copenhagen: Dansk Typograf-Forbund, 1969) and *Danske H. C. Andersen–illustrationer 1835–1975* (Copenhagen: Forum, 1975).

The main sources of information regarding Andersen and his writing are his biographies, his diaries, and the correspondence. The most extensive collection of letters is Andersen's correspondence with the Collin family: *H. C. Andersens Brevveksling med Jonas Collin den Ældre og andre Medlemmer af det Collinske Hus,* 3 vols., edited by H. Topsøe-Jensen in cooperation with Kaj Bom and Knud Bøgh (Copenhagen: Munksgaard, 1945–48), and *H. C. Andersens Brevveksling med Edvard og Henriette Collin,* 6 vols., edited by H. Topsøe-Jensen (Copenhagen: Levin and Munksgaard, 1933–37). Equally important are the letters exchanged between Andersen and his two close friends Henriette Hanck and Henriette Wulff: "H. C. Andersens Brevveksling med Henriette Hanck," *Anderseniana,* 9–13, no. 2, edited by Svend Larsen (Copenhagen: Munksgaard, 1941–46), and *H. C. Andersen og Henriette Wulff: En Brevveksling,* 3 vols., edited by H. Topsøe-Jensen (Odense: Flensteds Forlag, 1959–60).

The complete edition of Andersen's diaries is *H. C. Andersens Dagbøger 1825–75,* 12 vols., edited by Tue Gad, Helga Vang Lauridsen, and Kirsten Weber (Copenhagen: G. E. C. Gads Forlag, 1971–76); this edition is unannotated, but a number of annotated extracts from the diaries have been published separately, particularly in the journal *Anderseniana.*

Andersen's first attempt at autobiography, written in 1832, ends with a detailed, psychologically penetrating account of his love for Riborg Voigt. It was intended for publication in case of his premature death, and for many years the manuscript was thought to have been lost. It was found in the Royal Library of Copenhagen by Hans Brix and first published by him in 1926. Later it was published in an annotated critical edition by H. Topsøe-Jensen: *H. C. Andersens Levnedsbog 1805–1831* (Copenhagen: Det Schønbergske Forlag, 1962). For a planned German edition of his collected works Andersen wrote another autobiography, published in 1847 as *Das Märchen meines Lebens ohne Dichtung.* In the same year an English edition, *The True Story of My Life,* was published in London and immediately after reprinted in the United States (see below). The Danish edition, *Mit eget Eventyr uden Digtning,* edited by H. Topsøe-Jensen (Copenhagen: Nyt Nordisk Forlag), did not appear until 1942. The German autobiography was finally expanded and published in Danish in 1855 as *Mit Livs Eventyr* (Copenhagen: C. A. Reitzel). An American edition of this work, translated by Horace E. Scudder with additional chapters covering the years 1855–67, was published in New York in 1871 as *The Story of My Life* (see below).

The most important studies of Andersen as an autobiographer have been written by H. Topsøe-Jensen: *Mit Livs Eventyr uden Digtning: En Studie over H. C. Andersen som Selvbiograf* (Copenhagen: Gyldendal, 1940) and *Omkring Levnedsbogen: En Studie over H. C. Andersen som Selvbiograf 1820–45* (Copenhagen: Gyldendal, 1943). Topsøe-Jensen demonstrates how frequently Andersen's autobiographies are misleading, especially in giving the false impression that he was constantly persecuted and ridiculed.

The first scholarly book-length study on Andersen as a writer of tales and stories was by Hans Brix: *H. C. Andersen og hans Eventyr* (Copenhagen: Det Schubotheske Forlag, 1907). In his attempt to identify autobiographical elements in Andersen's texts Brix accepts at face value questionable material from the autobiographical writing, and some of his conclusions are based on speculation. However, Brix's work has influenced research to a great extent. Paul V. Rubow's *H. C. Andersens Eventyr: Forhistorien—Idé og Form—Sprog og Stil* (Copenhagen: Levin and Munksgaard, 1927) is another influential work. In addition to presenting a brilliant analysis of the language and style of Andersen's tales and stories, Rubow investigates various minor prose genres and the use Andersen made of them.

Reliable biographical studies by H. G. Olrik are collected in *Hans Christian Andersen: Undersøgelser og Kroniker 1925–1944* (Copenhagen: H. Hagerup, 1945), and Andersen's relations with England are discussed by Elias Bredsdorff in two very important books: *H. C. Andersen og Dickens* (Copenhagen: Rosenkilde and Bagger, 1951; for the revised English translation see below) and *H. C. Andersen og England* (Copenhagen: Rosenkilde and Bagger, 1954). Bredsdorff has also written the most important contribution to Andersen research in English: *Hans Christian Andersen: The Story of His Life and Work 1805–75* (see below). Surveys in English of scholarly works on Andersen have been written by Elias Bredsdorff, "A Critical Guide to the Literature on Hans Christian Andersen," *Scandinavica,* 6 (1967): 108–25, and by Erik Dal, "Research on Hans Christian Andersen: Trends, Results, and Desiderata," *Orbis litterarum,* 17 (1962): 166–83.

Within the last fifteen years a wide variety of critical methods have been applied to Andersen studies. Valuable works focusing exclusively on Andersen's fairy-tale universe are Bo Grønbech, *H. C. Andersens Eventyrverden* (Copenhagen: Povl Branner, 1945), and Niels Kofoed, *Studier i H. C. Andersens fortællekunst* (Copenhagen: Munksgaard, 1967). Eigil Nyborg presents a more controversial Jungian analysis of the tales and stories in *Den indre linie i H. C. Andersens eventyr: En psykologisk studie* (Copenhagen: Gyldendal, 1962). Arne Duve, a Norwegian psychoanalyst, utilizes a strict Freudian interpretation in *Symbolikken i H. C. Andersens eventyr* (Oslo: Psychopress, 1967) and *H. C. Andersens hemmelighet* (Oslo: Psychopress, 1969). A Marxist viewpoint is presented in Peer E. Sørensen's *H. C. Andersen & herskabet: Studier i borgerlig krisebevidsthed* (Grenå: GMT, 1973). Young scholars have recently tried other approaches—existentialist, linguistic, sociological, and structuralist—demonstrating that although Andersen's works have received much attention in the past, they continue to present a challenge.

In the following listing, only works in English have been included, except for the bibliographies and the journal *Anderseniana.*

BIBLIOGRAPHIES

Bredsdorff, Elias. "A Critical Guide to the Literature on Hans Christian Andersen." *Scandinavica,* 6, no. 2 (1967): 108–25.

————. *Danish Literature in English Translation, with a Special Hans Christian Andersen Supplement: A Bibliography*. Copenhagen: Ejnar Munksgaard, 1950.

————. "Hans Christian Andersen: A Bibliographical Guide to His Work." *Scandinavica*, 6, no. 1 (1967): 26–42.

Jørgensen, Aage. *H. C. Andersen litteraturen 1875–1968: En bibliografi*. Aarhus: Akademisk Boghandel, 1970.

————. *H. C. Andersen litteraturen 1875–1968: En bibliografi. Tilføjelser og rettelser. Supplement 1875–1968. Fortsættelse 1969–1972*. Copenhagen: Akademisk Forlag, 1973.

————. *H. C. Andersen litteraturen 1875–1968: En bibliografi. Tilføjelser og rettelser. Supplement 1875–1972. Fortsættelse 1973–1976*. Aarhus: n.p., 1978.

Nielsen, Birger Frank. *H. C. Andersen bibliografi: Digterens danske værker 1822–75*. Copenhagen: H. Hagerup, 1942.

EDITIONS OF ANDERSEN'S OTHER WORKS IN ENGLISH

Only first editions are listed, and are given in chronological order.

NOVELS

The Improvisatore, or, Life in Italy. Translated by Mary Howitt. 2 vols. London: Richard Bentley, 1845.

Only a Fiddler! and O.T., or, Life in Denmark. Translated by Mary Howitt. 2 vols. London: Richard Bentley, 1845.

The Two Baronesses. Translated by Charles Beckwith. 2 vols. London: Richard Bentley, 1848.

To Be, or Not To Be? Translated by Mrs. Bushby. London: Richard Bentley, 1857.

Lucky Peer. Translated by Horace E. Scudder. *Scribner's Monthly*, 1 (1871): 270–76, 391–98, 505–16, and 625–39.

TRAVEL BOOKS

A Poet's Bazaar. Translated by Charles Beckwith. 3 vols. London: Richard Bentley, 1846.

Rambles in the Romantic Regions of the Hartz Mountains, Saxon Switzerland, Etc. Translated by Charles Beckwith. London: Richard Bentley, 1848.

Pictures of Sweden. Translated by Charles Beckwith. London: Richard Bentley, 1851.

In Sweden. Translated by K. R. K. MacKenzie. London: G. Routledge and Co., 1852.

In Spain. Translated by Mrs. Bushby. London: Richard Bentley, 1864.

A Poet's Bazaar: Pictures of Travel in Germany, Italy, Greece, and the Orient. New York: Hurd and Houghton, 1871.

Pictures of Travel in Sweden, among the Hartz Mountains, and in Switzerland, with a Visit at Charles Dickens' House. New York: Hurd and Houghton, 1871.

In Spain, and A Visit to Portugal. New York: Hurd and Houghton, 1870.

A Visit to Portugal 1866. Translated and edited by Grace Thornton. London: Peter Owen, 1972.

A Visit to Spain. Translated and edited by Grace Thornton. London: Peter Owen, 1975.

AUTOBIOGRAPHIES AND OTHER WORKS

The True Story of My Life. Translated from the German edition by Mary Howitt. London: Longman and Co., 1847, Boston: J. Munroe, 1847.

The Story of My Life. Translated by D. Spillan. London: G. Routledge and Co., 1852.

The Story of My Life. Translated by Horace E. Scudder. New York: Hurd and Houghton, 1871.

The Fairy Tale of My Life. Translated by W. Glyn Jones. New York: British Book Centre, 1954.

Tales the Moon Can Tell. Translated by R. P. Keigwin. Copenhagen: Berlingske Forlag, 1955.

Seven Poems. Translated by R. P. Keigwin. Odense: Hans Christian Andersen's House, 1955.

ANDERSEN'S CORRESPONDENCE

Hans Christian Andersen's Correspondence with the Late Grand-Duke of Saxe-Weimar, Charles Dickens, Etc., Etc. Edited by Frederick Crawford. London: Dean and Son, 1891.

Hans Christian Andersen's Visits to Charles Dickens, As Described in His

Letters, Published with Six of Dickens' Letters in Facsimile. Published by Ejnar Munksgaard. Copenhagen: Levin and Munksgaard, 1937.

The Andersen-Scudder Letters: Hans Christian Andersen's Correspondence with Horace Elisha Scudder. Edited and translated by Jean Hersholt and Waldemar Westergaard, with an essay by H. Topsøe-Jensen. Berkeley and Los Angeles: University of California Press, 1949.

SECONDARY LITERATURE

Anderseniana. First Series, 1–13 (1933–46); Second Series, 1–6 (1947–69); and Third Series, 1–2 (1970–77).

Böök, Fredrik. *Hans Christian Andersen: A Biography.* Translated by George C. Schoolfield. Norman: University of Oklahoma Press, 1962.

Born, Ann. "Hans Christian Andersen: An Infectious Genius." *Anderseniana,* Third Series, 2, no. 3 (1976): 248–60.

Bredsdorff, Elias. *Hans Andersen and Charles Dickens: A Friendship and Its Dissolution.* Anglistica, 7. Copenhagen: Rosenkilde and Bagger, 1956.

————. "Hans Andersen and Scotland." *Blackwood's Magazine,* April 1955, pp. 297–312.

————. "Hans Andersen as an Artist." *Norseman,* 13, no. 1 (1955): 35–39.

————. "Hans Christian Andersen and the Brownings." *Scandinavica,* 14, no. 2 (1975): 135–39.

————. *Hans Christian Andersen: The Story of His Life and Work 1805–75.* London: Phaidon, 1975. New York: Charles Scribner's Sons, 1975.

Clausen, Julius. "H. C. Andersen Abroad and at Home." *American-Scandinavian Review,* 18, no. 4 (1930): 228–34.

Conroy, Patricia. "H. C. Andersen and His Audience." *Proceedings of the Pacific Northwest Council on Foreign Languages: Foreign Literatures,* 29, no. 1 (1978): 111–13.

Dal, Erik. "Hans Christian Andersen in Eighty Languages." In *A Book on the Danish Writer Hans Christian Andersen: His Life and Work,* pp. 137–206. Copenhagen: The Committee for Danish Cultural Activities Abroad, 1955.

————. Hans Christian Andersen's Tales and America." *Scandinavian Studies,* 40 (1968): 1–25.

Haugaard, Erik Christian. *Portrait of a Poet: Hans Christian Andersen and His Fairytales.* Washington, D.C.: Library of Congress, 1973.

Heltoft, Kjeld. *Hans Christian Andersen as an Artist.* Translated by Reginald Spink. Copenhagen: Royal Danish Ministry of Foreign Affairs, 1977.

Larsen, Svend. "The Life of Hans Christian Andersen." In *A Book on the Danish Writer Hans Christian Andersen: His Life and Work,* pp. 13–95. Copenhagen: The Committee for Danish Cultural Activities Abroad, 1955.

Marker, Frederick J. "H. C. Andersen as a Royal Theatre Actor." *Anderseniana,* 6, no. 3 (1968): 278–84.

———. *Hans Christian Andersen and the Romantic Theatre.* Toronto: University of Toronto Press, 1971.

Mishler, William. "H. C. Andersen's 'Tin Soldier' in a Freudian Perspective." *Scandinavian Studies,* 50 (1978): 389–95.

Møller, Kai Friis. "The Poet and the Fair Sex." *American-Scandinavian Review,* 18, no. 4 (1930): 220–27.

Mudrick, Marvin. "The Ugly Duck." *Scandinavian Review,* 68, no. 1 (1980): 34–48.

Niles, John D. "Andersen's 'Grantræet' and the Old English 'Dream of the Rood.'" *Anderseniana,* 2 (1974–77): 351–60.

Olrik, H. G. "Childhood Home in Odense." *American-Scandinavian Review,* 18, no. 4 (1930): 213–19.

Reumert, Elith. *Hans Andersen the Man.* Translated by Jessie Bröchner. London: Methuen and Co., 1927.

Rubow, Paul V. "Idea and Form in Hans Christian Andersen's Fairy Tales." In *A Book on the Danish Writer Hans Christian Andersen: His Life and Work,* pp. 97–135. Copenhagen: The Committee for Danish Cultural Activities Abroad, 1955.

Spink, Reginald. *Hans Christian Andersen and His World.* London: Thames and Hudson, 1972.

———. *The Young Hans Andersen.* London: Max Parrish, 1962.

Toksvig, Signe. *The Life of Hans Christian Andersen.* London: Macmillan and Co., 1933. New York: Harcourt, Brace and Co., 1934.

Topsøe-Jensen, Helge, and Paul V. Rubow. "Hans Christian Andersen the Writer." *American-Scandinavian Review,* 18, no. 4 (1930): 205–12.

Woel, Cai M. "Hans Christian Andersen as an Example for Writers." In *A Book on the Danish Writer Hans Christian Andersen: His Life and Work,* pp. 207–20. Copenhagen: The Committee for Danish Cultural Activities Abroad, 1955.